The Eyes of a King

❧ The Last Descendants Trilogy ❧
Book I

Catherine Banner

Doubleday Canada

Doubleday Canada and colophon are registered trademarks

Library and Archives Canada Cataloguing in Publication

Banner, Catherine, 1989-
The eyes of a king / Catherine Banner.

ISBN 978-0-385-66233-8

I. Title.
PR6102.A66E94 2009   j823'.92   C2008-906951-X

This book is a work of fiction. Names, characters, places and incidents are products of
the author's imagination or are used fictitiously. Any resemblance to actual events or
locales or persons, living or dead, is entirely coincidental.

Printed and bound in the USA

Published in Canada by Doubleday Canada,
a division of Random House of Canada Limited

Visit Random House of Canada Limited's website: www.randomhouse.ca

10 9 8 7 6 5 4 3 2 1

THE EYES OF A KING

*T*hese are the last words I will write. "Tell me everything from the beginning," you said. "Explain to me why you did it." I have. There is nothing left to tell you anymore.

The dust drifts across the paving of the silent balcony. A dark wind—the first wind of autumn—rifles through the pages and draws the stars behind it into the fading sky. Light and laughter are rising from the rooms far below; still farther below that, the lights of the city are emerging in the settling darkness. When you were here, half an hour ago, you lit a lamp for me. The breeze makes it waver now and turns the pages back to the beginning. This book is the past five years of my life. How can I close it now?

I do not have the strength to go down into the noise and the light

1

of the party. So I turn the pages of the book instead, tracing the words I wrote. There are parts of this story that still haunt my dreams, that repeat themselves in all my waking thoughts and refuse to let go. But I did not begin by writing about those things.

I began with the book, and the snow.

⤫

*T*he snow began to fall as I walked home. It was dark, though barely five o'clock, and cold. My breath billowed white in the darkness and everything was quiet. Even the jangle and thud of the soldiers' horses seemed deadened. The flakes were so cold that they almost burned where they touched my face, and they lodged on my clothes and stuck fast. I tried to brush them away and pulled my coat up tighter about my neck.

I was used to snow—we all were—but not at the end of May. It looked set to stay cold for at least a week. We got more than enough snow in the winter.

There was a sort of beauty in it, I suppose. The clouds had closed like a lid over the narrow squares of sky, and already the gas lamps were lit. The snow caked on their panes and glowed yellow. I stopped still, and then it was almost completely silent, without even the wet crunch of my footsteps. Quiet, not silent. Through the still air I could hear the feathery sound of the snowflakes settling.

I looked up into the sky. The way the snowflakes swelled in toward my face made me feel as if I was rising. It got darker. It got colder.

I started to think about going home, but I didn't.

I began to shiver, but I went on staring into the sky. It got still darker. I would have stood there all night, perhaps. It was like an enchantment. And I did not want to go home yet anyway. The constant frantic motion of the snowflakes made me dizzy, and my neck ached from looking upward. Still the snow fell. I was hypnotized.

Suddenly I felt someone was near to me. The spell was broken. I was back in the street again.

I looked around, but there was no one. Only a presence in the air, as if someone was hiding in the shadows. I felt sick suddenly. There were ghosts here perhaps, invisible spirits moving close by. I turned away.

Before I had taken three steps, my foot met with something heavy and I stumbled. There was a black shape in the snow, spotted with the flakes my feet had thrown up. At first I thought it was a dead animal—a rat perhaps—lying there frozen.

I bent closer. And I saw that it was not an animal at all but a book. Just a book. I reached out toward it cautiously. I could still feel a strange presence—someone else's thoughts like a vapor in the air.

I willed the book's cover to lift itself, with the slightest tensing of my fingers and my mind. It didn't stir. That was a trick I'd known for years, and it usually worked. Although it was only a cheap trick, no more. It did not even work on the Bible.

I was suspicious of the book. I did not know if I should touch it. Perhaps it would be better to leave it where it was. I turned to walk away. But I could not. I was going to pick it up; I knew I was. It was unavoidable. There was no point in reasoning with myself, then.

My fingers drew close to the dark leather of the cover even

before I had decided. I watched them hover above it for a moment, as if they were someone else's. I tried to pull my hand away. I couldn't. For a second I was frightened. Then my fingers closed around the book, and at the same moment the presence vanished. I picked the book up and flipped the cover open.

The pages were stiff and suntanned yellow, like sheets of bone. The first one was blank. I turned to the next. Nothing. The next one and the next one too were empty. I fanned the pages out loose, impatiently, bending the covers back almost to breaking point, so that the dry glue in the spine bristled. They were all blank.

The weather had changed while I had looked away. The wind growled through the narrow streets, the pitch of its voice heightening. The snowflakes dashed at my face like ground glass. My jaw ached with cold, and my fingers on the book's cover were raw and wet from the melting snow. I pushed the book into my coat pocket and set off for home.

Later, when I held the book to the light of the oil lamp in the bedroom, I wondered if I should have left it where it was. There was a strangeness about it that made me uneasy. I had been sure that there was someone behind me in the street, and I could not help connecting the book with that presence. Perhaps it was a stupid thing to think. It was only an empty book.

I turned away from the lamp and pressed the side of my face against the window to create a shadow that I could see out of. The wind had rent a hole in the snow clouds, and a few stars shone through. I liked looking at the stars. One of them was called Leo, but I did not know which one. I never knew which one. The snow was freezing hard in the streets. It caught every faint glimmer from the gas lamps and reflected it ice blue. Tomorrow would be cold—very cold.

A sound made me turn back to the room. "Leo!" came my grandmother's voice sharply. I pushed the book across the floor, into the darkness under my bed, and sat back on the windowsill. "Leo!" my grandmother said again, and she stepped into the room. She looked at Stirling, asleep in his bed in the far corner. Then she turned to me. "Leo, do you need that light?" Her eyebrows lowered, casting her eyes into shadow, like a skeleton's. "Put it out!" she told me. "You're wasting oil. What are you doing?"

"I was going to go to bed."

"Aye. It's late."

She gazed at me for a moment. She looked so old in the shadows, though she was only sixty-five. Her gray hair shone, tight across her head, and the loose wisps about her ears caught the light of the lamp. The lines around her eyes and mouth were pronounced, and her face was tense. Her face was always tense when she spoke to me.

"You were kept after school again?" she said. "Leo, I am losing count of how many times this month."

I did not answer. She looked at me for a long time without speaking. "What is it?" I said eventually.

I expected her to continue nagging me. But instead, she looked away and said, "You have grown so like Harold. His eyes were gray too when he was your age. That was what I was thinking."

"Grandmother?" I said, and stood up.

She turned back to me. "What?"

I changed my mind. "Nothing."

"Good night, Leo," she said sadly. "God bless you."

She looked as if she might reach up and put her hand on my shoulder, then seemed to decide against it. She left, and closed the door behind her. I heard the door of her own room rattle shut. It needed fixing. The screws were rusting, and one of the hinges had snapped. I would have done it. That door was going to fall soon. But it was hard to get hinges these days, when the factories only made bullets.

I waited for a moment before kneeling and reaching under my bed for the book. I felt a corner and caught hold of it. But what I pulled out was a different book altogether. Larger, and older. I blew the dust off the cover, as quietly as I could, and it prickled in my nose. This had surely been there a long time.

Then I remembered what it was. It was years since I had put it there. My grandmother would have gone crazy if she'd known I still had a copy.

The Golden Reign by Harold North. A hardback book, leather. It was a bestseller. Hundreds of thousands of people read that book. Then it was banned. They burned the entire second print run. My father was already far away. It was strange that my grandmother had just mentioned him, and now here was his forgotten book in my hand.

I ran my fingers over the cover. He was the best, my father, the best writer of our time. But seven years had passed now and I hardly remembered his face. I had been eight then, Stirling's age. Perhaps my father would not have known me either.

The cover peeled away from the title page reluctantly. Underneath the printed title my father's signature still stood out in yellowing writing. I remember he autographed it for me, because I asked him to. I said I wanted to be a writer, like him.

I slammed the cover down hard, pushed the book back under my bed, and turned to blow out the oil lamp. But I didn't have to. The oil was finished. The lamp flickered once . . . twice . . . and went out.

The next morning I woke to cold white dawn. White, not gray, because of the strange light of the snow. That was what I saw when I opened my eyes—the snow in the street, like pure white waves frozen in a channel, and above the dirty houses snow hanging heavily in the sky. Then I remembered that I couldn't see the street from my bed. Every morning, when I woke, I saw only the sky. But I was looking down into the street now.

I was sitting on the windowsill. My head was pressed hard against the freezing window, and it hurt to pull away. Why was I here? I remembered going to bed the night before, after the lamp had gone out. I stood up.

The book was lying on the windowsill, beside the stone-cold lamp. That book I had found in the snow. It was strange, because I was sure that I had left it under my bed, where I'd shoved it carelessly the evening before. I picked it up and fanned out the pages absentmindedly, blinking. It was early, and I was tired. It could not have been much later than six o'clock. Then I started. There was writing in the book!

I snapped the book shut. It had been empty the day before; I had checked every page. I opened it again. Yes, there was writing. Close-packed black writing that I did not recognize. Surely then, the book was more than what it seemed. It could only be evil. I put it quickly back on the windowsill, afraid to keep hold of it. I stared at it for a long while.

I knew that I was going to read it. I wanted to find out what the writing said. Perhaps I had been stupid to be afraid; a book could not harm me. I tried to open it again with my willpower. I concentrated my mind on it as hard as I could. My brain ached from the effort, but it didn't work. The book stayed shut. I considered it for a moment, then snatched it up and opened it.

There were several blank pages. I turned to the beginning of the writing and started to read.

As the first sunlight drove out the bleak gray dawn, it glowed through the curtains of the hospital room. The young man opened them quietly and looked out. He watched the light cross the railway lines and spread over the roofs of the square gray houses. It transformed the ragged weeds on the siding into clear purple flowers standing motionless in the silence of the morning. The tears were running down his face, but he stayed there at the window until they were gone. A train passed and faded again. He thought of the people just waking in the houses, and the people on that train, who thought this was an ordinary day, when the sun had risen so differently to him.

The young woman called his name. He turned and went to her, and laid one hand upon the baby's head. She did not wake. He took the woman's hand. His eyes fixed on her for a moment, though she did not see it. Her blond ringlets fell onto the baby's face as she held her, and she looked out the window, across the deserted tracks, to a broken fence where birds hopped and sang. They could not be heard through the glass, and the baby slept. The sunlight spread into the room and turned everything to gold.

A long time passed before the silence was broken. A middle-aged woman hurried in. She looked at the sleeping baby and began to cry herself and then laugh, and the younger woman was laughing too and hugging her mother. The baby's grandmother took something from around her neck. It was a gold chain with a heavy charm on it—a jeweled bird that caught the sun now and sent spots of light flying around the small white room. The baby opened her eyes suddenly, though it must have been chance. "Your necklace, Mam," said the young woman.

"I will give it to her now," said the older woman. "I will give this to my granddaughter." She handed it to the baby's father. "Keep it for when she's older. One jewel is missing, but it always has been."

"It doesn't matter," said the young woman. "Let her wear it now, Mam, just for a minute." Her husband fastened the clasp around the baby's neck and straightened the chain. The jewel came down almost to her waist, she was so small. In silence, they looked at the baby.

"I can tell already that she is going to be beautiful," said the baby's grandmother.

"I wish I could live to see her grow up," said the man, and he kissed the baby's face. A tear dropped from his eye onto her cheek, and she began to cry then too.

Far away in a lofty stone room, another baby was sleeping. His mother leaned over, pushing aside the velvet curtain of the bed, to watch him. Her husband had the baby in his arms while the priest spoke a blessing over the child. "Protect this prince and let him grow in wisdom," the priest was saying, making the sign of the cross, but the king was not listening. His eyes were on his wife's. The early sunlight reflected scarlet off her face, and her tiredness and that light made her look younger even than she was. The king tried to trace her face and his own in the child's, then stopped because it made the tears rise in his eyes. He was not yet eighteen and she was younger, and he felt like a boy now, with this baby in his arms.

Not long after the priest had gone, the baby woke. The king put him back into the queen's arms carefully and knelt beside her, and they looked down at him in silence. Already his eyes were strange— large and dark, with an unusual strength for one so small. The eyes of a king, the people would say later. An odd stillness hung over the room as they watched the baby. He did not even cry. "What will this boy's future be?" said the king, thinking of his own life.

"I have you, and now a son," said the queen, brushing the tears off her face. "If we are always like we are now, if we always stay together, I will never ask for more than this the rest of my life."

Five years passed and they were always together. And that last evening, the three of them were on the highest balcony of the castle when the queen heard shouts and turned to look down into the city. The prince and his father were fencing with wooden swords behind her. "What is it?" said the king, glancing at his wife.

"I cannot see." She turned back to them. "Go on with your match."

The king dropped the sword to his side and smiled. "I do not think I should be playing games like this." But he handled the toy as if it was a real weapon. The queen smiled too, to see that.

The prince, catching his father off his guard, knocked the sword out of his hand. They all laughed then, and the king lifted his son and swung him into his arms. "He would make a fine soldier," said the queen.

"Do not talk of that now," said the king, stroking the child's hair. "He's still a little boy."

Birds settled in the trees of the roof garden below. The sun was setting bloodred. They watched it in silence, standing together like any family anywhere. Then it was no longer silent; close by, people were shouting.

The castle gate fell with a loud explosion. Suddenly on their knees, the king and the queen stared at each other. "Don't move," the man told his son. Rebel troops were shouting below. Over the edge of the balcony, the boy could see them swarming into the castle yard like ants. The family clung together. The king drew a knife from his belt and it glinted red in the sunset. There was a sudden burst of gunshots in a room below. "They have guns," the man breathed into his wife's ear. "They have guns; is this possible? Who has been making guns?" She caught his hand; the small click of their two rings touching was harsh in the quiet.

Heavy footsteps were coming closer below the balcony door. The king stood up, and the queen followed. His eyes never leaving the door, the prince clutched at his mother's hand and found it. She moved between him and the doorway. The footsteps came closer.

The door shot open, the king ran forward, and two gunshots echoed suddenly around the towers and rooftops of the palace. The knife fell from the king's hand and clattered to the ground, and the king and the queen landed hard on the stone of the balcony. No one had resisted the attack. It had been too sudden.

There was silence. One minute the man and the woman had been living; the next they were not. The blood crept quietly over the stone, and no one moved.

The prince's tears stuck in his throat, and he picked up the knife and threw it at the soldier who had shot. It sliced into his eye and the side of his face and stuck there for a moment. The man dropped the pistol and fell to his knees, his hands clasped to his face. Blood spilled between his fingers, thick and dark, and spattered onto the stone. Another soldier raised his gun. "No!" cried the injured one, his hands still over his face. "Remember the prophecy! Do not kill the prince!"

They were on their way home. The girl—now five years old—and her grandmother. The radio was playing and the woman sang a few lines and turned it up louder. The little girl waved her arms like a dancer. Her grandmother laughed. "You'll be dancing on a stage one day."

"I hope I will, if I practice hard," said the girl, so earnestly that her grandmother laughed again. The bird charm still hung around the girl's neck, and her eyes had sharpened to a bright blue now— the same blue as the jewel in the center of the necklace, as though it had been made for her.

The lines of traffic moved fast. On the other side of the road, the cars stood in long queues, crammed close to each other. The girl began to doze in the evening light, rocking with every slight turn. Sandy shells and pebbles clattered on the dashboard. The woman reached across and touched her granddaughter's cheek as she slept.

Suddenly horns blared through the music. A lorry swung across the road, rocking. The girl woke, confused and already screaming in the swerving car. The last thing she saw before darkness was her grandmother struggling to turn the wheel one way then the other, while lorries loomed over the car and tires screamed somewhere close. "It's all right, it's all right," said her grandmother desperately, though the girl did not know why she was saying it. Then the car turned over and everything vanished.

The girl cried all that night in her mother's arms, in a cold white hospital with the dark close outside. They could have gone home, but neither of them thought of it. The little girl had been here many times before. This was the hospital where she had been born; a year later she had been carried here every day for three weeks while her father was dying. She had been here many times before, but this was the time she would remember.

The boy cried too, suddenly alone in a strange country, with only a stranger who could not comfort him. He looked out at the evening star, the star that was the first to brighten outside his window in the castle, but even the star was wrong and different here. It was pale and faded in a dull orange-gray night sky. "Come away from the window," said the stranger, putting a blanket about the boy's shoulders. "Try to get some rest." But the boy would not move. Not that night, or the next, or the night after that.

The girl lay on her bed and watched the same stars. She saw them appear in the evenings and fade in the mornings. She heard the clocks chiming in the city and counted each hour as it passed her by. But there was nothing they could do, either of them, to stop the time from passing.

The writing finished there. I sat still, the book open across my knees. The strange thing was that I had read this story before, I was certain. And it was not pretend. I was sure that it was real; it had really happened.

It might be, I thought, that the little boy was the prince who had been born the same year I had, the prince who was supposed to have been exiled to that legendary country. Prince Cassius. What was the country's name? Angel Land, or something very like. But that country was not real. Lucien's troops killed everyone in the castle that night; they killed the king, and the queen, and the prince. His advisor Talitha had been responsible for it; she had great powers, and it would have been an easy thing for her to kill a five-year-old boy. This was no more than a story, then.

But what about the girl? Some of the words in the passage about her I did not understand. What was a car, or a dashboard, or a radio? They sounded like foreign words. Perhaps she was in another country. Perhaps Angel Land too. Then she also was pretend.

"Leo! Stirling!" my grandmother called. "Get up quickly. It will take longer to walk to school in the snow." Stirling rolled over, muttering. I put the book into my coat pocket. I did not know yet what powers were in it, and I wanted to keep it with me.

As I went down to fetch water, I remembered that pretend country's name. That legendary land, in another world, that my grandmother used to tell us fairy stories about. It wasn't "Angel Land" at all. The name was "England."

***

On the way to school, I was still thinking about the book. Where had the writing come from? Perhaps I should not have picked it up. The story was nothing to do with me, and now I might be involved with it. But I was interested; I could not help wondering if that boy was the prince, and if so, whether he was still alive. If he was still alive, the prophecy could be fulfilled. But—

"Leo?" I came back from my thoughts. I was surprised to see the street and the snow and the houses still there. I turned to Stirling, jogging beside me. I had been walking fast, absentmindedly—too fast for him.

"What?" I said, slowing my pace.

"Leo, what are you thinking about?" he asked me. I shook my head, smiling at his upturned face, so serious.

"Nothing. Only a fairy story." I shrugged. "One of those old ones about England, but you probably won't remember."

"England?" he said. "Yes, I remember."

"What, then?" I asked him.

"England was the place Grandmother used to tell us about. The explorers went into a different world and found it."

I was surprised. He could not have been more than three years old when she used to tell us those stories. "And the prince went there," Stirling went on. "The prince was sent to England."

"Prince Cassius, who would have been Cassius the Third," I said. "You remember the stories too?"

"Yes, of course. Only I don't think they were stories."

"How do you mean?"

"I think the country is real."

"Real?" I said. He nodded. "How can it be real?"

"A lot of people think it is," he told me. "I'm not the only one."

"You are the only one these days, Stirling."

"No, I'm not," he insisted. "And I've thought about it a lot, and it makes sense, England being real."

As we walked on I watched him carefully, still startled that he could remember these things. "Why?" I said. "Why does it make sense?"

He thought for a moment. "The prince was sent there, for one thing. And the prince was real."

"Most people think that the prince was killed," I told him. "I don't."

I smiled at his certainty. "Is that all?"

"No," he said. "The poem that Grandmother's brother wrote said the prince would go there, not die."

"The prophecy written by the great Aldebaran." Aldebaran was our great-uncle, but we kept quiet about it. Harold North as our father was enough. "No one pays attention to those old prophecies these days," I told him.

"They should," he said. "It isn't old—it's sixteen years. Besides, they are usually right."

"Perhaps. What do you know of prophecies?"

"Not a lot. But all the real ones that I have heard of have come true. If the great ones who make them can actually see into the future, then they must be true."

"Well, perhaps this was not a real one."

"It was a real one," he said. "That means England is real."

"All right then," I said. "It may be that England is real." But I did not really believe it, now that I said it out loud.

"Speaking of the prophecy . . . ," he began.

"What?"

"I wanted to ask you—but . . ." We were nearing the school gates, and we always reduced our talk to harmless chatter when we got to this point in the road. It was understood, though we never said it—this point opposite the newspaper stand, on the corner of Paradise Way. "Later," he said.

There was no queue, so I bought a newspaper. "What's the headline?" Stirling asked.

"'Deadlock.'"

"What's that?"

"When a situation is going nowhere."

"The war, then. What does the rest say?"

"Too much to tell you now," I said.

"Will you read it to me when we get home?"

"All right." I folded it and put it into my pocket. "You know, you need to learn to read. You're eight years old."

"I can read, almost. Anyway, you can get clever without reading."

"I know. You think a lot."

"Yes," he said. "Mostly in class. And in church. Do you think that is bad?"

"No," I said. "Grandmother might, though."

Our grandmother took Stirling to Mass with her every day. His First Communion would be in July—July the twenty-first; the date was already set. I had never made my First Communion, and now that I was fifteen, Grandmother had given up suggesting it. And I refused to go to church except on Sundays. I think that it had as much to do with hating to be told what to do as with not being especially religious, though both were true.

"Yes." He laughed. "Grandmother might. Would God think that it was bad?"

"I doubt he even notices."

"He does. He notices everything. The sparrows and everything. So he'd notice for sure if people didn't listen in church sometimes. If it was bad."

"All right, all right," I told him. "Don't preach. And you know I don't like to be asked these religious questions."

"Why not? I'm only asking what you think."

"Stirling, leave it."

"Sorry."

He said it so humbly that I went on, more gently, "I'm sure he doesn't think it's bad. Anyway, I am the one going to hell, because I *never* listen in church." He laughed. "Come on," I said. "We're late."

The last boys were stumbling past us through the gate and rushing through the slushy snow in the yard to line up. Sergeant Markey, Stirling's teacher and the worst in the school, was surveying them with his usual expression, which was hard to identify as any emotion. It changed to contempt when he saw Stirling and me. He hated us and made no secret of it.

I glared back and gave Stirling the look I gave him every morning—a look of patient endurance, like a criminal resigned to his execution—and we turned to the gate. The look annoyed Sergeant Markey. "Boys, for God's sake, get in here now!" he spat. He must have been about the only person in Malonia who had no qualms about taking the name of the Lord in vain. I saw Stirling frown as he said it.

Sergeant Markey saw the frown too. We went in, but we didn't hurry. I made a point of dragging my heels, to annoy him. Sergeant Markey glared, but Stirling walked in so meekly that he could say nothing.

The snow was freezing hard as we walked home from school; it was treacherous. The streets were in shadow and bitterly cold. "So, do you think I could be right?" Stirling asked me again as we skittered down Paradise Way. "Do you think the land of England could be real?"

"It could," I said. "There is no way to prove it."

"But the prophecy—"

"All it said was that the prince would be exiled. It never said to where. And even though everyone thought it was England, where Aldebaran was sent, it wasn't necessarily."

"But it was another world."

"If he was exiled at all. If he was not killed. You know, death's another world. You cannot trust the words people use, sometimes."

"I don't think they would have killed him. They would have known there was a prophecy."

It was true that Aldebaran's prophecy had been respected once, and perhaps Lucien's men would have been reluctant to kill the boy because of it. The prophecy had definitely said that no one could harm the prince. It said that he would not be killed but exiled.

The snow made the yellow brick of the houses look filthy. I wondered if the clouds gliding together over the city were snow clouds or rain. The largest one, just above the church far below in the square, looked exactly like a stretching hand. It was so close to the cross on the building's top that I imagined it could reach out and touch it. But the movement was just the wind.

"So, it could be real," Stirling persisted.

"What?" He had been talking, but I had not heard.

"England could be real."

"Yes," I said wearily. "Cannot you stop talking about it now? I should never have brought up the subject; since first I mentioned it, you have not stopped. And we are never going to find out."

"No," he said. "But the prophecy . . ."

"What about it?"

"If it came true, then we would find out whether England was real or not. Because the prince would come back, and—"

"Stirling," I interrupted. "The prophecy—you were going to tell me something about it. Remember? This morning, you said you'd tell me later."

"Oh yes . . ." He glanced around. "All right." He lowered his voice to a whisper. We had stopped still now in the silent street.

A woman appeared suddenly round the corner and hurried past us, clutching a coughing baby wrapped tightly against the cold. Stirling waited until she had passed, then bent his head close to mine. "Remember when Grandmother burned Father's books?"

"Oh yes," I said. "I remember."

"You don't have to speak in that way."

"What way?"

"Like that. It wasn't her fault."

"He told me to look after them while he was gone. She made me break my promise, and—"

"About the prophecy . . . ," Stirling interrupted. We'd had that conversation several times before. "When Grandmother burned them, I took one. I still have it now; I found it again last week. And I worked out what it says on the cover."

"You read the cover?" I said. He nodded. "So what did it say?"

"It said this: 'A prophecy of the lord Aldebaran, written in the sixth year of the reign of Cassius the Second.'"

20

"That is the very same one," I said. "It must be."

"I thought so. And I wanted to ask you to read it to me. It took me an hour at least to read the cover, and you read fast, Leo."

I stared at him. "That is a very rare book. And I never even knew you had it." He grinned at that.

We resumed our careful walk. "If Grandmother knew, she'd kill you," I remarked. "You know that book is on the Highly Restricted list. You could get three months just for having it."

"Three months? Three months of what?"

"Three months in jail! It is a serious offense. Grandmother would be very angry if she ever found out."

"Yes, I know. Shh." He looked around anxiously. "Don't tell her, please."

"All right, I won't." I'd never intended to. I just wanted to caution Stirling. "And I can read it to you if you want."

"Thank you," he said. "Thank you, Leo."

"You still should not have it."

"I'm not the only one who's hiding books," he said, grinning.

"What?"

"You've got that one Father signed for you—*The Golden Reign*."

"How did you know about that?"

"You used to look at it all the time, when I was really small. When you thought no one was watching you. You used to—"

"Yes. Well," I said, cutting him off. "That's different. *The Golden Reign* is only Restricted. That prophecy is on the Highly Restricted list, which is serious. And besides, that book was mine. I didn't steal it. You took that—"

I stopped short. Reaching a meeting of the roads, we almost

careered into the middle of a group of soldiers on horseback. We stumbled upon them as they broke into abruptly raucous laughter. The nearest horse skittered sideways and the rider reined it into the circle again. We hurried on past the next block of houses. The snow on the ground quieted everything strangely, and we had not heard them.

◦❦◦

*W*e walked quietly, not looking at each other. "Do you think they heard us?" whispered Stirling when he seemed to judge that we were out of earshot.

"Of course not," I told him. "And it is no matter if they did." And I hoped he couldn't hear my heart beating as loud as I could. The sound of it angered me. I was not scared of the soldiers. It was just coming upon them suddenly that had startled me.

"Stirling, watch this," I told him. I pointed my finger at a deep snowdrift and sent a spray of orange sparks into it. Another trick. The snow leapt upward, leaving steaming pockmarks like bullet wounds where the sparks had landed. There was a loud bang, and I heard one of the soldiers' horses whinny, perhaps in surprise. They were not so far off as I had thought. But maybe it was just chance. They were used to gunshots, after all.

"Don't do that, Leo," Stirling whispered fiercely. "Stop showing off."

"Why are you so worried?" I demanded. "Are you scared of the soldiers or what?"

"You're the one that's scared, trying to pretend you're not," he retorted quickly. "It's true."

I turned away, quickening my pace. It was only a moment

before Stirling caught up with me and grabbed my arm. He had to reach up to do it. "Leo?" I ignored him. "Leo? Sorry I said you were scared of the soldiers. I know you weren't really." I still didn't speak.

Stirling hated it when anyone was angry with him. "Leo, that trick was good really," he said. "It's just because of the soldiers. I don't want them to put you in prison for doing magic. . . ." I gave in, and slowed my pace to let him catch up. "You know what, Leo?" I didn't answer. "I think," he continued, "I think you could be like Aldebaran one day."

I was pleased in spite of myself. "Really?"

"Yes, really. It runs in the family, doesn't it? Someone's got to have powers after him, and no one has yet."

"But they're just stupid tricks," I said. "Not real magic."

"Well, if you practiced, I think you could be really good. You could train in magic and be named a great one, the lord Leo. When you grow up, I mean."

"Stirling, I am grown-up. And I'm going to be a soldier."

He looked at me for a moment, frowning so that the freckles on his nose slid together. "But you don't want to be a soldier."

"I know."

He went on frowning as we walked. "Couldn't you train in magic instead? Aldebaran did."

"That was a long time ago. Before King Lucien. You know how it is with children who have powers these days. High-security schools, and they teach them a lot of rubbish. They are scared that if there was a revolution, those children could fight against the government; that's what I think."

"What's a revolution?" he asked. I could have sworn that he

knew all this. But I liked telling him things that I knew and he didn't, so I tried to explain.

We walked in silence after that. We were nearing home now. As we got closer to it, the castle rose over the white sky, high on its rock above the city. Flags were flying from every tower and battlement, and even from this distance below, I could make out the lion and the dove in the Kalitz family crest. That washed-out blue always made me think of school, because the flags were everywhere there too.

The castle rock was plastered with snow, even on the flat surface. The cannons watched us like a band of hungry vultures. Soldiers were constantly marching up and down the rock face on the zigzag road. Especially in these past months. King Lucien wanted more troops than ever to guard the city.

I would have liked to live in a castle like that. It used to look like an ancient temple, carved from the red rock of the very peak of the volcano itself. I could remember when it glowed like an orange coal in the morning—the first part of the city that the sun reached—and every window was a spark too bright to look at. Lucien had reinforced it with new guard towers and walls so that it no longer looked like it was part of the old island city.

But they said that from the highest balcony you could see the whole of Kalitzstad—the church, the square, the Royal Gardens—everything laid out like a map; and the river, winding round both sides of the city as it ran from north to south. To the west you could see as far as Port Hopeful and even the shadow of Holy Island on clear days; the other way, as far as the Eastern Mountains. Or that was what I'd heard. It was just a rumor. Everything seemed to be just a rumor these days.

"Is it a good thing, then?" said Stirling.

He was thinking aloud. "What?" I said.

"A revolution."

"Well, when Lucien took over, that was a revolution. I think. And that was a bad thing." I looked around when I said that. Luckily, no soldiers were in sight. That comment would probably have constituted high treason.

"Does it always turn out the same, a revolution? Does it always turn out bad?"

"I don't know. I only know about Malonia."

"Is it always by fighting?"

"I don't see any other way that you could take over a country."

"There must be other ways."

"Sometimes the only way to do something is by armed conflict."

"Sorry, but I disagree," he said firmly.

I laughed. "Listen to you—eight years old and talking like a lawyer." I was the one who had taught him the word "disagree." Before that, he used to say "I don't agree." And it used to irritate me, because he said it a lot. "Maybe you will be a lawyer," I said. "You like arguing, for sure."

"I don't think I'll be a lawyer," he said.

"All right, so what do you want to be?"

"A priest maybe. Like Father Dunstan. Don't roll your eyes. What's wrong with being a priest?"

I shrugged. "A priest doesn't earn much money" was all that I could come up with.

The streets were darkening as the clouds got thicker. A

ragged paper fluttered down the street, like a bat, and landed flat on the wall. It was a Wanted poster. I plucked it off as we passed it, and examined it carelessly before throwing it aside. "What was that?" Stirling asked.

"Just another dangerous criminal," I said. "Some kind old grandfather who apparently plotted to kill King Lucien."

He laughed.

We were rounding the corner of our street now—Citadel Street. It led to the castle eventually, though it was not the only street that did, and the apartments were cheap because of the constant thoroughfare of soldiers day and night. "What's wrong with being a priest?" Stirling said again. "If you don't want me to be a priest, Leo, I won't be a priest."

"Why are you so impressionable?"

"What's that?"

"Easily swayed by what other people say. I mean, if it's what God's told you to do, it is what you have to do. Who's more important, God or me?"

"But like Jesus said, if I hurt you, I hurt him. Like it says, 'Whatever you do to one of the least of these my brothers—'"

I laughed. "Stirling, shut your mouth and be a priest if you want to. I can't think of you being anything else."

"Unless I have to be a soldier too." He frowned. "Maybe there'll be another revolution by then. A good one. Maybe the prince will return."

"Shh, Stirling. Do you want to go to prison?"

"Sorry, Leo."

He began to hum, and we walked the rest of the way without speaking. It was not far.

The next morning I was disappointed to find that there was no more writing in the strange book. I had hoped that there would be. I had expected, even, that there would be. I went on checking the book when I remembered, but after a week with still nothing, I began to forget it.

One evening I came home late and alone. The snow was still frozen in hard gray slivers at the edges of the streets, where the sun never reached. It was the beginning of June now, but it might as well have been winter. I hurried. I did not like to approach people suddenly in the shadowed alleys when I did not know who they might be. But that day the streets were almost deserted. The air was so still that I could just hear the gunfire and explosions from the northeast border, where Malonia meets Alcyria. It was a long way away, but on days like this it could be heard.

I trudged down the alleyway beside the house and let myself in at the side door, shaking the hard ice off my boots. That day the sky was dark with clouds, and dusk was falling in the stairwell. My footsteps echoed coldly on the stone as I hurried up the stairs. I passed the two lower doors—reinforced steel, identical to ours—then reached the third one, second from the top. The top apartment had stood empty for years, and dust lay thick on the handrail and the steps beyond our door.

"I'm home, Grandmother!" I called, shutting the door behind me. My grandmother marched in. "Leo, where have you been? Where is Stirling?" I sat down on the sofa, dumped my coat beside me, and put my keys back into my pocket. "Leo, where is Stirling?" she asked again.

"He got kept in late," I told her. I spoke slowly, because I knew she wanted me to speak fast.

"Again?" She stopped in front of the sofa and regarded me, frowning. "What did he do this time?"

"He wouldn't do drill. It was target practice, and you know he never does that."

"Why wouldn't he today?"

"I didn't ask him."

My grandmother sat down in the chair beside the window, throwing up her hands in a gesture of despair. "Honestly, Leo!"

"What? What did I do? It's not my fault that Stirling is a pacifist, or whatever the hell he is."

"Leo, he is not a pacifist," she told me, standing up again restlessly. I looked at her but didn't say anything. "He doesn't even know what a pacifist is. He's only eight! You are a bad example to him, Leo, for one thing, and for another—he's lazy."

"I think you underestimate him sometimes," I ventured. "He's very clever. Anyone can see he's very clever and if—"

"Don't tell me," she interrupted. "However intelligent he is, he won't get anywhere with it. Intelligence is worthless unless it's applied to something. What use is a scholar in the family? No one needs professors or lawyers. We need soldiers and farmers and factory workers. Books and lectures do not put food on the table."

"It's easy for you to say that! My father did none the worse for being clever. How do you put food on the table, then? With the money from his books, that's how. You do not work."

"Would you have me work, Leo?"

"No. All I'm saying is that you don't."

"I don't have time, with looking after you and Stirling."

"You don't need to, because you have all the money from my father."

"Aye, and we are extremely fortunate that no one has found out. And look what Harold's cleverness cost him. My only son, fleeing in the night like a criminal, and now—" She stopped and began again. "Your great-uncle—so famous and powerful—his cleverness got him nowhere either. Dead. Is that where you want to end up?"

"Yes," I told her. I should have just let it go, but I was tired of her constant lecturing.

"Yes?" she repeated, her voice rising. "*Yes?* Well, that's where you are going to end up if you don't start working. I'm sick of you always complaining about school. Don't you know how lucky you are?"

"*Lucky?*"

"Don't you know what some boys would give to have the education you are getting? Don't you know how fortunate you are to be able to become a soldier? And you are so ungrateful as to say—"

"What's ungrateful?" I shouted. "What is there to be grateful for? All I said is, I'd rather end up dead. I mean it. I'd rather be dead if it means I don't have to end up as some bastard soldier. They think they're so bloody smart—"

"Leo!" I had not heard her shout so loudly in a long time. "Do not dare to talk to me like that!" I was always in trouble for swearing. "You are the one who thinks he's smart," she yelled. "Well, you've got a lot to learn! Including some respect."

She turned away, breathing heavily. Her face in the glass trembled, yellow with fury, and for a moment I thought I was frightened of her. I suppose I was remembering how I used to be scared when she shouted, when I was very young. I watched her for a moment. I felt suddenly like laughing at the response I had got so easily. I don't know why.

It got darker and darker in the room while I sat there. My grandmother made no move to light the oil lamp on the table. She stood as if she was carved of stone. The only sign that she was not a statue was a circle of mist on the window, getting larger and smaller, and then larger again, as she breathed onto the glass. The room was cold and I wanted to put my overcoat back on, but I was caught in the silence and I could not break it.

I wished then that I had not shouted at her. She was, after all, quite old, and I should have known better. I was not a little child. I should have made an effort. I vowed to myself that I would try to understand her better. I would try to control my temper. I wondered idly if she would ever move.

Eventually she turned back to me. The clouds were so dense outside now, and the light so dim, that I could not make out her expression. "Leo, why did you not wait for your brother?" she asked. She was carrying on the conversation, though her voice was shaky. She was still angry, I judged.

"I tried to wait," I said, "but Markey caught me."

"*Sergeant* Markey," she said, her voice tighter. "I want you to go back and meet Stirling."

"What? I stood there more than an hour before I came home—more like two hours. I'm still cold. It's below freezing out there." And it was a long way back to school. But I knew I was going to go.

"You heard me. It's not safe for him to walk by himself at six o'clock with the weather dark like this."

"All right," I said. That was it. I was going to try to control my temper. I crossed to the door.

"Leo." I turned to her. "Don't forget your overcoat."

I could tell by her voice that her anger was gone. It sounded like an apology. Stupidly, I had to take advantage of it. I reached out at the coat, and with a snapping like a bat's wing, it was in my hand. Another trick. It hurt my head to do that when I was tired.

My grandmother moved faster than I would have believed she could. She snatched the coat out of my hand and threw it back as if it burned her. Her eyes flashed with anger and something else. Fear. It was exhilarating. She was scared of me, I realized. She was actually scared of me. "What do I have to tell you about those stupid tricks?" Her voice was high. "Go back and pick it up properly." But I turned and marched out without a word, slamming the door behind me.

When I reached the school gates, it was nearly six-thirty. I was shivering cold without my coat, and I half wished I had not marched out like that. I looked about for Stirling. A light was still burning in a classroom window. I had waited here earlier, but Sergeant Markey had caught me and sent me away.

As I stood watching the buildings, a door opened and a small figure appeared against the light. It was Stirling. He trekked across the yard and through the gates. The snow was frozen in gray troughs and peaks, where many heavy boots had kicked it to slush during the day. I hurried to meet him as he stumbled across it.

As he got closer I saw that he was shivering too, and there

was a blue tinge to his face that was not just the strange reflection of the snow. Two white points stood out on his cheeks, and I realized that they were beads of ice. Frozen teardrops. He stood still in front of me. "Look at you," I said. "What have you been doing?"

He shivered. I put my hand to his shoulder, leading him away. I could feel him trembling. "He made me stand out in the cold until I did drill," Stirling said in a shaky voice.

"Who? Sergeant Markey?" He nodded. "For how long?"

"Since the end of school."

"But that's three hours! It's well below freezing point." Stirling didn't say anything.

"So you did drill in the end?" I asked.

"No."

"Why did he let you go, then?"

"He was closing the school."

I looked at him hard. "Stirling, have you been crying?" I did not mean to sound reproachful. But boys in our country don't cry. They just don't. It's a sign of weakness. Then again, Stirling was very small. He didn't answer. "Did he hit you?" I asked him. Stirling put out his hand. I held it in mine, toward the light of the streetlamp. On the white palm, three raw stripes stood out. The skin shone where it had been struck. His hand was cold, so cold—as if he was dead—and so small.

I let it go and shivered. "He didn't have to hit you three times. Not if you cried."

"That's not why I cried," Stirling said.

"Why, then?"

"He was saying things. Mean things."

"What things?"

He sighed shakily. "Just . . . mean things . . . It doesn't matter now, anyway."

"Tell me," I said. "I think I can take it."

He paused. "Just things about our mother and father. Nothing, really. It was stupid of me to cry, and—"

I interrupted him sharply. "What things?"

"He said . . . our mother was . . ." He glanced at me. "No better than a prostitute."

"No better than *what*?" I said, hearing my own voice rising.

"I told you."

I could not speak. I tried to, but I could not.

"He only said it to make me cry," Stirling muttered.

At that I found my voice again and began shouting.

"Leo, stop it," Stirling said. "Don't shout at me. Don't swear like that." He looked close to crying again. "Leo, please. This is why I didn't want to tell you."

"Sorry." I kicked hard at the snow in the gutter. It was frozen solid, and I only hurt my foot.

"You don't have to fight my battles for me, Leo," Stirling said, his voice still unsteady.

"How will you fight them if I don't?"

"The way you're supposed to."

"Which is what? Letting other people win? Turn the other cheek? Sometimes that's the wrong thing to do. People have to know when they're doing something bad." I glared at the ground. "Did he really say that?"

"Yes. Well, perhaps he didn't mean it to sound as bad. First he said, 'Don't think you're above becoming a soldier.'" His voice wobbled. "That's not what I thought. I never think I'm above anything."

"I know."

"Then he went on talking, and he said, 'You're lucky to have any chance in life at all, knowing what your parents were. Your father deserved worse than he got, making his money out of royalist . . . royalist . . .'"

"Propaganda?" I prompted him. I had heard these things before.

"Yes. . . . And he said, 'And your mother was no better than a prostitute.' That's what he said. So he didn't mean that she was a prostitute exactly."

I didn't speak. "She wasn't anything like that, was she?" asked Stirling tentatively.

"What?" I turned to him, grabbing his shoulder. "Stirling, you are clever enough to know that's a lie. She was a singer. A good singer—really good."

"And a dancer and all."

"Yes. But in theaters, not bars or anything. There's a difference between that and a prostitute. Just because Sergeant Markey is a stupid bastard . . ." I realized that I was shaking his shoulder, and let it go. "She was a singer," I told him again.

"Oh. I can't remember her, that's all. And when people tell you something, you get to think that it's true."

"I know." I spoke more gently.

"Listen, Leo," he said. "Don't tell Grandmother. Please don't. It would make her so upset."

I hesitated for a moment, then nodded. He was still shaking. "Here, let me give you my jacket," I said.

"No. . . . You don't even have an overcoat."

34

"It doesn't matter." I took off my jacket—regulation pale blue-gray—and wrapped it round his shoulders, on top of his coat. "Come on," I said. "The sooner we get home, the better."

When we got in, Grandmother fussed over Stirling, making him tea and putting him to bed. I sat by the fire and coughed and shivered. I had put on my jacket again, and my coat, but I was still cold. I stared into the fire, frowning.

Grandmother came back into the room, shutting the bedroom door behind her. "Sleeping," she whispered to me. She pulled her rocking chair close to the fire and sat down and began to sew together some squares of colored material, and she held them barely an inch from her face. She started humming. It irritated me. "All right, Leo?" she asked. I nodded. We never had much to say to each other. "I've put some soup on the stove," she said. I nodded again.

I watched the flames caper about the small pile of wood in the grate. It hurt my head to look at the brightness, and I shut my eyes, but I could still see colored spots blaring against my eyelids. And Grandmother went on humming, out of tune. I rested my head against my arms, and my arms on my knees. "I hope Stirling doesn't catch a chill," she said after a while.

"A chill?" I said, looking up sharply. "Did you see how he was shivering? He could catch more than a chill standing outside in the snow for three hours—"

"Don't shout at me about it, Leo," she said. She picked at the sewing without meeting my eyes.

"I'm not shouting," I said, lowering my voice. "And you are partly to blame. You think the teachers are angels of God who can do no wrong. He made Stirling cry! That bastard Markey is constantly bullying him—"

"Leo."

"Stop interrupting me!" I was shouting now. It made my own head ache, but somehow that made me shout louder. "Something has to be done. He made Stirling cry!"

"What was Stirling crying about?" she said, putting down the sewing.

I stopped then. I had promised not to tell her. I shrugged and rested my head against my knees again.

"I am on your side, Leo," she said after a minute. "I just want you to be happy. Happy with what you've got." I looked up at her. She picked up the sewing and continued with it as she talked. "I know that you do not like school, but you have to make the best of it. You have to get used to your life the way it is. That's why I take the teachers' side. It's not because I think you are in the wrong all the time."

I did not answer. "Could Stirling be moved from Sergeant Markey's class?" she said then. "I could speak to the headmaster. He's sensible, and he has always been kind to you both. He would want his teachers to be reported if they are behaving unacceptably."

"Perhaps," I said. "There is another Second Year platoon. I hardly know the teacher, though." Our school went right up from First Year to Ninth Year—from six years old to fifteen. With two classes for each year, that made over nine hundred pupils. All boys, of course. Girls hadn't gone to school in Malonia since Lucien took power. "I suppose you could speak to the colonel," I said, but I knew Stirling would say no.

"Oh yes," she said. "It's not headmaster; it's colonel. And a class is a platoon."

I laughed. "It's stupid, isn't it? You have to admit it's stupid."

"Perhaps. Perhaps it's good training." She put down her sewing again and went to stir the soup on the stove. I was still coughing. "Leo, are you sick?" she asked.

"No," I said. "I just got cold this afternoon, that's all."

But I went to bed still coughing. "I worry about Stirling," I told Grandmother when she came in to check on him. "I worry that he doesn't . . . defend himself. Do you know what I mean?"

"Blessed are the meek," she said. "There is more than one way of fighting life's battles, Leo." I sighed, turned over, and went to sleep.

In my dreams I returned to the story that had appeared, to the people and the places from the strange book. I could see the girl and the glittering necklace, and then the prince on that highest balcony with his mother and father as the sun set. I could see them clearly. And then, in my dream, another story began. An old man was sitting alone in an empty house when a stranger appeared at the door.

Although he had been listening for it all week, the doorbell startled Raymond. He had been certain no one would come after all. This was the last day, and no one had come yet. He put down his newspaper and struggled out of his armchair.

The bell rang again. It always made the glass cases in the hall rattle, now that they were empty. Raymond dampened the nearest one with the back of his hand as he passed, and hobbled to the door. He fumbled with the new locks, muttering, "Just coming."

A few feet back from the step stood a middle-aged man. He

was a gray-looking man—that was what Raymond thought first—gray like steel. Gray eyes, gray shadows of stubble on his chin, gray hair—not through age but naturally that metallic color.

"Al . . . er . . . Arthur Field," said the man, in an accent that was not English but not quite foreign either. "I have come about the butler's job." As he spoke, he held out a hand. And the hand that he held out was his left one. He was definitely not English, Raymond decided. He took the man's hand gingerly.

"Come in, then," Raymond told him.

The man set about scraping his boots on the doormat. While he did it, Raymond squinted at him, hands on hips. Arthur Field had a heavy cloak about his shoulders, and his clothes underneath were worn as though he had come a long way in them. Raymond caught the glint of a necklace at the man's throat, but the man pulled up his collar before Raymond could peer any closer. Raymond gestured to the drawing room door, and the man followed him.

Arthur Field looked even more out of place in the drawing room. He sat where Raymond indicated, in the armchair beside the window, and waited. Raymond lowered himself into the chair opposite.

Arthur was glancing at the glass cases around the room. "So . . . ," said Raymond, and the man's gaze fixed on him. "You wish to apply for the butler's job?"

"Yes. I saw your advertisement in the newspaper."

"And what training and experience do you have?" Raymond asked.

"I . . . er . . . don't have any formal training . . . as such," the man faltered. Raymond waited for him to go on, but he didn't.

"I see," said Raymond eventually.

"I could not help but notice the . . . er . . . reinforced vehicle on the grass," the man remarked, looking out the window, when the silence became embarrassing.

Raymond smiled. "It does look rather imposing there, doesn't it? It seems to scare away trespassers better than any guard dog!"

"I expect it would."

"It's a genuine First World War tank," Raymond continued. "Actually saw service in France, would you believe?"

"It must be rare to own one of those."

"Yes, but I've had it a long time, you see!" Raymond told him. "Many museums have approached me, but I won't sell it to them."

"You cannot put a price on something like that."

"No, indeed," said Raymond. "No, no, indeed." He chuckled. "So, you are interested in weaponry, are you, Mr. Field?" he asked.

"It is . . . yes . . . fascinating. Though I don't know much about it."

"I've built up some knowledge over the years," Raymond said, gesturing to the cases around the room. "And quite a collection too."

"May I?" the man asked, rising.

"Certainly."

Each of the weapons lay in its case on glistening red velvet and was labeled with a card as if it was a museum exhibit. "So these were made much earlier than the . . . er . . . First World War . . . ," Arthur ventured.

"Of course!" Raymond exclaimed. "These are all swords, daggers, and rapiers in this room, from the sixteenth century to the early nineteenth." He went to stand beside Arthur, who was looking into the largest case.

"This is my particular favorite," said Raymond. "A gentleman's rapier, which I'm pretty sure is Spanish, and it's in remarkably good condition, don't you think?"

"Yes."

"I rather like the decoration on the hilt," Raymond continued. "That's a fine example of the cup hilt, and it's a Toledo blade. I've always wanted to know for sure if it was Spanish, or an imitation."

"Are there experts who could tell you that?"

"I'm sure there are—though I've never really asked anyone. I tend to keep my collection a secret. You never know what a con man might try if he wanted to find out about valuable weapons."

"Would someone really steal antique weapons?" the man asked.

"Oh yes," said Raymond, with bitter triumph. "Oh yes, they would. Only a couple of months ago, nearly my entire collection of firearms was stolen. You must have noticed the empty cases in the hall."

"I did." The man frowned at Raymond, his eyes intense. "A misfortune indeed."

"I was sad to lose them," said Raymond.

"And have you been able to trace the thieves?"

"No . . . the police have had no luck as yet. It's my belief the criminals have smuggled the weapons into another country, but the police don't think so."

"Well, it would not be easy. Surely controls are tight."

"I would have thought so. I don't know how they'd have done it. But if they were determined enough, they'd have managed."

"How many of these weapons were stolen?"

"I had fifty-seven rifles and twelve pistols, as well as a Victorian revolver. Of them, fifty-three were stolen, and one of the most valuable ones was knocked to the floor and broken. The ones they left were the oldest."

"That is odd."

"Yes. Here's the strange thing: there was evidence of someone entering this room. They found fingerprints. Yet they took nothing from here. And I know that a good many of these pieces are more valuable than the guns were."

"Perhaps they wanted the weapons themselves, not the money."

"That may be."

Raymond limped back to the window and sat down heavily, motioning to the other chair. The man strode across the room but did not sit down. "It would take several people to carry fifty-three guns, would it not?" he asked.

"Oh yes. You know, I heard nothing, but it must have taken a veritable army to cart the things off."

The man leaned forward, gripping the back of the chair so tightly that the tendons in his hands quivered. "A veritable army indeed."

"It is most peculiar," Raymond went on. "I cannot think why someone would want to steal the least valuable weapons in the house."

"Perhaps . . . ," suggested the man, "they meant to replicate them."

"But whatever for?"

"To use."

"No . . . I can hardly see why. There are simpler ways of getting guns for hunting and suchlike; I would imagine even criminals have easier sources. And why take so many?"

The man seemed deep in thought for a minute. "Tell me," he said slowly. "Tell me—these weapons—are they very complicated?"

Raymond thought about that. "Certainly not compared to the modern standard-issue weapons. But they are very well designed, some of those old firearms."

"Do you think someone would be able to replicate them, if they had an original to work from?"

"I don't know. It would depend what they wanted them for. The decommissioned ones could have been reactivated, I suppose, and then copied. But most of them were antiques. The replicas wouldn't fool any serious collector."

"Well . . . say, for example, whoever stole your weapons wished to replicate them so that they would function. No more than function, simply so that they would fire. And then suppose they wanted to mass-produce them. Would they, in theory, be able to do that?"

"With only what they stole from me?"

'The man nodded. "In theory."

"Yes . . . ," said Raymond. "Yes, I believe they would." The man did not answer, so he elaborated. "A couple of them were sturdy bolt-action rifles. In the case of those particular weapons, their simplicity is what makes them so effective."

I woke suddenly. I was coughing again in the cold night air, and that was what woke me. In the darkness, I could see the light of the gas lamps on the cracks in the ceiling. I sat up. I heard that old man's voice echoing in my head for a moment, as if his spirit was lingering in the room even after the dream was gone. Then the building was silent. Stirling was asleep, his face turned to the wall. The church clock in the square was chiming two.

I realized that the book was lying on my bedcovers, that strange black book that I had found in the snow and all but forgotten. It was open. I picked it up, rubbing my eyes, and glanced at it. But before I had read half a page, I was wide awake and staring at the new writing.

I was frightened suddenly. It was not just that I felt I had read this story before. It was the same, even to the last word the old man spoke, as my dream. And in the book, the story went on.

❧

Raymond enjoyed talking about his weapons to one so attentive. "Yes," he continued. "I would go so far as to say that if time, money, and patience were no concern, someone could make a working replica of at least the simpler weapons."

Arthur didn't reply. "Please, sit down," Raymond told him, to break his unnerving stare. The man sat. "May I ask why you are so interested?"

"Oh . . ." Arthur laughed distractedly. "No reason really—just curiosity. It seems a strange crime."

"Yes, it was strange," said Raymond. And then he remembered why the man was here. "Anyway, about this butler's job . . ."

"Oh yes, of course," said the man, but the thoughtful frown did not leave his face.

"Look here," Raymond said. "I'd like to employ you, but you tell me you have no training or experience. Do you have any references at all?"

The man shook his head. "I was working in another country, in a very different field. I did not think references would be worth anything."

"Where were you working?" said Raymond.

"In Australia," said the man. He cast his eyes about the room. "Actually, I was in the army."

"The army!" said Raymond, leaning forward eagerly. "So when I asked you if you were interested in weaponry . . ."

The man laughed, showing all his teeth, like a skull. "Indeed."

"You were in the Australian forces, then?" Raymond went on.

"No," said the man. "I am not Australian."

"What were you doing there? Training?"

The man nodded. "In the desert . . . the Australian desert."

"What were you doing before that? Forgive me for asking; I'm rather interested in the army."

"Before that? We were carrying out . . . you know . . . operations . . ."

"Other than war?" said Raymond.

"Yes. How fast one forgets these things! Yes, we were working in various countries—I am afraid I cannot be too specific. It was highly secret."

"Of course." Raymond regarded the man with a new respect. "Anyway, about this job . . . Mr. Field, I would have liked to employ you—you're a decent sort of man, I can see—but if you've had no training whatsoever, I cannot pay you what I would pay an experienced butler."

"I think," said the man, "that we misunderstand each other. I did not expect payment."

Raymond looked up, startled. "I ask for nothing," Arthur Field went on. "I aim only to gain experience. I assume that whoever is employed will be lodged here?"

"Of course."

"That is all I ask for. I did not think you would assume that I wanted money while I was still training."

"I can't have you working here for nothing," Raymond began.

"You just said that you could not pay someone who had no experience."

"I meant that I could not employ someone who had no experience."

But he knew he was going to. He was under the strange man's power; the sinister gray eyes and the skull-like smile and the mind beneath the mask of casual indifference had drawn him in, and he was going to employ Arthur Field against his better judgment.

Later the new butler regarded himself in the mirror and smiled grimly. He did not like uniforms or groveling, or being called a decent sort of man by people who had half his intelligence.

Arrogance never did anyone any good, he told himself, rearranging the new black jacket impatiently. He was being arrogant. Here he had safety, a job, food, and shelter, and he was hidden. Here he was alive. Assuming an expression of subservience, he turned and marched out and down the stairs.

❧

*A*fter I closed the book, I sat in the darkness for a long time, thinking—and when I woke the next morning, the story was still in my mind. I wondered what the sixteenth and nineteenth centuries were, and the First World War. Were they English phrases? And if so, did that mean this story was connected to the other, the one about our exiled prince and that girl with the blue eyes? I was coughing all the rest of that week, and I could not shake it off, but I did not think about it so much as I would have done before. I was thinking about the book instead.

On Friday the cold weather ended suddenly. The rain streaked down the windows of the classroom, and I sat and watched it and thought again about that story. How did it concern me? If it was nothing to do with me at all, I did not know why I had dreamed about the old man and the stranger even before the writing appeared. It was very strange. I had tried to put it out of my mind, but I could not.

Something thudded on the desk in front of me then. It was a rifle. I stared at it for a moment, then blinked and looked up. Sergeant Bane was looking down at me, amusement in his face. "North, we are going out for drill," he said. "You were a hundred miles away." I saw that the rest of my platoon were already jogging out into the yard, the collars of their coats raised against the driving rain. "Hurry!" said Sergeant Bane. I stumbled up and fetched my coat, then picked up the rifle and ran out after the others.

We were training harder than ever now. We had shooting drill every morning for an hour, then weight training, and then we ran twenty times round the yard. But no one was making much of an effort that day, and by the time we got to running laps, we were all halfhearted. Even when the rain dwindled, the mud was still slimy, and I slipped and fell several times. I tried to run, but every few yards I doubled over coughing. "Keep going, North!" shouted Sergeant Bane from the shelter of the overhanging roof. I stumbled on.

It was while we were running that I thought of the book again and realized that the gun in my own hand was a bolt-action rifle. And I remembered suddenly that there had been a rumor, a long time ago, that our military technology had been developed in a country as far away as England. Just a rumor. I slowed to a jog and examined the gun in my hands. I did not know if it was a simple weapon, like the ones the old man and the stranger had been talking about. Perhaps in other places— places like England—they had guns that were far more advanced than this. I did not know.

Then Sergeant Markey appeared around the corner of the building, leading Stirling's platoon behind him. He stepped into the shelter beside Sergeant Bane, cast his eyes over us with a disparaging sniff, and said something that I could not hear. "North, you are going too slowly!" shouted Sergeant Bane to me. I was half a lap behind the rest. I ran to catch up, and that started me coughing again.

"One more lap and then you can go in," Sergeant Bane called as we passed him. I looked for Stirling in the crowd of younger boys and gave him a quick wave. He grinned back.

"North," said Sergeant Markey suddenly. "Come over here."

I stopped where I was. Stirling had stopped as well, but it was me that Sergeant Markey was talking to. "Come here!" he repeated. "Now."

I trailed over. I was coughing again, and I could not see his expression until I straightened up. He seemed to be smiling, but that did not reassure me.

"I noticed that North was not making an effort," he said, turning to Sergeant Bane. His voice was very reasonable. "So perhaps he can train for another hour and a half with my platoon. I will be very happy to supervise him."

"Given the state of his health . . . ," Sergeant Bane began, then seemed to change his mind. "Thank you, Sergeant Markey. Send him back in when he has finished."

After my platoon had gone back inside and Stirling's had started running, Sergeant Markey turned to me. "You think you're above hard work," he said, very quietly. "You think you're a bloody prince, North. This hour and a half will teach you better." He stared at me for a moment, and I could tell he was trying to make me look away. I didn't. "Thirty laps," he said then. "Get that rifle above your head. If it comes down, you will start again."

I began running, still coughing as I went. "One!" he shouted the first time I passed him. Then "Two!" I tried to think of the story again, so as not to feel the sharp pains that were rising in my chest, but it did no good. I got to six, then stumbled and dropped the rifle. I bent over, trying to catch my breath.

Sergeant Markey picked up the gun and put it into my hands, then pushed my shoulder hard so that I straightened up. "Are you going to give up now?" he said, his face close to mine. "I told you to run thirty laps and not to lower that rifle. Do you want to do some other training perhaps? Weights? Or just give up? Is that what you want?" I shook my head. "What's that?" he said.

"No," I muttered.

"No, Sergeant Markey!" he shouted, pushing my shoulder again.

"No, *Ser*geant Markey," I repeated. I spoke the word "sergeant" as if talking to someone insane who insisted on that inappropriate title. I should not have said it like that.

He watched me for a moment. I stood there coughing and trying to breathe. Sergeant Markey turned to survey the younger boys. "North, run faster!" he shouted at Stirling. "You're as lazy as your bastard brother! Do you hear?"

He turned back to me. "This is your first lap now," he said. "Start again."

I glared at him in silence. I decided suddenly to run the thirty laps even if it killed me to do it. I was coughing and gasping in air, but I started running again, keeping my arms locked straight above my head. They began to burn with pain, down to my shoulders, and the rifle grew so heavy that I had to slow to a jog. But I kept running. Every time I passed Sergeant Markey, he would stare straight at me, as though he was trying to put me off with his glare. My whole body was burning now, but my skin was cold with the rain and the sweat that was rising on it.

On the twenty-first lap, I fell to my knees in the mud. He was shouting something again. But suddenly I could not hear. I saw Stirling turn and say "Leo," and I could not hear his voice either. Then he ran to my side and caught hold of my arm. And after that everything went dark.

❧

Below me someone laughs, and I start and drop the book. My heart is beating fast at that faint sound. I get up and walk to the edge of the balcony. I must be losing my mind to start like that at such a slight noise far below in one of those lighted rooms. But I could not help it. I was far away and forgot that I was here at all. Perhaps that is crazy. You told me once that madness was a line, drawn only by humans and amounting to nothing more. But you know it as a theory. You have never been near that line.

I was trying to tell you about my old life, the way things were.

Perhaps I was too impulsive; perhaps I was too proud. But you have to understand that I felt trapped; I felt like I was being dragged in directions I did not want to go. And any response I got when I acted against this made me feel as if I was still alive. I drove Grandmother to exasperation and I argued with Sergeant Markey because I wanted more than anything to be free. I thought that no one could make me do anything. I used to look up at the stars and think, *That's Leo there, and no one can reach me.* I don't know if it was true.

All those years, I thought I was unhappy. I don't think anymore that I was. You told me something once that stuck in my head, about how thoughts are dangerous when you are in a bad situation. That if you let your thoughts console you and govern your life, you don't know what is true anymore. You don't see your life for what it is. You think that you're happy. I see now that it can go the other way. You can think that you're unhappy when you're not. That's what I did.

Standing at the edge of this highest balcony, I can see the lanterns strung out through the trees of the roof garden, the lights swaying as the breeze catches them, and the people walking there, just shadows among the trees. I can see the few carriages that move in the city streets, a long way below. I think suddenly that I would give anything to go back to those days.

I check the lamp, sit down against the wall, and open the book again. I will read the rest; I still have time. I cannot go back, but I can still read these words.

*T*he piercing blue of the sky was all that I could see when I woke. I lay and stared at it, thinking that I was in my bed at home. And then I heard a voice and saw that the windows above me were high and narrow, not the diamond panes of the window in the bedroom. "Leo, wake up," Stirling was saying. I turned over and remembered what had happened.

Stirling was kneeling beside me. He put his arm about my shoulders and made a sound like a sob. And it was, for when he drew back, I could see the tears in his eyes. "I'm all right," I said, trying to sit up. When I did, the room moved unsettlingly, and I lay back down again and shut my eyes. "Where are we?"

"The colonel's office." I felt Stirling take hold of my hand.

Then another voice was speaking, close by. "North, can you hear me?" I looked up. It was the colonel.

He knelt down beside me. "You passed out. You are not the first one to do this by any means. We brought you in here to recover."

"You were asleep for so long," said Stirling, clutching my hand. "I was talking to you all the time, and you didn't hear anything."

"It was only a few minutes," said the colonel. "That is nothing to worry about."

Everything was still strange and distant. I managed to sit up, and leaned back against the cold stone wall. Stirling would not let go of my hand. "You will need to go home and get some rest," said the colonel. He turned to Stirling. "You can take your brother home, can't you?"

"Yes," said Stirling. "I'll look after Leo."

"Good lad," said the colonel.

We sat there in silence. I was watching the sunlight on the papers that covered the colonel's desk, and the four-pointed stars it made on the glass cabinets around the walls. It was strange. Everything looked different since I had woken up. I can't explain it, but it felt as though I was in a completely different place. The world had changed. Or maybe it was just because the sun had come out. Stirling sat beside me and kept hold of my hand, and I let him. Then we got up and started for home.

"Grandmother will be angry," I muttered as we walked down Paradise Way. "Especially when she hears that I was being punished for not making an effort again."

But I was wrong. As soon as we stepped through the door,

Grandmother started up from her rocking chair, staring at me with such intent concern that I was startled. I went and lay down on my bed while Stirling explained. "Tell me again—tell me exactly what happened," Grandmother said, standing over me anxiously.

"I passed out when I was running," I said. "That's all. I should have stopped when I got tired, but I went on. I'm all right now."

She laid her hand on my forehead. "You don't seem to have a fever. But that cough of yours has been getting worse." She twisted her hands together. "I will get the priest to come and look at you," she said. "Father Dunstan will know if this is serious."

"It is not serious," I protested. "Grandmother, you don't need to send for Father Dunstan." But she was already hurrying out the door.

She arrived with the priest about half an hour later. "I pray to God that this is not silent fever," she said, hovering anxiously behind him while he took my pulse.

He shook his head. "It is exhaustion. That is why Leonard passed out." He turned to me. "Rest for a day or two. Get plenty of sleep. You have been training too hard for a long time, I think."

Grandmother and Stirling were still gazing at me in concern after Father Dunstan had left. I laughed at that. "I told you it was not serious. It's stupid, really. Usually I can run thirty laps without trouble."

"You didn't run thirty laps," said Stirling. "You ran more like fifty. Sergeant Markey kept starting again from the beginning."

"I should have seen that you were tired, Leo," said Grandmother, shaking her head. "I should have seen that all this army training was too much for you."

"It's not too much," I said. "It was that bastard Markey's fault."

And then I looked to see that Grandmother was not angry that I had sworn. And I was glad that she was not, which was strange. She did not reprimand me, either for that or for calling Sergeant Markey just "Markey." She only went on looking at me in that strange, concerned way and then tucked the blanket more tightly around me.

"I thought you would die!" Stirling exclaimed suddenly, clutching at my arm. "When I saw you fall down, I thought you would not get up again. I thought you were badly hurt."

"I'm fine," I said. "You don't have to worry. I'm sorry if I scared you."

"He's tough, our Leo," said Grandmother. "Thirty laps of that yard must be several miles." She took my hand, but her own trembled slightly. I could see the fragile relief in her face. She needed me, I thought, despite all our arguments. For a few minutes she had believed that I was very ill, and she could not have borne to lose me. The thought was comforting, because never before in my life had I realized it. We sat there, the three of us, talking as though we had not seen each other for days or years, while the sun came down through the window and lit up the whole room.

That afternoon Grandmother went out to the market, and Stirling sat beside my bed and talked to me. "Help me get up," I said after a while. "I'm going down to the bathroom."

"Now?" he said. "It might not be a good idea. I think you should stay in bed. What if you faint again?"

"I'll be fine," I said. "I will go carefully."

"I don't think you should go out in the cold," said Stirling. "There's always a bucket."

"I am not ill enough for that," I told him firmly. "Anyway, it's not cold. Look, the sun is shining." It had not stopped since I had woken up in the colonel's office and seen it slanting down through the high windows.

"All right," Stirling said doubtfully. "I'll help you, then."

He held on to my arm while I stood up, though I was not dizzy. I put on my army uniform—the nearest clothes to hand. I did up half the buttons on my shirt and pulled my jacket loosely round my shoulders. "Sit back down," Stirling told me, and he insisted on putting on my boots for me.

"Don't bother with the laces," I said. He still had trouble with laces. He took hold of my arm again and we started for the door. As I passed the mirror, I saw that there was mud in my hair and on the side of my uniform, and my face was still yellowish. "I don't look fit to be seen," I said, trying to flatten my hair.

"You're vain, Leo," Stirling told me, laughing. "No one's going to see you."

Everything was still strangely distant, and my muscles were shivering now from running too hard earlier. When we neared the bottom of the stairs, I began to feel sick again and darkness seared into my eyes. I could hear Stirling's voice, but over it was a painful thudding in the sides of my head. "Sit down," Stirling was telling me. "You're going to fall over." He pushed me firmly down onto the step. "Put your head down." I rested my head on my knees and shut my eyes. "I told you this was a bad idea," I could hear him saying.

After a moment my vision cleared and the blood flow in my temples lost its urgency. I stood up and we struggled down the last few steps. Stirling would not let go of me, even while he opened the door, and I was grateful for it. He held the door. But I started to feel dizzy again, and I couldn't see. Nausea bubbled up in my throat. I bent over sharply, retching, and my stomach stabbed.

Stirling did not let me fall. "You got up too quickly," I could hear him saying. "You should have brought your head up gradually."

And then another voice said, "Is he all right?"

"My brother's sick," said Stirling. And then, "Don't worry, it is not catching. Unless exhaustion is catching." And someone laughed.

I leaned on the door frame, gasping in air, and looked to see who it was. Someone was coming down the stairs, and as my eyes cleared, I saw that it was a girl about my age carrying some sort of heavy bundle in her arms.

❧

*T*he girl's hair fell carelessly over her shoulders, but as if she had arranged it that way, pushed it back so that it would fall forward over her ears. As she came closer, the light from the doorway shadowed her long eyelashes into spider-leg patterns on her cheeks. The jewels in her ears were expensive, but they did not make her look plain in comparison like they would have another girl.

There was something about her mouth that made me want to look at it. It was perfect. Her lips were parted slightly, self-consciously, as if she knew it made her look prettier but the action did not come naturally. I noticed I was staring at them, and looked away quickly. She was smiling. I tried to smile back.

"Do you live here?" the girl asked. I opened my mouth. Hell, she was pretty! She was like an ornament that should be kept locked up, for fear of ruining it. I shut my mouth again.

"Yes, we do," Stirling was saying.

"So do I," said the girl. "Since today. We just moved into the top apartment."

"I'm pleased to meet you," said Stirling. "I'm Stirling, and this is my brother, Leo. He's ill. He was training and he passed out, but he's all right now." I tried again to smile, without success.

"I'm Maria," she said. "This is Anselm." I realized that she was pointing to the bundle, and that it was a baby.

"Anselm?" asked Stirling.

"Yes, it's after a saint. A legendary English saint." She was standing next to us now. Stirling leaned over to look.

"He's sweet," said Stirling. "He looks like you. Is he your brother?"

"No, he's mine."

"Your what?" I tried to jog Stirling's arm.

"Mine," she said again, and she did not seem to mind. "My own baby."

"Oh," said Stirling. Then he asked, "Are you married?" I clutched my hand to my head before I could stop myself. The girl looked at me. "Do you have a headache? How thoughtless—I'm keeping you standing here in the cold when you are sick. I am sorry."

"Do not trouble yourself," I tried to say, without much success.

"Can you tell me where the bathroom is?" the girl asked.

"Out here," said Stirling, pointing out the door. "Across the yard."

"Thank you."

We followed her through the door, Stirling still supporting me. She stood still and looked round the yard, frowning at the grimy walls and the tall houses that blocked the sunlight. "I'm afraid it's not very nice," said Stirling, as if it was his own living room.

"Some plants would improve it no end, I daresay."

Then she realized we must be heading for the bathroom too. "You should go first," she told me.

"No . . . ," I said feebly, and wished we weren't having this conversation.

"Yes," she said. "The quicker you get back to bed, the better." I did not have the energy to insist. Stirling helped me across the yard to the bathroom door, and I went in alone. I could hear them still talking outside, and listened hard, in case they thought I could not hear.

"Your brother would not let you go into the bathroom with him." She was bold, for sure. "What if he was to faint again?"

"Even if he was dying, I don't think he would want to be helped more than he had to be."

"He is proud, then?" I could not hear Stirling's answer. "But pride is not necessarily bad. It is a virtue in some ways."

"That was what I meant," Stirling said. There was a short pause. The baby gurgled. Then Stirling's voice again: "Are you married?"

"No. Are you?" He laughed. The baby started to cry shrilly, and the girl said, "Shh."

"So is it just you and Anselm here?" Stirling asked when the baby quieted.

"My mother also."

"Where's your father?"

"Fighting at the Alcyrian border. Where your brother will be before long, I suppose. I see by his clothes that he is a soldier." I glanced down at what I was wearing, and remembered that my bootlaces were undone, and half my bare chest was showing, and there was mud in my hair. A fine soldier indeed I looked.

"He's in military school," said Stirling. "Then he'll have two and a half more years of training in the army."

"I thought by his looks that he was older."

"No, fifteen."

"Me also."

"I'm eight," said Stirling. "I'm in military school too. But neither of us like it. Especially my teacher—his name's Markey. Sergeant Markey, that is. He's really mean. I don't want to be a soldier when I grow up, and Leo doesn't either. He could be a—"

I opened the door hastily, and the girl said, with the faintest smile, "I see by your brother's face that he thinks you have said enough."

She pushed the door open with her free hand and looked in with disdain. "The bathroom's not very nice either," Stirling said apologetically.

"Never mind. At least there is a mirror, and a shower and a sink."

"Cold water, though."

"Ah, well." She shifted the baby higher up her arm.

"Would you like me to hold him for you?" asked Stirling.

"Your brother will be wanting to get back to bed."

"No, no," I told her. "I'll just sit here." I sat down and leaned against the wall.

"Thank you very much," said the girl, and she handed the baby to Stirling. "Keep your hand behind his head." She waited a moment to check that Stirling would not drop him.

When she shut the door, the baby began to cry. "Shh," Stirling said, the way Maria had, and jiggled him up and down, but he went on crying. The crying grew so insistent and so mournful that Stirling called, "Is he all right?"

"I think he's just hungry," Maria called back.

"I've got a sweet in my pocket."

"Don't give him that. He's still on milk."

"Oh. All right." Stirling went on jiggling the baby and put out his finger for him to hold. Anselm caught onto it and stopped crying long enough to draw breath, but then resumed his wailing louder than ever.

I was beginning to feel dizzy again. And my vision was going strange. My head and the back of my neck prickled sickeningly hot and cold. I looked at the ground, concentrating on the cracks in the paving stones to keep my sight straight. "You all right, Leo?" Stirling asked. I nodded.

I heard the bathroom door open, and the baby's crying subsided to a discontented grizzling. "You don't look well," Maria said. She was talking to me. I tried to lift my head. "Your face is very white," she said. "Oh dear. I am sorry to have kept you down here so long."

Stirling held out his hand and helped me up. I swayed and caught onto the wall. I held tightly to Stirling's shoulder as we struggled to the door. Maria held it open for us.

I could not see clearly where I was putting my feet, especially entering the dark hall suddenly after the yard. But I put one hand on the rail, and Stirling supported the other arm, and I managed to get up the stairs slowly. Maria followed us all the way, saying, "Sorry I can't help." And she really sounded sorry.

When we finally got to our apartment, Stirling had to get out his keys. I attempted to support myself while he did it, but the wall seemed to be sliding away. "Here, hold on to me," said Maria. She shifted the baby up to her elbow and held her other arm out. I tried to take it gently, but she slid it right around my waist and pulled me in to her suddenly. "I won't let you fall," she said. She was strong. I could not look at her face so close, but she was looking at me. I was painfully aware of her fingers, tight on my ribs, and her side, pressed right against mine, so that I could feel every breath she took.

Eventually Stirling got the door open and I moved over to him, still leaning heavily on his shoulder. "Goodbye, Maria," said Stirling. "Goodbye, baby Anselm."

"Goodbye," she said. "Wave goodbye, Anselm." She lifted the baby's hand into a wave, and he gurgled at us, dribble stringing from his mouth. And then, suddenly formal, she said, "It was nice to meet you."

"You too," said Stirling, and I managed a curt nod.

"I hope you get well quickly, Leo," she said, and went breezing up the stairs, but carefully, so as not to drop the baby.

I slept for the rest of the day. It was evening when I woke. I could hear hushed voices from the living room and something hissing over the stove. Stirling was standing in the light from the window, leaning on the back of the sofa and talking to Grandmother. I sat up, and he heard me and turned and came to the door. "You are awake, finally," he said, and sat down on the end of my bed. "Do you feel better now?"

I nodded. "I don't know why I passed out. Sorry to scare you, Stirling. I feel fine now." It was almost true. And when I got up, I was no longer dizzy. I dressed quickly, then followed him back into the living room.

Grandmother smiled at me from the kitchen. "I'm making you some soup," she said.

"You must be hungry," said Stirling as we sat down at the table. "It's broccoli soup, with potatoes in it and meat fat—"

"All right!" I said. "Please don't tell me about it." I was still feeling sick after that morning. "I'm sure I will feel hungry once I see it," I said.

Stirling had the newspaper in front of him, and he bent his head now and began trying to decipher the headline. After a while, he gave up and closed it. "I saw Maria again," he said, looking up. "I helped her carry some of her boxes up to the apartment."

"Oh yes?" I turned to him.

"She's like a princess," Stirling said. I nodded. "She's friendly, though," he went on. "Very pretty. Nice baby." It sounded as if he should be counting these out on his fingers as he said them. But he wasn't. "She was holding on to you close, wasn't she? This morning, when I was trying to open the door."

"Yes," I said cautiously, and then added, "Quite close."

"You should have seen yourself. You went bright red."

I was alarmed. "Did I?"

"I don't think she noticed. She didn't say anything about it this afternoon. She most probably thought it was just a fever." I laughed. "Did you think she was pretty?" he asked.

"Well, I suppose . . ."

"Who?" said Grandmother, setting the bowls down on the table.

"The girl we met today," said Stirling. "Maria. She has moved into the top apartment. She was very kind. She helped Leo when he was feeling ill, so I could open the door."

Grandmother sat down and began ladling out the soup. "Someone nice in the building—that will be a change after the last few."

"Can we invite her round here one day?" said Stirling. "We should invite her whole family round, to welcome them."

"Certainly," said Grandmother, quite unlike her usual self. "Who else is there? Her parents?"

"Her mother," said Stirling. "And her baby. His name is Anselm. He is very sweet, though he cries a good deal."

"Her baby?" said Grandmother. "How old is this girl?"

"Fifteen, same as Leo."

"And where is her husband?"

"She doesn't have one."

Grandmother raised her eyebrows. "I'm surprised she told you that so freely."

"But I did ask her."

"Stirling! You asked her if she was married?" Grandmother turned to him, frowning. "That was very rude! Do you know how rude that is, to ask someone if they are married? Especially if it turns out they are not."

"I didn't know she was not. That was why I asked. Anyway, she didn't mind."

"Well, perhaps not, but . . . ."

"Leo." He turned to me. "She didn't mind, did she?" I shook my head.

"She seems a brazen sort of girl," said Grandmother cautiously. "Not to feel ashamed at—"

"Oh, Grandmother!" I exclaimed. "Don't be so old-fashioned."

We were all surprised at that. "You are right," said Grandmother after a moment. "You are right. Sorry, Leo. Some of the people we have had here—respectable when you look at them, certainly, but so unfriendly. And I do not know the circumstances. I think that we should invite her round sometime. I would like to meet her."

❧

I had thought that I would rather be at home than at school, but by Tuesday evening I was growing bored. I was laying out my uniform ready for the next day when Grandmother came to the bedroom door. "Listen, Leo," she said. "I want you to stay at home at least until the end of next week."

I was surprised. "I thought you said Monday or Tuesday."

"There is a lot of silent fever in the city. It's too dangerous for you to go out when you are weak."

"Well, I'll be all right; I'll stay away from anyone who looks ill. I have not caught it yet, have I?"

"I am not worried about you. It says here that they think it might be carried by people who have been ill or exhausted, and then passed on to others." She held up the newspaper.

"They have said that before."

"Aye, but they are proving it now. In the hospitals at the border. Listen to this."

She sat down and opened the newspaper. " 'A report from the doctors at the hospital at Romeira . . . ,' " she began. She read slowly. I could hear when she got to the end of a line, because she paused while she found the beginning of the next. " '. . . states that most silent fever cases occur in soldiers who . . . have been in contact with those returning from the . . . hospital, or those diagnosed with exhaustion. . . . These convalescing or exhausted soldiers often have low . . . immunities, and so carry the disease and pass it to those . . . who are healthy. This is further proof of the generally . . . accepted theory that people who are unfit, especially those . . . recovering from illness, carry silent fever and pass it . . . directly to people they come into contact with. People with . . . low immunities are susceptible to the germs . . . which then pass remarkably easily to healthy people.' "

"You should not believe everything you read in the newspaper," I told her. "And it is pointless to worry about silent fever. It goes around and people catch it, and whether or not you are careful the chances are the same."

"That's not true," said Grandmother. "Being careful is always sensible. Exhaustion, Leo—that was what Father Dunstan said. And that is what these soldiers have, the ones who are passing on the illness."

It was pointless to worry about silent fever; I was not just saying it to aggravate her. No one really knew how it was passed or how to treat it. "People are only scared of it because of the symptoms," I told her. "Because you lose your sight and fall unconscious and can't speak. They think it's a serious disease, because the symptoms come on fast, when in fact most people recover."

"There are more serious strains," she told me. "Slow-developing silent fever, class B silent fever. Do you know about those strains, Leo?" I shrugged helplessly. "You are not going back to school," she told me. "You need to rest for a while longer." And I did not argue.

By Thursday evening I was going crazy with boredom. "I'm going out," I told Grandmother and Stirling, putting my boots on.

"Where?" asked Stirling. "Can I come?"

"You are not going out," Grandmother told me.

"I'm getting bored here in the house," I complained. "I need some fresh air."

"The air is not fresh; it is full of disease. Leo, stay in the house."

"Can I come to church with you later, then?"

"Stay in the house," Grandmother said. "Please, Leo. Or go out to the yard to get some air."

I went down to the yard. It was in shadow, although it was only five o'clock and the sun was shining in the street. There was a warm breeze blowing down the alley, and I stood beside the gate, where it was strongest. A breeze was unusual out here, for the houses rose so high on all sides that only a southeasterly wind could get in at all. Looking around the dingy space, I thought that Maria had been right: some plants would improve it. It could be a walled garden. A courtyard.

I paced round the walls, imagining that this was a garden. But the yard was too small. If I had a garden, I would like mainly grass, acres of it. If I was rich. Gentle slopes planted with trees, and a lake or a stream, like the grounds of a palace in the country. You could ride a horse across it. You can do whatever you want if you're rich. Maybe if I trained in magic and became as famous as Aldebaran. Or more likely, if I was high up in the army. But I'd never get anywhere in the army. I paced faster.

A noise made me start, and I turned and saw Maria coming out into the yard.

I noticed that I was walking in a circle, and stopped where I was. "Just . . . er . . . getting some fresh air," I said.

"Me also," she said, and crossed to the gate and leaned over to look down the alley into the street. "I am glad to see you well again."

"Thank you," I said. "And thank you for helping me . . . you know, the other day."

"It was nothing," she said. And then, turning to me, "You looked so tired and pale—you look quite different with some color in your face." Of course, she looked just the same as I remembered, only perhaps even prettier.

"Where is Anselm?" I asked her.

"He's asleep—for once," she said. "Upstairs. My mother is with him." She ran her hand through her hair. "Oh, he makes me so tired! It is a lot of work caring for a baby, and yet I get bored with it. I cannot agree with people who say that a woman's work is nothing but bringing up children and cooking and cleaning."

I laughed. "Then you are in a minority for sure these days."

"Perhaps I am." She smiled.

"Of course I love him dearly," she went on. "I don't mean that I don't. He is so sweet; who could not love him? But . . . I don't know! Today he cried for three hours, hardly stopping for breath; I was in despair! And then my mother came through the front door and said at once, 'He wants his blanket.' I told her that he already had his blanket, in fact two, and she said, 'No, Maria, his yellow blanket.' And she went and got it, and laid it on him, and he stopped crying straightaway. And then she said something about a 'mother's touch.' *I'm* a mother. She's not to be believed! I tell you what—she is the one who drives me to distraction, truly, not Anselm."

"It must be annoying," I said, into the silence. "If she always thinks she can bring up a child better than you."

"That's exactly what she thinks," she said. "But it's not as if he is her baby." I was watching her mouth as she talked.

"No," I said.

"I cannot be expected to know everything that she does, but she doesn't even give me a chance. And she has only brought up one child anyway. That does not make her an expert."

"Maybe that is why she is like that," I said.

"How do you mean?"

"Well, perhaps she feels threatened by you. As if she doesn't want you to be better than her at looking after children. I mean, not exactly that . . . but . . ."

"No—it's a good point."

"Just a thought."

We stood in silence. Maria twisted a loose splinter from the gate, frowning, and dropped it distractedly. "It annoys me," she said, "the way she's always telling me I'm wrong, or else looking disapproving, like this." She showed me, pulling her mouth into a tight line and raising her eyebrows. I laughed, but she looked beautiful even when she did it.

"I'm surprised if she really looks like that," I said.

She laughed too. "Well, perhaps not so bad, but you know what I mean by it. It's driving me insane."

"I'd guess that it would."

"What do you think I should do?"

"I don't know. I know nothing about that sort of thing, as no doubt Stirling will have told you." They seemed to have been talking often since Maria had arrived.

"Not at all," she said. "He never has anything but the highest praise for you. Only yesterday he was saying that he missed you at school because you always looked after him."

"Truly?" I was pleased. "Typical Stirling."

"You are too hard on yourself, perhaps. His praises seem to be justified." She caught my eye. "I'm sorry," she went on. "I see I have embarrassed you; I did not mean to." I put my hand to my face, and she laughed out loud at me then. "Come on, Leo! It is not as if I asked you to marry me or something!"

"Anyway, about your mother . . ." I said.

"Yes," she said. "What would you do if you were me?"

"If I was you. Probably . . ." I considered it. "I'd shout and swear. And throw things."

She raised her eyebrows, starting to smile at that. "Not at people," I said hastily, and she laughed out loud. "Seriously," I said, trying to think of what she wanted to hear. "I suppose you could . . . well . . . thank her when she offers you advice, and . . . keep on mentioning how helpful she is to you . . ."

"So that she doesn't find me threatening? Do you think that would work?"

"I don't know. You are asking the wrong person, to be honest."

"No—you are a good listener." I felt guilty then, because I had been watching her, yes, but some of the time I had not been listening. "It might work." She smiled at me. "Thanks, Leo."

But her smile faded, and I noticed how tired she looked. "I wish I could just leave home," she said desperately.

"Maybe you can, one day."

"Where would I get the money?" She looked, and spoke, as if she could get it right out of her pocket. But she was living on Citadel Street.

Watching her, I wished she would smile again. I spoke before I had even thought about it. "If you get tired of being with your mother," I said, "you can always come over to our apartment. I am there all day at the moment, and I would like to have someone to talk to. I'm not used to being at home all the time."

"Thank you," she said. "I might hold you to that. I get so lonely, and none of my girlfriends live near this part of town."

"I'd be glad if you came round. Anytime. Bring Anselm and all."

"Thanks," she said again. "Though I'd sooner leave him." And she laughed.

She pushed herself up off the gate, where she had been leaning. "I suppose I had better get back." I nodded. When she reached the door, she turned. "Thank you, Leo. I really need a friend." All I could manage was another nod. She slid round the door. The way that she did it, for a stupid moment I thought she was going to blow me a kiss. Maybe that was what was so enthralling about her mouth: it looked always as if she was about to blow someone a kiss. Anyway, she did not, and the door swung shut behind her. Lucky, really. I could not have coped with that.

$\mathcal{T}$he next morning there was a knock on the door at about eleven o'clock. I glanced in the mirror, straightened out my shirt collar, ran my fingers through my hair, and went to answer it. It was Maria, of course, carrying the baby. "Hello," I said. "Come in; my grandmother is out." She was wearing a dressing gown.

"Hello, Leo," she said. "You are looking dashing this morning." Dashing? She did it on purpose, for sure.

"Sorry about what I'm wearing," she said. She said this as if she had on a dress that was too old or too casual for a party, not a dressing gown in front of a boy. "Anselm threw up on my clothes—little angel—and the rest are drying."

"Don't worry," I said. "Er . . . sit down." She did.

"This is a change from sitting about by myself," she said.

"What—sitting about with me?"

She laughed. "Your mother's always out?" I asked.

"Yes, she works at the market full-time now. At the fruit and vegetable stall."

"Mr. Pearson's?"

"How did you know?"

"My grandmother talks to him sometimes. I don't know him well."

I was trying to think of something to say before the silence drew out any longer, when the downstairs doorbell jangled loudly. "Probably my grandmother," I said.

"Should we answer it?"

"Mrs. Blake downstairs will. She always does."

I stood up to go to the apartment door. But the voice that came from downstairs was not my grandmother's; it was a man's deep monotone, asking a question that I could not hear. Mrs. Blake answered quietly. The man spoke again, more loudly, and I could have sworn that I heard "Leonard North."

"Did he just say my name?" I whispered, frozen in midstep halfway to the door.

"Is your real name Leonard?" Maria whispered back.

"Originally."

"Then he did. It was 'Leonard North.' "

"But who—" A loud thumping on the door interrupted me. I stepped forward and opened it without thinking.

The man looked to be about fifty, with a sharp-boned face and reflective glasses that captured the whole room. I saw the worry in Maria's face reflected there and, stupidly, smiled at her tiny reflection. I realized I was actually smiling at the man. He did not return it. Instead, he flashed some sort of official pass at me but snapped it back down to his side before I could see what it said.

"Ethan Dark," he said. "Truancy officer. Are you Leonard North?"

"Yes."

"Are you aware that you should be in school?"

"Er . . . yes, I'm aware of it. . . ."

"Why aren't you there, then?"

72

I explained what had happened the week before. "You passed out?" said the man, as though he was not impressed by that. I nodded. "So that was last week," he said. "And you are still at home."

"I'm supposed to be resting. It's dangerous to go out with so much silent fever about." The man smiled, curling his lip up like a snarling dog, as if I was an anxious old woman, and I did not appreciate that.

Anselm began a shrill wailing. Maria tried to quiet him, and the man frowned. "Legally, I am not required to be in school," I told him loudly.

"I think I know better than you what the law is on this matter."

"Most fifteen-year-olds are working. You do not trace them like this because they are not at school."

"Mr. North, you are among the privileged few. You are officially registered as a military cadet. If you wish to work, clear that with the authorities. If not, you are required to be in school, eight-thirty to three-thirty, five days a week. Do I make myself clear?"

"Is this standard? Do you hunt down everybody who misses two weeks' school?"

"Mr. North, I am not here to argue with you. I have other important business to attend to. If you are not in school next week, this visit will be followed up."

"Who sent you here?"

"I said I am not here to argue."

"Can I see that pass again, please?" But he was already on his way back down the stairs. Anselm's crying settled to a quiet grizzling, then stopped altogether, as if it had been the presence

73

of the man that had upset him. Perhaps it had. He had a very brash presence.

The man turned again and called back, "You will be in school on Monday morning, or this will be followed up. I trust you value your future career as a soldier." I leaned out the doorway and stuck two fingers up at his retreating back and my future career as a soldier.

As he let himself out the front door, he collided with my grandmother, and she looked up at me, question in her face. When she reached the apartment, I took her shopping from her and shut the door behind her. "Who was that?" she said, rubbing her hand where the basket handle had cut into the palm.

"Truancy officer." She looked at me with evident concern and then saw Maria and Anselm.

"Hello, Mrs. North," Maria said, standing up. "I am Maria, from the apartment upstairs. Leo said I could come over. I hope you don't mind."

"Oh, not at all . . . ," said Grandmother. She was looking at Maria's dressing gown.

"Oh yes, sorry about this," said Maria. "I'm afraid my baby was sick on my only clean clothes, and . . ."

"Ah," said Grandmother. "No matter, anyway. I am glad to meet you, Maria. I have heard a lot about you." She held out her hand and Maria took it, shifting Anselm up her arm to do so. "And what a charming baby!" Grandmother exclaimed, looking at Anselm. "He looks very like you."

"Yes, people say that often."

Baby Anselm stretched out a small hand to her, gurgling, and my grandmother smiled. "May I hold him?"

"Of course." Maria tipped the baby into her arms. He flapped his hands and feet but did not start to cry again.

"So, what is this about a truancy officer?" Grandmother asked, rocking the baby.

"That man was apparently a truancy officer," I said. "And he says that I have to go back to school on Monday or he'll follow up the visit. He was very insistent."

"He looked angry. You weren't rude to him, were you, Leo?" I opened my mouth, then closed it again. She turned to Maria. "Was he?"

"Only where it was justified," Maria said.

Grandmother laughed reluctantly. "Aye, for sure. Leo is so disrespectful—the number of times I have told him!" Her face grew serious then. "But who has sent this man? The headmaster told Stirling only yesterday that it was perfectly all right for you to go back next week. Surely they do not need to send the truancy officer round here."

"Perhaps it was Sergeant Markey," I said. "You know that he hates Stirling and me."

"Well . . . it may be . . . ," she said. "We will not find out, anyway." And we did not speak about it again.

❧

On Saturday evening I was staring out the window, and Stirling was lying on the floor, trying to read the newspaper. "N-O. No. R-E-S . . . R-E." It said "No Rest at the Border," but I didn't tell him. Grandmother was sewing more of those squares I had seen her making before when she suddenly exclaimed, "Oh—I had forgotten about that!" and stood up.

"Forgotten about what?" Stirling asked her, but she had already left the room.

"She is almost as bad as you," I told him.

Grandmother returned and touched my shoulder. "What is it?" I asked, then saw that she was holding out a book—that strange black book I had found.

"It is yours," she said. "I am sorry to have taken it. It was on the windowsill and I picked it up."

I had forgotten again about the book until I saw it now in her hand. I was sure that I had not left it on the windowsill. "Did you read it?" I said.

"No. I intended to, but I changed my mind." I glanced up at her, and I could see that she was telling the truth. In any case, Grandmother never lied. "It would not have been right to read it," she said. "I knew it was yours."

I was surprised. I had always thought that she didn't trust me. I took it silently and put it into my pocket. She patted my shoulder briefly, and I gave her a quick smile. "I am sorry I took it," she said.

That night I looked through the pages to check if there was any more writing. There was none. Stirling asked what it was, so I told him. "It's like a story," he said. "Finding a magic book. As long as it is not evil magic."

"No," I told him. "I do not think it is."

But how could I be sure? I put the book in the chest under the windowsill, right at the bottom. It would have been better to put it under my pillow, but I felt somehow as though it would be dangerous for it to be so close to my head.

The stars were bright that night. I stood at the window and watched them and wondered who had written in the book.

Stirling could barely print his own name, and Grandmother wrote with difficulty. It was neither of them, and it was not me. Then who? I might find out. But I was beginning to doubt it. It was one of those unexplainable things, that was all.

I looked for the star called Leo, but I had never known where in the sky it was. It might be any among those thousands; it was pointless, then, to search for it. But still I did, and often. There was one that I thought it might be—one of the palest in the center. Then again, perhaps it could not even be seen from here. It always made me sad when I didn't know which star was Leo. I don't know why. Later, when I fell asleep, I was still trying to guess.

When I woke on Sunday, the sunlight had already reached my bedcover. I got up straightaway. A heavy thud on the floor-boards made me start; I had knocked something onto the ground. Looking down, I saw that it was the book.

I stared at it and then at the windowsill, where I remembered leaving it. I had put it right into the chest there, under my clothes, the day before. I had not touched it since. I would have sworn it on my life.

Stirling would remember. He had seen me do it. I left the book where it lay, taking care not to step near it, and went out into the living room to find him.

On the table was Friday's newspaper, "Gone to church" scrawled on it in my grandmother's shivery handwriting. Then it was past ten o'clock. The writing carelessly marched across the face of Lucien's man Ahira, an artist's impression. They always drew him from the left-hand side—his left, that is—because of the scar across the right side of his face. Underneath the picture was the headline: RETREAT IS NOT SURRENDER. The war was not going well, then, although it was hard to tell from the newspaper.

I went back into the bedroom and frowned at the book. It had fallen spine up, so that some of the pages were folded against the floor. When I picked it up, the bent pages forced it to flap open, and I saw at once that the crinkled, written-on section was thicker. Someone had written in it again!

I sat down on the windowsill and found the place where the previous writing had ended. It was very strange. The text finished halfway down one page, and the next page was blank. There were several more empty pages. I flicked through them until I found where the next section of writing began.

⚜

"Field," said Raymond one day. The butler had been with him several months now. "Would you drive me to the seaside? I have not been for so long, and I thought we might take a drive up there."

"The seaside?" The butler nodded. "Certainly, sir. I will go and get the car ready. Anywhere in particular?"

"Graysands Beach," said Raymond. "It is not far."

It was the beginning of the tourist season. They went out to the little island. They were the only ones on the boat, which clanged in mournful tones as they moved over the wide, dark sea. "Was there any special reason you wanted to come here?" asked the butler as they walked along the gravel beach that ran around the island. The sun had come out, and spring was stirring in the air. A couple of mangy seagulls flapped and screeched overhead.

"I used to come here when I was a lad," said Raymond. "With my friend, I used to come here. We'd walk for hours around this island."

The butler was eating chips. He threw one carelessly into the oily water and watched the seagulls fight over it, screaming. "What happened to this friend? Did he go away from here?"

Raymond sat down on a rock and rested his walking stick against his knee, frowning at the carved handle. "He went away, yes. He joined the army and went to war. You should have seen the medals he won! They sent them to me after he went. They aren't part of my collection, of course. They're just in a box somewhere in the attics."

Raymond looked up then. He found it hard to judge the butler's reaction from his expression. "I am boring you, perhaps," he said warily.

"No, no. On the contrary." The butler frowned slightly. "I am surprised you never went into the army yourself, sir. That was my thought."

"Yes." Raymond gazed out over the dark water. "I used to want to be in the army once, you know."

"Truly, sir?" The old man had never mentioned it before. "What made you change your mind?" And then, "Sorry, sir. I am forgetting my place."

Raymond always thought that it seemed to amuse Field to say things like "I am forgetting my place." "No, no, do not apologize, Field," he said. "It was a long time ago, and I ought to . . ." He twisted the carved top of the walking stick in his palm. "I failed the medical."

The butler nodded but did not say anything. "The problem was my heart," Raymond went on. "I've always had trouble with it." He smiled faintly. "It's funny. It mattered to me so much at the time, not getting into the army, and I never really got over it. Even now, if I could change something—one thing—about my life, it would be that. If I could have done."

"I daresay your mind was set on it for a long time."

"Yes. Ever since I was a young boy."

"And I suppose you used to plan it with your friend. I expect you always thought you would go together." The butler scattered the last chips for the seagulls and folded the paper. "Perhaps you were walking up and down this beach planning it and came home to find that Britain had declared war, and you swore to go together."

Raymond stared at the butler. "How did you know that?" he demanded.

The butler studied the gravel in front of his feet. "Just a guess. I hope you do not think I am speaking out of line."

There was a silence. "It's still cold this time of year," said Raymond then, getting to his feet. "Doesn't do to sit still."

The sun was setting as the boat rocked away from the island. The butler leaned over the side and threw something into the water. "What was that?" asked Raymond.

"Nothing. Just a stone."

Raymond thought he had seen something glitter before it sank, but he was weary that day and had no strength to question the butler further. He had learned, anyway, in these past months, that it was pointless. Field told him what he wanted to, and nothing more than that.

"You know," said Raymond, looking back at the island. "I think I'm going to die. I really do. I'm going to die soon."

"No, sir," said the butler. "No, you are not. You may live twenty years more."

"Now I've seen that island again, it doesn't matter. It's funny; it used to look beautiful to me in the old days, but it's nothing special."

"I am glad to have been here," said the butler, turning back to watch the sun spread, glittering, over the sea.

❦

"Sir?" said the butler as they drove home through the darkness. "Sir, I have been meaning to ask you something ever since I came here."

Raymond turned in his seat to face the butler. "I wondered if you ever knew a lady called Emilie," Field continued. "She used to live near here a few years ago."

"Emilie?" said Raymond, frowning. "A French name. It is familiar. What was the lady's surname?"

"Field."

Raymond was startled. "A relative of yours, then?"

A bird leapt into the headlights, and the butler swerved. "My brother's wife," he said, tightening his grip on the steering wheel. "His wife or his partner—I don't know. My brother was in England before me, several years ago. He was very close to this lady, but he did not treat her as he should have done. Harold was not the best of men."

"You have never spoken about your family before," remarked Raymond. The butler did not reply. "But tell me, what did your brother do wrong?"

"I understand he lived with this lady for some years. Even if

81

they were not married, there were certainly children. Then he got up one day and left them all. I don't know why. I have never understood Harold. But I wanted to find this lady, this Emilie, and set things right. I believe that she lived near here in those days."

"There was an Emilie Devere in the village," began Raymond slowly. "Yes, she worked in the Red Lion. She had two little girls—Monica and Michelle, I think their names were. But she moved down south about twenty years ago. I saw the husband once, actually, when he was around. A flashy sort of man, and very high-spirited."

"That is Harold," said Field quietly. "It must have been." He glared at the dark road ahead.

"Was he really so bad, your brother?" said Raymond.

"He was a great gambler when he was a young man. It nearly ruined us all. His behavior made my sister ill with worry on several occasions, and I find that hard to forgive. She was always so devoted to him. She even named her son Harold. And he treated her like that in return. You know, sir, all the time he was in England—six years—we none of us knew where he was. But then, he was never in higher spirits than when people were crying over him and he could come sauntering in and make everything all right."

The butler shook his head. "I should not speak of him like this, I suppose. He told me once that I was arrogant and self-obsessed." Field laughed, then stopped as if remembering. "Well, perhaps he was right. There are two sides to the story, and he can no longer tell his."

"What happened to him?" said Raymond.

The butler stared ahead into the darkness. "Like your friend, he went away to war. That was what made me think of him."

A motorbike overtook the old car and disappeared ahead,

leaving the hedgerow shivering. "You have never told me about your family," said Raymond. "Are any of them here in England?"

"No," said the butler. Raymond watched him, but the car was swinging into the drive now and he did not elaborate. And by the time he came in from the garage, he seemed to have forgotten that he had ever mentioned a woman called Emilie or a brother and a sister in a foreign country. Raymond did not dare to ask him again.

That was the end. I sat and stared at the page for a long time while the sun rose higher at my back. This section was just as familiar as the others had been. I closed my eyes, and vague images of those people drifted into my head—the old man and his butler, the blue-eyed girl, and the prince. I could see them all, as if I had met them before. It was very strange. And when I closed my eyes and concentrated harder, I could almost see what was going to happen next.

Then the door opened loudly, and Stirling called, "Leo! We're back!"

I started and dropped the book. I could hear them talking in the living room. I opened the window seat chest hastily, dropped the book in, and turned to the door to meet them.

"What? Not even dressed yet?" Stirling exclaimed. "You had better hurry. Maria was at church and we've invited her over for dinner, and her mother too. They will be here any minute!"

❧

*M*aria and her mother knocked on the door while I was still washing my face and Grandmother was hastily chopping vegetables. I motioned to Stirling to wait to open it, but he pretended not to see. I grabbed a towel and dried the cold water off my face and ran a comb through my hair while Grandmother was saying, "Please, come in. Hello, Maria. Hello, Anselm. So nice to meet you, Mrs. . . . ."

"Andros," said Maria's mother. I had not known that until now.

She was a slight woman, shorter than Maria. She wore a scarf around her head, but tendrils of her brown hair escaped about her face. It would have been much like Maria's, I think, if she had let it fall loose.

Anselm began to cry, and Maria rocked him and said, "Shh, shh."

"Give him to me," said her mother.

"He's all right," said Maria, turning away.

But he began to cry again. "Sit down, please," said Grandmother over the wailing. Maria's mother sat on the sofa, and Maria, still rocking the baby, sat down next to her, flashing Stirling a smile and me a sort of look from beneath downcast eyelids. It made my heart stumble over a beat, and I hurried into the bedroom to get another chair. Half my mind had still been on that strange book, trying to work out what it meant, but I gave it up completely now.

"He spoke very impressively," Mrs. Andros was saying when I returned. "I must say, I thought he seemed young for a priest, but he is a good one."

"Aye," said Grandmother. "He is a clever man, and kind."

"Very. He was so friendly when he introduced himself to us, was he not, Maria?"

"Who?" asked Maria distractedly, still trying to quiet Anselm.

"Father Dunstan, Maria."

"Oh . . . yes."

"He noticed that we were new to the church, and came straight up and talked to us," Mrs. Andros went on. "He made us feel very welcome, which is more than many people do these days, I must say." Here I thought I saw her eyes move toward Anselm for a second, and Maria turned her shoulder away, as if to shield the baby from the glance.

"True, people are often so hostile in these difficult times," said Grandmother. "I am glad of the kindness of Father Dunstan and the congregation."

I watched Maria rocking the baby. At some point she must have started watching me too, because then we were looking at each other across the group, and I was not listening to Mrs. Andros anymore.

After a while Grandmother went to the kitchen to finish preparing the dinner, and Mrs. Andros went with her. We could still hear their voices and the sound of Grandmother chopping vegetables. Stirling sat on the sofa next to Maria, who smiled at him without moving. He looked down at Anselm and whispered, "Is he asleep?"

"Nearly," said Maria. I pulled my chair up closer to the sofa. It grated on the floorboards, and Anselm's eyes sprang open. He began to wail loudly again.

"Sorry!" I exclaimed.

"Don't worry," said Maria. "He would not have slept for long; he is probably hungry."

"We have some milk in the kitchen," said Stirling, seemingly triumphant at remembering their conversation. "Would you like me to go and get him some?" I could see where this was heading.

"Thank you, Stirling," Maria said. "But it is cow's milk, I guess, and he can't drink that. I think it would make him sick."

"Oh? I thought you said he would have milk."

I started coughing. Why did we always get onto the most embarrassing and inappropriate topics with Maria? "I see your cough is not quite recovered," said Maria. I shook my head and she gave me a faint smile.

Stirling held out a finger to the baby and he caught onto it and stopped crying. "He must like you," said Maria into the sudden quiet, and Stirling looked pleased.

"When are you going to teach him to talk?" he asked.

"He will learn by himself, I think," said Maria. "But not yet; he is only two months old."

"Two months?" Stirling said. "That is young." He stared at the baby. "It's only two months since he was born?" he demanded again, incredulously.

Maria laughed. "Yes. Why are you surprised?"

"I thought he had been alive longer. Just thinking that two months ago he was not here at all."

"It does seem a short time."

"So . . . his birthday is in April?" Stirling said.

"Twenty-second of April."

"How did you remember?"

"I would not soon forget it," said Maria. "It is an important day, after all."

"I always forget when my birthday is," said Stirling. "I know it's in the winter."

"It's the twelfth of November," I told him.

"Did you have a party?" Maria asked. Stirling shook his head. "Why not?" she said.

"I don't know." He turned to me, seemingly bemused. "I've never had a birthday party, have I, Leo?"

I thought for a moment. He might have had a first birthday party when Mother and Father were still here; I could not remember. "I don't think you have," I said.

Maria would not believe that. "I always used to have a party when I was a little girl," she said. "You must have had one once, Stirling. You must have done."

He shook his head. "I'm having a party for my First Communion, though."

"Well, it seems a shame not to have a birthday party. Why not have one now?"

"We could go for a picnic!" said Stirling suddenly. "Me, you, Leo, and Anselm. I always wanted to go for a picnic."

"Why not?" Maria said.

"Why not?" Stirling repeated. "Let's."

They sat there side by side, Stirling's finger still clasped in the baby's hand, and began planning this picnic. "Let's go next Saturday," said Maria. "It will be the last day in June."

"Really summer," said Stirling. It was true. It had crept up entirely while we still thought we were wearing jackets and lighting the fire and complaining about the cold. I glanced out the window now at the sunlight on the roofs across the street.

"Leo?" Maria was saying then. "Where shall we go? Somewhere pretty, like a garden."

I turned back to them. "Where is there that we can go for a picnic in this city?"

"There must be somewhere," said Maria. "Come on, Leo; it is an excellent idea!"

"I'm not denying it's excellent," I said. "I'm just saying, where? All I can think of is the graveyard."

"That is not nice for a picnic!" said Maria.

"It is for the worms."

"Leo, stop it!" Stirling told me.

"You'll be giving him nightmares," Maria said. She thought for a moment. "It's a shame we cannot go to the Royal Gardens. I heard they are beautiful. People used to be allowed into them."

"We could climb over the gate," I said, not really serious.

"With Anselm?" She laughed and shook her head.

"The eastern hills!" said Stirling suddenly. "That is a good place for a picnic."

Grandmother leaned through the door and called, "Leo! Stirling! Will you set the plates out, please?"

"The eastern hills are a good idea," said Maria. "I think we should do it."

"But why?" I asked. "Why this sudden notion of a picnic?"

"Because it's fun, Leo," said Maria, as if it was obvious.

Stirling brought plates from the kitchen. I cleared Grandmother's sewing and the newspaper off the table and put them on the sofa beside Maria. She looked at the picture of Ahira and then turned it over. "Why did you do that?" I asked.

"I hate him," she said quietly. And the hairs on her arms had risen, as if she was cold.

"I hate him too," I said.

"If you live a hundred years, Leo, I don't think you'll get to hate him as much as I do," she said, in the same quiet voice. I didn't dare to ask why. And then she shrugged and smiled, and we went over to the table.

I did not go back to school on Monday. I could tell that Grandmother was worried by the set of the edges of her mouth as she waved goodbye to Stirling, but she did not mention the truancy officer and I didn't either. That morning it was very quiet in the apartment, with Stirling at school and Grandmother at the market. I read through the book again, then put it away and wandered from room to room.

I had hoped that Maria would come to the door, but I could hear Anselm's wails drifting down the stairs all morning. When I passed Maria in the yard, she was still trying to quiet the baby, who was screaming in her arms. "He just won't stop crying," she said, and she seemed close to tears suddenly. "I was going to come and see you, Leo. As soon as I settle Anselm, I will." But time passed and I could hear the baby still shrieking upstairs.

That evening Grandmother got back from church before Stirling. I went to the door to meet them. Stirling was coming along behind, talking to Maria. She waved when she saw me, and came jogging up to our door. "Listen, sorry I didn't come round earlier," she said. "Anselm just would not settle, and . . ."

"I understand," I said, because she wanted me to.

"Thank you, Leo," she said. "I knew you would." She looked far less harassed now without the baby as she went tripping up the stairs.

About five minutes later the shouting began. Shouting has to be really loud to be heard through the ceiling. I stood still and listened. "I am not your child-minder!" Maria's mother was yelling. "If your baby can't get to sleep, you stay home with him."

"You always want to tell me what to do, but when it comes to helping me with one small thing, you complain!" Maria shouted.

"Aye, one small thing! You're trying to lead a double life, Maria! Thanks to your own stupidity, you now have a responsibility to look after a baby. And yet every day I'm minding him while you go to visit one of your friends, or to the market, or—"

"Or to church! To *church*!"

"*I* wanted to go to church, and *I* have not been stupid enough to deserve to have to look after a baby day and night!"

"Stupid? Are you saying it was my fault?"

"Yes!" Anselm's crying rose into uneven, raucous screams.

"My fault? Are you—"

At that moment Stirling came into the room. "Leo, what are you doing?" he said sternly.

"Just . . . er . . ." I crossed to the chair and picked up my jacket from it, as if I had only just come into the room to get it.

"You shouldn't listen to their argument. It's not your business."

"All right, preacher." I followed him out to the living room, where the shouting could not be heard. "Happy now?" But I could not help smiling at him. The way he always tried so earnestly to be good, to do the right thing. "You'll make a good priest, Stirling, I swear." He took it as a compliment.

I was restless all that evening. "Why don't you read something?" said Grandmother, looking up from her sewing.

"If there was anything to read, I would."

"Have the newspaper," she said. "I have finished with it."

I did not much feel like reading the newspaper, but I did not argue. I took it back to the bedroom and read the reports of the war at the border. The shouting above had subsided now, though I could still hear the baby crying.

I was reading the casualty figures when Stirling came running in, took something out of his chest of drawers, and pushed it into my hand. It was a book. "What's this?" I asked him, turning it over.

"The book that Aldebaran wrote," he said. "Remember, we were talking about it. The prophecy."

I glanced toward the living room. "It's all right," said Stirling, grinning. "Grandmother is downstairs visiting Mrs. Blake. Will you read it to me? You said you would."

I put the newspaper down and examined the book. It was very thin, bound like *The Golden Reign*—like a book that would sell many copies. They used to print all the books like that—even these great prophecies that they printed first like Bibles, for rich people. There had been thousands of different books printed every year when I was small. My father had listings and charts of the titles on the wall above his desk, I remember. "Leo, will you read it?" Stirling said.

I came back from my thoughts. "All right. When will Grandmother be back?"

"Not for an hour." He sat down beside me.

I began to read. " 'A prophecy of the lord Aldebaran, written in the sixth year of the reign of Cassius the Second.' " Stirling listened in silence. Most of the text was background information, a long introduction that discussed the context and the meaning of the prophecy. "Who wrote this?" I said when I finished reading that section to him. "It is like Father's style."

"Is it?" said Stirling, leaning over my shoulder though he could not read the words. "Could he have written it?"

"He could. They always used renowned writers to interpret the prophecies." I began turning the pages of the old book. It was the custom to leave out the name of the author; I knew that, but it didn't stop me searching for his name.

"Grandmother will be back soon," said Stirling. "Go on reading, Leo."

I gave up looking for my father's name. "All right." I turned to the end of the introduction, where the actual prophecy began. It was no more than a few lines. I began to read. " 'I, Aldebaran, witnessed these things, in the sixth year of the reign of King Cassius the Second, and I wrote them faithfully, without elaboration or reduction or alteration—' "

"What does that mean?" said Stirling.

"It is required by law. It means he didn't change what he saw."

I read on. " 'I dreamt, and I saw myself beside a lake in a strange country, and I heard these words in the darkness:

Mourn for Malonia, cry out for her cities;
    for trouble like a shadow will fall on our country, days of
    fighting and unrest.
But though many die, the boy will not be killed;
    the prince will live and he will not be harmed.
His destiny is in his eyes and his destiny will endure;
    but in these years he will be a stranger in a strange land.
The boy will live; he will not be killed.
If a man lifts his hand to strike him, that man will be struck down;

if a man lifts a sword against him, he will fall by the same blow.
If anyone dares to kill this boy, the same will come to him;
retribution will fall on anyone who harms him.
The boy will be a stranger for many years;
far from his people, he will mourn for Malonia.

But change will come to our land again;
the prince will return and his kingdom will be restored.
The silver eagle will be lost and it will be found;
the prince will mourn and he will be comforted.
And the one he loves will see him return;
the eagle will be restored by this beloved one.
The boy will choose between his duty and his heart;
between love and obligation, which will prevail?

'And I, Aldebaran, swear that this is a faithful record of what I saw.' "

I put down the book. "That does not mean anything to me," I said.

"It means the prince will come back," said Stirling. "It said he would not be killed. It said he would return. I told you, Leo." He picked up the book and traced the letters with his fingers, as though they were magical symbols. "It means the prince is coming back."

"Stirling," I began, "just because Aldebaran supposedly wrote this book . . ." Then I gave up. Why shouldn't he believe it? I watched him tracing those letters, every so often spelling a word or two of the text aloud.

"Leo?" he said then, looking up. "Can you see into the future like Aldebaran can?"

I was startled. "I don't know. I don't think so. My powers are nothing like his."

"Try," said Stirling. "Shut your eyes and try to."

I shut my eyes and concentrated all my willpower. But I couldn't see anything. I opened my eyes again and laughed. "Nothing," I said. Maybe it was because I didn't really believe that I could. I didn't really believe that anyone could. But the strange thing is that prophecies come true. People really can see into the future, and you can deny it no more than you can deny that the earth is round or the stars are fire.

At that moment we heard Grandmother's key in the door. "Quick—hide it!" whispered Stirling. I shoved the book back into the chest of drawers, and when I went into the living room, Stirling was talking innocently to Grandmother about some incident at school. I could not help smiling at that. For all his goodness, he could be very like me.

❧

$\mathcal{W}$e had just started dinner when there was a sharp rap on the door. Grandmother went to open it anyway. "Ethan Dark," I heard. "Truancy officer." I turned in my chair. The man was standing right on the threshold, glancing from me to Grandmother behind those reflective glasses. "Are you the legal guardian of Leonard North?" he demanded.

"Yes." She wasn't, but she said it anyway.

"Are you aware that he has failed to attend school today after a previous warning?"

Grandmother tried to explain about the incident the week

before in training, but he waved it aside. "Yes, I know about all that. So why is he still at home?"

"There is a lot of silent fever about," Grandmother said. "I don't want him to catch the germs. They say that if you are suffering from exhaustion—"

"Mrs. North," the man said wearily. "We are all in difficult circumstances. But we cannot just hide in our houses. There is a war going on, and there are more profitable things that I could spend my time on. I do not wish to come here again."

"But the headmaster of Leonard's school has said—"

"That is of no consequence. As another member of staff pointed out to us, Leonard has failed to obtain a doctor's note."

"But there are no doctors to obtain a note from." That was outspoken for Grandmother. I got up and went to stand behind her, and Stirling followed me.

"Then I suggest he gets himself back to school with all due haste," said Ethan Dark. "He has been warned already. If I receive another complaint from the military academy, there will be serious consequences. Last year we expelled over a hundred boys for consistently failing to attend military training. They have lost all chance of a career in the army now. But when they reach eighteen, they are still going to be called up to fight at the Alcyrian border as civilian soldiers. Evidently not where Leonard wishes to end up."

"Very well," she said after a moment. "He will be in school tomorrow."

"Thank you," the man said, and turned and marched down the stairs.

While we were all still standing at the door, Maria came

jogging down with what looked like baby sick on the front of her dress. "Look what Anselm did, bless him," she said through gritted teeth, holding up a slimy hand. "Who was that?"

"Ethan Dark, truancy officer," I recited. "He loves saying that."

"Shh, Leo," Grandmother said, but the man was already gone.

Maria laughed, and when she did that, I saw suddenly that she had been crying. I could see it in the way her smile faded and the glitter of her eyes. "I suppose you will be going back to school, then," she said to me. I nodded.

"You will have to," said Grandmother. "You could be expelled, Leo!"

"Don't listen to him," I said. "It's only Sergeant Markey stirring up trouble."

"You were getting bored at home anyway," said Grandmother.

"Now that I have to go to school, I don't want to," I said. "I'd sooner stay at home."

"Ah, well," Maria said. "At least you are not stuck at home forever with a demon baby."

"True. But he will not be a baby forever."

"That's also true."

"And there is the picnic to look forward to," I said.

"Are you coming?" said Maria. "You didn't seem very keen before."

"I've come round to it," I said. She smiled at that.

"What is this about a picnic?" asked Grandmother when Maria had gone on down the stairs and we had returned to the cooling dinner. Stirling explained.

"I don't know," said Grandmother. "The soldiers march through there on the way to the border. What if they practice shooting? Or what if stray explosives fall there?"

"The war is miles away," I told her. "We are not going to go far. We will just go through the graveyard and beyond that a short distance. Explosives cannot travel fifty miles through the air."

Stirling looked relieved when I said that. Grandmother put down her spoon and frowned into the soup. "But what if the soldiers don't let you back into the city? Remember last time, when you thought it would be so smart to go walking along the river, and then when you tried to get back in, you were nearly shot."

"I wasn't nearly shot," I said. "And that was years ago. It's different now. There are barely any controls on the bridges anymore; you've read it yourself in the newspaper. Lucien pulled his men back to the castle and now he doesn't care."

"I'm still not sure," she said. Stirling glanced at me but did not speak.

"How about . . . How about I wear my soldier's uniform?" I suggested suddenly. "Then there will be no trouble at the bridges. They will know I am no revolutionary."

"I did say I'd never let you out of the city again," she said slowly.

I knew I was winning now. "You are going to have to relent sometime," I told her.

"I don't see why." She smiled. "You must really want to go on this picnic if you are prepared to wear your uniform during the weekend."

"Yes, I really do."

She hesitated, then nodded. "All right. It is a good idea, after all. You never get any fresh air, you boys; it is no wonder you were so tired last week."

I began to clear the empty bowls off the table. She put her hand on my shoulder and looked at me for a moment. "What?" I said.

"You've changed, you know, Leo," she said. "I cannot remember the last time you got so enthusiastic about something. You've changed for the better since that day you fell ill."

"I know it."

❦

I was lying in the mud of the yard, leaning on my elbows and looking down my Maracon 14. It was one of the more beaten-up guns: the bolt had a tendency to stick and then fly back suddenly, catching your fingers. I had forgotten how you had to be quick to get the new ones at the beginning of shooting drill.

I was facing directly east, and the sun was not quite yet overhead, so I had to squint to see the target. That is, a chalked cross on the heart of a warped board that was roughly human-shaped and painted dull green—the color of the Alcyrian army uniform. My mind wandered; I thought of the empty hills, through those layers of drab houses, and Saturday, when we would be going there.

"North! Wake up!" It was Sergeant Bane. He sounded as if he had said it more than once already. North—that was me. There was some raucous laughter from the other boys.

"Er . . . sorry, sir, I—"

"Fire, North!" he shouted before I got the words out. I

pulled the trigger hastily, and the bullet skittered off somewhere near the bottom of the board. We did not fire with real bullets, of course, and I had always thought that with real bullets it would have been a lot easier to shoot straight.

"Bullet collecting, North," Sergeant Bane told me as he shepherded the boys inside again. "You need to learn to apply yourself." I did not even pretend to mind. Bullet collecting was tedious in winter, when the yard was waterlogged and the wind bit sharply, but now it was summer and I would rather be outside.

A breeze was blowing in from the east. Alone in the yard, I wandered round by the far wall, picking up the fallen bullets. The clouds were rolling across the sun in rags, so that it seemed bright and then suddenly overcast, and then bright again, and their shadows were projected onto the mud.

I liked shooting drill, though I did not admit it. In my more vindictive moments, I used to move the rifle a fraction of an inch toward one of the other boys or Sergeant Bane and then imagine that I was going to turn it suddenly and shoot him dead. I could have done, I used to tell myself. Although the bullets couldn't kill easily, and I had not such a good aim as to hit the target every time. But I had changed now, I realized. Everything had been different since that day when I had collapsed in training and woken up in the colonel's office.

I hated school—of course I did—but I could not help but think that things were improving. I had realized my blessings, for one thing. Grandmother had changed too. Since that day, she had not nagged me once about anything. She had kept me at home in spite of the truancy officer, and she was letting us go on this picnic on Saturday. I could not remember arguing so little with her since my mother and father had gone away. And there was Maria. I had not had a single friend before now. There was something calming about her, the fact that she was nearby, that made me think before I acted. Maybe it was the need to impress. I never cared what everyone else thought of me. But I wanted her to like me. I did not want to act in a way that she would despise.

In history class, we were studying the Liberation again. At the moment we were concentrating on the Iron Reign—the rule of the royal family of Donahue—the very same era referred to as the Golden Reign by my father's book. I felt the old sense of frustration with school returning. It was stupid. It was a waste of time to teach Malonian history like this. They should just tell us the facts and let us decide for ourselves, I thought.

"Gone was the old regime!" Sergeant Bane was declaiming. "When King Lucien overthrew the dictatorship our country had known for so long, he brought equality back. Everyone now has the chance to work and fight for their own country, and vote for their own government. He has made Malonia a land of which we can be proud." He glanced over the class as he spoke, and I assumed a look of disparaging boredom. "North!" he said. "Name one thing that was done away with when King Lucien's army brought an end to the Iron Reign."

"King Cassius the Second," I said.

"No!" he said. "Wrong!"

"Well, actually, technically—"

He cut me short. "Raise your hand if you want to hear what North has to say." No one did. "Thank you, North," he said. "May I continue?" I did not bother to reply.

Sergeant Bane's speech dragged on. I stared out the window and looked for shapes in the clouds. But I could not find any; they were moving too fast. The yard was bare except for an apple core lying in the mud, and I fell to frowning at it and trying to make it lift into the air. I had tried that with objects before, and it worked if I concentrated hard enough. I managed to make the apple core rise an inch or two. I could not keep it there for long, though; it was like holding your breath. When I let it drop, my brain hurt, as if it had endured great pain. It was very strange. Magic is not miracle at all; it is just effort and willpower.

My father used to tell me about it when I was a little boy. The training the great ones took was based on physical exertion, and even torture. The best were able to smile while plunging their hands into boiling oil. Really smile, not grimace, and that is a difficult thing to do. And they concentrated so hard that they were protected by their willpower, and so there were no burns or scald marks on their skin, though they still felt the pain.

I was thinking about that all the rest of the day—magic and willpower—and Sergeant Bane's lecturing passed me by. On the way home from school, I remarked on it to Stirling. "Do you remember about the great ones, the ones who train in magic?" I asked. "How they can endure torture?"

"Yes," he said after a moment. "I think so. You used to tell me stories. . . ."

"That's right." I used to tell my father's stories to Stirling after my parents left. Those were not Grandmother's sort of stories.

"I remember," he said.

"I was thinking that it's strange how it works," I said. "They rely on their minds—their willpower and strength of character. They don't do miracles. Anyone can do magic."

"Yes. They just believe that they can do something and they can. Like those ones that used to bend iron bars. They just believe they are bending a straw, don't they? That was what you told me."

I nodded. "I suppose you have to have the right mentality. Not everyone can do impossible feats. If you started to doubt yourself, you would not be able to do it."

"And not everyone has enough willpower," said Stirling.

We walked on down Paradise Way. Then Stirling said, "Speaking of the great ones, I want to see Aldebaran's grave again one day. I can't remember what it looks like. And I think it's pretend—a pretend gravestone." When I did not answer, he continued, "Because he was exiled. Talitha sent him to England."

It was true that the grave was made a long time after he had disappeared. I did not remember Aldebaran, but I remembered when the grave was made. And it was also true that nobody had thought he was dead for sure until the rumors started spreading. "They say he died in prison," I told Stirling. "He had been in a secret prison for several years."

"How do you know that's true?" Stirling said.

I didn't. "All right, why don't we go and see the grave?" I said. "Let's go and see it now."

"Now?" said Stirling. "I don't know if we should. You were tired last week after you got ill in training. If you do too much today, you will be tired again tomorrow."

"Well, I might be dead tomorrow," I said. Stirling looked confused. "All I mean is we can't just keep worrying about tomorrow. If you want to go and see it, we will go and see it. Today. Now. Come on." And I turned down a side street.

"What about silent fever?" Stirling asked, trotting after me.

"Stop worrying."

"You know what you are, Leo?" he said. "Repulsive."

"Repulsive? What are you talking about? You mean impulsive."

"I mean you only just had the idea and already—"

"Come on. You wanted to see it." He laughed and followed me.

⚞⚟

*I*t was about two miles to the graveyard. We walked briskly. "Are you sure this is a good idea?" Stirling would ask at intervals, and I kept replying, "Yes. Don't worry."

"I think we are going the wrong way," he said a couple of times.

"We will get there anyway," I told him.

As we got nearer to the edge of the city, the streets grew wider, and the breeze stronger. "We've come completely the wrong way," Stirling told me.

"You're right."

"Stop walking, then. Should we turn around?"

"Let's keep going until we get to the wall. And then we can follow it round to the graveyard. It will not be far."

I couldn't remember ever being in this part of Kalitzstad before. I could tell the houses here were not divided into apartments: all the curtains in any one house matched each other. Some even had gardens about them. And there were no soldiers here at all. There was never any trouble in a place like this; this was as still as the realm of the dead.

"It would be boring to live here," said Stirling. "It's so quiet and pressing."

"You know," I told him, "sometimes boring is good." But I knew what he meant. There was a thick atmosphere of stupefying wealth and conformity and safety that hung in the streets like damp, soaking even into your brain. I would rather have lived here than Citadel Street—of course—but you'd never feel alive. I did not believe in the people who lived in these perfect houses. Living here, you'd wake in the morning and wonder if your feeble heart had faded in the night, never having anything to beat against. That was what I thought. And then I thought about the hot water and the carpets in the bedrooms and the streets empty of soldiers and was not certain. We had lived like this once, and I still remembered faintly.

Suddenly, abruptly, we came to the city wall. It continued this way all around the city island, lower than Stirling's height and two feet thick, no more. The city needed no defense beyond the river. The wind lifted over the wall and caught us face on as we approached.

We strolled over and leaned against the wall, looking out into the hills over the wide gulf of the river. "It's nice," I said indifferently. "I would not mind living here." But really, I could have stood there forever.

The houses behind us looked as if they should face others on the opposite side of an ordinary street. But instead, across the cobbled road there was only the wall, and beyond that, space. The whole street was built of clean gray stone, leaning out like the side of a ship. The buildings here were not old; the oldest in the city were made from the volcanic rock of the island itself.

I leaned over to look down into the gulf, and Stirling caught my arm, exclaiming, "Be careful, Leo!" The river was at least sixty feet below. The dirty water flowed fast, darkened by the shadow and the red reflection of the cliffs. But there was a beauty in the volume and power of the water foaming over rocks as it ran southward.

Stirling was still tugging my arm. "Leo, stop leaning over like that," he said. I stopped and looked out over the sunlit eastern country instead. On the other side of the gulf, lower than the city, ran the Circle Road. Four soldiers on horseback were cantering around it toward the north end of the city. We could see the Northeast Road from here, a straight line drawn across patchy farmland. Just before it slipped into white mist, I thought I could see Ositha, the halfway point between Kalitzstad and Romeira. And to the east were the hills, fresh with their new coat of summer grass and spotted with white flowers. The sun spread from behind us, over our heads, out across the country, and flushed the distant Eastern Mountains with lilac.

"It was all right to come here without Maria, wasn't it?" said Stirling.

"Yes. I mean, we've seen it before."

"But I didn't remember it as beautiful as this."

"She will not mind. The hills are different when you're in them, and we won't go into them until Saturday."

"Are we going to Aldebaran's grave, then?" asked Stirling. "I think we should go before it gets late. If you still want to."

I rose from the wall, where I had been leaning, and we turned to walk toward the graveyard.

I was watching the water flowing past us when Stirling

jogged my arm. "What?" I asked, looking up. The door of one of the houses slammed shut ahead of us, and looking to the sound, I saw a familiar figure jogging down the steps.

"It is Sergeant Markey," I said.

"Yes. Can you believe he lives here?" said Stirling.

"Oh, I can well believe it."

"He is coming this way," said Stirling through the side of his mouth.

Sergeant Markey marched briskly toward us, and when he looked as if he recognized us, Stirling said politely, "Good afternoon, sir." We both nodded to him. He gave the briefest hint of a nod, so small that we could have imagined it, and quickened his pace as he passed us, looking away.

"How impolite!" said Stirling in mock indignation when he had passed. And then he said again, "Can you believe he lives here?"

"I always assumed that he was poor, for some reason."

"Me also. Most of the teachers aren't rich."

"Well, they're not this rich. That's probably why he's so mean and irritable at school. He probably can't bear to be away from his perfect house with its perfect street and its perfect view. He probably can't bear to see all the ugly streets and shabby kids when he's used to this."

"You shouldn't be jealous, Leo."

"I'm not jealous. I'm just saying that it explains a lot."

The street sloped shallowly downward. Soon we saw that there was a dead end ahead, cut off after a house by railings and then a sheer drop, and we turned off to the right.

As we walked south we reached a street I remembered. We were out of the wealthy area, without having noticed where it had ended, and back among the familiar drab houses. We had to walk slowly, jarring our legs, this road was so steep. At the school I used to go to when I was a little boy, before the military schools were opened, they had taught us that the streets here sloped so sharply because this was the point where, thousands of years ago, the volcanic rock had slumped. I told Stirling that as we walked.

At the bottom of the street was the huge building of Zenithar Armaments. I think it used to be a hospital. There was a triangular space of mud in front of it, gouged with the tracks of many heavy carts. "Left here," I said. Industrious metallic sounds seeped out from it as we passed. Not long after they had died away behind us, we reached the bridge.

There were five bridges from Kalitzstad. Lucien renamed four when he took over: the North, South, Northwest, and Southwest bridges. The one that we came to now remained the Victoire Bridge, named after the man who designed it; it was the only name that had not had royal connotations. It was the bridge that Lucien's troops entered the city by when they took power.

This bridge had stood for over two hundred years, but I still wondered if it was safe as we crossed it. There was so much empty air between the bridge and the water. The old saying used to go that the city was built on willpower alone, because of the long tradition of training in magic here, and because of that gravity-defying bridge, and the castle on its rock, and the harbor that was hollowed out of the west side of the island, an enormous cave under the edge of the city.

We entered the graveyard through the stone archway at the end of the bridge and were instantly among the graves. Most on the perimeter were new, sunk from the settling of the earth or mounded up still too high, and marked only with small wooden crosses. A short way to our left was an empty grave, newly dug. Stirling glanced at it as we passed.

The graves were arranged traditionally, in circles. In the center of the middle circle, a long way away from where we stood now, there was a large monument—a stone cross with the figure of Christ on it, surrounded by a circle of trees. Nearest to it were the graves of the royal family, going back about four centuries, and a lot of empty grass, which had been left for the rest of them for a long time to come. It would have been strange to be a young prince or princess in those days and walk up here and see, to the nearest foot or two, where you would lie until you returned to dust.

"I can't remember where the grave is," Stirling said. "It's all changed."

"I know it was over this way," I said, weaving in and out of the headstones. I glanced at the nearest one. "A long way further in. These are only dated about a year ago."

"I think it was in that direction," Stirling said, pointing.

"Here, we are getting close. Read the dates."

"I can't."

"I forgot. I will find it; we are near to it now." We were about fifteen rings in toward the center. "It's in this circle, for sure," I told Stirling. "It's around here." He jogged over, and we both peered at the headstones. It was like a macabre sort of treasure hunt, and we were taking a strange delight in it.

"Is this it?" He pointed.

I looked. "Yes, I think so."

"A-L-D . . . ," he spelled. I let him. "A-L-D-E-B-A-R-A-N. Aldebaran, that says. It is his grave."

*I*t was an ordinary cross, blotched with mustard-colored lichen, bearing only his name and the dates of his birth and death. "How old does that say he lived to?" asked Stirling.

I worked it out. "Sixty."

"Younger than Grandmother," said Stirling. "So how old is he now?"

"He would have been seventy."

"Would have been? If he was alive, you mean?" He looked at me steadily. "I still think he is."

"Perhaps." I shrugged.

Stirling began to stamp on the grave. "What are you doing?" I demanded.

"Testing if I can hear a coffin echoing."

"How would you know if coffins echo? And it would have rotted by now."

"Oh." He stopped stamping.

Now that we were here, it seemed stupid. How would we ever know if the grave was real just by looking at it or stamping on it? Or even digging it up? If people want to lie, they can lie, and you never know if they're telling the truth.

"Do you know what?" Stirling said, casting his eyes about the graveyard.

"No, what?"

"Their heads are far apart, but their feet are all nearly touching."

"Whose?"

"The bodies in the graves. That's the problem with putting them in a circle."

"Stirling! What a thing to think of! I must be a bad influence on you!"

"You sound like Grandmother!" he told me, and I laughed but hushed quickly. It was like laughing in a church. Even if you are quite alone, the spirits in the air tell you that you should not do it. "I don't mean to be disrespectful," he said. "They're not really here."

An urgent breeze snagged in the branches of the trees. The sun had lost its warmth without our noticing it, and the rays were casting long shadows behind the gravestones. The dark stone angels on the royal graves twitched. "Come on," I told Stirling, shivering. "Let's go home."

"Are you scared?" he asked me.

"No—just cold. Come, we should be getting back."

He followed me in and out of the gravestones. But before we reached the gateway, a figure emerged through it toward us—a somber, cloaked figure.

It was a priest. Behind him came four men bearing a small coffin—a child's—about the height of Stirling. A young couple pressed close behind it, and a small family group a little way behind them. The man was wearing a soldier's uniform. They were both crying and made no attempt to hide it. There should have been no one here to see.

I stood still, guilty because my laughter was still fading from the air, and Stirling stopped beside me. The people went and gathered around that open grave, and as soon as we could, we slipped past them toward the bridge. As we went, the man broke away from the group and staggered back to the gateway. He leaned there as though he could not support himself, sobbing openly, his hands over his face. Stirling glanced at me, and we edged past him. He did not even look up.

We walked back in silence. The child must have died from some infectious illness; that was the reason for burial so late in the day. It was the tradition to bury people in the morning, so that they would rise with the sun. But it was the law to bury people after five o'clock and before sunrise if they had died of an infectious disease. Some people thought that just before dawn was closer to sunrise. Some people thought that the last light of the afternoon was. But the thing is neither of them is actually sunrise.

I had half expected Grandmother to be angry that we were late back, but she was not. We told her we had been for a walk, and she did not question it. "I'm glad that you were not kept in after school again" was all she said. Then she and Stirling went out to church.

I could not settle to anything. I wandered around the apartment, thinking about Aldebaran's grave and whether it could be fake, as Stirling said. It had looked the same as all the others. Just the fact that he had a gravestone had always made me believe that he was dead for certain. But I was not certain anymore.

I began looking for that black book. Several days had passed since the last writing had appeared, and I wanted to check it again. I thought I had put it back in the windowsill chest, but it was not there. I searched the room. I found it eventually, under the mattress on my bed. That was strange, because I knew I had not put it there. And when I opened it, there was more writing in it.

I was less unnerved by the book than I had been at first, but I still hesitated before reading it. Not only was writing appearing in it, someone was moving it too. But what harm could it do just to read the next section? I flipped the next blank pages over, found the writing and began before I could change my mind.

❧

"Field," said Raymond, looking up from his newspaper. He found it increasingly hard to read, but he could make out most of the headlines. "Field, you know that gardening is not the butler's job."

"Sorry, sir," said the butler, wiping the lawn mower oil from his hands. "The grass needed cutting."

"How many times have I had to tell you, Field?" said Raymond. "You needn't work so hard. You aren't a slave."

"It is no trouble, sir. Hard work is good for me."

Several years had passed, and the butler had not aged. "Maybe that's true," said Raymond, chuckling.

"Well, I have always been accustomed to it."

"I suppose the army was very tough physical work."

"The army? Yes, of course."

"I would not have managed," said Raymond. "I've never been healthy. Look at me now: I'm barely seventy and I'm at death's door."

"I wouldn't say that, sir. A heart attack takes some getting over, but I would not say you are at . . . death's door, as you put it." But Raymond shook his head.

The butler knelt and lit the fire. The swords, in their cases, glimmered in the falling dusk. "Field, would you pass me the envelope from the top drawer of my desk?" Raymond said then. "The brown one."

The butler fetched the envelope and handed it to him. "I've asked my lawyers to come by this evening," Raymond said, taking out a few papers. "I needed to set some things in order." At that moment the doorbell rang. "Show them in, Field, if you will. You don't need to stay. I'll call you if I need you."

"Very good, sir."

As soon as the butler reached his room, he went to the cupboard. He got the book out, sighing in exasperation when he saw that there was still no more writing than his own unanswered messages. He began scrawling into it furiously, the ink·spurting sharply from the pen with the force that he exerted on the nib. *The twentieth of August, in the twelfth year of the reign of King Cassius II,* he wrote. *Talitha.*

I started and held the book closer to my eyes, reading that one name. Talitha—I had not misread it; that was what it said. Talitha, Lucien's closest advisor, the one who had killed the king and the queen and exiled Aldebaran and the prince. This man was not a stranger after all. And the date he had written— the twentieth of August in the twelfth year of the reign of King Cassius II—that date was three days before the Liberation. I read on quickly.

Talitha, it has been two months since you replied to me, and yet I know you are in no danger. Cannot you even write me one word?

From what I can see of the country, which is not much, I can tell something is about to happen. But my attempts to see are being blocked. Could you investigate this? I fear there are traitors among us. Be careful. If a rebellion is stirring, I am sure it is the Kalitz family on Holy Island that is behind it. Could you not get someone to watch them? I suspect Lucien Kalitz. I know that you say this is unfounded, but please, check again before you cast aside my concerns so quickly.

Measures need to be taken. And from what I can see, nothing has been done. Of course, I leave the protection of Malonia to your far superior judgment, but can you tell me what you are planning to do about this? Please reply, Talitha—I am worried. If there is any risk of an attempt at revolution, we ought to move first and tighten security. You have not seen these English weapons. Willpower is nothing against them. We must be absolutely certain that someone is not mass-producing rifles to equip a rebel force. These are not impractical firearms like those that are beginning to be developed in Malonia. These are highly effective machines.

I beg you once again to reply to me. Your servant, A.F.

After scratching in his initials, the butler pushed the book back into the cupboard and began to pace about the room, flexing his fingers so as to loosen them from their grip on the pen. He rubbed at his head; he was tired from the effort of trying to see into Malonia. Why could not Talitha reply?

Two days later a message appeared, scribbled hastily in slanting lines across the page. A.F., Situation under control. Do not attempt to communicate with me again—I cannot be sure that you are not being watched. No one is plotting a revolution, least of all the Kalitz family. I know you bear a grudge against them, but kindly keep it out of these matters of state. Do not reply. Talitha.

Arthur Field slammed the book shut and frowned into the darkness outside the window. He respected Talitha less and less every day. But she was his superior in every way; what right had he to accuse her of failing to do enough? She had not time or strength to spare to communicate with him constantly, after all. He watched the lake growing darker under the fading sky and ground his teeth together absently, digging his fingernails into the cover of the book. "Talitha," he said then, addressing the darkness. "Talitha, answer me." He closed his eyes and spoke louder. "Answer me."

The darkness remained silent. Talitha, if she had heard him, chose not to reply.

And then I realized who the man was—the butler, Arthur Field. I felt as though I knew what was going to happen next, as if I had witnessed it long ago and almost but not quite forgotten. I stared at the page. The writing had grown more sloping and uneven, scratched deep into the old paper, since the story began. And this was the end.

I was distracted the whole of that evening, still thinking about the book. Lying in bed that night, staring out at the stars between the curtains, I was still confused. If the butler was Aldebaran, which was what I was beginning to believe, and if this story was true, then he had been alive in England just before the Liberation ten years ago. And if he had been alive at that time, why would he have been writing to Talitha? Could she have tricked him into believing she was on the side of the king, as she had tricked others? I was not sure. But if anyone could have tricked the great Aldebaran, it would have been her.

Then another thought made me sit up in the darkness. If

those trained in magic could communicate through a book, perhaps that was what this book was too, the book that I had found. And if so, did that make it dangerous? Maybe I should never have picked it up. How did I know it was not the property of someone great and powerful, someone who could be watching me now as I turned the pages?

I did not sleep until the clock in the city had struck two. Lying there, I was wondering uneasily whose writing I had intercepted—and whether they knew that I was reading it.

⟨~⟩

The lamp gutters and goes out altogether. I sit for a while in darkness, then cross the balcony and look out over the city. I can hear the music still rising from the rooms of the castle, the notes faster and wilder now that it is late. The church clock, away across the roofs below, is chiming twelve. I used to hear the clock chiming in those days too, those days when I sat up at nights reading the book.

I remember how that book troubled me. I always thought that something was only evil or only good. Never both. I lay awake at nights wondering which the book was. But there is never only evil or only good—that is what you said. There are particles of good and particles of evil, and they are mixed. And sometimes they stick together in clumps, and sometimes they diffuse out of an area, or an age, or a life. The evil particles have more energy. More strength. Like when one dead fly ruins a jar of perfume.

You use science to explain everything. It annoys me sometimes. But I think in a way you are right. I can say that about my own life. This book was my confession to you—that was why I began it. My sins have been great, I should tell you now. Or at least, they had great strength.

I hear a woman's heeled shoes on the stairs. She is saying something in a soft, well-spoken voice like Maria's, and a man replies. After a while their footsteps fade again. Alone on the balcony, I walk along the parapet and watch the lights of the city. And then the moon rises from behind the clouds.

I can see by that light, even without the lamp. I will read on, now that I have started. I will finish reading what I wrote.

On Thursday morning I woke late. It was Stirling's occasional coughs that eventually jolted me awake. "Hurry, Leo, or we will be late!" he said then, and I sat up. He was beside my bed, already dressed and putting on his boots. "It's past seven-thirty," he said.

"Why did you not wake me?" I said.

"I thought you would be tired after walking such a long way yesterday."

"I'm not tired," I said, though I was yawning as I spoke. I hurried down to fetch the water.

We ran half the way to school, but we were still two minutes late. Sergeant Bane did not much bother about lateness.

Sergeant Markey did. "He will keep you in again," I told Stirling as we ran through the gate. I was out of breath and coughing with some of the old violence that had faded.

"If he does, you go home by yourself," Stirling said, turning to me.

"I will wait for you," I told him.

I had fully intended to, but a cold drizzle started just as school finished, and I was tired, and I ended up leaving without him. "He will only be half an hour," said Grandmother. "And the evenings are light now anyway."

I was sitting on my bed, reading the newspaper, when Stirling got back, more than an hour later. He came trotting into the bedroom. "Sorry I didn't wait," I told him, folding the newspaper.

"I don't mind," he said.

He took off his boots and put them down by the side of his bed, in line with each other exactly, and trailed the laces out to the sides so that they didn't touch each other. "Why do you have to do that?" I asked him. He'd always had to put his boots like that, ever since he was small.

"I don't know." He shrugged. "I don't like the boots to stand on the laces."

I laughed at him. He sat down on my bed. "Do you know what Sergeant Markey made me do as punishment? I had to run around the yard five times, with weights—"

"That is hardly a punishment," I told him.

"No, then he hit me. Look at this." He held out his hand and laughed to hear me gasp.

I could make out the stripes of a stick on it, but there were so many that it was impossible to distinguish any unwounded flesh. It was red—raw meat red—and shiny, and blood seeped in the palm lines. "How can you laugh at that?" I said, alarmed. "Does it not hurt?"

He shook his head.

"But it hurt when he did it?"

"No."

"When he actually hit you, I mean."

"No. I promise it didn't hurt. That's what is funny. I never felt it. I knew it would hurt, but it didn't, and I sort of smiled because it was strange. And he looked scared. I was humming a tune, and he shouted at me to stop it."

"You were humming a tune?" I said, taking hold of his hand and staring at the stripes crossing it.

"The hymn we sang at Mass yesterday."

"Why?"

"I don't know many other songs except hymns."

"No, I mean why were you humming?"

"I didn't notice I was doing it."

"A hymn." I let his hand go but went on staring at it. "He probably thought that you were a prophet, come to send him to hell."

"Do prophets send people to hell?"

"I don't know; he probably thought God was helping you or something."

"Stirling!" Grandmother exclaimed from the doorway.

"Yes," he said, turning to her, his bloody hand gleaming grotesquely in the light from the window.

"What happened?" she asked, hurrying over. "Why did you not show me?"

"It was Sergeant Markey."

"That man! My poor baby!" She clutched him to her.

"I'm not a baby, Grandmother. And it didn't hurt—don't be so worried."

"That man!" she said again. "I must report him to the headmaster. I should have done so much sooner, only with Leo getting ill I forgot. He is a vicious bully. I will go to your headmaster tomorrow."

"Don't do that," Stirling told her.

"Stirling, something must be done about him," she said. "And this is not the only time he has been so cruel."

"No. But I don't think he will be again. It scared him, because he couldn't hurt me."

"He couldn't hurt you?" said Grandmother. Stirling explained.

"Perhaps Stirling has powers," I said to her.

"No," she said. "I hope that he does not."

Grandmother bandaged Stirling's hand, and he sat frowning at it while he drank his tea. "Does it hurt now?" I asked him. He shook his head. "Have you completely lost your sense of feeling?"

"Punch me; see if it hurts."

I hit his arm, just hard enough that he should feel it slightly. He didn't even move. I punched him harder.

"I can't feel anything," he said.

"Stop that, Leo," said Grandmother, coming in from the kitchen at that moment.

"It didn't hurt," Stirling assured her. She regarded him anxiously.

That evening Maria came back from church with Stirling

and Grandmother. She had Anselm with her. Stirling told her all about the incident, the three of us sitting around the table in the living room, Maria holding the crying baby. We had to shout to be heard, though we were barely two feet apart.

"Perhaps you will grow up to be a saint, and this is your first miracle," Maria remarked.

"You shouldn't joke about that," Stirling told her.

"I was being serious," she said, laughing at his earnestness.

I noticed that he was clutching his bandaged hand. "Is it beginning to hurt?" I asked. "Are you getting back your sense of feeling?"

"I think so." He unclenched it. "Yes, it hurts for sure."

"I'm glad," I said.

"You're glad that my hand hurts?"

"No—only that you've got your feeling back. It was strange when it didn't hurt at all. Unnatural."

In the silence that followed, I held up the newspaper, which I had been reading until they came in. "Look at this." I turned to the front page and read the first few lines: " 'The Alcyrians must be crushed. We will not retreat until we have taken back the land that is ours. Those who are truly loyal to our country would count the casualties a small price.'"

"Who said that?" said Maria.

"Ahira," I told her. "Who else? Does he seriously think that we will win this war?"

"No," she said quietly. "I . . . don't suppose he does."

"He came to our school once," said Stirling. "Ahira. He gave a speech."

"Oh yes." I laughed. "He said, 'Boys, you are soldiers of new Malonia.' Things like that. I tell you, the teachers bowed to him as if he was God himself. He shook all of our hands. And when he came to me, what I thought of him must have been written on my face, because he nearly broke my wrist."

"There's something about him," said Stirling. "Something that makes you—I don't know—scared of him but you have to listen to him."

"Compelling," I said. "He's a strange man." And then I saw Maria's face. "Anyway, what about this picnic?" I said.

And we talked no more of Ahira. We told her that we had been to the graveyard and seen the hills from that side of the city. "We should go that way when we walk out there," I said.

Anselm was still wailing. "Is it sensible to bring him?" Maria asked.

"It seems unfair to leave him here alone, when we are having fun," Stirling remarked, stroking Anselm's head. "Shh," he told the baby, and Anselm stopped crying. But only for a moment.

"Babies don't find that sort of thing fun," said Maria. "They like sleeping and eating and . . . staring at things. I can't think what else, to be honest. They don't like being carried about for miles; it just makes them miserable. And being in the sun all day will annoy him, and he will need changing all the time, and feeding."

"It is a bad idea to bring him, really," I said.

"I should leave him with my mother."

"Will he mind?" asked Stirling.

"We can go on plenty more picnics, when he's older. He will not be a baby forever; soon he will be able to do things like that. We can take him around with us then."

"It still seems unfair," said Stirling.

"People probably left you behind when you were a baby," Maria said. "That's just the way. He would prefer to stay at home. He likes it at home."

"Well, I suppose," Stirling said. "We will have to make it up to him, though."

She laughed. "Remember that, Stirling, and in a couple of years we will take him on a picnic and tell him it is because you said so." Anselm looked up at us, silent for a moment, as if he knew that we were talking about him.

"I won't forget," said Stirling.

On Friday evening Stirling was coughing again. "Are you cold?" Grandmother asked. She felt his forehead. "No, you are warm. I hope you don't have a fever."

"I'm fine," Stirling said, and insisted that he was well enough to go to Mass.

"I hope you aren't coming down with something," said Grandmother as they left for the church. "I think we have had enough of illness in the family for one year." Watching him skipping down the stairs, she laughed suddenly. "Perhaps I am too anxious. Ever since Leo's incident in training, when you came home so dramatically, I have been worrying too much about you boys."

"That cough will be gone by tomorrow, I'll guess," I told her.

I met Maria down in the yard that evening, and we stood at the gate and talked for a while. When I eventually turned to the door, she caught my arm. "Is Stirling all right now?" she said.

"His hand is hurting him," I said. "Why do you ask?"

"No reason." But she did not let go of my arm. "I was just thinking—a lot of illnesses begin with loss of, you know, faculties. I was reading about it in the newspaper. . . ."

"Loss of sight or hearing," I said. "Not feeling. And you know what that newspaper is like."

"True," she said, and laughed, but she didn't sound convinced. "You know, we can always go on that picnic another weekend." Then the kids from the first-floor apartment came running out into the yard, banging the door, and she let go of my hand and smiled. "It is nothing to worry about, I suppose. It was just that he was coughing and I wondered if he was feeling all right now."

"He will be fine tomorrow," I told her. "You'll see."

And he was. When he woke, even the cough was gone. I could tell that Grandmother wanted to keep him at home, but he was determined to go. "I feel fine," he insisted, skipping about the kitchen as we got the food ready for the picnic. We had some bread, a small piece of cheese—all that was left—and some apples that were slightly too old. It was hardly a feast.

"Use the cloth to polish those apples, Stirling, not your shirt," Grandmother said, hovering distractedly in the kitchen doorway. "Are you sure you are well enough to go?"

"I'm sure."

Grandmother opened her mouth to speak again, but at that moment there was a rap at the door. "That will be Maria," Stirling said, and ran to open it.

Maria had brought a basket with a lot of fruit and vegetables but not much else. Still, we had plenty of bread, and the apples she had brought were better than ours. Maria and I sat talking while Stirling and Grandmother finished wrapping up the food. "Come on, let's go," said Stirling then, dragging us both out the door.

"Take care," Grandmother called after us.

Walking down the stairs, we smiled at each other as if we were little children going out alone for the first time. It was strange to be leaving the building with Maria. "I keep thinking that you have forgotten something," I told her as we went out the side door.

"What is it?" she asked.

"Anselm."

She laughed. "Yes, it's strange to be without him."

Maria looked like a sophisticated lady, carrying the basket on her arm. The way she walked, too, was elegant; I had not much noticed before. She was wearing fairly ordinary clothes—a long-skirted dress with a tight bodice and a colored shawl—but she wore them as if she knew she was pretty, and it made them into more than what they really were.

Stirling walked ahead, humming. He was always humming, but it didn't annoy me like Grandmother's humming did, because he had a sweet voice. Maria suddenly linked her arm with mine. I started, and she laughed at me for it. But I soon got used to the weight of her arm on the inside of my elbow. And with Stirling walking ahead and Maria holding my arm, I fell to imagining that we were married, Maria and I, and Stirling was our little boy. It was a stupid thing to imagine, but I imagined it anyway. I was a soldier, on leave for the weekend. Stirling was . . . better make him about five or six years old—no matter, he was small. He could be our son Leonard, named after me. And we were—

"Which way is it?" Maria was asking me. "Leo?"

I started. "Oh, sorry. Right."

"Why don't we go to that street?" asked Stirling, falling in beside me. "The one that looked over the river. Maria would like to see it."

I turned to Maria. She shrugged. "Why not? See how the rich people live." We laughed and turned off to the left so that we would come to the edge of the city further north.

There were a lot of people about. Five soldiers on horseback swept down the street toward us at a brisk rising trot, and we stood to the side to let them pass. The first one raised his hat to us. "Perhaps the war is going well," Maria remarked. "They are not usually so friendly."

"They are probably going down to the harbor," I said, looking back to see which way they turned at the crossroads. "Yes, they are going in that direction. Perhaps they are being stationed over in the west; that is the best place to be at the moment."

"I wish they would station my father somewhere else," said Maria.

I had forgotten her father was at the border. "Is he a soldier?" I said.

"No, he just got called up for the Alcyrian war. He was a banker before that. You know the bank by the market square?"

"What—the one that is owned by Zenithar Armaments?"

"Yes. That was his. It used to be—"

"Andros Associates," I said. "I remember."

"Why aren't you rich?" Stirling exclaimed.

She laughed carelessly. "We used to be."

We were walking slowly, Maria swinging the basket on her arm, her other arm still linked with mine. Stirling strolled along, his hands in his pockets. Suddenly I heard a voice from somewhere close by: "Is that North—Leo North from school?"

"Yes, it is," someone answered. "Call him—go on." Casting my eyes around, I saw two faces leaning out an upstairs window, two boys from my platoon—Seth Blackwood and Isaac Sadler.

"It's that bastard Leo North!" shouted Seth, grinning and waving to me. Isaac leaned out the window and made to spit on us, but he was not serious.

"Piss off," I said, laughing in spite of myself, and we hurried out of spitting distance. "Is that his girlfriend?" I heard Isaac whispering. Then more loudly: "North, is that your girl?" I ignored it. "Leonard!" Isaac called louder still.

"Mr. Leonard B. North, Esquire, kindly answer!" shouted Seth. And then he added, "B for 'bastard,' that is." Maria turned round and gave them a look. They retreated from the window, Seth hitting his head hard on the window frame. "See you in school on Monday!" he called.

"All right," I called back.

We turned a corner in the road and were all suddenly laughing. But I was surprised at their comparative friendliness. "Nice boys at your school," said Maria. Stirling caught her eyes and choked with laughter.

"Do you always talk to each other like that?" Maria demanded. I nodded. "Leonard B. North was priceless," she said. "That wounded Leo deeply; I could see."

And we could barely draw breath for laughing until we reached the edge of the city.

"Oh, how lovely!" Maria exclaimed as we came out onto that cobbled street. "I wish that I lived somewhere like this."

"Me too," said Stirling. He leaned his chin on his hands, on the top of the wall. "See the hills? That's where we are going."

But Maria had her back to the hills. She was looking at the houses. She seemed far away in her thoughts, and she did not reply. "We haven't been out of the city for ages, have we?" Stirling said, turning to me.

"Not for years," I said.

Maria stood gazing at those houses. She did not seem to want to go on yet, but it did not matter; we were in no hurry anyway. We stood in silence beside her. I wondered if this street made her think of her old life, when she was a banker's daughter. I had thought she must have been wealthy before, because of the way she talked. But I had not guessed how wealthy.

"Look who it is!" Stirling exclaimed then, and we both turned. A hired carriage was standing outside a house ahead and someone had just stepped out of it. "It's Sergeant Markey," Stirling told Maria.

"So that's what he looks like," she said. We stood and watched him.

"He's helping someone out of the carriage," said Stirling. Sergeant Markey stooped and lifted a child. She must have been about nine or ten. She clung tightly around Sergeant Markey's neck and began to wail.

"Shh," he said. "Papa's got you." He stroked her head. Her hair was a fine ice blond, like Stirling's would have been if he did not wear it short, and her face was pretty, though it was red from crying now.

"What is it?" Sergeant Markey said. "What's the matter, angel?" But the way he said it, he didn't seem to expect her to respond. The girl murmured something, her eyes darting about nervously in her thin face. She buried her head in his shoulder and began to wail again. A lady came after them down the carriage steps—a lady in uniform who looked like a housekeeper or a nurse. She hurried to open the door, and shut it behind them, cutting off the girl's cries.

There was silence. "Well!" I exclaimed.

"I thought you said he was nasty," said Maria.

"I thought he was."

"He looked sweet with his little girl. Not many men can look after children like that."

"I didn't even know he had a kid," I said.

"She looked sick," Maria said. "Did you see how bony her face was? Probably some sort of illness has left her an invalid."

"Yes. Something like silent fever, I'll guess. Poor child."

"No wonder he is not high up in the army, then," said Maria.

"What, you mean harboring unacceptables? That's why he has to teach school?"

"You know what they are like about that," said Maria. "I'm not saying it's good, the way the government treats sick people. I think it's terrible."

"Yes."

We gathered ourselves to walk on. "All right, Stirling?" I asked, turning to him. He was leaning heavily on the wall. "What's wrong?"

"Boys!" It was Sergeant Markey's voice. I turned to see him coming back down the steps of his house. "What are you doing loitering around here?" he demanded, in his usual manner.

"We can loiter around wherever—" I began, but at that moment Maria exclaimed, "Hey, Stirling!" I turned. Not in time to catch him as he passed out. He smacked down hard on the cobblestones. I fell to my knees beside him, and so did Maria, dropping the basket. He was out cold.

Sergeant Markey knelt down next to me. He turned Stirling over and pressed his hand to his forehead. "He has a high fever," he said. "You need to get him home quickly. This looks as if it could be something serious." Then Stirling came to. He stared at Sergeant Markey, whose hand was still pressed down on his head.

"You fainted," I said.

"Oh . . . ," he said distantly.

I waited for the color to return to his face. "Can you sit up?" I asked. I put my arm around his shoulders and pulled him into a sitting position, Maria supporting his other side. We moved him round so that he could lean on the wall. Then I noticed that Sergeant Markey had gone. Not unlike him, I thought. Typical, in fact.

I felt Stirling's forehead. The heat was rising off it like steam. "He can't walk home like this," said Maria.

"Give him a minute," I said. "He'll feel better in a minute." I turned to him. "Stirling, will you be able to walk home?" He made no answer. "Stirling, can you hear me?" I passed my hand in front of his face. "Stirling?" He did not seem to mark it.

"How is he going to get home?" asked Maria.

"Well, he's going to have to, somehow," I said. "I can carry him if it comes to it."

"All the way?"

"I'm not doing all this weight training in school for nothing."

"Still, it's—" Someone touched my shoulder, and I realized it was Sergeant Markey, holding out a glass of water.

"Here, give him this," he said. So that was where he had gone.

Stirling drank some of the water and seemed to be listening to me when I spoke to him. "Will you be able to walk home?" I asked him.

"I don't know," he mumbled after a moment. "Yes . . . I think."

"Take my carriage," said Sergeant Markey.

"Excuse me, sir?"

"He cannot walk like that. Take the carriage. I can wait until the driver gets back."

"I'm not sure you can get to our street by carriage," I said, not looking at him.

"He can take you as far as possible, anyway. Where do you live?"

"Citadel Street."

"Ah," he said as if I had just told him, "The sewers." Or perhaps I only imagined it. "If he took you down to the market square, could you come up to it from there?"

I couldn't think properly. "Maybe," I said, dabbing the water onto Stirling's forehead with my jacket sleeve.

"I think you could," said Sergeant Markey. "The sooner you get him back home, the better."

He bent and picked Stirling up, then carried him briskly across to the carriage. Stirling's bandaged hand fell limply across Sergeant Markey's back. We hurried after them. "Get in," said Sergeant Markey, and he laid Stirling on one of the seats.

I smiled at Stirling as we sat down, to try to reassure him. "The young lad's been taken ill," said Sergeant Markey to the driver on the front. "Will you take them as near to Citadel Street as you can get? I'll pay you when you get back."

"Yes, sir." The man shook the reins, and the horses moved off.

I had not thought that Sergeant Markey would be paying. I did not want to be indebted to him. But it couldn't be helped now.

"All right, Stirling?" I asked. He nodded. It looked to be a big effort. "We haven't been in a carriage before, have we?" I said, trying to keep my voice calm. He shook his head and managed a faint smile.

"We used to have our own carriage," said Maria. "It was not much use except for going out of the city. I had my own pony as well, but that was a long time ago." She reached across and took Stirling's hand. "Nearly home, Stirling."

His head was jolting against the seat. I swung over onto his side of the carriage. "Here, put your head on my knee," I told him. Maria helped him up so that he was leaning against me. He began to shiver then. She spread her shawl over him. "I should not have made him come out," I said. "I didn't know he was ill."

"You weren't to know," she said. "Anyway, he was better this morning."

"I still feel guilty." I touched his shoulder. "All right, Stirling?" He nodded.

"It's not your fault, Leo," Maria said. "That's how it is with illness. You cannot plan for it."

The streets were crowded, and the people had to stand aside to let the carriage pass. Kalitzstad was not built for carriages; we rarely saw them. We were descending toward the market square, on one of the main roads. We drove close past the church and around the edge of the square, then turned off toward the castle and Citadel Street. "The way we came was quicker," said Maria.

"Sergeant Markey's paying anyway," I said. She laughed, but Stirling didn't even smile at that. His eyes were closed, and his forehead was still hot when I passed my hand over it. I opened the window, leaned out, and called to the driver, "Can we go any faster, please?" He raised his hands helplessly. The people went on thronging past the carriage doors.

Stirling coughed feverishly. "He's had that cough for days," I said. "I thought it was nothing. I should have known he was getting sick."

"A cough by itself is not serious," she said. "And you fainted yourself the other week. It often happens." She paused. "I think a doctor needs to see him, though."

"What doctor?"

"Father Dunstan, then. He knows about medicine. Your grandmother should ask him to come and see Stirling."

"Yes, I'll guess she will. She always does when we're sick."

"Just in case it's something serious. I'm sure it's not."

We continued in this uneasy way until the carriage slowed, halfway up Citadel Street. "Sorry, this is as far as I can go," called the driver, and he opened the door for us. "Need a hand to get the boy out?"

"No, I'm fine," I said. "Come on, Stirling." I lifted him over my shoulder.

"Are you sure it's all right to do that?" Maria said anxiously. "You don't want to do yourself an injury."

"I'm fine," I said. She followed me.

I carried Stirling up the street slowly, so that I would not jolt him too much. Maria went ahead to unlock the door, and held it open, and I maneuvered us through it, trying not to catch the door frame. "I'll run ahead and tell your grand-mother," said Maria while I was still lifting Stirling up the stairs. "It will give her such a shock if you suddenly burst in like this."

"Poor baby!" cried Grandmother when I brought Stirling in. "Put him on his bed." I carried him through the bedroom door and laid him down carefully. "What exactly happened?" she asked, feeling his pulse. "His heart is beating fast! And he has a fever! He was fine this morning."

"He just suddenly fainted," I said. "He was fine, and then he fainted."

"Stirling, can you hear me?" Grandmother said.

"Yes," he whispered, though his eyes were unfocused.

"Tell me what you feel like. Dizzy? Sick?"

"I can't see properly. Grandmother?"

"Yes, it's all right. You're safe at home now." He clutched at her, but his hand went wide of her shoulder as if he could not see where it was at all.

"Can you see this?" I asked, holding my hand before his face. He made no sign that he could.

"What?" he croaked.

"Leo, will you go and get Father Dunstan?" asked Grandmother. "Hurry. Go at once."

I shut the front door and ran down the stairs.

*F*ather Dunstan was kneeling at the altar. "Leonard!" he said, turning as I clattered through the door. He always called me Leonard, because he didn't really know me. "Glad to see you well again."

"Could you come and look at Stirling?" I said. "He is sick."

"Certainly, yes." He stood and picked up his cloak from where it lay over the front pew. "Now Stirling? This is sudden, is it not?"

"Yes." He strode out of the church and I followed him. "He's been coughing for a couple of days, and then he just fainted suddenly, and he's been bad ever since."

We hurried through the square and up toward our street. Father Dunstan shot the occasional question at me as we walked. He led the way, and I jogged behind him.

"Do you think it is serious?" I asked when I had told him all the symptoms.

"I cannot say," he replied. "But sometimes illnesses appear serious at first, and then turn out to be only mild. Let us hope it is one of those."

Maria was still there when I got back, and I was glad of her company while I waited in the living room. Father Dunstan was in the next room with Grandmother and Stirling, and I could hear their low voices but could not judge anything by the tone.

I picked up Grandmother's sewing absently, then stabbed my finger on the needle, swore and dropped it again. Maria did not notice. She was staring out the window.

"Maria?" I said after a while. "What did you say you read in the newspaper? About diseases that start with loss of feeling?" She turned to me. "You were talking about it yesterday."

"Oh yes," she said. But she did not go on.

The previous day's newspaper was lying on the table, and I reached for it now. "Is it in here?" I said.

"I . . . I think so, yes. But it was not a very serious article. You said yourself that this newspaper . . ." She trailed off as I searched through the pages.

I went through it once, then again, impatiently. She took it from me and turned to a page near the back, scanning it for a minute without showing it to me. I leaned over her shoulder to read the headline: WHEN I GOT BACK, I REALIZED I'D BEEN SHOT.

"It sounds like comedy," I said, though I was not laughing. "Hold it still; your hand is shaking."

She did not speak while I read it. It was a real account of a soldier who had had what he'd thought was a close escape in battle. He rode back to camp alone. When he got there, he saw that his leg was bleeding, and he realized that he had actually been shot. But he could not feel any pain.

I glanced up at Maria, but still she did not speak. "What did he have, this soldier?" I asked quietly. "What illness?"

"Silent fever," she said.

I stared at the page. The words were drifting in front of my eyes. I tried to read on, but I couldn't. "It's a different strain, they think," said Maria. "Slow-developing silent fever."

"What does the rest say? Tell me."

"It says they are just discovering this disease. Some of the symptoms are different, so they always thought it was a different illness. It doesn't pass on between people like ordinary silent fever. You know how with marsh sickness you catch it from drinking bad water, not contact with people who are infected? They thought it was something like that. But then they found at the border that people were getting sick with this disease because they came into contact with silent fever carriers."

She ran her finger down the page. I followed where she was reading: " 'The illness always begins with temporary periods of loss of senses—in most cases sight or hearing; but in many, taste, smell, and occasionally feeling can be lost too, as in the case previously described.' "

I looked at Maria. Neither of us said anything. At that moment Grandmother gave a cry from the next room. We both clattered to our feet in a rush, still staring at each other in blank horror.

At the bedroom door Maria paused for a moment, but I pushed it open and she followed me. Father Dunstan knelt beside the bed, one hand clasped in Stirling's. Grandmother's head was pressed against his shoulder, and she was sobbing. The only one who noticed us enter was Stirling. We stood in silence while Father Dunstan attempted to comfort Grandmother and she cried. I tried to catch the priest's eye, to ask him in a look what was wrong, but I couldn't, and at last I blurted out, "What is it?" Neither of them answered.

Then Stirling murmured, "Silent fever." At the words,

Grandmother's wailing grew louder. We had known it already, but this confirmation from Stirling himself made it seem so final.

I ran to his side, but he did not seem troubled, or even quite conscious of what was happening. Grandmother's sobs rose. Even Father Dunstan, who saw people sick like this every week, had tears in his eyes. Why was I not crying? All I felt was selfish disappointment that just when I had thought everything was perfect, this had happened.

I turned to look at Maria kneeling beside me, and a tear fell from between her eyelashes and landed on her cheek. Impulsively, I reached up and brushed it away, and I kept my hand there, pressed to the side of her face. Then I was suddenly angry with myself. Stirling was ill—seriously ill—and all I could do was flirt shamelessly. I dropped my hand, my fingernail catching on her cheek, and stood up and left the room. No one even called after me.

❧

I met Maria down in the yard the next morning. She was there, with Anselm half asleep in her arms, when I stepped out of the bathroom. "Are you all right?" she asked.

"Me? Yes." I was still putting on my shirt. It was early, and I had thought I would meet no one.

"You look tired," she said. "You look as if you haven't slept." The baby murmured, and she jogged him absently. "How is Stirling?" she asked.

"Not so bad. Better than he was yesterday, anyway."

"Good." I stepped away from the bathroom door to let her in. "Are you going to go to church this morning?" she asked. I nodded. "I'll see you there, then. Give my love to Stirling."

I was almost at the door when she said, "Leo?" I turned. "I have had silent fever," she said. "I had it, and I got well again quite soon. It will be the same with Stirling, I think."

"Are you telling the truth?" I said. "Are you serious?"

"Yes. Of course."

Halfway up the stairs I thought of something and ran back down again. "Maria!" I said. She was still at the bathroom door, struggling to quiet Anselm, who was beginning to grizzle. "How did you get well again?"

She hesitated, rocking the baby. "I just . . . got well."

"Just like that?" I persisted. "Was there no medicine?"

She began arranging the baby's little shawl carefully. "I had some medicine. Not much."

"What was it? Tell me the name."

She did not answer for a long time. Then she said, "Bloodflower."

I stood still and stared at her. I knew about the Bloodflower. It was the one certain cure for silent fever. I knew about it, and I knew what it cost. "Where did you get that?" I said eventually.

"People used to find it in the mountains. It used to be more common than it is now. I had silent fever about eight years ago. It has got much rarer."

"But they still find it," I said thoughtfully. "You read about it in the newspapers sometimes."

"People recover without it. That's what I wanted to tell you. My father's doctor gave it to me as a precaution, even though I was recovering already. I think Stirling will recover just the same."

"But if we had the Bloodflower . . . ," I began, then stopped. I wandered back up the stairs.

I was at church alone. Grandmother would not leave Stirling. He was the only one of us who had slept the night before, and he seemed better for it, although he complained that his head hurt, and he still had a high fever. This was how Father Dunstan had said the illness would go: he would sink and then rise again. Until one day, I thought, he would sink below the surface.

When I thought that, such fear caught me that I felt as if I was falling. Really falling. The whole world stayed where it had been, but I dropped through it, into darkness, as if it just wasn't there. I gripped the front of the pew and went on mouthing the words of the prayer. When the bells jangled at the front, they started my heart beating fast, though they always rang at the same point in the service.

I felt the panic rise again in my heart when I heard Stirling's name listed in the prayer for the sick. Stirling North, among so many others who did not even seem real. Of course, they were real to someone. But to me they were just names—not actual people who were actually sick. And now—

I was breathing fast. I pressed my hand to my mouth and wished that I had sat nearer the back of the church, where I would not have been so exposed.

I caught Maria's eye as she filed past me behind her mother on her way back from Communion, jogging Anselm up and down to stop him from crying. I gave her as much of a smile as

I could, and she smiled faintly back. She looked tired in the cold light of the stained-glass windows. Maybe she had been worrying too.

After the service I waited behind for Father Dunstan. He emerged from the vestry, knelt for a moment at the altar, and then turned and saw me standing halfway down the church. "Leonard," he said, approaching. "How is your brother?"

"Better today," I said.

"I am glad to hear that."

"I . . . wanted to talk to you," I said. "I just wanted to ask, is there anything that can be done? For Stirling. To . . . save him."

He looked at me for a moment. "Leonard, you should not give up hope like this." I stared at the floor. "Many people do recover from silent fever—even this strain, which seems to be more serious. Stirling has always been perfectly healthy." I nodded. "If he is improved today, that is a good sign."

"Yes. But they don't recover very often, do they?" I heard my voice rising in spite of my efforts to control it.

"They do recover. If they have proper care and plenty of rest."

"Is there anything that I can do?"

"The only thing really to be done is to let it run its course. I won't lie to you, Leonard. We know very little about this illness. The slow-developing strain even less than the common one."

"Is there no treatment? What about that herb—the Bloodflower?" When he did not answer, I went on. "Would that cure even slow-developing silent fever?"

He hesitated for a moment. "It has been known to. Yes, it would cure any strain of silent fever. But I haven't heard of anyone who has found the Bloodflower for a long time. It can't be cultivated."

"Doesn't it grow in mountains, or hills?" I said. "What about the eastern hills? People find it there."

"It is important to remember, Leonard, that Stirling has a very good chance of getting well without it. Sometimes people even develop what seems to be silent fever and then recover again after a few days. The symptoms are so varied—"

"But if we had the Bloodflower, then he would be safe no matter what. If we had it—"

"Leonard." He said it with an air of finality so that I had to stop and listen. "The illness of a loved one makes us feel helpless. We want to do something about it, so that everything is not out of our control. But if you can just—"

"I had better go," I interrupted. "Sorry, Father, I . . . said I would be back—well, anyway—" I tried to smile at him. "Thank you for your help. Really." Then I turned and walked out of the church.

The square was deserted. I started along the side of it, breaking into a run, down the center of the main road, toward the edge of the city.

❧

*I*t was almost dark by the time I stumbled into the apartment that evening. Grandmother marched through the bedroom doorway, hands on hips, eyes shadowed by her frown. "Leo, where have you been?" she demanded. "You have had nothing to eat all day. I expected you back after church, and now it is nine-thirty. Where have you been?"

"Just . . . out." I shrugged and sat down heavily on the sofa. "Places . . ."

She went on firing questions at me. I was too tired to answer. I took off my boots and dropped them on the floor, and the thuds fell heavy in the silence, one after the other.

"Leo, where have you been?" she shouted suddenly. "I am not in the mood for this! Stirling is very sick, I didn't sleep at all last night, and I do not need you to add to my worries with your stupid, childish behavior!"

"I said, I went out."

"Leo!" she exclaimed through her teeth. From the other room, Stirling groaned. "See what you have done?" Grandmother said. "He was asleep, and now you have woken him. You will drive him into the grave with your stupidity, and me too if you can manage it!" She marched into the other room.

"Well, I am not in the mood for this lecturing!" I said. "You always think I'm so stupid and childish, but you don't know anything about me. You don't know where I went today—"

"No!" she interrupted. "Of course I don't know, because you will not tell me!" Then, to Stirling, "What's wrong, my angel?"

"All right," I went on, marching across the living room after her. "I was in the hills looking for the Bloodflower herb to save Stirling's life! What the hell is stupid and childish about that? While you sit here doing nothing, I'm trying to—"

"That's childish, Leo. I'll tell you why: because you will never, ever find it. That's typical of the way you act—always thinking—"

"Stop!" As I rounded the corner, I saw that Stirling was sitting up in bed, breathing heavily with the effort of shouting. "Please, stop!" He fell back onto his pillows, his face gray. "Please, don't fight."

"Sorry, Stirling," said Grandmother, her voice breaking with tears. She sighed and turned to me. "Leo, I was just worried about you."

"I'm sorry," I said, with effort. "I should have told you where I was going."

"That's better," said Stirling, like a parent sorting out two rowing children.

I went over to join Grandmother at the side of his bed. My anger was burned out, leaving only tiredness. "How are you feeling?" I asked.

"Better," he said. "Oh, much better. I think I will be well again quite soon."

"Good. I'm glad." I took off my jacket and laid it on my bed.

"Why did you go to the hills?" he asked.

I told him about the Bloodflower herb. "I think I will get well again without needing it," he told me. I nodded. "What was it like there?" he said. "What were the hills like?"

"Oh . . . green . . . big . . ." I rubbed my aching head.

"Tell me about them," said Stirling. "Sit here." I sat down on the side of his bed. Grandmother stole out of the room.

I was exhausted, and I could barely speak, let alone entertain him. "You don't have to," Stirling said then.

"I know what," I said. "I found a place for the picnic. There's a little stream—a rocky stream—that runs between two hills. The valley is shaded, and there's a meadow of wildflowers. All different colors—like a picture. You would like it, for certain. It is not too far from the city either."

"It sounds pretty," Stirling said. "When I am well, we can go there, with Maria. As soon as I am well."

"Yes. You would like that place."

"Tell me some more about it."

I told him about the valley, how the flowers were taller than he was and how there were butterflies glittering everywhere, how green the grass was, and how blue the sky. Perhaps I elaborated it slightly. "I can really imagine it," said Stirling when I had finished telling him. And then he said suddenly, "I missed you, Leo. Don't go to the hills again."

"But what if I was to find the herb?" I said.

"I don't think you will find it. Anyway, I'm almost sure that I will get well without it. Perhaps I have the illness only mildly. I don't feel so bad today."

"Maybe it is so."

"I think it is. Father Dunstan said it was difficult to tell, anyway, even whether it was silent fever or not."

Later that evening, Stirling suddenly lost his sight.

∼⌒⌒∼

*H*e did not shout or cry out; he just remarked, "I can't see," almost calmly, and we went to his side. But a couple of hours after, when it grew quite silent in the room, he called out in fright, "Grandmother!"

"I am here," she said. She had not left him.

"Leo?" he asked.

"I'm here too," I told him.

He held out his hands to us. "I couldn't hear you. I thought you'd left me."

"No," Grandmother said as we took his hands, one each. "We will not leave you." The one I took was his right one, the bandaged one, and I could feel the heat radiating from its still-raw palm.

His hand grasped mine tightly, as if the bond between them was the only thing that anchored him to this earth. His fingers were hot and dry, and I could feel the quick pulse in his wrist beating against mine, so tightly were they pressed together, until it seemed that the veins beat as one and it was my heartbeat that was keeping him alive.

Later, when he slipped into a fretful sleep, Grandmother said, "Why do you not get some rest, Leo? It's well past midnight, and you must get up early for school tomorrow."

"I won't be able to sleep," I told her.

"Leo, you must. This illness may draw out for months. You will have to sleep in that time."

"You need it more than me; you have been working harder. Go and get a few hours' rest; I will stay here with Stirling."

"Leo, go on. I can rest during the day tomorrow."

My previous sleepless night was beginning to catch up with me; my eyes were dry and prickly and my head ached sharply. I started to separate my hand from Stirling's, which was still clenched around it tightly. But I was suddenly so afraid that if I did, he would slip away forever, as if the cord that held him in life would be severed and his heartbeat would slow into silence, that I could not do it. It was silly, but I sometimes imagined things so vividly that I made myself believe them. So I stayed where I was.

And then I must have fallen asleep, because I dreamed.

❦

"Come and talk to me, Field," said Raymond.

"Very good, sir," said the butler, crossing the room to stand beside the old man's chair.

"Come and sit here." Raymond gestured to the armchair opposite him, and Field sat down. "I'm frightfully tired, and I can't think why. I'm getting old. I'll be dead soon."

"You shouldn't keep saying that, sir; it is bad luck."

"Bad luck?" said Raymond. "I've never heard that before."

"In my country—" The butler stopped then and glanced away. "In Australia, where I spent so many years, they have a saying . . ."

When he looked back, the old man was regarding him with a faint smile. "What is it?" said the butler.

"I never understand you, Field. You're mysterious, aren't you?"

"I would hardly say mysterious, sir."

"You dropped your guard for a minute. You are always on your guard. I don't think I know you at all."

"Perhaps you don't."

There was a silence. Then the butler shook his head. "I am sorry if I appear distracted. I was thinking about—" He paused. He was thinking about the message from Talitha that had appeared the day before. But he did not mention that. "I was thinking of other things," he said. "Shall I leave you in peace for a while, sir?"

He got up to leave. "Stay with me," Raymond said suddenly. "Won't you stay and talk to me and keep me company?"

The butler turned back to him, surprised. "Of course, sir, if you wish me to." He sat down again and leaned back in the chair, gazing out over the darkening lake.

"Field?" said Raymond after a while. "Will you tell me about what you did before you came here? You never have."

"Never?" said the butler. "Surely I must have told you."

"All I know is that you were in the army. If that's true." Raymond watched the butler steadily. "And I wouldn't mind too much if it was not," he continued. "I'm not so fixated on the army anymore, Field, you know."

"I had noticed."

"Can't you tell me something about yourself?" Raymond went on. "For instance, how did you come to be in England? You are not English by birth."

The butler hesitated, then shook his head. "No. Not English."

"Why did you decide to come to this country?" Raymond persisted, certain that Field would deflect his questions as usual. "And why did you decide to apply for the job here? You have not always been a butler. Tell me about yourself, Field; I could do with some entertainment."

The butler laughed, showing his teeth in the way that he always did. He never smiled at all, and in fact his laugh was more sinister than his darkest frown, because it made him look, to Raymond, just for a second each time he saw it, like a skull. "I'll tell you," he said then. "It would do no harm to tell you."

Raymond had not expected that. The butler was still gazing out the window, watching the shadow of the tank lengthen on the grass. "I have not always been a butler, true," he said. "I was a very famous man in my country. Highest but one in the secret service. And I did not *decide* to come to this country. I am only here because things went wrong." He turned to Raymond, who was watching him in startled silence. "I could tell you how I came to be in England. It would pass the time to tell you that story. But one thing, sir?"

"What is it?"

"You will not pass this on."

It was not a question; Arthur Field knew that the old man would not pass anything on after that night. But Raymond shook his head. "Of course not, Field."

*W*hen I woke, slumped against Stirling's bed, his hand had drifted away from mine and lay loose by his side, and he was breathing peacefully. I had been dreaming; at the moment I woke someone was about to tell me a story. I was forgetting it now. I got to my feet. All my muscles ached, and my whole head and face hurt with tiredness, and I could hardly keep my eyes open. I couldn't continue like this for much longer.

I was irritated with myself for being so weak, scarcely able to endure two sleepless nights for the sake of my own brother. I could continue like this, I resolved, and I would.

There was a rap on the door when I had only just come back upstairs from the bathroom. Grandmother went to open it, shutting the bedroom door behind her so that Stirling would not wake. It was Maria; I could hear baby Anselm crying. I was still putting on my uniform, but I stepped nearer the closed door. From the low rise and fall of their voices, I made out a few of Maria's words. "I don't want to bother you when Stirling is so sick," she was saying, "but I could come and sit with Stirling if you need to get things done, or fetch your shopping for you." Then more low murmuring.

"You are very kind to offer," Grandmother was saying.

"It is nothing." She said it sincerely, not in the way that

people ordinarily say it, when custom has made them forget its meaning. When Maria spoke, she meant what she said.

Grandmother came to the bedroom door not long after. "That was Maria," she said, in an undertone, so as not to wake Stirling. "She is a very nice girl, you know. Very nice indeed."

"She is."

"She was offering to help us. And she has had silent fever; would you have guessed? Lots of people recover from it, after all; it has done her no harm." I nodded.

"Some people would be afraid of bringing a baby near here," Grandmother continued. "But then, I suppose Maria is a sensible girl, and knows what is dangerous and what is not. She said that having silent fever yourself means that your children are born immune. She saw a trained doctor when she had it, and he told her so."

"This strain is not catching anyway," I said. "At least, I don't think so. What did the newspaper say?"

The article about the soldier was still open on the table, and she scanned it again now. We had both read it several times already. It did not make much sense to either of us, but it was all we had to go by except for what Father Dunstan had told us.

"You had better hurry or you'll be late for school," said Grandmother, looking up. "You have had no breakfast. And you ate nothing yesterday either."

"I'm not hungry."

"Go and get yourself something to eat."

I swallowed a dry piece of bread, cut a couple of slices for my lunch and grabbed an apple, and stuffed them into my jacket pocket. "I'll see you this evening," I said. "Don't worry if I'm late."

Once I shut the door, I wished that I had said goodbye to Stirling. But he would still be there when I got back.

I never walked to school alone, and noticing it made me worry. Every step reminded me that Stirling was ill, and by the time I reached the gates, I was almost too afraid to go in. You have to be strong to go to school. I wanted to turn back. But I didn't.

"We saw you at the weekend, North," Seth Blackwood told me when I walked into the classroom. Usually everyone treated me with cold indifference.

"I know. I spoke to you."

"I didn't know you had a girlfriend," said Isaac.

"A girlfriend? Well . . . ," I began distractedly.

"Damn pretty girl too," Isaac announced to the rest of the platoon.

"She . . . ," I began again. But they were not listening, and I was too weary to explain.

About halfway through the morning, another whisper started. I had only just noticed it when Seth Blackwood called across to me again: "North, is it true your brother has silent fever?"

I swallowed and said, "Yes."

He swore quietly, more pity in his tone than anything else. "What are you doing in school?" someone else said. "You could pass it on."

"It's slow-developing silent fever. That's not catching."

"How do you know?"

I didn't trouble to answer. Wherever I looked that day, someone had stopped working and turned to watch me. I wished that they would not, because it made me feel suffocated.

152

I was so afraid for Stirling, so afraid that he would die, and always people were watching me. I was used to being invisible.

I got home late again that afternoon. I made myself push the door open quickly, or I would not have done it at all; I thought suddenly that Stirling was gone. But I saw at once that the bedroom door was open, and Maria was sitting beside the bed, talking to him. I hurried in, my heartbeat slowing again.

"Leo!" said Stirling, smiling and turning toward me, though he was not looking directly at me. "Where have you been?"

"The hills," I said. I had walked farther this time, but I had still not searched as far from the edge of the city as I would have liked. There was a long distance to go yet.

"I missed you," said Stirling. "I wish you would not go there."

"I have to. What if someone else found the Bloodflower, and it was somewhere I could have been looking myself? Near to the city. It's possible."

"You are looking for the Bloodflower?" said Maria. She watched me in silence. "But do you not think that everywhere you search, someone else will have searched first?"

I sat down on the end of Stirling's bed, kicking off my boots. "You look terrible," said Maria. I laughed shortly. "No." She smiled. "I mean terribly tired."

"Do I?" I stood up and looked in the mirror. It was true. "I will get used to this in time," I said. "I have walked a few miles today, that's all."

"Stirling seems good, though," said Maria. "We both think he will get better by himself anyway."

"Yes," said Stirling. "You do not need to find that plant."

"Well, when you get well by yourself, I can sell it and buy us a house on the edge of the city, better than Sergeant Markey's even." They laughed at that.

"Where is Grandmother?" I asked.

"She went down to take a shower," said Maria. "Which is good; she needs to do something other than sit here worrying."

"She could go to church this evening," I said.

"If you can persuade her to leave Stirling."

I managed to get her to go, with Stirling's help. She could see that he was better, at least today, and it would take me two minutes at most to run to the church to get her. I was sitting on Stirling's bed after she and Maria had gone when he said suddenly, "Leo, where are you?" I had forgotten that he could not see.

"I don't know," I said. I wondered afterward why I said it, but at the time I could not help it.

"What?" There was real fear in his voice, and it brought me back. "Leo?"

I put my hand in his. "I am here. I am here, Stirling."

"I can't see. You scared me. What did you mean? I thought I was dying."

"No, you are safe."

He clung on to my hands. "Keep talking," he said into the silence, "so that I know you are there."

"I'll stay here."

"Keep talking. I get afraid, otherwise, in the dark all alone." There was panic rising in his voice. "Keep talking. I don't like the silence."

But suddenly I could not. "It's hard to talk when you are commanded to," I told him.

"Say anything. Tell me a story. Like when we were small."

I tried. But I must have forgotten how, because they kept sticking after the first line. I had not the imagination I used to have. "I can't make up stories anymore," I told him eventually. "I'm sorry." I rubbed my head. It was aching again. "I suppose I could read to you."

There was no newspaper; Grandmother had not gone to get it and I had forgotten to. "What about *The Golden Reign*?" I said. "That is all we have. Or the Bible, which I'll guess you know by heart anyway."

"No, I don't." He did not notice the intended joke. "Read me *The Golden Reign*."

I let his hand go and he left it stretched out, as if he wanted to keep the smallest possible distance between us. "I am still here," I said. "I'm just going to get it. I'm walking over to my bed; it is under my bed." I walked heavily so that he could hear that I had not left the room. "I'll be back in a second." I bent down to get it, wondering if the pages of dry information would really draw his mind away from the fear. *The Golden Reign* was a history book, except for a couple of chapters. "It's not that interesting, though, Stirling," I said. Then I thought of the other book—the one that I had found, with the strange writing.

"Stirling?" I said. "Why don't I read you that other thing I told you about—the story that appeared in the book I found?"

"Yes," he said after a moment. "That is a good idea. I want to hear that too."

"Perhaps you will be able to make something of what it says."

"I hope so. Yes, read me that."

I got the book out of the windowsill chest and went and sat

back down on Stirling's bed. But when I opened it, I saw at once. "There's more writing in it!" I told him.

"Really? Lots more writing?"

"A few pages. And there is a gap before it. The writer leaves gaps between the writing. I don't know why."

"Will you read it?" said Stirling. "Start from the beginning."

"All right." I turned to the first page and began. Stirling lay still, listening carefully, his hand on my knee.

Somehow reading it out loud made it seem less real, as if it truly was just a fairy story after all. But when I paused after the first section, Stirling said, "That was about the Liberation, wasn't it? I told you they didn't kill the prince."

The story was working as a distraction; he had forgotten his fright and was becoming involved with it. "I know this makes sense," he said, seemingly frustrated, after I had read the second section. "I know it makes sense, but I can't work it out. My brain won't work."

"Don't worry," I said. "It's because you are ill. Just listen."

It took a surprisingly short amount of time to finish reading the rest, to say how long I had spent thinking about it. "The man must be Aldebaran," said Stirling when I had finished. "He sounds like he is trained in magic, and they said the country was England—lots of times they said it. I think he really is Aldebaran."

"I think so too."

"But why was he writing to Talitha?" said Stirling.

"I don't know. Perhaps she tricked him. She tricked some people. She was on both sides—openly working for the king and secretly leading the revolution. It was only after Lucien took power that everyone knew."

Stirling frowned. "But Aldebaran is a very great man."

"Talitha is powerful too—maybe more so."

He seemed to be thinking. I was impatient to read on, but I waited. "So that's what happened with Great-uncle Harold," said Stirling. "He went to England and had a wife and children there."

I nodded. Grandmother rarely talked about him. Even less than she talked about Aldebaran. "That must be what happened," I said. "All I knew was that he disappeared for years and then came back."

"Then we have relatives there," said Stirling. "Think of that! English relatives."

"I suppose we do," I said. "That is the strange thing. If the man is Aldebaran, then this is a story about our family. Who would write a story about our family?"

"When did this happen?" said Stirling.

"Ten years ago. The date in the letter is just before the Liberation."

"And when did Great-uncle Harold die?"

"I don't know. Long before I was born."

"And when was Aldebaran exiled?"

"When I was a baby."

"This story is too confusing," said Stirling. "It must be true."

I laughed. He laughed too, and when he did, he started coughing like an old man. The sound of it frightened me. "Stirling," I said. "Stirling, are you all right?"

He nodded and tried to smile. "Read on," he told me.

The next section startled me. The butler was lighting the fire and preparing to tell the old man a story. It was the same as what I had dreamed the night before. I hesitated and thought of telling Stirling that. And then I changed my mind. I did not want to frighten him just when he seemed to have grown calmer.

"The butler *must* be Aldebaran," said Stirling. "The things he said about the secret service. Don't stop, Leo. We might find out."

There were more blank pages and then the writing began again. I turned them over and read on.

⚜

"I could tell you a thousand stories about my life," began the butler. "For the first few years it was ordinary enough. My parents were farmers on Holy Island, off the west coast of Malonia. I grew up working on the land. There were three of us—me, the eldest; my sister, Margaret, who is five years younger than me; and then our baby brother, Harold. In the daytime I would be out in the fields; in the evenings Margaret and I would sit in front of the fire with the baby, singing to him and telling him stories. I was just another boy, a farmer's son, except for one thing: I was born with powers."

"With what?" said Raymond. "And where is Malonia?"

"Just listen," said the butler. "There is no time to argue."

Raymond, startled by the butler's tone, fell silent again. "I was discovered by the great Sheratan when I was thirteen years old," the butler continued. "And from then on my life has never been ordinary. Sheratan took me as his apprentice. I became a tough man, trained with torture and exertion. I was very skilled by the end. And when I was still young, I was offered a place in the secret service."

There was a silence. "All this is true," the butler said then. "I have not always told you the truth, sir, but all this I tell you now is true."

"What did you say this fellow did?" demanded Raymond. "This man who trained you. And what do you mean by powers?"

The butler folded his arms. "Sheratan was a great one—that is what we call them in my country. And by powers I mean the ability to perform superhuman feats. Great willpower; great strength of mind. We call it magic, although that does not mean the same thing in my country as it does in yours. We call it magic for want of a better word."

Raymond stared at the butler, then began to laugh. "Is this a joke of yours?" he said. "Making me swear not to tell a soul and then spinning some ridiculous story? I must say, you took me in for a minute."

"Sir, what I am telling you is the truth."

Raymond went on laughing. "But, Field—"

"There is no time for this," the butler said suddenly. "I am telling you the truth. There is no time to argue about it."

"Explain what you mean, then," said Raymond, suddenly uneasy. "Tell me what magic means in your country. You mean that you learned witchcraft, casting spells and suchlike? I can't believe that. It's a fairy tale, Field."

"The great ones do not cast spells," said the butler. "There are no magic spells; there is only willpower. You can do anything you want if you have enough strength of mind."

"Magicians cast spells, in all the stories," said Raymond.

"Call them magicians if you like," said Aldebaran. "Those with powers do what appears to be magic. Impossible, superhuman feats. But everyone has willpower."

"So anyone can do magic? Is that what you are saying?"

"Not anyone. There is a sort of spirit required. It is hard to explain."

"Try," said Raymond. "If you are going to tell me this story, Field, I will have to understand."

"Very well. Suppose someone has willpower, and a talent for music, and good training. That person might become a musician. With a great one it is the same. Different people have the spirit—or talent—to do different things. The spirit of a magician is an absolute belief that when you apply the force of your mind to something, it will obey. You believe it is possible to do what other people would think impossible. You do not lose your nerve."

"So why are there no real magicians here in England? If that was true, there would be."

"There are. You just do not see them. There are people in England with the right traits to train in magic, even if they do not have the training itself."

"So nothing is really magic?" said Raymond. "It is just willpower."

"You could say that. Or you could say everything is magic. I'll tell you what is magic, though: what is magic is the human spirit. It is what gives us the power to do great things. I prefer to say that everything is magic."

"Perhaps you are right, Field."

"It is just what I think."

The fire shifted in the grate and the old man started. The butler got up and turned the coals over. It was summer, but the old house was still cold at nights, and the butler always lit the fires. Raymond watched the back of his head, frowning. "Field?" he said then. "If you really had powers, as you say, you would be able to prove it. You could show me a trick."

The butler placed a coal in the closest flame. "I don't want to give you another heart attack, sir."

Raymond smiled. "I see."

"I can do it if I want to; do not mistake my meaning."

"Then do one of these impossible feats, Field, if you can."

"Are you challenging me?" said Aldebaran.

"Yes." Raymond laughed. "Yes, I am."

The butler turned and stood up, brushing the coal dust off the knees of his trousers. "What would you have me do?"

Raymond glanced out at the clear sunset over the lake. "Start a thunderstorm."

"I am too tired for that. Think of something smaller."

"Why not the thunderstorm?" said Raymond. "Can't you just say a word and wave your hand?"

"No," said the butler. "You have to be careful. Talitha, the head of the secret service, is the greatest magician in my country, but there are things that even she could not do. She tried once to create a permanent doorway into England. It had never been attempted before, but she thought she could do it. It was too much. She nearly died."

"Field . . . ," Raymond said. "Fascinating as this is . . ."

"I still have not shown you any magic." The butler sat down again. "So what shall I do?"

"Make that book on the table there lift into the air."

"Very well, sir." The butler frowned at the book and it lifted.

It did not look magic; there was nothing special about it except that it was defying gravity—no aura of light about it, no puff of smoke, no sudden bang. Raymond had to look at it twice to see that there was anything different, and then realized that it was several inches above the table. He leaned over and passed his hand under the book. It did not fall.

"You are not impressed," said the butler with a faint smile, letting the book drop back to the table.

"Doubtful," Raymond muttered, staring at Field. "But this is a very elaborate setup, if it is one. That gave me quite a turn." He pressed his hand to his heart; it was suddenly beating fast.

"Sit still for a moment, sir, and you will feel better."

Raymond went on staring at the butler. "Do you know how strange it is when you suddenly realize that nothing is like it used to be?"

"Everything is exactly what it used to be," said the butler. "Only you did not know before what it was." He laughed. "That was an obvious trick. You could have asked me to do anything at all. It is not even my area of expertise, manipulation of forces."

"What is your area?" said Raymond weakly.

"Prophecy," said the butler. "Even when I was a young boy, the future would come to me in dreams. Once I predicted a storm that would have ruined our harvest. And when I was thirteen, I saw myself as a middle-aged man, tortured and banished. That came true, unfortunately. Everything I've ever predicted has."

"Predict the future, then," said Raymond. "Tell me what you see in my future." He thought for a moment. "Tell me the day I'm going to die."

"No," said the butler, serious again. "I think I should go on with the story. This is not a game. None of this."

Raymond was suddenly frightened, though he could not have said exactly why. "Yes, go on, Field," he said.

✳   ✳   ✳

"Prophecy was my main role in the secret service," said the butler. "At least at first. I moved up the ranks and became very famous. The people would read in the newspapers that Aldebaran had uncovered a plot against the king or broken up a chain of arms dealers, and so 'Aldebaran' became a familiar name. There was an old prophecy about a great one who would come from the west of the country. People began to connect it with me. But it was only my taken name that was famous—the name I took on after my training. In the secret service, you remain anonymous. No one knew my face."

"Aldebaran?" said Raymond. "That was the name you took after you trained in magic?"

"Aldebaran is my name, yes. After a star. That is the custom—to name the great men and women after stars, constellations, planets—you know."

"Are there enough?" said Raymond, glancing out at the first stars that were appearing over the mountains.

"They haven't run out yet," said Aldebaran.

"So your name never was Arthur Field?" said Raymond.

"It was Arthur Field once," said the butler. "But all those years in the secret service I was just Aldebaran."

"Go on with the story," said Raymond, leaning forward in his chair.

"There were very distinguished men and women in the secret service," Aldebaran went on. "Most of them had powers; I was no one extraordinary there. Talitha was the greatest. She was the same age as me, but she always undertook the most serious and dangerous missions. She was far more powerful than I ever was. She had more raw talent to begin with, and more ambition. She

163

was head of the entire Malonian secret service by the time I was in my late forties. But I was just as famous by that time. Perhaps more so after that, because now I was gaining glory on the most difficult missions while she was directing operations from the city.

"Anyway, one day a task came up that Talitha nominated me for. The king, Cassius the First, had died the year before, and his son, aged only ten, had suddenly had to take up the throne. As a result of this, security was tightened, for fear of revolution. For a long while, the Kalitz family on Holy Island had been suspected of plotting an uprising; Marcus Kalitz had been an advisor to King Cassius the First, and had been fired in a mystery that no one quite understood.

"Now Mr. Kalitz was advertising for a tutor for his children. The plan was for me to infiltrate the family and keep a close watch on them. I thought that I was far too well-known for such a job. But for some reason Talitha had fixed it in her head that I was the only one to go. I suppose it was logical. I am a native of Holy Island myself. It is a separate state, ruled by the Kalitz family rather than the monarch, and the accent and the customs are very distinctive. I had that accent and I knew those customs. It was my home, which I loved, and though I did not admit it, I thought that I would prefer teaching a couple of children to negotiating politics. Those were the wrong reasons, perhaps. But I agreed."

I put down the book. There was a silence. Then Stirling whispered, "He is Aldebaran."

"Yes," I said. "We were right."

"And Margaret is Grandmother, and baby Harold is Great-uncle Harold," Stirling continued. "His family, that he was talking about at the beginning."

I turned back to that page. I remembered Grandmother telling us once about the three of them growing up on Holy Island—a long time ago, before she stopped talking about Aldebaran. She had told us about how they used to sit in front of the fire with the baby, just as Aldebaran had told the old man. It was strange to read it again here.

"He must miss her," said Stirling. "Aldebaran must miss Grandmother. She's the same to him as I am to you."

"I suppose she is." I had never thought before about Aldebaran being Grandmother's elder brother, and how they probably walked to school together and argued and talked for hours like Stirling and me. Aldebaran seemed too much of a legend for that. "Shall I read on?" I said. Stirling nodded. We had half an hour before Grandmother would be back from church, and there were several pages left.

❧

Outside the window it had grown quite dark, but Raymond made no move to turn on the lamp. "Go on with the story," he said. "Tell me about Holy Island."

The butler gazed out over the lake again. "This was what I was going to explain about. This mission that went wrong." He seemed to be thinking for a moment, then began again. "Talitha ordered me to leave at once. I went to the harbor and boarded a ship that was going south to the coast, then northwest to Holy Island. All the time I traveled, my heart was lifting, because I was going home. The roads grew familiar as I neared Valacia."

"What is Valacia?" said Raymond.

"The capital. The Kalitz mansion was outside it a short

way, not ten miles from where my parents used to farm. But I would not be able to communicate with my family. I knew that I would be as good as a prisoner in that place; I could not go out and risk being recognized, and besides, the Kalitz family lived set apart, behind high fences. They had an army of servants too, half of them guards. They were all lined up along the drive as I approached, just for show, even though I was only the children's new tutor."

"Did you say they were royalty?" asked Raymond.

"Not exactly. They are nobles. But they are royalty as far as Holy Island is concerned, and they expected to be treated as such. Anyway, the only one I could stand was Anneline, the little girl. Mr. Kalitz did not even come down to greet me when I arrived, and barely spoke to me in the weeks that followed. Most of the time he maintained a sullen silence. The only one he really spoke to was his son, Lucien. He would lecture him for hours. He preached to him against the monarchy as if he was a priest proclaiming the gospel."

"Why did he hate the monarchy?" said Raymond.

"He hated the royal family—the Donahue family—mainly because of the argument between him and King Cassius the First. The king said that Kalitz had tried to assassinate him, and Kalitz said it was a misunderstanding. But the Kalitz family all hated the royal family."

"What about the others?" said Raymond.

"Celine was just as irritating as her husband. She spent all her time comparing others to herself and finding them inferior. The servants were considered a lower race."

"Surely you were not a servant?" said Raymond.

"I was counted a servant in that house. Not by Anneline, but by everyone else. Even the boy, Lucien, would order me about. He was eleven when I arrived, and as ambitious as his father. Often it happens that a child so pressured by a parent will rebel against this with all his strength. I have noticed that here in your country too. But Marcus Kalitz could not have wished for a better first-born in Lucien. He was even more ferociously antiroyalist than his father."

"What about the little girl?" said Raymond.

"Anneline," said the butler. "I could never find a single fault with her, even now. She was nine years old when I arrived, and very timid, but she changed. That was the one good thing that came out of this mission, perhaps—that I taught her."

Raymond shifted in his chair, his eyes still on the butler. "It is important that I tell you all this, sir," Field said suddenly. "Even now, I am trying to work out what went wrong. You do not think that I am wasting your time in explaining this to you?"

"Of course not. Go on telling me. I want to hear."

The butler nodded. "Well, I did try hard to be a worthy tutor to them. I did not think it was fair that their education should suffer because I was an impostor. Anneline was an attentive pupil, easy to teach even when I was struggling with some fact that I had got out of a book the day before. But Lucien did not concentrate. He was clever, but he would not work. And the parents encouraged it. They thought he was a natural genius, born to be a great man."

It was almost completely dark in the room. Raymond sat motionless, listening, the last firelight glinting on his glasses. "Things started to go wrong early on," said Aldebaran. "I should have pulled out. Instead, I got too involved. I was starting to think I was a real tutor. I taught Anneline to sing the national anthem. That was my first mistake. I was not thinking. I was just aston-ished that she did not know it, and I did not think it would be

167

outside the role of a real tutor to teach it to her. She had a lovely singing voice. She was a very accomplished pianist too. She used to play for her parents' guests when they gave parties.

"Anyway, at one of these parties I heard her picking out some of the tunes I had taught her, adding the chords herself. She could improvise like that even at nine years old. And then she started the national anthem, and suddenly all the voices stopped together. A moment later Celine was shouting. I heard Anneline mumble something, and I knew it would only make things worse if I went in and explained, so I thought it best to retreat upstairs.

"I heard Mr. Kalitz come running up the stairs not long after, a glass of spirits still in his hand. He was shouting like a madman. 'You have been indoctrinating my children! You have been corrupting them with your royalist values! You know how I feel about the monarchy!' And so on. He grabbed hold of my shirt and threw me against the door."

"What did you do?" said Raymond.

"Well, I could have done anything," said Aldebaran slowly. Then he shook his head. "I just let him grab hold of me. I was a servant there, not a great one. I kept saying, 'Yes, sir; sorry, sir,' trying to calm him down. He threw the glass at the wall and went on shouting. And then some of the guests were coming out to see what the commotion was, and he had to quiet down. 'Never ever let me hear report of this again,' he told me. 'You teach them the real history of Malonia, the real geography, the real literature. Is that clear?'

"I just said, 'Yes, sir,' again to that, and he let me go. 'I am disappointed in you, Field, more than I can say,' he told me. And then he turned and marched back down the stairs. I nearly felt guilty about that, to tell you the truth. He was so passionately

168

antiroyalist. Although his feelings were not justified—not really—I felt sorry for him because of the sheer fervor of them. And I was supposed to be inconspicuous here. I had gone against my duty to the secret service in teaching Anneline that song, and caused her all kinds of trouble from her family. From then on I tried to teach the children in a way that would not cause any more problems."

Raymond reached out his hand to turn on the lamp, then drew it back. He would not break the stillness of the room. "How long did you stay there?" he said.

It was a while before Aldebaran replied. "The days just passed," he said eventually. "I don't know how. Three years were gone before I had even noticed being there one. I had barely communicated with Talitha. I panicked then, when I realized how long I had been there. I tried to contact her."

"How?" said Raymond. "By telephone? Wouldn't the family be watching your every move?"

"Telephones do not exist in Malonia," said Aldebaran.

"Telephones exist everywhere," said Raymond. "Surely, Field—"

"My country is not like England," said the butler. "No, I used my willpower. I wrote in a book, and used my willpower to transfer the words into another book as I wrote them, a book in Talitha's possession. That was my own idea. It was difficult, but it worked. I thought that communication by magic was the safest. I was worried, because somehow I had been there for so long, and I had tricked even myself into believing that I was a tutor. I had stopped reading the newspapers. For all I knew, revolution could be imminent and I might never have known it. So I did not want to waste time with letters."

"Why did you forget to contact Talitha?" said Raymond.

"What about being on your guard? I thought you were supposed to be a very famous spy, Field."

"There was something strange about that house. A kind of stupefying atmosphere that made me stop being careful. That alarmed me, when I realized it. I am always on my guard. It must have been magic. That is all I can think now." Aldebaran shook his head. "I should have realized."

He paused, then went on. "Talitha only replied when I suggested in desperation that I come to the city. She wrote briefly that all was under control, and that on no account should I move from the house. So I tightened my watch on the family, and began to practice my skills again. I had begun to forget how to use my willpower.

"That was when I started to suspect that someone was watching me, because no matter how hard I tried, I could not seem to see any more than an ordinary person; someone was blocking everything I did. I wondered if I was losing my powers. That has been known to happen. Sometimes the great ones grow out of their powers. And then, one night, a vision came to me."

"Vision? How do you mean, a vision?"

"I dreamed, and I wrote a prophecy. So I knew that I had not lost my powers. I began to suspect that the rebels were stronger than I had thought, and that someone knew who I was and was controlling what I did."

"What did you do?" said Raymond.

"Continued teaching Anneline. There was nothing else to do. Lucien was taught solely by his father now, and I could see enough to understand that there was some large plan in their minds. But above that I could tell nothing. It could have been a party, for all I knew of it. We were allies more than ever in those years, Anneline and I. She was almost completely ignored by her family, and I was uneasy and had too little to do even as a tutor. I went on teaching her, and she used to come to me for advice also. She began to talk about leaving when she was still young. She hated that house. She wanted to go to the mainland.

"So the first young man who proposed to her, she almost accepted. She was only thirteen when the sons of nobles and rich traders started asking for her hand in marriage. Her parents said that she should wait, and I agreed with them. I did not realize what they meant—not wait unconditionally, but wait for something. They wanted her to marry the young king. The two met at a ball when she was fourteen and he was sixteen, and it was barely six months before he proposed to her too. Marcus and Celine had known that would happen."

Aldebaran frowned at his hands clasped on his knees. "I am not pretending that Anneline did not love Cassius," he continued. "She did; I knew her well enough to see it. And Marcus and Celine pretended to disapprove of their daughter's marriage. But they had been trying to engineer meetings between the two for months—even I could see it. The thing was, Marcus and Celine were antiroyalist, but they were deviously antiroyalist. They were ruled by reason. Lucien—he was passionately antiroyalist. The day she announced her engagement was the last day that he spoke a word to her. Hatred of the Donahue family flowed in his very blood. He left the house while Anneline prepared for her wedding. He refused to step back through the door until she had gone.

"The evening before she left, just after her fifteenth birthday, I was in the empty schoolroom with her, helping her to pack her last belongings. We were sad to part; she had almost become a daughter to me. I said as much to her then. 'If it were not for you, I would

171

have gone mad in this house, Aldebaran,' she said. What was strange was that she used my taken name so pointedly. I had given the name Arthur Field in that house, as I gave to you, my name before I was trained in magic. That was how she knew me."

I stopped there and rested the book against my knees. The clock in the square was chiming the quarter. "This is Lucien's story as well," said Stirling.

"Yes. I never knew that Aldebaran was his tutor when he was a boy."

"They don't teach us this at school," said Stirling.

I laughed at that. "No. This would be Highly Restricted if it was a real book."

Stirling looked worried. "It's all right," I said. "I haven't told anyone about it, except for you. And anyway, I am not to blame. I do not write these words."

"Who does?" said Stirling. "It's strange. Do you think it's someone with powers trying to communicate by magic, the same way Aldebaran was trying to communicate with Talitha?"

"I thought about that," I said. "But why would a great one write this? Some of it is important, but some of it only means anything to you and me."

"Maybe . . . ," said Stirling, "maybe it's someone trying to communicate with us."

I was startled by that. "Who?" I said eventually. "Aldebaran himself?"

I had been joking, but Stirling did not notice. "It could be!" he said. "If he is still alive. Read on. There might be a clue. Read on, Leo."

Across the lake, a church bell was chiming. The butler glanced toward the sound, as though it had brought him back from his thoughts. "What did you say when she addressed you as Aldebaran?" asked Raymond.

The butler laughed. "I don't think I said anything at all; I was too startled. I just stared at her, and she said, 'I know you are the lord Aldebaran; I have known it for a year or more.' She began to laugh then; it must have been the way I was staring.

" 'How do you know?' I said eventually.

" 'I guessed,' she said. 'I guessed, and I think my mother and father know too—but they did not guess it; someone told them. But Lucien does not know. If he did, he would have killed you.'

"She was only half joking. We were all of us slightly afraid of Lucien—even I was, to tell the truth.

"She was glancing edgily at the door, and she stepped closer to me. 'There is something I want to talk to you about before I leave,' she said. 'I am afraid that my family are developing some sort of underhanded plan. I hear things, though they would never tell me.'

"I asked her what kind of plan, but she could not say. 'It is just that Father, when he goes out with Lucien, does not drive out on the estate as he says,' she told me, whispering now. 'I do not know where they go, but I have seen them leaving on the road. And you know how long they stay away for. Days and weeks sometimes.'

"It was true that they were developing some plan. Of course they were; that was why I had been sent there to begin with, because they were suspected of plotting revolution. 'I think the same,' I told her. 'But what do you want me to do?'

"She took my hand and said, 'Escape far from here. Go tonight, when I leave.'

"Again, I was too startled to reply. 'I think that there are very powerful men and women involved in this,' she said, 'and perhaps they will try to kill you. And if Lucien finds out who you really are, he will strangle you with his bare hands while you sleep. You know him. He has a mad streak. Truly.'

"'Are you frightened of him?' I asked her. She was looking up at me as if I was her own father.

"'Yes,' she said. 'Of course I am frightened of him.'

"'You are good,' I told her. 'He cannot harm you. The good are protected.'

"That is what I would have told her if she had been my own daughter. It was not true, and she knew it. She always saw through me when I struggled with some point of science or history in one of our lessons; she had a way of lowering her eyes, though she was too polite to say anything. She was looking like that now. 'I think you should leave,' she said again. 'I am not going to change my mind. I think you should leave.'

"I was still not convinced. But she caught hold of my hand and went on begging me to escape. 'You are valuable to our country, and you must protect your life at all costs. You have great powers. You are a very important man.' She went on. And then she looked at my hand in hers and let go of it, as though she did not have the right to do that now she knew who I was. 'Sir, you must leave,' she said.

"It was strange to hear her call me 'sir' like that, and I started to tell her not to, but she was already impatient to say something else. 'Take this with you,' she said, and put something in my hand.

"'What is it?' I asked. But even before I had finished asking, I realized."

"What was it?" Raymond demanded, leaning forward in the darkness of the room. "Field, you keep pausing at the most important points."

The butler laughed, though he had been doing that on purpose. "Sorry. It was a famous and valuable jewel—probably the most famous and valuable in all Malonia. It is a necklace in the shape of an eagle. The silver eagle, all the stories call it."

"A necklace?" said Raymond.

"Do not look so disbelieving. I'll tell you the story. Long ago, Malonia City was under siege and the people were almost starved. All the great ones—the magicians—sure that they would die whatever happened, decided to preserve their power. One of them, a rich man, had a valuable necklace that had been in his family for generations. It was common sense to choose the most valuable object, because it would never be lost or thrown away. And even if it was, silver and jewels endure. So they put their power into this necklace, killing themselves in the process."

"But they would have died anyway?" said Raymond.

"No. By some strange turn of events, those in the city actually defeated the enemy. Anyway, the silver eagle had been lost for years, but it was generally thought that some powerful magician, some great one somewhere, owned it. So I was astonished to see it now in my hand. 'Where did you get this?' I said, and she lowered her voice still further.

" 'From my father's cupboard. He should not have had it. Take it with you when you go.'

" 'I cannot take it,' I told her. And I was not even sure that I was going.

" 'You have to,' she said. 'You must escape, now. There are prophecies concerning you—about how you will save the country in a time of trouble. If you don't escape, what will happen to us when that time comes and you are dead? And this necklace is dangerous in such foolish hands as my father's.'

"It was against my judgment, but I took the necklace. Then, for some reason, I went and got the prophecy I had written, and gave it to her. 'It will not come true,' I told her. 'It was a mistake.'

" 'I will keep it safe,' she said, as if she believed it might.

"I tried to tell her what I had been meaning to—to be wary of her parents, and of Lucien. I tried to suggest that her parents might use the marriage to further any plot they had against the royal family. But I could not say those things straight out; it would have hurt her too much. So by the time Celine called her to leave, I was not sure I had made her understand.

"A carriage arrived to take her away to the harbor, to travel to mainland Malonia for her wedding the next week, and I gathered my things and escaped as fast as I could."

"You did what she said?" asked Raymond.

"For the better or the worse, I did." The butler shook his head. "I was being watched—she was right—and they came after me as soon as I left the grounds. Once I was out of that house and its strange atmosphere, I could see the danger clearly. What could I have done? If I had stayed, I would not have lasted long. And yet as soon as I went, I was followed. I reached the mainland, but they found me that same night."

Aldebaran put out his hand and turned on the lamp. "But I won't talk about that," he said, staring into the black night. "You did not want to hear a story about torture. And that's all in the past now. . . ." He stopped. "I was too confident, I suppose. I always thought I could deal with anything, until I had to. I never imagined that the rebel groups would have men and women with powers equal to my own. There was one—a woman whose face was hidden—who was far stronger than I was. I did not dare to fight. I had that necklace hidden around my neck, and I tried to comply with them and wait for some chance to escape while I concentrated on protecting it with my willpower. Perhaps that was a stupid thing to do.

"Anyway, I was weak and faint by the end. They had chained my hands and gagged me. We marched through the rising dawn, and I did not know where we were going. We were in a dense forest. We started up a hill, through bushes and undergrowth, and then we stopped and the woman whose face was hidden stepped forward and released my hands."

Aldebaran was silent for so long that Raymond almost spoke. The butler looked up then. "That was the last I saw of my homeland," he said. "That forest was where I disappeared. I did not know it. It was darkness all around me for a long time. Then I woke up shaking from torture and in a strange country. I woke up here. I was an exile. It was what I had seen when I was a thirteen-year-old boy."

"They exiled you?" said Raymond. "How?"

"Some people develop these skills—what you call curses. I would never dare. It seems to me too dangerous, to force new rules on the world, to send people out of their own country and into other places where they do not belong, to confine a person's life with false rules that mean nothing real but that could kill them if they are broken." The butler shook his head and gave up trying to explain. "Anyway, I may not approve of these skills, I may not understand them, but she had developed them and I could not fight it. So that was it. I was here, in England, with nothing but the clothes I wore and the necklace. They had not taken it."

"Why not? I thought you said it was important."

"All I can think is that no one knew that I had it. Perhaps they had only seen enough to know that I was escaping. And I worked so hard to protect it all the time we were walking through that forest. It was all I did; I barely struggled or fought, but I protected that necklace. They know now, of course, that the silver eagle is here. But they exiled it when they exiled me."

"So that was why you came here?"

"Aye. Because I had no choice. And a few weeks later I arrived on your doorstep and you employed me as a butler, and I have been here ever since."

There was a silence. Then, "Very good, Field," said Raymond, clapping. "Very good indeed."

"Thank you, sir."

The butler looked up and saw that the darkness outside had fallen completely. "I have not heard such an entertaining story for a long time," said Raymond.

"But not a story. Is that not partly why it was entertaining—because it was true?"

"Perhaps. What happened in the end?"

"It is not finished. It is not a story; it is my life. At the present moment, I am cut off more than ever and I cannot communicate with Talitha at all. I don't know why."

"But, Field . . ." Raymond began, with a faint smile. "The way you told that story, you made me believe that Talitha was not to be trusted. I thought that would be your surprise ending. I thought you were going to reveal the fact that she had betrayed you all along."

The butler fixed his eyes on Raymond. The old man's smile faltered. "That was what you made me expect . . ." he said, then trailed off altogether.

"Not to be trusted?" said Aldebaran. "You are speaking of Talitha, the head of the Malonian secret service?"

"But that was what you implied yourself. First she sent you on a mission that turned out to be a trap, then powerful people were tracking your every movement and blocking your powers. And this woman who exiled you—I was certain you were going to tell me that it turned out to be Talitha herself."

Aldebaran leaned forward in his chair. "Sir, you understand nothing about what I have just told you. How can you suggest that Talitha—"

"I did not mean anything," Raymond said, startled. "It is only a story. I was only entering into the story."

"You understand nothing," the butler said again, raising his voice. "How can you accuse Talitha of that? The great ones are revered in my country; they are not traitors."

"Field, you are worrying me with this," said Raymond. "Stop pretending now. It was a good story while it lasted, and it passed the time, but really! You must know that if this is a real lady you are talking about, then I don't mean to insult her, or anyone else for that matter. It was just a story. Field?"

Aldebaran did not answer. He was watching the moonlight on the lake outside. And then he began to feel uneasy. Something rose into his mind; he could not tell what it was exactly, but it made him anxious. Something in Malonia—some change just out of his sight. He felt these things still, the shifting fortunes of his homeland, in the same way he felt his old injuries ache in damp weather. He stared at the blank window and tried to see, but he could not concentrate.

"I think I have made a great mistake, Field," said the old man slowly.

"A mistake?" said the butler, without turning.

"In respect to my will. I think—" Raymond started up out of his chair. "Fetch me a pen and the envelope from my desk. Quickly!" There was panic in his voice suddenly. "Field!" He held out his hands as if he could not decide which he would rather— that Aldebaran went from him or stayed. Then he fell facedown on the carpet, his glasses splintering on the floorboards under the side of his cheek.

The butler knelt beside him. He lay still.

Aldebaran turned the man over silently. He was already far beyond calling, so the butler remained silent. He stayed there kneeling for a moment, then stood up and went to the desk. He took out the brown envelope from the top drawer and opened it. Inside was a thin sheaf of papers. "This is the last will and testament of me, Raymond Spencer-Grange . . ." He skimmed through it quickly, searching for the key phrase. He found it soon enough, for the document was short: "I give the whole of my estate to Arthur Field."

The darkness grew thicker. The butler stood there, motionless, and stared at the will. Images came into his head, and he could not stop them.

The prince was crying while men talked above his head about exile and revolution. Anneline and Cassius were already lying dead.

And Emilie, Harold's Emilie, was close by. Her car had just turned over on the way back from Graysands Beach. The silver eagle was round the neck of the little girl crying in the hospital room.

And Talitha. He was cursing himself suddenly for not

understanding before. What were powers worth, if someone who could see so far could blind themselves so entirely to the truth?

Every plan had gone wrong, and Aldebaran was powerless to do anything about it. He stood and read the old man's will, staring at those words through the tears in his eyes, and waited for the chaos of the worlds to subside.

We sat in silence for a long time after I closed the book. "Is that the end?" said Stirling then.

"Yes," I said. "For now, anyway."

"So that's what happened to Aldebaran. He went to England, like I thought, and then got the old man's house when he died?"

"But this was a long time ago, even if it's true. Talitha may have gone into England and killed him since then."

"I think he's still alive." Stirling frowned for a moment. "And I think the story went on. He is very clever; he can do all kinds of things. He would not just let his plans come to nothing like that."

"Maybe," I said.

"That little girl is a relative of ours," said Stirling suddenly. "That girl who has the necklace is a relative of Great-uncle Harold, so she is a relative of ours. If her grandmother was Harold's wife."

"You are right!" I said. "But this story can't be true. Someone must be making these things up."

"I don't think so. I think she is living in England now, that girl. And Aldebaran too. And the prince."

I was silent for a moment. "Stirling, what do you think this book is?" I asked then. "You've heard everything in it now."

"I don't know," he said. "It's magic, though."

"I think so too." I hesitated, then went on. "And listen—every time I read this writing, I feel as if I know what is going to happen next in the story. Is that not strange?"

He nodded. "So tell me what's going to happen."

"I don't know exactly. I just feel as though I have read this, or witnessed it, before. I have dreamed about some of this, and then it appeared in the book exactly the same."

At that moment the front door opened, and Grandmother called, "I'm home!"

Father Dunstan followed her into the room. "Hello, Leonard," he said. I nodded to him and stood up, keeping the book behind my back. "Hello, Stirling. How are you feeling?"

"Not so bad," said Stirling. "Maybe even better." I could not tell if he was saying that out of bravery or because it was true. I watched him carefully. Father Dunstan sat down on the edge of the bed and took out his watch, holding Stirling's wrist to feel his pulse. He examined the whites of his eyes and rested his hand on Stirling's forehead. We watched in silence. "You are doing fine, Stirling," he said after a moment. "Your pulse is almost normal, and your temperature is down slightly. I am surprised."

"What does that mean?" I demanded. "Does it mean Stirling is getting well?"

"I will be happier when his sight comes back," said Father Dunstan. "But these are good signs. I will come again tomorrow." He turned and looked up at Grandmother and me. "Sometimes these things do turn around. We will have to wait and see."

That was all he said each day. Two weeks passed. Stirling stopped coughing and grew less confused. We waited. If Stirling was getting well, his sight would come back. Often when I sat beside his bed, I felt myself holding my breath. I did not sleep much. To keep myself awake in the silence of the dark apartment, I read and reread that book.

And then one day I stepped round the door of the bedroom and he turned and looked at me—straight at me, not slightly to the left or the right as he had before. I shouted to Grandmother, and she sent me running to the church for Father Dunstan.

The priest sat for a long time without speaking after he had checked Stirling's pulse and his temperature twice or three times. Then he shook his head and finally smiled. "This is not like slow-developing silent fever—at least no case that I have ever heard of. I would almost say . . ." He shook his head again. "I must have made a mistake."

❧

Stirling was almost completely well. Just like that. And we suddenly realized that it was the middle of July, and it would soon be the day of his First Communion. "I want to keep the date the same," said Stirling imperiously from his bed—quite unlike him. "We have to keep the date the same."

"But you have missed some of the classes with Father Dunstan," Grandmother argued. "You have missed them all the time you have been ill. And what about the invitations? And we will have to have a party, of course." She was smiling anyway.

"I want to keep the date the same," he said again.

"What matter is it if he doesn't know what the seven deadly sins are, or how to decorate a pulpit?" I said.

"No, Leo. Don't be childish. The classes are important."

"I do know what the seven deadly sins are," he said. "Sloth, envy—"

"There is always next year," Grandmother said.

Stirling nodded. "I suppose so, but . . ."

"Very well," said Grandmother. "I had better start writing the invitations." She went to the cupboard and fetched the box of invitation cards she had been saving. She was humming in her old way as she began to write them, but today it did not irritate me.

"It is nearly six o'clock!" she exclaimed then, looking up.

"Why does that matter?" I asked.

"I am not ready for church." She sighed. "I don't want to go today, but I feel guilty when none of us is there. Oh dear—I suppose I can go tomorrow instead."

"I am going!" I told her. I had already put on my boots. I shut the door on the atmosphere of astonishment and ran as fast as I could and cared not at all when people turned to stare as I shot down the street.

It was humid in the city. There was a humming silence, and dark clouds sat heavily among the roofs. There were voices in the air; no matter how quiet it was, they would always be just too far away to hear, but the very atmosphere was buzzing with them. That weather usually comes before a change.

The thunder began as I reached the edge of the square, and then the rain fell as if it was pouring straight out of buckets. It came down so hard and fast that the empty pool in the center of the square filled up almost immediately, and the water dashing

184

horizontally off the horse statue's lower lip made it look as if the fountain was working again. I jogged across the square, toward the lighted church doorway, my clothes already soaked.

"Leo!" someone called from behind me, and I turned and saw that it was Maria. She did not have Anselm with her. She ran toward me, holding up her skirt so that it would not trail in the streaming mud, and supporting her jacket over her head with the other hand.

"Maria!" I shouted, spinning around where I stood.

"You are coming to church on a weekday?" she yelled through the rain. "Can this be true?"

"Yes!" I announced, mad from the storm and the exhilarating relief that Stirling was well. "Yes, I am coming to church!"

"And why might that be?" She laughed at my wild eyes. "What has happened to you, Leo?"

"Stirling is well! It is not silent fever after all! His sight has come back!"

The lightning slashed the sky in two and made the pool flare. She reached me and looked up, smiling. There was water on her eyelashes and shining on her cheeks, and a drop fell from her full bottom lip. On a sudden impulse I grabbed her and kissed her. Just like that.

"Leo!" she exclaimed breathlessly, pushing me away. "We are outside the church! What will people think?" She was laughing, but uneasily.

"I don't know," I said. "What will they think that matters?"

"They will think you're Anselm's father, that's what."

"Oh." I stepped away. "A fair point. Sorry."

"And if you want to kiss someone, you should ask them first." She was smiling again now.

"Sorry. It will not happen again."

"For your sake, Leo, it better had not."

"No. Next time I will ask." I turned to her, laughing. "Can I kiss you, Maria?"

She slapped me, but not hard. "Get into the church, Leo. Get into the church and repent of your sins!" We stumbled through the door, suppressing laughter. I was embarrassing myself. I didn't care.

The church was almost full, in spite of the torrential rain outside. "I have never seen you this happy," she whispered as we sat down in the back pew. But she was smiling too, and I realized suddenly that there were tears in her eyes. She wiped her face on her sleeve. "I can hardly believe that Stirling is well. I saw he was much better when I sat with him yesterday, but I thought it was too much to hope . . ." I reached out and took her hand. She let me.

But people were glancing at us then, and I slid along the pew to a respectable distance. "Maria?" I asked.

"What?" But at that moment the bell rang at the front of the church, and everyone stood up.

Church was not dull and meaningless that day. That day it was true.

I walked home with Maria. The rain had stopped and left a dripping stillness and a quiet evening sunlight. A rainbow shone in the east, over the hills, where it was raining yet and the sky was thick and gray. "I think everything makes sense now," I said suddenly.

She laughed. "What?"

I spread my arms wide and lifted my face to the sun and yelled, "Everything!"

"Stop it, Leo. You're scaring me."

"Sorry. I mean, I believe in God and all."

"Oh . . . good . . . ," she said hesitantly. "I mean . . . is it? Why are you telling me this? You have been going to church all your life."

"But now I believe in God. I really do. I did not used to, but I was wrong. There is a God."

"I always thought so," she said mildly.

"Everything makes sense."

"No, it doesn't."

"Doesn't it?"

"No. Nothing makes sense at all, Leo. But that does not have to stop you from believing in God."

"How do you mean?"

"Everything doesn't make sense. If you think that everything makes sense, you will only be disappointed when it does not."

"How do you know everything doesn't make sense?"

"Just look around you." I looked around at the street. "I meant metaphorically."

"Everything does make sense," I insisted. "I am beginning to see it."

"One day, Leo, you will see that is wrong. It doesn't make sense now. It will, when we reach another dimension, but it doesn't now. You'll see it one day. You watch out." She was laughing.

"I do not think so. There is an order to everything, if we could only see it."

"All right, preacher. Are you going to become a priest now?"

"Calm down! Not too much in one day. I went to church

already." We turned down the alleyway to the side door and both got out our keys. "It would get me out of joining the army, though," I remarked, unlocking the door.

"Leo!"

"It was a joke. Don't worry."

A faint wailing ghosted down the stairwell, a mournful sound that could not help but stop our laughter. The smile slid from my face before I could catch it. "Anselm is not happy," I said to Maria.

"That isn't Anselm," she said.

"Oh? That's strange." We started up the stairs. "It must be one of the kids from the first-floor apartment. I hope it is nothing serious."

When I opened the door of our apartment, the crying broke into the corridor like a wave. And with a sudden jolt to the stomach, I realized for sure that it was Stirling. How had I not known? Only it sounded so unlike him. "What's wrong?" I exclaimed in fright, running to the bedroom doorway.

There was Stirling, clutching his head and wailing. Grandmother was trying to comfort him. His whole head was red and blotchy, even through his stubbly hair. His eyes were squeezed shut and tears burst out of them and ran into the wet edge of the sheet that he clutched up to his face. He was crying so hard that spit spilled from his mouth and soaked the sheet too. I ran to him. "What happened?"

"He suddenly got a lot worse again," Grandmother said. "He isn't responding to a thing I say. Go and fetch Father Dunstan. Go, Leo! Run!" I tried to catch Stirling's eyes, but all I saw reflected was pain and fear. He did not even seem to recognize me. He continued his strange wailing; it was unself-conscious, as if he could not help but let it pour wildly from his mouth.

"What is it?" I asked her. "A headache or what?"

"Go! Quickly!" I hurried out the door. "Run!" she called after me.

We had done this before. All of this we had done before. We could not go back again. I didn't have the strength. But I ran anyway, because I had no choice.

❧

"Stirling!" said Father Dunstan sharply, through the wailing. "Stirling, can you hear me?" He put his hand to the side of Stirling's face. Stirling looked at him for a moment. Then he scrabbled backward into the pillows, hitting his head on the bedstead. He did not seem to notice.

"No!" he cried. "Do not harm me! Help! Help me!" It didn't sound like his own voice at all. Wild screams ripped from his throat, and I felt myself flinching.

"Stirling, it's all right. It's me, Father Dunstan."

Stirling went on crying and struggling backward on his pillows. "Stirling, you are safe," Father Dunstan said clearly. "You are safe." He put his hands on Stirling's shoulders to hold him still. "Tell me—can you see?"

"Can I . . . can I . . . ," Stirling groaned feverishly, over and over, thrashing his head from side to side.

"Can you see me?"

"Please, take them away! They're trying to get me!"

"Who?" said Father Dunstan.

"There—look—there!" Stirling gave a sudden harsh shriek.

"Oh God!" I exclaimed, my voice sounding like someone else's, far, far away, and as if I was praying rather than blaspheming. "Is he possessed?" No one heeded me.

"Can you see me, Stirling?" Father Dunstan asked again. Stirling was mumbling something about ghosts, and he did not seem to hear. "He is hallucinating," said Father Dunstan. "He does not know what he is saying. Fetch me a cold cloth; I will try to bring down the fever."

"Look!" squealed Stirling suddenly, his breath snagging in his throat. He sat straight up and stared wildly into the corner of the room. "Oh, look! Why is she here?"

"Who?" asked Father Dunstan.

"That lady—don't you see? She is reaching out? There!" He screamed again and twisted his bedcovers onto the floor with his snatching arms. Father Dunstan held him down, to keep him from throwing himself onto the floor too. Stirling jerked upward, trying to break free, his shallow breaths themselves almost screams.

"Stirling! Stirling, calm yourself," Father Dunstan told him.

Maria, shaking, put a cloth into the priest's hand. He pressed it to Stirling's head, though Stirling tried to struggle free again. "Save me! She is reaching out at me! To get me—stop her!"

"You are safe, Stirling."

He stared into the corner of the room without moving. "Who is the lady?" Father Dunstan asked.

Feeble wails came from his mouth as he gaped at nothing. "She says . . . she says . . . she says . . ."

"What does she say?"

"She says she is my mother—a ghost! Please, save me!" He screamed again. The noise shattered up into the back of my skull.

"Stirling," said Father Dunstan. "Your mother is not a ghost, and she will come back to you one day. Stirling. Stirling."

Stirling turned to him then, suddenly still. There was a silence, in which not one of us breathed.

"Father Dunstan?" he asked weakly after a moment, gasping as if his lungs had been pierced.

"Stirling, can you see me?"

"Yes." Then we all breathed out together.

"Were you imagining things? Pretend things."

"Was it a dream?" said Stirling.

"Aye, you are quite safe. But you are ill."

"Who was the lady?" he said after a moment.

"That was a dream."

"It was real. She was talking to me. She said she would take me with her, and I didn't want to go."

"Perhaps it seemed very real," said Father Dunstan, the only one of us who was still quite calm. "But you are safe. Lie still for a while. Tell me, how do you feel?"

"My head aches, and my throat—here." He gestured feebly to his neck. "And I feel sick. I'm too hot. My head hurts."

"All right." Father Dunstan put his hand to Stirling's forehead. "You have a fever."

"Am I going to die?" asked Stirling.

"No . . . ," said Father Dunstan. "Not right now." He said it jokingly, as if to reassure Stirling, but Stirling did not understand.

"Not right now?" he asked. "But maybe soon?"

"We cannot tell what God's will is, Stirling, nor can we change it." I almost hit him then, but instead, I sat down hard on my bed to stop myself from passing out. But Stirling seemed comforted by his words.

Grandmother did not want to leave Stirling even for a moment, though Maria was with him. So Father Dunstan had to tell us quickly. "I fear it is more serious than I had thought," he whispered, shutting the door. "Hallucinations are a sign of the advanced stages of the illness." He paused then, as if he expected us to respond, and raised his hand to his forehead. "He may recover well, but he relapsed very suddenly, and that is usually a bad sign. I cannot tell exactly how serious it is. He will deteriorate rapidly now; be prepared for that. I will visit as often as I can. If you know of any medical experts, by all means call them in—anyone at all. They will not do as much harm as they may do good."

"Thank you, Father," said Grandmother eventually. "Will you stay for a while?"

"Of course I will," said the priest. "I am sorry for my mistake—I truly thought that I had got it wrong when I told you it was silent fever. He seemed so much better. But do not despair. There is still much cause for hope."

We all sat around Stirling's bed. I don't know why, only we did. He lay so still and so quiet that we could not tell if he knew what was going on around him. Dull conversations staggered into nothing until we gave up and sat silent. It was as if we were already keeping vigil about his coffin. When that thought struck me, I could not sit there any longer. I stood up and left the room. The circle and the intense atmosphere were broken, and Maria and Father Dunstan got up to leave.

The echo of conversation was still fading from the bedroom, as if it was the end of a party. "All right, Stirling?" asked Grandmother. He nodded. "Sorry we were all in your room," she said. "Everyone wanted to be with you."

"It's all right . . . ," Stirling said, with effort. He looked as if he would like to say more, but he did not. Grandmother went to the kitchen to get together some food. "I liked it . . . with everyone here . . . ," said Stirling eventually.

"Good," I said.

"I would like . . . my First Communion . . . the party . . . to be . . ."

"To be like that?"

"Yes . . . with everyone here."

"Everyone will be." He gave a weak smile. "Do you find it difficult to speak, Stirling?" I asked him.

"No . . . just to think."

I pulled the chair up beside his bed. "Will you . . . will you . . . read . . . to me?" he muttered a moment later.

"Read to you? What do you want me to read?" He did not reply. "You don't mind? The Bible?" He nodded.

Perhaps it was the lingering of Father Dunstan's presence that made me suggest that. Or perhaps the lingering of my brief religious mania. Only I thought that Stirling would like me to read from the Bible. That was why I suggested it. "Thank you, Leo," he said. "I know . . . you do not . . . like to read it. . . ."

I smiled at him, got the Bible out of the cupboard by his bed and opened it at random. "The book of Eccles—Ecclesi—" I faltered.

"Ecclesiastes?"

"Yes." I sat down and began to read. " 'The words of the Teacher, son of David, king in Jerusalem: "Meaningless! Meaningless!" says the Teacher. "Utterly meaningless! Everything is meaningless." '

"How true," I said bitterly. "How very true."

<hr/>

*W*hen Grandmother came into the room, I carried on reading. " 'There is something else meaningless that occurs on earth: righteous men who get what the wicked deserve, and wicked men who get what the righteous deserve. This too, I say, is meaningless.' "

"What are you reading, Leo?" she asked. I held the Bible up to show her. "Why do you not read Stirling a nice story? Read from one of the gospels."

"No . . . ," said Stirling. "Leo . . . reads well."

"Oh, I have no doubt that he reads well; it is what he is reading."

"The book of Eccles . . . ," I attempted again.

"Ecclesiastes?" she said. "At least you are reading the Bible. I hope you are getting some morals from it, Leo." She was still trying desperately to be jovial.

"Everything is meaningless?" I said.

"You have not got to the end of the book. No wonder, then, that it is not very cheering. Stirling, you should be going to sleep soon. I have made you some soup. Will you eat some?"

Stirling shook his head.

"You must," said Grandmother. "You need to keep your strength up."

"I will be sick . . . ," he said wearily. "I'm starting to feel sick."

"Well, eat some anyway," said Grandmother.

"It's a bad idea," I said.

"I didn't ask you, Leo," she told me.

Stirling was violently sick after he ate that soup. Grandmother had anticipated it with a bucket. "Leo, take this down to the yard to wash out," she said, handing it to me. Stirling was still gray-faced. "Bring the other bucket from the cupboard in the kitchen," she called after me. "Before you go down."

"I knew it was a bad idea to give him the soup," I said, quite good-naturedly, when she handed me the other bucket on my return from the yard.

"That is not helpful!" she told me shortly.

"How long is this going to go on for?" I said, with slightly less goodwill, the fourth time I had trailed upstairs again.

"Sorry," Stirling croaked, which made me feel guilty.

"I was joking," I said. "I do not mind."

"Why the hell can we not have bloody running water?" I demanded, about the tenth time. I stood there and told her what I thought of our apartment, banging the bucket down on the floor.

"Leo!" exclaimed Grandmother. "Stop swearing like that."

"And why do I have to keep rinsing them out only for him to throw up in them again? It barely takes up any space in the damn bucket. Can't he throw up twice in one, and then I'll take it down? Or can't he come downstairs to the bathroom?"

"Leo!" shouted Grandmother. "Do you not understand

what is wrong? It's silent fever! No, he can't come downstairs! Heaven and earth—I despair of you, Leo!"

"I . . . could . . . try . . . ," said Stirling, attempting to get up.

"Stay where you are," said Grandmother. "Leo, go downstairs and wash this out." I went, muttering curses and slamming the door. I was suddenly exhausted, and I had no energy left for kindness.

Maria came out into the yard as I was swilling out the bucket into the drain. "Leo," she said. I nodded to her. "What are you doing?"

"Pouring vomit down the drain," I said heavily after a moment. She smiled. "It's not bloody funny," I told her.

"Sorry." Her face was serious again. "It was just the way you said it. Sorry. Do you need any help with anything?"

"Like what?"

"Just . . . anything. It must be hard work for you and your grandmother to look after Stirling, and I would like to be of help to you."

"It has only been one day," I told her.

"True. You look tired, though."

I sighed. "Do you know how many times I've washed this thing out?" I demanded, punctuating the sentence with several curses.

"A lot, I'm guessing. I don't know." She refused to let me draw her into an argument. I wished she wouldn't. I needed someone to shout at.

"Neither do I. I've lost count." I went to the tap, poured more water into the bucket, and trailed back over to the drain to pour it out again.

"I could have helped with that."

"Why the hell would you want to wash vomit down the drain? For your own amusement, or what?"

"You have hardly slept all the time that Stirling has been ill, Leo," she said, still standing there. "Even when we thought he was getting better, you were sitting up with him. I worry about you."

"Well, you are the only one who does."

"Tell your grandmother that I will come and help with anything. Any time, day or night. If you cannot ask your friends for help, Leo, who can you ask?" I gave in at last and tried to smile at her, by way of an apology, though without much success. She came over and took the bucket from me. It was reasonably clean, except for a tidemark of yellow scum near the bottom. She put her hand to my face and pushed my hair back from my forehead.

"Try to get some rest," she said, looking at me with concern. I hardly even noticed how pretty she was anymore.

∽∾

I was woken at four the next morning by Stirling's screaming. I was sleeping on the sofa in the living room so that Grandmother could be near Stirling. She had only just persuaded me to go to bed. "Help!" Stirling was crying again. "Help me!"

"Stirling," Grandmother was saying. "Stirling. Stirling." The way that Father Dunstan had, except her voice was not calm. I got up.

"What is it?" I asked sleepily. Stirling was thrashing about wildly, as if a demon was in him.

"Stop him, Leo," pleaded Grandmother. "He will make himself worse. Hold him still." She sounded so childlike it frightened me to hear her. I crossed to the bed and kneeled down beside it, catching hold of Stirling's arms.

He cried out again. *"Help!"*

"Stirling. It is me, Leo. I will not harm you. You are safe." He lay still. "Shh," I told him. "It's all right."

Suddenly his arm burst upward out of my grasp, his fingernail catching my eyeball. I swore, clasping at it, and let go his arms. He struck out at the air as if there was something just out of his reach in front of him. "Help me!" he wailed. "Oh, help me! Help! *Help!*" The words were drawn out and distorted as if he was crying out in a different language.

"He is hallucinating again," said Grandmother.

"No!" cried Stirling. "No! Help me, Leo!" He looked straight at me then, and the look was so eerie that I drew back from him. He reached out to me. "Leo! Can't you hear?" And he began to wail again.

"I am here. What is it? What is wrong?"

"My head! Help me! My head!" He wailed, clutching at it.

"It's a headache?" I said. "Tell me, Stirling."

"My head's going to break! My head! Oh!" A tear burst from his eye and landed halfway down his cheek. "Help me, Leo! Grandmother!" She took his hand and he clung to her, crying.

"Shall I get a cloth to put on his head?" I asked.

"Yes," said Grandmother. "Shh, Stirling. Shh."

There was still some water in the jar in the kitchen. I poured some onto a cloth, wrung it out over the basin, and brought it back in. Stirling was still sobbing, his arms around Grandmother's neck. She took the cloth from me and pressed it to his forehead. "There," she said soothingly. I sat down on the end of the bed, rubbing my head. I was feeling a lot worse for getting some sleep; I had not known how tired I was before.

Stirling lay down again, more calmly. His crying subsided into breathless hiccups. "Shh," Grandmother continued quietly. "Shh, Stirling." He clasped at his head in a sudden movement. She took his hand and placed it back down at his side. "All right. It's all right." More tears squeezed from his eyes and rolled sideways over his cheeks and onto the pillows.

"All right," Grandmother said again. He coughed shakily and caught onto her hand. "All right."

I found that I had somehow ended up bent double, with my head resting on my knees. I was falling asleep. I sat up quickly, my feet scuffing on the floor, and they both turned to me. "Shh, Leo," Grandmother mouthed, frowning. Stirling just stared at me, as if he had not recognized who I was at all. I stood up and crossed to the window. Without thinking, I began to draw back the curtains, but light stabbed into the room. Stirling clutched at his head and began crying again. "Leo!" whispered Grandmother. I shut them again hastily. Stirling's creaking sobs came faster and faster, as if he could not breathe. "Shh," said Grandmother, dabbing the cloth on his forehead. "Shh." She stroked his head. "My poor Stirling. Poor baby."

"Oh—my head," he moaned. "I am getting worse! I am getting worse! Why can't I just die now?"

"It's all right, Stirling," Grandmother said. "You are not going to die. You are going to get better. The worst will soon be over. It's all right."

"But my head—"

"Calm down; you are hurting it more by crying. Concentrate on breathing. That's it. Breathe in. . . ." He took a rattling gasp. "Breathe out. Slowly." He clutched at his head again, and again she removed his hand.

"Shh," she whispered over and over again as if to lull him into sleep. His sobbing breaths went on, but they grew slower, and he grew calmer and shut his eyes. After perhaps half an hour had passed, Grandmother turned carefully to me. "Go back to sleep, Leo," she mouthed. I tried to shake my head, but she turned to Stirling before she could see, and I found myself trailing into the living room and falling heavily onto the sofa.

I did not think that I had fallen back to sleep, except I woke. I dragged myself up off the sofa; it felt as if I was waking from death. Then I remembered why I was there: because Stirling was sick. I could hear him crying in the other room. I stumbled through the door. Grandmother was still sitting on his bed. "Leo, stay with your brother for a minute," she whispered. "I am going down to the bathroom." I sat on the bed, rubbing my eyes. Stirling caught my hand, his own palm feverish and dry.

"All right, Stirling," I said sleepily.

"I'll only be a moment." She hurried out.

"Leo!" Someone was shaking me by the shoulder. "Wake up." It was Grandmother. "Leo, you will be late for school."

I sat up. "What is it?"

I was lying slumped half on Stirling's bed and half on the floor. I must have fallen asleep.

"Hurry. You will be late for school."

I stood up. "School?"

"Yes, it is already a quarter to eight, and you haven't got the water yet."

"Cannot you do it?"

"No, I can't carry it."

"Neither can I," I said stupidly, but I had to get it.

It was ridiculous even to think of going to school, but I was so tired I hardly realized I was going until I got there. Sergeant Markey met me in the front yard. "You are fifteen minutes late, North." Why did he have to say everything at such a high volume?

"Yes," I said, taking a step back.

"Go and wait outside the colonel's office." I wandered off in the direction of the school. "Hurry, North! We don't have all bloody day!" I walked even more slowly. "North, come back here!" he shouted. "I expect an apology for your lateness."

"I'll apologize to the colonel when I see him," I called over my shoulder, and walked into the school.

Sergeant Markey was on duty, so Sergeant Markey was the one who would punish me. I had forgotten, of course. "Why were you so late, North?" he demanded.

"Er . . . my brother's ill. . . . I did not get much sleep . . . ," I muttered.

"That is no excuse." I did not answer. "That is no excuse at all," he said.

"I didn't say it was a damn excuse; you asked me why I was late, so I told—"

He hit me, and I fell backward hard against the corridor

wall. "You need to learn some respect, North!" he told me, his hand still raised from striking the side of my face. "Some serious respect."

"Like hell I do," I said. And I turned and walked out.

"North!" he said. "North, come back here this instant! My God, you'll be sorry when you get back!" I marched out into the yard, and the door cut off his shouts. I was not going back.

I put my hand up to my stinging face once I was out of sight of the yard. That would come up with an ugly red mark. I swore out loud at him, not caring who heard it. At that moment there was no one I hated more than Sergeant Markey. I stalked down the street, fuming, and was halfway home before I realized it. Grandmother would ask questions. Still, it could not be helped.

I met Maria on the stairs. "What are you doing here, Leo?" she asked, jogging the baby up and down. "I thought you were at school. And what happened to your face?" Anselm began to wail.

"Bloody Sergeant Markey," I said loudly, over the noise.

"What—he hit you?"

I nodded. I was still breathing fast with anger. "I walked out," I told her.

"Out of school? Will you not get into trouble?"

I shrugged. "They expelled a boy the other year for walking out of class."

"That's serious, then. Why did you do it?"

"What do you mean, why did I do it? Should I just stand there and take it?" I was raising my voice.

"Shh," she told Anselm, rocking him. And then to me: "Don't be aggressive. I didn't say you should stand there and take it. I just asked why you walked out."

"I felt like it."

She looked worried. "Are you set on ruining your whole life, Leo?"

"This is coming from who? Righteousness herself, evidently, with a baby at fifteen."

The concern froze on her face. "Leo, that is unfair!" I looked at the floor. "That is what you think I am, is it? Some sort of slut? Is that what you think of me?"

"No . . . ," I began. "Maria—"

"I am glad to know you have such a high opinion of me."

"I'm sorry. I did not mean that." She turned and walked out the door. It slammed shut behind her.

I marched up the stairs. "Leo, what are you doing here?" Grandmother demanded when I edged around the bedroom door. "And was that you I heard shouting and stamping about in the corridor? I hope to goodness it was not." I did not reply but trailed over to my bed and sat down heavily. "Leo, what are you doing here?" she said again. Stirling was asleep, his face to the wall. "Leo! Answer me!"

I did not answer, but she went on hissing questions at me. "I left school!" I shouted eventually. "I left school because of that bastard Markey. I wish all his descendants would follow him to hell." I said several other things before she cut me off.

"*Leo!*" she exclaimed. "Do not dare to use that language! And what do you mean, you left school? Why? Why did you leave school?" I shut my eyes, but she went on. It turned into another argument.

"Oh, Leo!" she exclaimed then. "Why are you such a trouble to me? Count yourself fortunate that you are not ill like poor Stirling. Why can you not look at your blessings, instead of being so bad-tempered and—"

"Bad-tempered? Bad-tempered?" I stood up. The thud of my boot against the floor woke Stirling, and he turned, gasping with fright.

"What's going on? Grandmother?"

"It's all right, Stirling. I am here."

"What's going on?" He clasped at his neck. "My throat hurts."

"You call me bad-tempered?" I continued. "Well, I—"

"Leo, shut your mouth!" Grandmother told me sharply. "No one wants to listen to you. You are not important. Stirling is important now, because he is sick. I don't have time to mind you like a baby."

I marched to the door. "I do not need to be patronized like this!"

"Oh—my head!" Stirling moaned, his voice hoarse. "Grandmother? Grandmother!"

"It's all right, Stirling," she said. "Shh."

I walked back out the door as Stirling began crying with pain again. I felt guilty. At that moment, I cared more about my own anger than about him.

I tried to go to the hills, to look for the Bloodflower herb. But every time I stepped out the front door, I thought I was falling. Eventually I went back, let myself into the apartment quietly, and sat at the table and listened to Stirling crying. While he was crying, I knew he was alive. He didn't stop until six o'clock.

❧

"Leo, I need to talk to you," Grandmother said the next evening. I had not gone to school that day either, but she hadn't tried to make me. We were sitting with Stirling, who shifted fretfully in his sleep, his face red and puffy with fever.

"What about?" I asked.

"Duty. You know, everyone has a duty of some sort. For example, my duty is to look after you and Stirling. Or Maria's duty is to look after baby Anselm. Or Father Dunstan's duty is to—"

"I understand you."

"Some people have duties that they do not necessarily like but still have to fulfill. You, Leo—you have a duty to go to school, not to get into trouble, and not to get expelled. You have a duty to me, and to Stirling, to help us when we need you to. Do you understand? People can't just stop fulfilling their duties, can they? Because there would be chaos. So I want you back in school tomorrow with no complaining. All right?" I did not argue.

There was a silence. "Do you think that Stirling is better?" I asked then.

"No. I fear he is worse." We watched him. He turned over and muttered something, clutching out his hand. "Leo—I'm so afraid he will die!" she said suddenly.

"Shh," I said. "He will hear you."

"I could not live if we lost little Stirling."

"We will not," I said. "In a year's time we will look back at this, and it will be no more than a memory. It won't be real anymore; not like it is now."

"You are right," she said. But she was crying. "I cannot bear seeing him in so much pain; I am powerless to help him. He calls out to me to help him, and I can't."

"He knows it."

"But think—" It came out as an uncontrolled wail. She took a breath and continued. "Think of how much pain he must be suffering. Crying out for help all the time he is awake."

"Pain like this is soon forgotten. Many people have had silent fever."

"True." She sighed and dabbed at her eyes. "I'm only worrying because I am so tired."

"I can sit with him tonight, Grandmother," I said. "You should get some sleep."

But Stirling screamed the whole night through, and neither of us got any sleep as it turned out. "It's a mercy that he will soon be unable to speak," I grumbled the next morning, thinking of the next stage of the illness.

"Leo!" Grandmother exclaimed, and I remembered that it was Stirling I was talking about.

"I did not mean it," I told her in horror. "I did not mean it at all."

I did not go to school. She seemed too tired even to mention it.

That afternoon Stirling lost his voice. "It is perfectly normal," said Father Dunstan. "They say the disease does something to the vocal cords. Your voice will come back, Stirling."

I sat with him while Grandmother was in the kitchen cooking dinner. He stared at me, the tears slipping down his cheeks, and his eyes making constant tiny anxious movements. "What is wrong, Stirling?" I asked him. "What are you crying about?" He opened and closed his mouth, but the only sound was the hissing of his breath. "Does your head hurt?" He nodded. "And your throat?" He nodded again and gave a silent sob. "Crying will make it worse," I told him.

He lay down on the pillows, but he went on crying. "Do you

feel sick?" He nodded. "What else?" He put his hand to his chest. "Your chest hurts? Your heart? Your lungs? Do you find it difficult to breathe?" He nodded again.

The silence pressed in on my brain. I had hated Stirling's constant shrieking, but it was better than this. If I was not by his side, I would not know even if he was dead. "Let me read to you," I said. "Then you won't be frightened."

I fetched the black book. With every step I took across the room, I was praying there would be more writing. I saw my own hands shaking as I opened it.

There was another section, a few pages. "Shall I read it?" I said. Stirling did not respond, but he was watching me, still crying. I began, trying to keep my voice steady. This story was not about Aldebaran. It had returned to the girl—that girl Stirling had said was an English relative of ours. Those days when we had read the book before—they already seemed years ago. I rubbed my aching eyes and began to read.

❧

When she was nine years old, the little girl woke suddenly from a dream. And when she sat up, her grandmother was beside the bed. Emilie used to sit there often while her granddaughter fell to sleep, and the girl did not think it strange to see her there now. "Nan," she said quietly.

"Anna," said Emilie.

Anna had been thinking about her grandmother that afternoon, about the days when Emilie had first taught her to dance. That afternoon she had put away her ballet shoes. No one could pay for lessons anymore. She had not thought she minded until she saw her grandmother sitting there.

Anna began to cry. She said, "They want me to give up dancing."

"Listen to me now," said Emilie. "Never give up dancing."

A church bell was chiming three, away over the rooftops, and Anna was sitting up in the darkness. There was no one else there.

She got up and turned on the light. She took her shoes out again and put them on. She began to dance.

Her mother was at the door then. "What are you doing?" She caught hold of the girl's arm. "Anna, answer me!"

"I want to dance," the girl said.

Anna's mother bent and looked into her face, still holding her by the arm. "Were you crying, Anna angel? There are tears on your cheeks."

"Nan was here," Anna said. "She was sitting there by the bed talking to me."

Her mother let the girl's arm fall and stared at her. Anna could see her eyes moving, as though she was trying to read Anna's own. "Maybe it was a dream," said Anna. "But she told me not to stop dancing. Please let me dance."

"For how long?" said her mother. "Another year of lessons?"

The girl shook her head. "Forever."

That same night the boy could not sleep, so he wandered down through the empty house to the library, where the light was still burning. Aldebaran was at the table with a pile of books in front of him, but he looked up when the boy entered. "It is late," said Aldebaran. "Past three o'clock, and you should be asleep." He smiled and set the books aside. "Tell me what is troubling you, Ryan."

"Uncle?" said the boy. "The place where I used to live—my own country—I think I have nearly forgotten it now."

"You must not forget," said Aldebaran, rising to his feet.

"I know it."

"Here," said Aldebaran. "Come here." He picked up an open book from the top of the pile and blew the ink dry. "I am going to read you a story."

"What story?" said the boy, pulling a chair up to the table.

"It is called *The Golden Reign*," said Aldebaran. "This is the last chapter."

Aldebaran opened the book. "'The Betrayal of the Royal Family,'" he read.

I stopped reading and turned to Stirling. "We know this already. The next part is the last chapter of Father's book. Do you really want me to read it to you?" Weakly, he nodded. The tears were drying on his face, still catching the evening light. "All right," I said. "I will read it. Maybe I have forgotten it, anyway, and I would like to hear it again." But really, I could have told it to him by heart.

King Cassius I had an advisor by the name of Marcus Kalitz, in whom he placed absolute trust. Kalitz knew every secret of the country. One night King Cassius woke, and Kalitz was in his room, holding a dagger. He was cast out from the king's service. But Kalitz always maintained that he had heard a sound and gone to investigate, thinking that someone had broken into the palace. It was never known whether Kalitz had meant to assassinate the king that night, but from then on the two were enemies, and their families after them. And the old hatred rose again between the Kalitzes and the Donahues.

Five years later, a son was born to the king and the queen, and in the same month, Marcus Kalitz's wife, Celine, also gave birth to a son. The king's son was named Cassius also, and Kalitz's son was named Lucien.

While he was yet young, the king fell ill, and he did not recover. On his death, his son became King Cassius II, at the age of ten. There was fear of revolution at this time of instability. The lord Aldebaran of the secret service went undercover to the Kalitz mansion on Holy Island.

Talitha, the head of the secret service, told Aldebaran that he was going to Holy Island to keep watch on Marcus and Celine Kalitz. But Marcus and Celine knew who he was. They hated the royal family with a ferocity, and Aldebaran was working for the king's government, but they kept him there. He was the one who was being watched. Talitha had sent Aldebaran to Holy Island for one reason only. She wanted him far away and carefully guarded.

Talitha was secretly working for the rebel group that was planning to take over the country. But as head of the secret service, she was responsible for the hunting of the rebel leaders. Without Aldebaran it was easy to cut down the country from the middle of the ranks. Many of the powerful royalists working in the secret service died in dangerous operations and suspicious circumstances during the following years. Many wasted time looking the wrong way, sent far away on pointless missions. An atmosphere of fear rose over the country. Meanwhile, Marcus Kalitz was developing an army and a dictator—his son, Lucien.

Now, Anneline, Marcus Kalitz's daughter, did not know of the plans of her family. She met the young king at a ball and they fell in love. They were engaged when she was fourteen. Lucien hated his sister from that day onward.

Anneline suspected her family of plotting something, though she did not know what. She found the silver eagle, an ancient and powerful charm, in her father's possession. She gave it to the lord Aldebaran. Anneline knew that Aldebaran was in danger from her family, and she advised him to flee. He gave to her a prophecy that had come to him as a vision.

Just before Anneline's wedding, the great Aldebaran escaped the Kalitz mansion and the bonds of magic that Talitha had placed upon it. Aldebaran's power did not match that of Talitha, although he surpassed her in wisdom. Talitha caught him, and she and others exiled him from the country.

The king married Anneline Kalitz, who was beautiful and good. A baby was born to the king and the queen, and he was named Cassius also. He would have become King Cassius III. From the first, the boy had the eyes of a king, and he was loved by the people. And when Queen Anneline saw this, she began to suspect that Aldebaran's prophecy had meaning, and so it was made into a book, as were all the prophecies of old.

The silver eagle contained great power—the power of freedom. And Aldebaran knew that it must be protected by any means. It was part of his prophecy, and if Lucien found it, he would destroy it. So Aldebaran hid the talisman where no one could find it.

After his father's death, Lucien Kalitz grew even more fiercely determined to take over the country. There were many whose allegiance he could buy. He set up factories to mass-produce foreign firearms—weapons that had not been seen in this world before. He had imported them from somewhere far away and employed some of the country's cleverest scientists to discover how they worked.

One night Lucien Kalitz's army stormed the castle. There was no one who could withstand the foreign guns. At Lucien's orders, his soldiers murdered the king and the queen, who was Lucien's own sister. But when they came to the prince, they were afraid, because of the prophecy. So they took him to Lucien. Lucien commanded Talitha to exile the boy. It would have been unwise to kill an innocent child who was so loved by the people. So the prince was exiled to England, where Aldebaran also was. And the lord Aldebaran took the boy into his care and sought to bring him up as one fit to rule Malonia.

Lucien's army took control of Malonia, and he named himself Commander of the Realm. Less than a year later, his government were calling him King Lucien instead. And he turned away from the prophecy, cast it aside as if it was a joke, and pretended he was invincible. But perhaps he remembered it sometimes, because others believed it was true. There was a chance. He knew that something must be done to prevent its fulfilment, so that the people would look away from dreams, back to reality.

Lucien knew of the powerful charm that Aldebaran possessed, and he sent his soldiers to England, to seize it. But they could not find it, and torture had no power over Aldebaran. Talitha was needed for the war that Lucien now waged on Alcyria, and she could not afford to be weakened by searching in vain for the silver eagle.

Then a rumor began: the prince had never been exiled; he had been shot with his parents on the night that Lucien took over the country. People had seen it happen. A child's body was found, and it could have been the boy's. The rumor spread like a germ through the country. The prophecy was forgotten. The people accepted Lucien as king. They stopped waiting for the boy's return. They were a broken nation. They had no guns, no money, and no power. And they had no hope either. And we ask who started that rumor.

I tell this story as I see it, because this is what I believe about our country. This is what I have seen. To write these words is my God-given right, and I will not be silenced by fear. I will give everything I have, and I will give my life, if it is my own destiny to lose it for this cause. The prince is not dead. He will return. We should not give up hope because the Golden Reign is ended. The earth circles constantly from day to night, and back again to day, and when we are in night, we have the day to look forward to, but in the day we have only the night. And I tell you truly that the Iron Reign is begun.

Perhaps it was fortunate that I could tell that story by heart, because tears had been blinding me for a long while now. I breathed in silently and blinked them out of my eyes. Stirling's face was distant, and he did not seem to have noticed. "I have lost the page," I said, bending over the book and leafing through it. "Wait a minute."

I went on reading hastily.

Aldebaran closed the book. "Do you understand that story?"

The boy nodded. "This is the story of my family." He got up and went to Aldebaran's side. "Who wrote this?"

"My nephew, Harold North. I have been copying it down

chapter by chapter using my willpower. You know that I can see what he writes."

"He wrote it like a legend," said the boy. "Like one of the old stories you used to tell me, about good and evil."

"He told it like that because he wanted to make people listen," said Aldebaran. "He will suffer for this book, but he wrote it anyway. You know that this story is real. You have seen Lucien and his military commanders and the great Talitha. You have seen the marks of torture on my arms and legs." The boy nodded. "Here in England, they used to believe that the king was appointed by God," Aldebaran continued. "That is not true. It is chance that you were born the son of the king of Malonia. But there are people in your country who would die to see you take the throne again, because of the prophecies surrounding you, because your father and grandfather ruled the country well, and because they are already dissatisfied with Lucien. People like Harold North. People are prepared to die for you, and you in return will give your life to them."

"That is why I have to remember about Malonia," said the boy.

"Tomorrow I will begin to teach you," said the man. "So that you do not forget."

The last light lay, glittering, on Stirling's hair. He did not seem to notice that I had stopped reading. I wiped my face on my sleeve. I was almost glad that he seemed barely to register what was going on around him while I was crying like that over some story about my father's book.

It was true that he had suffered for it. That chapter had been one step too far for the great Harold North. They put a price on his head and banned every royalist book in the country. And now here we were, his two sons, who he would not have recognized, sitting here reading his declaration of freedom. Those were the last words he wrote before he left us for good.

"I think you were right," I said, wiping my face and trying to keep the tears out of my voice. "Aldebaran did not die, or the prince. If this story is true, they went on living in England."

Stirling had shut his eyes, and I did not know if he heard me, or if he was sleeping. I put away the book, then took his hand and sat beside him in silence until Grandmother returned.

"I heard you talking," Grandmother said when she came in with a bowl of soup for Stirling. "Were you telling a story, Leo?"

I shook my head and let go of his hand, standing up. Stirling turned to her weakly as she sat down where I had been, on the side of his bed.

She tried to spoon soup into his mouth, but he vomited it straight back up. We went through this process about three times every day, because he had to keep his strength up. He had to, otherwise he would not survive the final stage of the illness, which was unconsciousness. The next stage.

When I trailed back upstairs with the washed-out bucket, Grandmother asked me, "Leo, will you go to church?"

"What?" I said, trying to get my brain to work.

"Will you go to church?" she repeated. "To pray for Stirling."

"You can go," I said. "I will stay with him."

"No—I'll not leave him."

"Father Dunstan prays for Stirling at every service," I said.

"I know, but . . . please, Leo . . . please go . . ." She took my arm.

"Every service," I said. "Morning and evening."

"I want one of us to be there."

I was too tired to go, but I was too tired to argue. So I went.

I did not hear a word of the service. It seemed as if there was a wall of glass round about me that filtered every normal sensation and made it strange and distant and dreamlike. After the service had finished, I remained where I sat. Gradually, everyone else left.

"Ah, Leonard," said Father Dunstan when he emerged from the vestry. "I was meaning to come and see how Stirling is getting on. Shall I see you back at your house?" I nodded without focusing my eyes on him, and it was five minutes after he'd gone before I realized what he had said.

I walked to the back of the church slowly and stood looking at the rack of candles burning there. Through my tired, watering eyes, the lights made diagonal crosses, which stretched in the breeze from the open door. A storm was blowing up outside. The wind was snarling in the narrow streets and snapping newspapers against the empty fountain in the square. The door rattled open and shut again, banging against the frame.

The wind lulled for a moment. I took a candle, lit it, and put it in the rack, for Stirling, apart from the rest so that I could tell which one it was. I knelt down beside the candles, judged the distance wrong and crashed my knee against the floor, and had to bite back a curse. I bowed my head in guilt.

"Please, God, please let Stirling live," I whispered, so quietly that I could not tell whether I had really whispered it or just thought it. "Please. I know that I am evil, but should he be punished for it? I promise that if you let him live, I will never swear again. I will come to church every day. I will read the Bible morning and night. I will give anything. I would have my arms and legs cut off, if that was the only way Stirling could live." For a moment I was uneasy, as if this bargain was final and it might actually happen. And then, kneeling there, I was paralyzed with guilt that I valued my arms and legs over my own brother.

"Please—I will do anything," I went on whispering. "Let me catch silent fever and die if someone must, only spare him. He is the good one. He is too good to die—do you not see?" I was speaking out loud now: "Do you not see?" But there was silence. God was too far away to hear. "Only do not let him die to punish me."

The door swung and crashed against the wall in a sudden gust of wind. The candle flames bowed low and rose again in unison. Except for one. Stirling's candle, the youngest and the tallest, separate from the others and closest to the door, went out. A narrow thread of smoke coiled upward, and then the wind snatched it away. I stared at the space where the flame should have been, then stood up and ran out the door. I believed in bad omens. Truly, I did, and there was no point in pretending not to.

*H*itting my elbow on the front door frame in my haste, I slammed the door shut and clattered into the bedroom. Grandmother and Father Dunstan turned to look at me. Stirling lay still.

"He is unconscious," said Grandmother.

I stood there and looked at him, panting and clutching absently at my numb elbow. "Come and sit down, Leonard," said Father Dunstan. "Do not be alarmed. This is a normal stage of the illness."

I had thought that Stirling was dead, just for a second. But I knelt beside the bed, put my hand in front of his mouth, and felt the breath there. "How long?" I said.

"This will probably not be over quickly," said Father Dunstan. "All we can do is wait."

We sat there in silence, watching Stirling. Stirling's body, that is—for wherever his spirit was, it was not there. There was a strange calm about him that made me think that he was dreaming. Whenever he moved the slightest amount, Grandmother would leap up with a cry, only to sit down again when he fell back into stillness.

For some reason I was not worried. The calm of Stirling's breathing made my breathing slow also, and I could hear Father Dunstan's watch ticking and my own heart beating, but nothing else. My mind wandered to other things. I began to wish Maria was here. But she had brought some shopping earlier; she would not call round again that day. She would not want to see me, anyway. Why had I said that to her? Why?

How could I have said that? I screwed up my eyes and pressed my fists into them at the thought of it. How could I have said that?

When I opened my eyes, I saw that Father Dunstan was looking at me. I stopped grimacing. He smiled kindly. "All right, Leonard."

I felt so guilty then that I made myself imagine that Stirling was dead. Gone forever. I would walk to school on my own. Grandmother and I would go to church on our own. If someone asked me if I had a brother, I would have to say no. His bed would be empty, and his place at the table, and his desk at school taken by someone else.

I imagined myself looking out the classroom window one day, seeing Second Year Platoon A training in the yard. I would see that one whose front teeth had been missing for a year, and the colonel's nephew with the orange freckles, and the one who was smaller than the rest and always started fights—as usual, I would see them all—but I would not see Stirling, no matter how long I looked, because Stirling would not be there. Stirling would never be there; he would not even exist, except as a memory.

My heart was rattling against my ribs. I looked quickly to see that he was still breathing. Slowly but regularly, he was. I pressed my hand to my heart, and after that I did not take my eyes off him.

Father Dunstan stood up to take Stirling's pulse at midnight. We were sitting in the dark, and it had been dark for two hours, but it was only then that I noticed. No one made a move to light a lamp. "How is he?" asked Grandmother.

"It is hard to tell," said Father Dunstan. "It is very hard to tell." And he sat down again, and we went on staring silently at Stirling.

After about half an hour, my eyes grew heavy. It hurt to keep them open. I pushed fiercely against the heavy blinks. Could I not even stay awake one night for the sake of my own brother? What if he died while I slept?

But it was no good. I was falling asleep, and no one made a sound to stop me; the stillness in the room was lulling me into sleep, and Stirling's slow breathing, and the darkness, and I just could not keep my eyes open.

❧

I woke up and saw Stirling lying there, and started to my feet. "Grandmother, why didn't you wake me?" I demanded. "How is Stirling? Worse?"

"The same," she said. He was lying still, just as he had been before. Her chair was drawn up close to his bedside, and she was pressing a cold cloth to his forehead.

While I had been asleep, I had forgotten that Stirling was ill, and my heart was beating fast again now. "Where is Father Dunstan?" I asked.

"He went to take the eight o'clock Mass," said Grandmother. "He thinks that Stirling may lie like this for a couple more days without changing."

"And then what?" I said.

"I don't know," she said. "For now, we have to be patient. Sit quietly, Leo."

But I couldn't sit quietly. I had gone to sleep resigned to

waiting and watching in silence. I had woken up and could not wait anymore. Overnight I had lost whatever calm I'd had. I began pacing about the room. I tripped over my boots on the floor, and Stirling's forehead furrowed for a second. "Leo, why don't you go to school?" said Grandmother.

"School? How can I go to school?"

"I think it would be good for you. Or else go down the road and buy some bread; we are out of food, and neither of us have eaten since yesterday lunchtime."

"What if Stirling gets worse while I am gone?"

"I will send Maria to fetch you. She will do that; she has said she will. Why don't you get ready to leave at least, then you can decide?"

I was already in my uniform; I had fallen asleep in it the night before. I splashed some water on my face and hurried back into the bedroom. "Maybe he is worse," I said, looking at Stirling. His face was flushed with fever, but then, it had been like that before. "Father Dunstan is coming after the service," said Grandmother. "He will be able to judge whether Stirling is worse or not."

"Grandmother, I don't know why, only I'm worried. You know I have powers. If I am worried, there may be a reason."

"But Father Dunstan said—"

"Does Father Dunstan have powers?" I demanded.

"Leo, what use are your magical powers to Stirling? What use is anything that you can do? What can you possibly do to make Stirling well? He may lie like this for days before he wakes up, and all we can do is wait. Sit down or go out for a while, but will you please try to be calm and sensible?"

It made me suddenly almost cry with anger that she could be

so unreasonable. "Grandmother, why are you trying to pretend everything is normal?" I began. "Do you seriously think—"

"There's nothing you can do, Leo," she repeated.

But there was. There was something I could do. I could not sit here waiting, but I could do something. So I left.

⁂

I ran. That was all I did, just ran—out of the city and through the graveyard. There were no soldiers at the gate to stop me. I went on. Something was driving me out into the hills to search for the Bloodflower again. If you have powers, you cannot ignore them.

I did not stop running. Even as the hills grew steeper, I kept up the same pace, pounding on uphill and downhill, toward the horizon. I ran straight through a stream, and water soaked my boots. I raced from valley to valley, trying to find some clue that would tell me where to look. But there was nothing, and in desperation I searched everywhere.

My eyes began to ache with hunting for a flash of red petals that was not there. I looked more and more meticulously. I ended up circling about the same patch over and over, snatching impatiently at the grass stalks. I stopped still and realized there was nothing there at all. And suddenly I was sick of this place; I wanted to get out. I ran up the nearest hill.

I could see a long way from there. I turned and looked back; I had come several miles. My bones were aching, and my head was throbbing from too little sleep. I collapsed where I was and stared upward.

The sun was overhead and the sky was artificial blue, like

dye, thick and dazzling with color. It hurt my head to look at it, and I shut my eyes, putting my hand up to my face to shield it from the brightness. My forehead was running with sweat, though I had not realized it.

I did not have the energy to get up again. And suddenly I did not want to either. Everything was in control while I lay still. If I did not move, nothing else would. I lay there, irritated with the heat and the grass stalks pressing against the backs of my arms, until I began to drift away.

I opened my eyes, and I did not know whether I had slept or not. A bird was singing close by. Looking upward, I found it, a dark shape against the sky. It flew ever higher, until it was no larger than a dust speck, and then it was gone. Had it gone right out of the atmosphere? Or were my eyes too weak to see it? It could have gone right into heaven, for all I could tell.

That made me think of an old story that Grandmother used to tell us, about the little children who died. Their souls became birds so that they could fly up to heaven. I remembered her telling us, "They flew up and up, and the earth grew smaller and smaller, until they could see it no longer. They flew through the clouds, and they were free. They forgot the earth and all their troubles there, because they were going home." That was Stirling's favorite part of the story. "Imagine not being able to see the earth," he used to say. "Imagine that, Leo." He had never been afraid of death. Never. I was the one who was afraid.

My eyes were watering from the bright light. I stood up, but the tears went on falling. They were rolling down my cheeks and soaking the collar of my shirt. I tried to wipe them away, but more fell, and I sunk to my knees and found that I was pressing my hands to my face and rocking and wailing like a baby. I wasn't going to find the Bloodflower; it had been stupid to think I would. Stirling was going to lie unconscious, and then worsen and then die—and I would be left behind and there was nothing I could do about it. I took a shuddering breath. What the hell was wrong with me? But I kept on crying. I could not stop myself.

I stopped only when all the tears in my head had fallen. I opened my eyes, coughing miserably. The grass was gleaming wet in front of me. My stomach was watery and heavy from crying so long. I began, wearily, to get up. It was no good staying out here any longer.

Then I stopped. Because I saw something. There, in the wet grass, as if it had sprung up from my tears, was a plant.

I stopped breathing and stared at it. It had blood-red star-shaped flowers with yellow centers; the leaves, veined with red, were a deep green. It was the same as the pictures I had seen. It was the same as the descriptions I had heard. It was, as far as I could see, the Bloodflower.

I sat and stared at it. Then I reached out and touched it. The teardrops on the flower centers trembled, but it did not disappear. It was really there in front of me; it had been there all the time.

❧

*M*y heart was beating so fast that I could hear it in my head. I began scraping at the soil around the plant, terrified of damaging it. I was glancing around all the time, in case someone else had seen, but the hills were deserted. I worked faster. The ground was dusty and the plant came out soon enough, roots and all.

My hands were shaking. I took off my jacket and laid the plant in it, covering it carefully so that I would lose none of the petals. Because the petals were the part that cured silent fever. With that thought, I got up and ran.

Our building looked different when I staggered up to it. It was because I was different. Tired and dusty as I was, I felt suddenly like an immortalized hero, greater even than the lord Aldebaran. I had found the flower to save Stirling's life. I unwrapped my jacket and checked that it had not vanished, that it was still the same flower it had been out in the hills. The leaves were already limp and thin; the stem had wilted; but the petals were intact. I stood still for a moment at the door, because nothing would be the same now and it made me dizzy. Then I clutched the plant to my chest and went in.

I was running again. I had thought I was tired, but it was not true. I clattered up the stairs two at a time. "I'm home!" I shouted. "Grandmother! Stirling! I'm back!" I tumbled through the door, shouting like an excited kid. "See! See what I have found!"

THE END

❧

I close the book and for a moment I can feel myself smiling when I remember that day. It is growing quieter on the balcony. The lights of the city extinguish one by one. The music has faded now that they have shut the doors against the rising breeze. I get up and walk across the moonlit stone, the book still in my hand.

Now that I read this again, I remember the day I wrote that part of the story. I was sitting at the window, and I could tell someone was behind me even before I turned. I laid down the pen and turned and smiled. "Remember that, Stirling?"

But whatever I wrote then, it was not the end.

I stumbled through the bedroom door. Grandmother and Father Dunstan were both in the room, facing Stirling, so that their backs were to me. "Grandmother!" I called. "Father Dunstan! Stirling! See what I have found."

"Shh, Leo," said Grandmother, without turning. I ran into the room and opened my hand and held out the plant.

"Stirling," I said, more quietly, but he did not answer. "Stirling?"

I didn't know why I was trying. He never would answer, no matter how loud I called. But my brain had stopped ordering what I did. "Stirling?" I shouted. "Stirling!"

"Leo, stop shouting," Grandmother told me. And when she

227

said it, she began crying, and she turned to me, and she didn't look like herself anymore. And Father Dunstan didn't look like himself anymore. And I wasn't myself anymore. The only one of us who still looked the same was Stirling. And he was gone.

And that was why I wrote "the end." Because that was the end of everything.

I stood and stared at Stirling, and I fell down on my knees and went on trying to wake him, because my brain still did not realize it. But my heart did, and my stomach, and my lungs; they had all stopped working. I felt as if they were dissolving.

Stirling's hands were still warm. As if he might open his eyes and grin at me, with his uneven teeth and his freckles and his crew cut that was lighter than his skin. "He looks very calm," said Father Dunstan, crying too. "He was not in any pain; he slipped away peacefully."

I pressed my head down into the quilt and placed my hands on Stirling's. Eventually I said, "Why didn't you—?" And then I could not finish. I tried again. "Why didn't you send for me?"

"He passed away just a minute ago," said Father Dunstan. "He asked for you earlier, when he woke for a short while. We sent Maria to your school, but you were not there."

"Just . . . ," I began.

"Just a couple of minutes ago."

I dropped the bundle in my arms. The flower fell to the ground and lay there silently; that was all. So I ran into the living room, picked up a chair, and threw it at the window. The glass shattered, and I heard shouts from outside when it fell. "Leo!" Grandmother was exclaiming in a frightened voice. "Leo, what is wrong with you?" Father Dunstan got up. I tried to overturn the table, but he ran in and caught my wrist before

I could. He held on to me while I struggled. "Calm down, Leo," he said. "It's all right to feel this way—to feel like destroying everything. It is perfectly normal."

But I did not want to react in a normal way. Because this was not a normal thing; it did not happen to everyone else. That was why I punched Father Dunstan.

I had not meant to hit him hard. But he fell back onto the table, sending the newspapers flying from it like a cascade of leaves in the wind. One of the legs broke and it crashed onto the floor beneath him. "Leo!" cried Grandmother. "Leo!"

The priest got to his feet, one hand over the side of his face. "It's all right," he said. "I am all right." He had let my wrist go. Then I was back in the bedroom, and Stirling was lying so still, like he was sleeping, and the flower was there on the floorboards. I crushed it under my foot.

And suddenly I didn't know what to do. I had been following my anger like an actor's part; I did not know what else to do. I turned around once, my hands over my face. And then I was punching and kicking the wall, while all the time my heart was cold and stunned. "Leo, don't!" Grandmother was gasping through her sobs. "Oh, Leo, Leo, don't." She tried to pull me round to face her. I shouted back but I don't know what I said.

"Calm down," Father Dunstan said. "Just calm down, Leo."

Grandmother sunk to the floor beside the crushed flower. "Leo . . . was this . . . ? Leo . . . ?"

And suddenly I could not reply.

"It was the Bloodflower?" said Grandmother. "It was the Bloodflower." Her face collapsed with tears. "Leo!" she wailed. "Oh, Leo! Leo! Why did you not run faster? Oh, if only you had run faster."

"Mrs. North," said Father Dunstan gently. "Margaret. It was not anyone's fault. No one is to blame for this." Grandmother clutched to him, her back bent, and sobbed. "No one is to blame. No one can change what God intends." And then he was talking about the flower, how it would have had to be prepared, how this might not be the Bloodflower anyway and it looked to him like the wrong color, how when you were in difficult circumstances it was easy to mistake what you saw.

I wanted to shout and scream at him as loud as I could, but as loud as I could would not be loud enough. And I felt as if there were so few words. So I stopped talking.

I looked at Stirling, and I wished it was only him and me here, without Grandmother's hysterical crying or Father Dunstan's misguided wisdom. There were too many people. I could not think. I needed silence. I wanted to tell them to leave us alone. But I didn't speak. Eventually Father Dunstan helped Grandmother up and they went out and shut the door.

I fell down beside Stirling and touched his face. His skin was cooling. "Oh . . . no . . . no . . . ," I whispered. "Stirling, wait." I pulled the covers up around his face desperately, trying to keep him warm, trying to stop his spirit from drifting away. But it was already gone. I caught my arms around his neck and sobbed. "Please, Stirling. You can't leave me. I'll die, Stirling, I'll die."

And then I did a strange thing. I hugged him so tightly that my heart was beating against his silent chest. I closed my eyes and imagined that my heartbeat was bringing him back. I concentrated so hard that everything slid away, and the only thing was the one heartbeat, going on and on, in a circle. I wasn't breathing, but I wasn't holding my breath either. The only thing that was left in the whole earth was the heartbeat. And then I saw myself beside the bed, with Stirling in my arms, and I was drifting away. I was dying. And he was coming back.

Then I thought my head had exploded. My whole body was shaking, and my teeth were rattling uncontrollably, and I landed on the floor. My brain throbbed against my skull, and I reached out for Stirling, but I was too far away.

And there was nothing that I could do. My powers were not enough to save him.

I couldn't move. My brain had come disconnected from my body. I dragged myself a couple of inches across the floor and caught Stirling's hand and lay there, gripping it, while it grew as hard and cold as marble. And then I passed out.

I dreamed that everything that had ever existed was dissolving into Nothing. Nothing is not darkness. Nothing is further than darkness. There was no earth; no sun or moon, no stars, no magic; no heaven, no hell; no demons, no angels—there was no God—only Nothing.

Then Grandmother's crying woke me, and it was worse than the dream, because it was real. I came back and felt the floorboards under me. I was still here beside Stirling's bed in the cold daylight, the flower crushed and Stirling gone. "What happened?" she was saying, shaking me by the shoulders. "We only left you for a few minutes. Leo, what is it?" But I would not answer her.

I did not speak again. That night Stirling was laid out in an open coffin and carried to the church so that we could keep the vigil there. There was nothing between him and the stars as we processed across the quiet square. At the church, we all stood about him in silence. Almost the whole congregation was there. Maria cried all evening—I could see her at the other side of the room—and I hated her for it, because I couldn't cry. I just stood and looked at Stirling and did not speak and thought of nothing.

I had to look at Stirling. Otherwise, it didn't seem real. I felt as if there was someone missing, and he would come running in and reach up to catch my arm and grin at me. But how could he while he lay there so still in the coffin?

For a moment, when I looked at Stirling's face, I saw myself lying there. I thought I was losing my mind. But it was only that he looked like me. A part of him was the same as me. A part of me was dead. But it didn't feel like part. It felt like the whole of me. What did I have without Stirling?

At dawn we returned to the house to put on our clothes for the burial. He had to be buried between five o'clock and sunrise. I thought we should refuse and give him a proper morning burial, but I did not speak. "Stirling's soul is already in heaven," said Father Dunstan. "He is at God's right hand whether we bury him before dawn or after; I am certain of it."

"Wear your army uniform," said Grandmother to me. She was still crying, and her nose was running like a baby's. I almost spoke then; I almost shouted that Stirling would hate it if I wore my army uniform, but I clamped my mouth shut and went and put on ordinary black clothes. "Please, Leo," she said. "Stirling would have liked to see you looking smart—not like that. Anyone who sees you will think you do not care." I dug my fingernails into my hands until they bled, and remained silent.

"Please speak to me, Leo," she said. "Why so quiet? I'm so alone, Leo. I feel so alone, and my heart is breaking." I turned away; it was time to leave, anyway.

When I had tried to bring Stirling back, everything had slipped away from me, and it was still distant. My brain wasn't working well enough to tell me to feel anything at all. I felt dull, like I wasn't real. Like nothing was real. I wanted to cry so badly, but I couldn't. Outside in the alley I crashed my head against the wall. For a second I was aware of nothing but the pain in my head and the darkness that veiled my eyes.

"Leo, what are you doing?" Grandmother exclaimed, trying to stop me. I had not seen her come out the door. "Leo! Stop!" I put my hand up to my head and fell back against the wall. "You will harm yourself." She tried to look into my eyes. "Don't do that." I shut them.

She held my hand as we walked to the church. I wished that she wouldn't. It held me down in reality. But still I didn't cry. The longer you go without crying, the harder it is to do.

I felt as if maybe this was a joke. Or a dream. Or maybe we'd all made a mistake, and he was still breathing. Or maybe I was only imagining that he was dead, and he'd run along the street and put his hand in mine, and we'd walk to Mass together—me, Grandmother, and Stirling. But he didn't. And every second that he didn't, I felt as if something important was out of its place, and I could not rest until I had brought it back. Stirling wasn't where he belonged. He was alone in a coffin, in the darkness of the church, not here with Grandmother and me.

We stood at the side of the coffin when it was closed for the last time. When the coffin bearers picked up the lid to put it on again, I raised my hand and they held it. I had not had time to say goodbye to him forever. I went on looking at his face, desperately, but Father Dunstan gestured to them and they put the lid down anyway. "You will not forget him, Leo," he said. But already I was.

We processed to the graveyard as the gray light of dawn diffused into the indigo sky in front of us. Father Dunstan went first; then the servers from the church, in procession; then the deadpan coffin bearers with Stirling; then Grandmother and me—which was all the family party. There should have been relatives, but there were only us two. Mother and Father were far away, maybe dead, Aldebaran dead, Grandmother's parents dead; Great-uncle Harold dead; and if Great-uncle Harold had any relatives, they were in England, if it really existed. Or dead.

There was silence in the procession, except for our hushed footfalls, and Grandmother's soft crying like rain, and the rhythmic clink as the burning incense swung from side to side on its chain. It rose in claws about us. Its strong perfume was sharp in the back of my throat, and in my eyes and my nostrils. The two flames of the acolytes' candles blushed feebly through the mist and the darkness ahead of us. Occasionally someone coughed or let out a breath tentatively, and the silence would fall all the more oppressively after that.

I was angry with myself for being so slow to realize what had happened. Stirling's dead, I kept repeating, over and over in my head. Stirling's dead. Stirling's dead. But I repeated it like a rhyme and forgot its meaning. And I kept looking for him in the procession. Maybe he'd just marched ahead, humming to himself. Maybe we'd catch him up.

The coffin bearers slowed when we reached the steep hill that led down to the Victoire Bridge. The coffin slanted, and I thought of Stirling, in the dark inside it, sliding down. I wished I could tell them to be careful.

At the bottom of the hill, beside the Zenithar Armaments factory, two young soldiers stood talking and laughing. They stopped abruptly, taking off their hats and pressing them to their chests, casting their eyes down as we passed. I suddenly hated them so much, because they were like me but their brothers were not dead, and they could laugh like that as though the world was still ordinary.

One of the soldiers looked up, the smile still fading from his face, and I realized that it was Seth Blackwood from school. It was another five minutes before I wondered why he was dressed in a private's uniform, on guard duty for the army, but by then we were far past them.

Stirling was buried farther round the outside ring of the graveyard than the other coffin that we had seen buried before. I thought of that day, when he had spelled out "Aldebaran" and stamped on the grave to hear a coffin echo. And when he asked me if I was scared, and pressed close behind me when the priest came through the arch, like I could protect him because I was his big brother. That was Stirling. That was who we were burying. Not the peaceful, dead Stirling, who looked like he was sleeping, but the living, breathing, laughing Stirling—the one who wanted to be a priest and tried to teach himself to read from the newspaper.

At the head of the pit, there was already a small wooden cross, marked *Stirling Gabriel North*. That's his middle name. Gabriel. Was his middle name. And the dates below it—only eight years, and already in the past. This was the end. His life was cut off here, like a story that stopped in the middle, and it would never continue, and Stirling North would never be on this earth again.

I wanted to cry like I had out in the hills, uncontrolled and wild. I wanted to cry so hard that I could not think, until all the sadness was out, but I could not. I just stared silently, dry-eyed, while Father Dunstan spoke a prayer over the coffin, and Grandmother and I stood alone at the side of the grave. He read from the scriptures, but I did not listen to the words. Then the coffin was lowered into the ground. Grandmother cast a handful of earth into the grave and motioned to me, and I did the same. The lumps of soil burst and scattered on the new wood of the coffin, and the grave was filled in swiftly as the procession returned to the church and dawn rose. But I remained where I was.

"Come, Leo," said Grandmother as the rain started. It began suddenly, without warning. The grave digger had left, the grave was compacted and covered with turf, and everyone had gone. I was thinking of nothing, just staring at the grave and the cross with Stirling's name on it. "Come, let us go home." But there was no home without Stirling; there was nothing without him; he was the only one I cared about in this world.

I could stay here beside the grave forever. Until I died of tiredness or thirst or starvation, and then I could be buried here too, in the next grave, and I would never have to leave Stirling. But all flesh rots away, and graves are sometimes moved, and who could tell what would happen to this graveyard in the future? And even if I was buried in the cold, dark earth beside him, he was not here. I could never reach him. But still, I felt as if he was. And I didn't want to leave him here in the dark by myself.

An ache that was too much to bear was rising in my chest. I looked around, and Nothing was coming up over the walls, like the hands of ghosts, and the rain in the air was shivering, and the ground was tipping so that there was nothing that could stop me from falling off. I dropped down onto the grave and began scrabbling in the earth, as if to dig it up.

Then Grandmother had hold of me, trying to pull me to my feet. "Leo! Leo, please. I need you. Don't lose your mind." The ghosts vanished, and the earth righted itself, and the rain fell so hard that it hurt. I turned and followed her.

As we got farther and farther away from the graveyard, I felt that a cord was being stretched taut—a cord that ran between my heart and Stirling's grave. The farther away we got, the tighter it grew, and the more painful. I could actually feel it— real pain aching in my chest. I never understood until then what people meant when they said their heart was breaking.

✦

When I came upstairs from the bathroom later that morning, Grandmother looked up from her sewing and called out, "Stirling?" I walked into the range of her searching eyes. "Oh, Leo," she said. "But where is my little one? Where is my Stirling?" I wouldn't talk. I just looked at her. But she wasn't looking at me. "Dead and buried?" she said, though I had said nothing. "What—has it been six years?" She was talking to someone in the space between me and her, but there was no one there.

Then her eyes caught me, and she came back from wherever she had been. "It's barely three hours," she murmured. Tears brimmed from her eyes. "Oh, Leo, I forgot—how could I forget? I don't know what happened."

She was clutching at something that was lying across the arm of the chair. I went to her side and looked at it. "For little Stirling's First Communion," she said, holding it up. It was a patchwork quilt, nearly finished, and she was sewing in the last square. The outside squares were embroidered with a pattern of birds and leaves, and the central ones with stars. That was what the squares of material had been, the ones I had seen her sewing all this while. "Oh, Leo!" she wailed. "How will we survive? How can we go on without him? How can we?" She crushed the quilt down in her lap and sobbed, rocking back and forth, her eyes unfocused. I walked around the room. I walked in circles, holding my breath each lap. That was all I had done since we had returned from the graveyard. I was losing my mind; I knew it. We both were.

Father Dunstan found us that way later: Grandmother still rocking and crying, me still pacing, though I broke off to open the door for him. The rain sheeted down behind the broken window. He'd had to leave to attend the service; it was the twenty-first of July, the day on which Stirling should have made his First Communion but instead was buried.

Father Dunstan arrived about one o'clock, and he cooked us some soup. Neither of us ate any. He spoke quietly with Grandmother, and I went on walking about the apartment. I could not concentrate on anything. I tried to look at the clock, but I couldn't tell what time it was from it. I tried to sit and look out the window, but I started up again and went on pacing. I couldn't do anything else.

I had been avoiding the bedroom, but I didn't want to talk to Father Dunstan, so I marched in there. Grandmother had laid the patchwork quilt on Stirling's too-neat bed. His Bible was on the cupboard next to it, and his army uniform was folded on the chair, next to mine. And his boots, at the end of his bed, stood exactly in line with each other, with the laces trailed out so that they didn't touch. His things looked just the same. But all their life had flown away with Stirling's spirit. The boots would not be worn, and the uniform would stay neat and folded, and the Bible would never be opened.

I sat down on my bed, picked up Stirling's gold christening bracelet, and traced the letters with my finger: *Stirling Gabriel North*. Stirling Gabriel North, eight years, eight months, a week, and two days. That was it. He could never be anything more than what he was then. As if he was frozen where his life ended. I cried then, for who he would never be. But I didn't cry for long. I couldn't. I lay on my bed and turned the bracelet around in my hands. And then I could not stay in the apartment any longer.

Grandmother called after me as I went down the stairs, and Father Dunstan said quietly, "Margaret, let him go." I did not know where I was going. I met no one on the stairs. The yard was deserted, except for the falling rain. I crossed to the bathroom and bolted the door behind me.

It was half dark already in there. I sat down on the grimy edge of the shower and rested my head against my knees. The rain outside was like a mournful tune, sounding different notes as it fell on the roofs and the mud and the rusted water pump and the old window ledges with the paint peeling. I could hear the baby from down here; he was repeating the same angry wail over and over. I shut my eyes. I sat there and wished with all my soul to be somewhere else. I could not stand any longer being Leo North; it was too much. I was scared that my heart would break, really break, if I thought again about Stirling.

I couldn't pray to God, so I prayed to Aldebaran. I prayed to him to take me to another place, as though he was an angel who could save me now. I concentrated all my mind on it, and all my powers. A long time passed.

An hour or more I must have sat there without moving. Perhaps I fell asleep; I could not tell. But next thing I knew, I was dreaming. I could see mist in front of my eyes. I was certain that I was dreaming—that it was not real—but I knew more than anything that I did not want to wake. Fog was drifting like smoke around me, and I fought to keep it there. And then I could hear voices speaking from a long way off.

~~~~~~

Aldebaran forgot what he was doing and gazed into the mist that was thickening over the English hills. "What?" said Ryan, beside him.

"Nothing," said Aldebaran after a moment, bending his head over the engine of the old car. "Nothing. Try that again."

Ryan turned the key. The engine gave a shuddering cough. He leaned against the side of the car and shivered. "It is growing colder. The middle of July and it might as well be winter."

"English weather," said Aldebaran. "It is very—"

But Ryan never heard what he had been going to say about the

English weather, because he frowned, still gazing into the mist, and then bent over the engine again. "It is unpredictable," said Ryan. "Uncle, we are in the middle of the road; perhaps we should move the car."

Aldebaran did not answer.

A few yards away, beyond the mist, Anna was walking toward them. She had been lost on the hill for half an hour when she heard the car engine coughing and started toward the sound. The fog was clinging to her hair in droplets and she tried to brush it off now, shifting her grip on the suitcase with her other hand. The headlights were cutting beams through the mist. She could make out the dark shape of the car and two people, a middle-aged man and a boy moving beside it. The man looked up as she approached.

"Are you lost?" he said. "If you need directions we can probably help you." He went on looking at her thoughtfully, as though he recognized her.

An engine was approaching from somewhere. A motorbike appeared suddenly out of the mist and swerved to avoid the car, its tires screaming on the road. The man turned, startled, as it vanished again. "We should move the car. Ryan, help me."

The boy put his shoulder against the side of the car. Anna put down her suitcase and went to the other side, behind the man. "You are very kind," he said, turning to her. "Go carefully, and stop when I tell you. There is a steep drop a few feet farther on this side."

Across the roof of the car, the boy's eyes met Anna's. His were dark as water, close to black. Even after the car was resting safely on the verge, their eyes remained on each other's for a moment before they looked away. "You had best wait here for a while," the man told Anna. "Do not think about trying to go on. The road does not widen for a mile or more in either direction, and cars come up suddenly in this fog." She nodded. They waited in silence while the man bent over the engine again. Somewhere beyond the mist, a bird sang a few high notes.

"Where are you going?" the boy asked Anna then, leaning on the side of the car and fixing his dark eyes on her. "You must be on holiday, with that suitcase."

"No, I'm working. At Hillview Hotel, somewhere on the other side of the valley. My aunt runs it; I'm working for her."

"The manager of Hillview is your aunt?" said the boy. "She is our nearest neighbor; we know Monica Bailey well."

"Monica Devere," said Anna, without thinking. Bailey had been her aunt's married name and she never used it now.

The man straightened up suddenly and crashed his head against the raised hood of the car. "Monica Devere?" he asked her.

"Yes," said Anna. There was a silence. "Why do you want to know?"

"No reason." The man folded his arms and looked out into the mist, then turned back to her. "The Devere family have a history in this part of England, don't they?"

"I suppose. That's why Monica came back here: all our family used to live here."

The man nodded, his eyes still on her, then adjusted something in the engine and slammed down the hood. "Should you not be in school?" he said. "How old are you?"

"Fifteen. It finished yesterday. It finished for the summer, so I came up here."

"I am not at school," said the boy. "My uncle teaches me at

home." He ran a hand through his black hair. The way he did it was careless and nearly arrogant. He held out his hand. "I'm glad to meet you. Ryan Donahue. My uncle is Arthur."

"Arthur Field," said the man, taking her hand in turn. She shook his hand, then wiped the oil off her fingers. "Sorry," said Arthur Field. "Anyway, I am glad to meet you."

"But I have not asked you what your name is," said Ryan.

"It's Anna."

"That would be Ariana originally?" said the man. He wiped his hands on a rag, then threw it into the backseat of the car and straightened up with a faint smile.

Anna was staring at him in silence. "How did you know?" she said eventually. "It's only on my birth certificate."

"Just a lucky guess."

The boy touched her arm, making her start. "You must not let my uncle worry you," he said. "He likes to pretend to be a mind reader. But where we come from, every Anna is an Ariana. It is one of the old names there."

She nodded, but she was not entirely convinced. There was something about this man. He had turned back to the car, and they both watched him in silence. "It will work this time," he said. "This will be the time." He turned the key. The engine coughed, and coughed again, and rattled to life. "And the fog is clearing at last," he said, leaving the engine running. He went to the edge of the verge and looked out into the expanse of white.

Anna glanced around. It looked as dense as ever, blurring even the wall at the other side of the road. And then suddenly it was drifting backward. A tree emerged, and a rock. And a few minutes later, the edge of a stretch of water was glinting far below them, and hills appeared against the sky.

Someone was hammering on the door of the bathroom. I raised my head from my knees and came back. It was raining hard outside. "Leo?" someone was calling. It was Father Dunstan's voice.

I opened the door and blinked at him. "You look exhausted," he said. "Were you asleep?" I did not know. I had been dreaming I was far away from here, but everything was coming back to me now. Stirling.

I caught hold of the door frame to keep myself steady. "You have not slept properly in days, after all," Father Dunstan was saying. Grandmother was beside him, peering at me anxiously through the tears in her eyes. "Leo, listen. There is a man here—" said Father Dunstan.

"Is this the boy?" said someone else, whose voice I did not recognize. I looked up and saw that a soldier was standing at the edge of the yard. He approached me now, blinking against the rain. "Are you Leonard North?"

I nodded. "Sorry about this," he said, turning to Grandmother, the priest, and then back to me. "You have been called up to report for military service."

❧

I just looked at him, still confused. He was holding out a uniform, asking me to put it on, and trying to hand me a rifle. "What?" exclaimed Grandmother, panicking already. "What are you talking about?"

"Have you not read the newspapers?" he said.

We all looked at him in silence. "Due to the heavy casualties at the border, we have had to pull out all the troops we can spare from elsewhere. As a result, we are obliged to bring in cadets from all major cities to fill in the vacant posts."

"You cannot send children to fight your war for you," said Father Dunstan. That was the only time I ever heard him out-spoken about anything.

"No, no," said the man. "You misunderstand me. None of the cadets will be fighting; they are only carrying out simple duties—guarding the gates, running messages, patrolling the city, and so on. I assure you, they will not see frontline action. And the only cadets we are bringing in are Ninth Year pupils, who are almost ready to join the army anyway. We need to free the privates who are currently carrying out these duties, so that they can fight. I know this is regrettable, but—"

"He buried his brother only this morning," said Father Dunstan in an undertone. I still heard it. "Can you expect him to go now?"

The soldier tried to apologize to me, but I turned away. "If he speaks to the sergeant, I am sure he will be released," he said to Father Dunstan. "We are not strictly enforcing conscription in circumstances like this. If Leonard puts this uniform on, just for formality, and speaks to the sergeant—"

It was too loud suddenly, and I didn't want to hear any of this. I took the uniform from him and went upstairs to put it on. I could still hear Father Dunstan arguing with the private, but at least it was quieter in the apartment.

I put on the uniform. There was what looked like a bullet hole in the jacket. I wondered if they had taken it off a dead man. I didn't care. Seeing Stirling's christening bracelet where I had left it, I picked it up and put it onto my arm, sliding it up so that it lay beneath my own and the names Leonard Joseph

North and Stirling Gabriel North were together. It was all right, because I had been told to do something and now I was doing it. There was no choice about it, and no thought. It was still raining; I picked up my overcoat and put that on too.

They were standing in the hall when I went down. "Where are you taking them?" Father Dunstan was asking.

"I cannot tell you," said the private. "This is a confidential operation; I cannot tell you where troops will be deployed."

"The border?" cried Grandmother. "It is the border, isn't it? You cannot take him! He will catch silent fever, and he will die. Please, keep him in the city."

The private was trying to reassure her, but she went on wailing. "Sergeant Daniros will probably send him straight back," the man said. "Come out and speak to him now."

I went to the door and the man followed, Grandmother and Father Dunstan behind us. A group of soldiers were huddled against the front wall of the building, trying to shelter from the rain that gusted in all directions. There were about twenty—cadets, like me, but wearing privates' uniforms. "Leonard North?" said a man—the sergeant—looking down at a soaked piece of paper.

The other soldier nodded. "That is him. Sir, this boy—"

"I want you to fetch the others and catch us up," the sergeant interrupted. "We are running late. Go now. Here is the list."

The private glanced at me, then hurried off through the rain. The sergeant turned to us. Grandmother was clinging to my arm, openly crying. "I will not let him go!" she told the sergeant. "I will not."

"I really feel that Leonard would be better off here in the

city," began Father Dunstan, stepping close to the sergeant. "The circumstances are such that—"

"I do not want to hear about your circumstances," said the sergeant. "We have had these scenes at every bloody house."

"But, sir—" began Father Dunstan again.

"Listen," said the sergeant. "The boy is perfectly willing to come. If he does not want to join us, we can talk about your circumstances then. If he wants to come with us, there is nothing further to discuss. North, are you willing to join up?"

They all looked at me in silence. I glanced from Grandmother, tears and rain running together down her face, to Father Dunstan, who still looked as if he would argue. I turned back to the sergeant and he took it for consent. "Good," he said, and clapped his hands. "Then let's go. Come on, boys."

I hesitated, then followed them. Grandmother was wailing behind us, and some of them glanced back, avoiding my eyes. At the corner I turned for a moment, and she took a few steps toward me, reaching out like a child. "Hurry, will you?" shouted the sergeant. I followed him.

Perhaps I should have spoken to him. Perhaps I should have refused to go. But the private, when he reappeared, seemed to have forgotten it. And I would not speak. I could not. So there was nothing I could do. That was why I left. I had no choice.

Morale was low in the small group. We did not even march in file, just walked in a dejected trail. I lagged some way behind. The other boys were apprehensive. The sergeant and the private were edgy. We walked around the castle and out across the North Bridge. The river was heaving with milky brown water, and for a second it made me feel as though I was going to fall. And then I stopped thinking about that. Outside the city, the sergeant stopped and surveyed us. "Boys, I will not lie to you," he said. "We are going to the Alcyrian border."

The others muttered and glanced at each other, but I felt nothing. They resumed their dejected walk, and I followed in silence. I had prayed to be somewhere else. And here I was, on the road to the border.

❧

*W*e must have walked for hours, because when I looked up, the sky was growing dark. The clouds were still low, and the copper light and the heavy atmosphere made my head ache. After a while the clouds began to roll away, back toward the city, and we caught up with the weak evening sunlight. The rays were cutting down onto golden fields. I had never seen a corn-field until that day. I remember that part of the journey. Nearly all the rest has gone forever.

I was thinking of nothing. I stared ahead and saw only what was there and made nothing more of it. It was the way to sur-vive. I could pretend that I was someone else, because I had nothing that reminded me of who I was; I was walking through a landscape I had never been in before, with none of my belong-ings and no one I knew or had ever met. Only the weight of the extra bracelet on my arm reminded me that I'd ever had a brother called Stirling, or that I had ever been Leo North, or that I had a grandmother at home who might wonder where I was.

At some point while we were walking, I began to cry. I had forgotten for an instant that Stirling was dead, and when I remembered, suddenly I was so frightened, and it seemed so real. More real than it had before, even when I had seen him lying in the coffin.

The boys sneaked embarrassed glances at me, turning their faces hastily away and whispering to each other. I went on crying, and they pretended they couldn't hear. But then one of them, a boy with a silver tooth, dropped back from the group and fell in beside me. The tears in my eyes made his tooth glint like a star. "Are you scared about going to the border?" he asked. I shook my head wearily, looking away from him. He was silent for a moment while I tried to stop crying and he tried to think of something to say. Then he was asking if I was tired or ill. I did not reply. "Do you speak?" he said. I shook my head. "Are you a mute or what?" I shook my head again. He did not question it. "I guess we will reach Ositha soon," he said. "It is getting late."

I had thought that we were going to the border, but I realized then that it was too far to walk in one day. The sound of the explosions and gunfire was still faint. It was growing darker. The sky, patterned in shreds of dark blue and pink, was lying reflected in the puddles along the road. The reflections looked more real than reality, and the puddles were so close together that it was like looking at one large picture through windows in the ground. I imagined that I was looking into a different world—into heaven, where Stirling was. Maybe I'd catch a glimpse of him through one of the windows.

But they were just puddles. I marched straight through them, and the light in the water vanished. When I looked up, the boy was walking ahead again, and he didn't look back.

At first I had just wanted to get away. Away from Grandmother's crying, and Stirling's empty bed, and sanctimonious

Father Dunstan. And I had got away from those things, and I was glad of it, but what I hadn't got away from was the ache in my heart. Still, I was glad to be walking. I began to think that just walking would stop me from falling or realizing that Stirling was gone. I wished we could go on all night, but the gray lump of the barracks was in sight already. Then I grew tired and I stopped thinking. A strange sort of calm fell.

A line of carts came up over the crest of the road. We stood to one side to let them pass, and I thought at first that they were filled with sleeping people all piled on top of each other. But then I realized that they were dead—dead bodies, still in their uniforms.

"Silent fever," I heard the sergeant say. "It's the only thing that's killing them. They sit in the mud all day waiting to catch it. It's not a war. A hundred men shot a week, and most of them by accident. We don't need the cadets. Bloody waste of time bringing in kids."

I listened. It was something to fix my mind on to stop it from drifting. "If you ask me," said the private, "Lucien is only pulling the cadets out of the cities for fear they will revolt. They are the ones who are not being paid for their obedience to the government. And with these revolutionary groups gaining strength . . ." He must have gone on, but I did not hear.

We walked a way farther. The sun had almost set. The private was telling the sergeant that if he was Lucien, he would get out of the country. "Last time there was an atmosphere like this, the king ignored it," he said. "And next thing, he was dead."

My mind was drifting away. I tried to force myself to listen rather than think. "People are hauling in that old prophecy again," the sergeant said. "The atmosphere is full of rumors. Is that what you mean?"

"The lord Aldebaran is communicating with the revolutionaries," said the private. "It is not just rumor—it is fact."

And then I was back with Stirling, walking through the snow that day when we had talked about Aldebaran and the prince. And I started to realize that things would never be like that again. Tears were rising in my eyes. I willed them not to fall, and went on trailing after the others. We were in the town now. We passed through an empty square where cannons were standing in rows, then a waste ground turned into a shooting range with half a house still standing at one side. The wind was wailing through the gutted building.

There was an atmosphere of disquiet in that strange town. Horses shifted and puffed steam in the damp evening air, and the men who walked around did not talk or smile. There were Malonian flags everywhere, grubby and damp, and they flapped like sickening birds against the buildings. Reaching a small house, we stopped. "All right, boys," said the sergeant. "You will stay here tonight. We will be at the inn down the road." He pushed the door open and led us into the deserted room. The floor was covered in dust, which was swirled all around where people must have lain before. I traced those shapes in my mind while the sergeant was talking.

Time must have passed, because darkness had fallen completely and the sergeant and the private were gone. The others were spreading out blankets on the floor. I stood still at the back window, and the other boys paid me no attention, except for casting uneasy glances at me from time to time. Someone lit a candle. I watched the reflections in the glass. The boy who had spoken to me earlier, his silver tooth glinting in the dusky room, was showing off a pistol that he had brought. A couple of the others lifted their rifles and aimed them at each other, laughing, then tried to fire at the wall, only to find they were not loaded. They had not given us bayonets either; the sergeant was evidently more thoughtful than he seemed. "This is loaded," the boy assured the others, holding the pistol sideways along his palm. They looked suitably impressed.

He slept with the pistol in his hand. The candle had run down to the ground and it was too dark to find another. Eventually the last whispers died away, and when I turned from the darkened window, I saw that they were all asleep. I had not even taken my rifle off my back. I shivered in my damp clothes. I stood there and watched the stars come out.

The heavy silence, and the coldness of the stars, and the dismal, shadowy room were dispiriting. But at least I was alone. I stood at the window and cried, not madly but silently, and partly because of those cold white stars, and I felt quite calm. As if I could cope. As if I could already see the way forward.

It was stupid to think it. I turned, and the sleeping boys reminded me of Stirling sleeping at the other side of the room at home. And then I really cried. Not for who Stirling might have been, or who he used to be, or the part of me that was lost, but for who he was—Stirling, my brother. Because I felt so desperate, and more than anything I wanted someone to comfort me, and the one who I wanted was Stirling. He was so far away.

My breath came in fast sobs that shook my whole body, and I pressed my hand to my mouth and sunk to the floor. I sat slumped against the wall and cried, letting out wavering wails like an animal. I didn't care how stupid I sounded or if any of the other boys would wake. I think you can quickly get to a point where you're so unhappy you just don't care about anything anymore.

If only I had run faster. Why had I not run faster? If only I could go back in time and run faster; I could have, but I had thought I was safe. Then, in the dark room, I realized that no one is ever safe. I could have run faster, and I didn't. If only, if only I had. Why had God not warned me to run faster? But there wasn't a God. And Stirling wasn't there to tell me that there was.

He was nothing but gentle and good, all the days of his life. And I never told him that he meant anything to me. I never told him that I loved him. I was a poor brother to little Stirling. Alone in the darkness, I remembered every cruel thing I'd ever said to him. I hadn't thought of him dying before I could take them back.

Tears coursed down my face, over my mouth, and onto the collar of my coat as if they would not stop. Even when I pressed my eyelids tightly together, they ran through my eyelashes and went on falling.

Stirling was so good, and I was so bad, and now I was left while he was gone. I wished that I was the dead one. Or else that I was dead too. Then maybe—maybe—we could be together. And even if we were not together, perhaps I could stop being and just lie there in the earth. Perhaps I could stop thinking. That was the only thing I really wanted. I could see nothing else in my bleak future.

When I stopped crying, it was beginning to get light. My cheeks stung with the bitter tears that were still lying on them. A dismal calm had descended on me; it was worse than wild grief, because it would endure forever. I could feel it in my stomach, in my head, in my very bones. I was too tired to move. I looked at my reflection in the window, a stranger looking back from the glass.

I had not stopped crying for any reason I could understand. The sadness in my heart was no easier to bear than it had been before. It was strange, because I suddenly felt so weary of being unhappy. I wished that I didn't have to cry. I wished that I could laugh. I wished that I could worry about inconsequential things like whether I had to be a soldier. I wished that I could flirt with Maria. I couldn't understand it exactly, only that the old Leo— the Leo who was dead now—wanted to do all those things, but the ghost that was left behind didn't have the heart or the strength to do anything at all. I would never be doing those things now. I felt far removed from everything I used to be. And then I remembered that it had been less than two days, and I felt so desperate I wished I was dead.

Very quietly, I moved. My muscles were stiff from standing so long in wet clothes, but I managed to limp across the room to where the boy with the silver tooth lay. I knelt down beside him and watched him breathing slowly in and out, and my breathing slowed to match his. Then I put my hand on the gun. It was a Delmar .45—the army pistol.

I prized it from his fingers, took off the safety catch and cocked it, then got up and went back to the window. I stood with my back to the light and pointed it at each of the boys in turn. I don't know why I did that. Then I closed my eyes and imagined dying—pain for a moment, and then nothing; escaping from this, from everything, into white silence.

I held the gun to the side of my head. I was not frightened.

And the weight had lifted off my heart, and I didn't feel as if Stirling was dead anymore. I felt as if I was fighting against God—against God and his plan for my life. And then someone spoke. It was me, but it sounded like someone else, and I couldn't tell if it was out loud or in my own head. "Even if you're dead," said the voice, "Stirling still will be too." But I won't know it, I thought. I won't know anything. There will be nothing. "Hell comes after death," said the voice. But I didn't believe in that.

And then I saw Grandmother crying as I turned my back on her and walked away into the rain. And suddenly I changed my mind.

Someone pushed the door open. It was the sergeant, looking the worse for his night at the inn, clutching his head and carrying a bag of food. He caught my eye, and I caught his. Then, slowly, I took the gun from my head and pointed it at him.

He stared at me silently. He dropped the bag and made the slightest move for the pistol at his side, identical to the one in my hand. I made a move, even slighter, with my head, to tell him not to. He stayed still. I gripped the gun more tightly, with both hands, so that it would hold steady. He didn't believe I would do it. If he had, he would have gone for the pistol. He thought I was joking. I thought I might be too—I was not sure.

There was irritation in his face, but also a hint of what was almost amusement. As if I was a child dragging a game out far too long. It reminded me of how my father had looked one time when I was about five years old, when I stole his expensive watch and ran round with it, sick with laughter, while he got later and later and didn't know whether to laugh or shout or chase me. I was angry because he had to go out to an interview almost every day that month, when *The Sins of Judas* was published. I kept running, because once I'd gone so far with the game, I couldn't go back. And then my mother gave him her watch and he jogged off down the street, and when he turned to wave, I saw that he looked tired and he wasn't smiling. The laughter died in my throat and I wished I'd given it to him to begin with.

I came back abruptly from my thoughts and tightened my hold on the pistol. Then I think the sergeant realized I was serious.

We stared at each other. Then, "Put that down," he breathed, quiet as ice. I pulled the trigger.

⚜

*T*he gunshot surprised me with its loudness, and the recoil made me stumble. The other boys woke at once, shouting out. I opened my eyes and saw the sergeant again and expected him to sway and go down like a felled tree. He looked as if he expected it too. But he didn't move. A lump of plaster dropped from the wall, and I saw where the bullet had really struck— three or four feet wide. I was not used to firing this type of gun; I would not have missed with a Maracon rifle.

There was silence in the room while everyone stared at me and I went on grinning stupidly. "I could get you imprisoned for attempted murder," said the sergeant, his voice high. "Do you know that?"

"The hell you could," said the loud voice in my head, "while

I still have the gun." But I didn't say it out loud. I walked toward him without lowering the pistol. They were trained to get to their weapons quickly. I watched for a sudden movement. But everyone was still. It was like walking through a gallery of statues.

I was within a few steps of the sergeant, and I nodded to him to move away from the door. He did it. I went out, and then I lowered the gun, turned, and walked off. He could shoot, and I knew it. I braced myself for a bullet in the back of the head at every step, but none came. "He took my pistol," I heard the boy with the silver tooth complaining in the house behind me.

"Shut your mouth," the sergeant growled. "I swear to God, the blood of whoever he takes it into his head to shoot now is as much on your hands as his."

"He's sick," the boy said. "There is something mentally wrong with him. He's possessed by a demon."

Then I realized what I had done. I started laughing, feeling the fear rise like a prickling current in the air from the house that I had left. I laughed and laughed, falling down on my knees in the street. Men passed me, staring, but I could not see them properly.

When I opened my watering eyes, the sergeant's voice came quickly behind me. "Don't move." I tried to turn anyway, but he fired a shot. "The next will be in your head, so stay still if you value your life." I didn't value my life, or I never would have tried to shoot him. But there is something frightening about a gunshot, something that makes you freeze automatically. He stepped forward and kicked the pistol from my hand. I did not even try to catch it as it fell.

"Pick up the gun," the voice in my head was shouting. But I couldn't. It looked like a dead insect lying there on the ground, with its shining black barrel and the crisscrosses on the butt, like a fly's wing case.

"Stay where you are," said the sergeant. He was tying up my hands. I tried to turn. "Don't move," he told me warningly, and pressed the gun to my back as he pulled the knot tight about my wrists. "Stand up," he told me then. I did it.

Footsteps were approaching behind us. "What's going on here?" It was the private.

"He tried to shoot me," muttered the sergeant. The private laughed incredulously. "It is not a joke." The sergeant bent and looked into my face. "You will be in prison for this. You do understand that? You will be imprisoned for this crime."

I did not answer. I had heard about the military prison in Ositha.

"Perhaps you are being too hard on him, sir," said the private. "Perhaps he did not mean to shoot. He is probably still in shock. I was surprised you brought him at all."

"In shock?" said the sergeant.

"You know," the private said, lowering his voice. "After what happened with his brother."

"What did happen with his brother? Because this boy has not told me."

There was a silence between them. I looked at the floor. Then the private was explaining.

"Hey, don't cry," he said, turning to me. My nose was running, but I couldn't do anything about it because my hands were tied. "He should be with his family," said the private. "This is a misunderstanding, and I am partly to blame."

The sergeant forced me to meet his eyes. "You should have told me," he said. "I wouldn't have made you come if you'd told me."

I looked away. They went on arguing, but I did not listen. Then the sergeant was speaking again with his face close to mine. "Listen. Whatever the circumstances, you are guilty of attempted murder. That is final. I'm sorry."

I did not know what that meant. I sat down on the floor and closed my eyes. "Watch him," he told the private quietly, and went to get the other boys ready to leave for the border. The boy with the silver tooth was still complaining that I had taken his gun, but the sergeant ignored him.

It was then I realized that the pistol was still lying at my feet. I opened my eyes.

The sergeant was inside the small house, with his back to me. I glanced at the private. He was sitting on the doorstep of one of the deserted houses, studying his clasped hands. I wondered if he was paralyzed with guilt because he had forgotten to tell the sergeant about what had happened, or if he was thinking of something else entirely. I moved slightly. He did not look up. And then I decided to escape and get back to Kalitzstad. And the weight lifted from my heart.

I was remembering a trick I used to practice when I was a little boy. I clenched my fists and imagined the ropes dissolving from around my wrists. I concentrated so hard that for a moment I could not see. The knots loosened. I went on forcing them outward. I stopped thinking of anything but getting my hands free. I could move my wrists now. I stopped and breathed again.

But once I had stopped, I felt suddenly as if I would fall. I remembered that Stirling was dead. I was so frightened of falling into Nothing. I told myself that if I got back to Kalitzstad, everything would be all right, and was only faintly surprised when I began to believe it. I shut my eyes and tried to stop my heart from beating so quickly. Then I held my breath and snapped every knot. The rope loosened, but I held it so that it did not fall.

The private glanced up. "Look," he said, in a low voice, "I really am sorry. I don't know what to do about this." I did not answer. He got up and paced away from me, down the street, and raised his hands to his face. In that moment, I moved. I picked up the gun.

The sergeant, suddenly at the door, shouted, "Saltworth, I told you to watch him!" He swore and took a step toward me.

This time I aimed properly. I shot the glass out of the windows of the house. The sergeant threw up his arms to cover his face, and the other boys were shouting and jostling to the door. I turned and ran.

❦

I could hear them shouting behind me, but I did not listen. I raced down a side alley, then cut across the yard of an inn and came out on a different street. I went on running. Soldiers turned briefly as I passed them, but they were all preoccupied and no one stopped me. I fought my way through an old barbed-wire fence and across a stretch of waste ground, and then I was running through the narrow streets again. Somewhere ahead a church bell was chiming. I could see the cross on the tower suddenly, and hills beyond that, and I ran in that direction. For some reason I could not get my arms and legs to work properly. I stumbled and fell more than once. But every time I stopped, I thought I heard shouting voices behind me, and that drove me on.

I came up to a fence, and beyond it was the churchyard. Soldiers were filing in at the gate, but I ran past them and dropped down on a stone seat beside the door. I could no longer hear shouting. I breathed out. My hands were bleeding from climbing through that barbed wire. I rubbed the palms against my trousers and shut my eyes.

When I opened them again, a young private was watching me with what looked like faint amusement. The other soldiers had gone into the church; he was the only one left. He lingered in the doorway. "Mass is about to start," he said. "You are not coming in?" I shook my head.

A hymn began inside, and it made me think of Stirling humming on the way back from church. And I realized that even if I got back to Kalitzstad, nothing would be all right again. I wished I had let them put me in prison. Sometimes physical hardship makes you forget to think. "Are you all right?" said the soldier, still watching me. "You seem troubled by something. You must be one of these cadets that they have called up suddenly."

The hymn finished and he glanced into the church but did not move from where he stood. "You are not religious?" he said, turning back to me. I shook my head again. "I'm not," he said. "But I'm going to the border. I want to go to Mass before I leave. Maybe that is bad religion." He shrugged. "I have a brother at home about your age," he went on. "He would be fifteen. He works down in the harbor. He promised to take care of my wife and my little girl."

I did not answer. My heart was beating so loudly that some of the time I could not hear him. He did not seem to notice. He hesitated, then sat down on the bench beside me, searching in his pocket. He took out a sheet of paper and smoothed it carefully. "My little girl drew this. She's only three but she can draw. Look." He began pointing out what the picture was supposed to be. I went on watching him in silence. I could barely follow what he was saying to me, but I did not want him to leave me here alone either. He traced each line of that child's drawing, then folded it and put it back into his pocket.

The psalm had started by the time he got up to go into the church. He looked at me for a moment then, frowning as though he had only just seen me properly. "Is that your gun?" he said. "They are giving the cadets pistols?" He frowned again, then shrugged. "To be honest with you, nothing would surprise me anymore, with this war. Let me see that."

He took the gun from me silently and examined it, then adjusted the safety catch. "Did they not teach you?" he said. "Leave that on. You don't want to have an accident." He handed it back. "Goodbye, then. I am glad I spoke with you." Then he turned and went into the church.

I waited for my heart to slow, but time passed and it didn't. Then I got to my feet and crossed the churchyard. I could see, beyond the fence, the lines of war graves, row on row of them, all identical. They stretched across the hills for a mile or more. I stopped at the fence, where the summer flowers and the long grass ended abruptly, and looked out over those endless graves. And then I looked beyond, across the cornfields and the marshes and the edge of the eastern hills. Kalitzstad, a hazy red island, was visible in the distance. I thought about climbing over the fence and walking back there.

And then I was on my knees in the grass, with the tears pouring down my face. The pain in my heart was so bad that I thought I was dying. I wondered if I really was. You can die just by wanting to be dead. We had a dog, when I was about four years old, that died like that. My parents sold its only puppy, and it just lay like a stone on its rug until one day it didn't wake up. That's what I felt like. As though if I let myself think about Stirling being dead, my heart would just stop beating.

And then someone spoke, close by. I turned. But I was alone. It was the Voice, speaking quite differently from how it had before. "If you get back to Kalitzstad, things will be all right," said the Voice. "If you get back to the city. You'll see." I was not even surprised at how loud it sounded. I did not care.

My legs were shaking, and I could barely keep hold of the gun, my hands were growing so weak. I don't know why I didn't let myself think about Stirling, but forced myself to get up, still crying, and climb over the fence and begin walking. For the same reason I froze when the sergeant fired that shot. Not because I valued my life, but because life still had possession of me.

As I stumbled across the open country, I asked the Voice to protect me, to take me somewhere else so that I did not have to think. I remembered that dream—the English mist, the girl, the prince, and Aldebaran. I wanted to go back to a time before Stirling was gone, or a place where none of us existed—not Stirling, or Grandmother, or the sergeant I had shot at, or even me, Leo North. I concentrated all my mind on it. And maybe it was because I was so tired, but I began to see things. Aldebaran, at a desk in that other country, leafing through papers. The prince standing beside him. The girl, Anna, dancing.

❧

"Ryan, you are not paying attention," said Aldebaran, pushing back his chair.

"What?" Ryan turned.

Aldebaran shut the book and went to stand beside him at the window. "What are you looking at?" he demanded.

"Just the hotel." Ryan pointed to the white stone building, a quarter of a mile away, along the shore of the lake. "I was thinking, Uncle. I'm sorry."

"Shall I read that to you again? I was going over the messages from our allies. I wanted your opinion on whether we should condone a campaign of sabotage or tell them to wait until your return to the country is imminent."

"Uncle, whatever I say, you will do what you yourself think best."

"That may be so, but I want your opinion. The time will come when you will have to rule alone. Ryan, you are not listening again."

"That girl we met . . . ," Ryan began. "Anna."

"What about her?"

"Why did you look at her like that? As though you recognized the name Devere."

Aldebaran sat down again and examined the pen in his hand without speaking. Then he said, "If I tell you, you will not pass it on to her. I know you have been there and spoken to her."

"I was passing on the road this morning, that was all."

"This is a serious matter. Do you understand? Not to be passed on."

The boy hesitated for a moment. Then he turned to Aldebaran and said, "Yes, Uncle. I understand."

Anna was spinning in the middle of the empty hotel dining room, and her eyes were on the window where Ryan stood. From this distance she could not see that he was there. But the glass was catching the sunlight, and she fixed her gaze on it to stop herself from moving from the spot. "Will you come and help me with this ironing?" Monica called from the kitchen, but Anna did not hear.

It was only when Monica took hold of her arm that she started and turned, landing hard on the floorboards. "Will you come and help me?" Monica repeated. Anna followed her.

In the corridor, guests were passing on their way out of the building. Daniel, the chef, was at the sink, washing the last sauce-pans from breakfast. "Is that where Ryan and his uncle live?" Anna asked. "That house you can just see on the edge of the lake."

"Yes, that's Lakebank," said Monica. "It's an old manor house. Here, take this. I'm trying to fix the kettle."

"A manor house?" said Anna, taking the iron from her. Monica examined the dismantled parts of the electric kettle strewn over the kitchen table. "Do you know them well?" said Anna.

"No one does. They keep to themselves. That's landed gentry for you."

"Is that what they are?"

"Apparently. Mr. Field is a sort of recluse, I think. Why else would you live in a big house like that, with gates ten feet high and all the rest? I speak to Ryan, though, when he passes. He's a polite boy. The uncle is strict with him."

"He seems like a strange man," said Anna.

"He's eccentric, but there is nothing wrong with him."

Daniel hung up his apron and picked up his car keys from the sideboard. "You will never fix that," he told Monica, leaning over her shoulder to look at the kettle. "You shouldn't have taken it apart yourself. Buy a new one—that's what I think. I'm going to Lowcastle; I will be back in a couple of hours." He turned and left the kitchen. Monica frowned after him, pushing her hair off her face. She had the same blond ringlets as Anna's mother; they caught the light now as she shook her head impatiently.

"What were we talking about?" she said. "Oh yes—Mr. Field. There is not much more to tell you. He has lived here fifteen or twenty years, they say, and he is a stranger to everybody."

⁓

*T*he Voice was telling me a story as I walked, in fragments and faint images that were hardly real. Perhaps I wanted so desperately to be somewhere else that my mind had conjured these things—the prince, the girl who was our English relative, Aldebaran as he appeared to a stranger. And after a while I grew too tired. All I could see now was what was there in front of me—the marsh and then the hills, deserted, with the wind sweeping over them. It was so bleak and empty that the tears ran down my face as I walked, and I thought of Stirling and no longer had the energy to stop myself. But I kept walking.

Eventually it grew so dark that I could not go on. I could see the lights in Kalitzstad, but I couldn't see where I put my feet. I stumbled and fell. I did not get up after that. I lay down, with my head on a rock, to wait for sunrise. I could not understand why I hadn't reached the city yet, but it was several miles away and I could go no farther.

It was eerie in the hills at night. I could hear slow footsteps on the grass, coming closer and then moving away again. And someone breathed. The darkness pressed in close, but I saw something glint in it. Perhaps someone was watching me, waiting for my eyes to close. Only I wasn't quite sure if it was real, or if I imagined it all, or if I was dreaming.

This is what it's like all the time for you now, Stirling, I thought. Lying alone in the dark, with only the dead for company. I couldn't bear it. "Stirling's in heaven now," said the Voice, sounding like Father Dunstan or Grandmother. "Now go to sleep." I shut my eyes.

Listening to the footsteps, I imagined it was the Voice, incarnated in the safety of the dark, where I could not see its form, padding gently around me like a guardian angel. As I drifted into sleep, I realized that the footsteps were only my own heartbeat.

And even in the wilderness, I dreamed. It was England again, and night there also, and over Aldebaran, the prince, and Anna, the same stars were shining.

❧

"Anna, stop dancing now," Monica was calling. "It's late; you will disturb the guests."

"I have to practice," said Anna.

"I know. But please—can't you do it tomorrow? And dancing in those shoes will damage the floor."

"I didn't have time to go up and get my ballet shoes or I would have done."

"Have you finished sweeping?"

"Yes. I put the broom away."

Anna stopped where she was and leaned against the stack of tables in the deserted dining room. Through the open doors she could see the constellations, patterns she knew well. Monica was walking about the kitchen putting things away, her heeled shoes echoing on the tiles. "Are you looking at the stars?" she said then. Anna nodded. "I remember when you were four years old and Mam bought you that astronomy book. You were so determined to learn them. Michelle thought you were too young for a book on astronomy. But maybe she wasn't the one who knew you best."

Monica fell silent. Anna was thinking then of the clear nights that winter after her Nan had died, when she had propped the book on the radiator under her window and learned the patterns of the constellations. Monica, leaning against the kitchen doorway, was thinking of the same thing. In the darkness they could hear the waterfalls. They were close, somewhere out there beyond the open doors.

Monica was still standing there when Anna came back to the kitchen. She was looking at the line of photographs on the windowsill. "Do you know what is strange?" she said, turning.

Anna came to stand beside her. "What is?"

"We're the only ones left—Michelle, you, and me."

It was true. Half the people laughing so surely in the photographs were gone now. "That's why I came here to help you," said Anna. "We're still a family."

Monica turned to her and seemed about to speak, then put her hand on Anna's shoulder for a moment. "I don't know what that picture of Richard is doing still there," she said then. "I should take it down." She picked up the photograph of her former husband and brushed the dust off it, then put it back.

Anna thought of something then. "Monica, your father?" She glanced toward the photograph.

"Yes," said Monica, her voice changing. "What about him?"

"Was his surname Field?"

There was a silence. "That's what Mam told us," said Monica then. "It made no difference anyway. Why do you want to know about him?"

Anna shook her head. "I don't. Sorry."

"Go up to bed now, will you?" Monica said. "I want to start breakfast at quarter to six."

When Anna was almost at the door, Monica spoke again. "Listen, I will make sure you have time to dance tomorrow. I know this audition is important. All right?"

Anna nodded, then turned and trailed along the darkened corridor, rubbing the aching muscles in her arms. A car swung past on the road outside, the distant yellow of the headlights glittering faintly through the jewels of her necklace. She twisted her fingers through the chain absently as she climbed the stairs. It was the same necklace, the bird necklace with one jewel missing, that she had worn all her life.

Anna fell to sleep that night with the necklace in her hand. She dreamed she was dancing, years from now. In the dark beyond the stage were her family, all the people in Monica's photographs and the photographs beside her bed, as though they had never been gone. And in the dream she could see her future family, a tall man and a child, gazing up at her with the light edging their faces, gazing up proudly with their faces turned to gold.

* * *

"I can tell what you are thinking," Aldebaran said.

"Uncle, I know you can," said Ryan, yawning. "Your greatest gift is prophecy."

Aldebaran laughed at his tone. "Do not be so disparaging. No one needs powers to tell what you are thinking, gazing over at the hotel like that."

"I was thinking that it is very clear on these summer nights," said Ryan. "You can hear the waterfalls. That was all."

They sat in silence for a moment, listening. Then Aldebaran said, "Go over that again. The principal causes of the Alcyrian border war. I am not convinced that you have got it right."

Ryan yawned again. "It is late. . . ."

"Ryan." Aldebaran pushed his chair back so that it sent a pile of books toppling. "You know that this is important. These are the principal causes of the war; they are also the principal failings of Lucien's government. Do you know what he has done today? He has ordered cadets to the border—boys your age—and he has ordered the army to march on a Sunday. Monarchs have lost a country for less. So go over it again."

Across the lake, the church bell chimed twelve. Ryan began again.

⁂

Sometimes in dreams, or entering a bright room from the dark, I think for a second that Stirling is there. Even while I was writing this—while I was lost again in the days before he was gone and the days straight after—I would begin to think he was standing there, just out of my sight. Always, I start up and begin to speak to him. And then I remember. He's the only one I speak to now, but he never does answer. And yet sometimes I am so sure.

I lean on the parapet and watch the lights of the carriages moving down the castle rock. Half the guests are leaving, but the music goes on, faintly. I listen in silence. I can see every place I tried to describe to you in this book—the fenced waste ground where my school used to be, Citadel Street, the graveyard. I tried to remember the places that once captivated me, but they seemed suddenly like ghost realms. Kalitzstad is a dead place. When Stirling's spirit left, the life was sucked out of everything else too.

When I was a little boy, I used to believe my mother and father would come back. I fully believed it. I used to kneel beside my bed to say my prayers, and after that I would take my gold christening bracelet and turn it round three times and whisper a few words, and imagine that I was working a charm to bring them back to us. But time passed, and they did not come. That kind of magic drifted away years ago, and I knew they never would. I didn't have proof. I just knew. There are some things you know in your heart without proving them.

But there was another magic that I always took for granted. Before Stirling died, there was a kind of power that glittered behind everything and gave it life. Maybe it was its potential always to be greater, or better tomorrow. But Stirling can never be more than eight years, eight months, a week, and two days, and everything in this world has stuck too. Now I know there is no magic. There never was. All magic ended forever when Stirling died.

I will continue. There are many other things. This was my

confession to you, and it is not finished. But I cannot read on yet. I stand here alone instead and let the book fall from my hand. The breeze is rising over the parapet and catching in the leaves of the trees below. I will go on. After a while, I will pick up the book and read again. Not yet.

I woke out in the hills, and I did not know why I was there. I was lying in the cold grass, with my head on a rock and my overcoat pulled up over me as a blanket. There was a layer of silver dew across it. I had been dreaming about Aldebaran. I stood up and stretched out my painful arms. Then I remembered what had happened the day before, and that Stirling was dead. I fell to my knees again and stayed there, unable to move. I think I was praying that I would wake up as someone else. But I had already woken as Leo, and the sickness and shock did not release me no matter how long I knelt there.

"You can go quicker now that you have rested," said the

Voice. And something made me stumble to my feet, pick up my coat, and start walking.

My legs were aching so that I could hardly lift them, and my head thudded sickeningly. I did not know where this tiredness came from, but it was real and it stopped me from thinking of anything except walking. I was glad at least of that. But I wondered if this was all my life would be from now on— violently doing something else so as not to remember Stirling was dead, and the sudden realization, which was worse than thinking of it all the time. I willed the Voice to tell me a story, as it had the day before, but no words came.

After I had been walking for several hours, I tripped at the summit of a hill and began to stumble down. I landed on my back in a shaded valley. Then I realized that I knew this place—it was the valley that I had told Stirling about. The valley we were going to when he was well. I walked down into the expanse of wildflowers. They were already dying, and that made me start to cry. Since Stirling had been gone, everything I touched had turned bitter.

When I stopped crying, the valley was in shadow, and birds were flitting across the fading sky. I stood up and hobbled down to the stream. I washed the tears from my face. "Get back to the city," said the Voice. "There are still a few hours of light. Get back to Kalitzstad and everything will be all right."

Perhaps I really believed that everything would be all right if I got back to the city. Anyway, I kept walking. As I staggered on, faintness would rise to my head; every few yards I had to sit down until it subsided. The hills were small, but they seemed like the largest mountains. I was sweating and shivering. I was not well. But I was getting there. I began to believe that the reason for everything—for my tiredness and faintness, and the miserable weight on my heart, and Stirling's death even—was that I had not reached the city yet. As soon as I stepped through the gate, everything would be all right. I felt nothing anymore; I thought only of the city and the distance and the Voice.

Eventually the hills became flat ground. I walked through the overflow graves, scattered like knocked-out teeth, where the Unacceptables were buried. I crossed the Circle Road, swayed, staggered on, and reached the graveyard gate. There were soldiers on guard duty—cadets, by their look. Their shadows stretched out toward me, running long over grave and ground alike. It must have been about six o'clock. They shouted to me as though they thought they were important men, but I ignored them and walked on past.

I had not been in the graveyard since Stirling's burial. I hadn't thought of what I would do when I reached the city; now I found myself searching for his grave. I walked among the headstones. There was a thick light, like yellow dust hanging in the air; it irritated my eyes. I found the grave. It was in the shadow of the wall, and not quite where I had remembered it was. The ground had sunk where it had been mounded up, so that the turf sagged in the middle. There were flowers on the grave, and the wooden cross now had an inscription under Stirling's name: *Be faithful unto death, and I will give you the crown of life*. Grandmother had chosen that without me. Stirling would have liked it, anyway.

Then I thought suddenly that he would not be able to read the words without someone to help him. Why did I think that? I had been imagining, just for a moment, Stirling looking down and struggling with the inscription on his own cross the same way he had spelled out Aldebaran's name. Because I felt as if he could see me, when I stood there beside his grave. "Can you hear me, Stirling?" I asked, but only in my head. "Can you see me?" There was no answer. Perhaps he could not.

I fell to the ground there on the shaded grave, so that my head was at the cross and my feet stretched over onto the path. Stirling was a good two feet shorter than me. The flowers smelt sickening and dusty close to my face. I lay there, as if I was dead and this was my own grave, and thought of Stirling there—so close, under the earth. I wished that I could see his face again.

I had become accustomed to crying now. I cried for myself, because I was hot and tired and sick, and it was still a long way home, and because I could never be happy again. I was tired with being unhappy. Whenever I thought of Stirling now, I was unhappy. When I thought of him before, when he was alive, I would recall some funny thing he had said or the last conversation we'd had, or I would think about what he was doing at that moment. Now I only thought of his illness and his death. And everything reminded me. My life seemed interminable, stretching out into a dark, blurred mist as far as I could see. "Help me, Stirling," I said in my head. "Help me, Stirling. I can't go on."

❧❧❧

I was dreaming again. They were becoming more and more real, more and more haunting. The girl was taking down washing in a gray side yard, with tears in her eyes. I could see her as

I imagine spirits looking down on Malonia from somewhere above it. And the boy was approaching across the lawn, but she could not see him.

"Anna," said Ryan. She started and looked up. He smiled at her. Overhead, clouds were gathering. A few raindrops crackled against the sheets on the line. "Let me help you with that," he said.

"I'm fine. Don't worry."

Then the sky split with thunder and the rain came down, clattering on the roofs of the cars and making the trees shudder on the hillside. Ryan pulled down the last of the washing and ran after her toward the hotel door.

In the kitchen, he put the washing on the table and laughed, running his hand through his already wet hair. "Thank you," said Anna.

"I had better go," he said. "I see you are working." She shook her head. "Then perhaps I will wait until the rain stops."

"Shall I make some tea?" she said.

He nodded. "Thank you. I am glad to be stranded here, to tell you the truth. My uncle woke me up at six to go over some point of history he thought I got wrong yesterday, and he has been like that all day. I sometimes wonder if he is entirely sane." Then he laughed edgily, as though Arthur Field might hear him. "Still, you must get used to this in my occupation. That is, in the occupation I will take up."

"What's that?" said Anna, trying to light the broken gas ring with Daniel's cigarette lighter.

Ryan shook his head. "Nothing of consequence. But tell me, Anna—I have been meaning to ask you—when I came past here yesterday, and the day before—"

"When I talked to you?"

"No, other times. I saw you dancing, and I wondered what it is you are practicing for."

"An audition for dance school." She said it without turning.

"Are you serious?" Ryan raised his eyebrows, with a faint smile. She set a pan of water on the gas ring. "No wonder you are so good!"

"I'm not really good," said Anna. "You have to work hard at something. Everyone does."

"You must be good to get the chance to audition."

"It's luck. All of it. Everything is."

"Is that what you really believe? You can dance like that—you must have trained for years—and you believe that everything is luck?"

Anna shook her head. She had been thinking just now of the day when she was five years old and her Nan took her to Graysands Beach. They had run over the sand for miles, filling Emilie's leather handbag with shells and stones. Then the sunlight started to fade, and Emilie said, "Time to go home, Anna angel." Anna wanted one more shell, and then another one. Emilie laughed and did not mind. And then, suddenly, Anna decided they had enough. They turned and started back, hand in hand. It was late by then and they were caught in heavy traffic. If Anna had collected one less shell, or one more, what happened next would never have happened.

"Everything is luck," she said again. "Whether you become a dancer or whether you don't—that's luck."

"How did you get the chance to audition for dance school, then? Was that luck?"

He was grinning, but she answered seriously. "The principal

of Clara Nichols Performing Arts School toured in Russia with my dance teacher. It's a personal favor to him. A scholarship place came free at the last minute, just a couple of weeks ago, and my teacher asked if I could audition for it before they give it to one of the people who came close in the auditions in the spring."

Ryan laughed, and she smiled, but reluctantly. She turned back to the pan of water and watched the bubbles rising in it. "This seems to be what you English do," said Ryan. "You have your dreams. And it is a good thing. You will dance professionally one day; I know it."

"Monica offered me a job yesterday," she said. "For when I leave school. What do you think?"

Ryan started to his feet, and she turned. "You should go to dance school," he said. "You should do anything rather than give up on it, if it's what you want to do. If you ask me, you should not even be here helping her now if you have to practice for an audition. You should let your family take care of their own affairs."

"I had to come up here," said Anna. "Monica couldn't run a business like this without family to help her. You can do whatever you want, Ryan; you don't have to earn your living."

He did not reply for a moment. Instead, he sat down again at the table. She poured out the tea and set a cup in front of him. "If I had been an English boy, I would have wanted to be an artist," he said. "But my ambitions are taken out of my hands."

"What does that mean?" said Anna.

"Nothing. It means nothing. It means that I know luck is important—of course it is. If I had been born someone different, I could have done whatever I wanted. That is why I think that you should not give up on dancing. It is in your own hands, whatever the struggle, far more than my future is in mine."

She couldn't think of anything to say to that. "You wanted to be an artist?" she asked eventually.

"Well, I used to be drawing all the time when I was a little boy. I will draw you a picture someday; then you can judge for yourself if I ever could have made one."

"All right." She smiled, but the smile faded fast.

They drank their tea in silence. Upstairs, children were running heavily up and down one of the corridors, making the ceiling creak. "You seem sad today, Anna," Ryan said.

The way he had said it made her look up at him. As though he knew her well and cared about that. "No," she said. "Not really."

The rain thudded more heavily on the glass with a gust of wind. Ryan looked out. "Is that your family?" he said then, standing up to look at the photographs.

"Your mother looks like Monica," he remarked. "But the other lady looks so much like you. Is she your grandmother?" Anna nodded. "And the man is your father?"

"Yes. He died."

Ryan glanced at her. "I am sorry." He turned to examine the picture again. "He looks like a good man."

"I didn't know him exactly. He died when I was one year old. But he was a good man—from what my mother has told me."

"What do you know about him?"

Anna knew many things about her father; he had become a legend to her from years of Monica and Michelle's stories. But she couldn't tell them to this boy who she barely knew, even if she talked to him every day now. "Nothing," she said. "I don't really know anything."

"He looks young in this picture," said Ryan, touching the frame lightly.

"He's eighteen there. Just after they married. A year before I was born."

Ryan went on staring at the picture of her father, as if it was a window into another world. "I don't have any family myself," he said.

"Except for your great-uncle," said Anna.

"Of course—yes. And one uncle, my mother's brother, back where I come from. But I hate him. There is no one—almost no one—I wish dead more than him."

"Don't you feel bad to say that about your uncle?"

"Perhaps I should. You have not met him."

"What about your mother and father?" said Anna.

Anger rose from him suddenly and overtook the room, though his face didn't change. "They are dead." His cup was rattling suddenly on the saucer in his hands. He put it down and stared out the window.

"I am sorry," said Anna. "I didn't mean . . ."

"I am not angry with you," he said.

But his eyes, when he turned back to her, were angry.

<hr />

"Harold! *Harold!*" I had been asleep and dreaming. "Harold? What are you doing here? You should be at school." I opened my eyes and saw a black silhouette, low down over the sky. Grandmother. "What are you doing here?" she demanded again.

I didn't know, and I wondered why she had called me

Harold. I looked about me, turned over, and felt the grass beneath my back, printed in my shape, and the flowers crushing out pollen under my head. I sat up. I must have fallen asleep on Stirling's grave.

"Why are you not in school, Harold?" she asked. I just looked at her. She stared back at me as if she didn't know me.

She turned away as I stood up, and placed a new bouquet beneath the wooden cross. She arranged the flowers and began to hum and cry at the same time. I stood awkwardly behind her. The notes were high and out of tune, but I thought it was a hymn that she sang. She stood back and regarded the cross for a moment, her eyes losing their focus. I touched her arm.

She started and turned to me. "Leo?" I nodded. "You startled me. What are you doing here, Leo? Where did you come from? I did not see you arrive. Did you come in from the gate while I bent to lay down these flowers?"

I did not answer. "So late, though . . . ," she said, and she was not watching me. "So late to return. I thought you were dead. It's been six years." I was frightened. This was like a nightmare, when nothing makes sense. I shook my head fiercely. She watched me for a moment, then turned away again.

"Oh yes. It's six years. How the time has raced by for you, Harold. You said you would contact me. A letter—a message with a friend—anything. Two words would have been enough. But you did not. And your son Leonard hates me because I would not let them come to you in Alcyria, and Stirling cries for his mother, but what else could I do? I would not risk the lives of your boys when I had no word. Why did you not contact me?"

I almost spoke. But it was like a promise, and I would not break it. She stared at me blankly. Then she looked at the grave, and when she turned back, she seemed to see me properly again. She reached out and put a hand on my shoulder. "You are back," she said quietly, continuing from where she had left off. "Oh, I have been so worried, Leo. You are back to stay now?" I nodded, and she gripped my shoulder tighter. "Thank heavens."

She stepped back and looked at me then. "Why are you so dirty? And you look pale; have you eaten since Saturday?" She put a hand to my face. "What happened, Leo? I thought you were going to the border. Did you decide to come back?"

When I made no reply, she took my arm. "Come, let us go home." It reminded me so suddenly, and so exactly, of Stirling's burial that for a moment I was back there, in the darkness and the dismal scuttling of the raindrops, beside the new grave.

"Come, Leo," she said, and I followed her.

We reached home about seven o'clock. "I have missed you, Leo," said Grandmother. "I was so lonely. I have lost Stirling, and I had lost you. Nothing but my thoughts, and no one to talk to—no one to share the burden of Stirling's death." Then she began to cry. I wished she would not talk about it if it made her cry. "Talk to me, Leo," she said. "Say something to comfort me." I could not have done, even if I had been willing to speak again.

She clasped my hands in her own trembling ones, and they felt frail and bony and weak as paper. "I try to forget Stirling's death, but how can I?" she went on. "Everything here reminds me of him; everything reminds me that he is dead. And what is there for me to do? I cannot work; I have no friends; even Father Dunstan cannot be here all the time. Church is my only comfort. I can't bear to sit here alone, crying and thinking of Stirling."

Then she tried to smile and put a false cheeriness into her voice. "But it will be better now you are here, Leo. You know how I suffer; I know you are suffering too. We can help each other to bear this." I nodded, trying to pull my hand away. "Look at you, Leo," she said, in a different tone, brushing the tears from her face. "You look unwell. Go down and take a shower, and I'll make you some soup."

I took a shower, then folded that uniform, put the pistol underneath it in the windowsill chest, and put on my ordinary clothes again—black ones. Grandmother was wearing black also. It was the custom to wear black for a month. I vowed then that I'd wear black forever. Anyhow, I thought dismally, a month was as long as forever when it had been only three days. From the bedroom I could hear Anselm's thin wail and the sound of shouting—Maria and her mother arguing again.

"You look like you need a good hot meal, Leo," Grandmother said when I opened the door. She was cooking onions in oil; the juice in the air caught at my eyes. I felt sick to think of Grandmother saying cheery things and cooking so soon, as if she had already forgotten. I wished I was back in the hills, sweating and stumbling, where at least my life reflected the pain in my heart.

"I'm going to have to look after you now," Grandmother said. I did not ask, "Now what?" but she said anyway, "Now I do not have Stirling to look after, that is," and began crying. So did I. I tried not to, because I did not want her to comfort me, but it was no use. "Come here, Leo," she said, holding out her hand, but I shook my head and went into the bedroom and shut the door.

"Leo!" I heard her calling, in a tear-choked pretense at

jollity, a few minutes later. I got up from my bed and went out, though I didn't feel hungry.

We ate silently, on two sides of the table, with Stirling's empty chair between us. I stared straight down at the vegetable soup as I shoveled it into my mouth. I ripped a large piece of bread and crammed it in defiantly, the food pushing out of my too-full mouth, and the tears pushing out of my eyes. I felt guilty, eating so greedily, but I did it anyway. I willed the tears not to brim over.

"I think I forgot something," mumbled Grandmother. "This soup doesn't taste quite right." It was true—it tasted different from how she usually made it—but I did not care. "It is different, is it not?" said Grandmother. "And I burned the onions. Sorry, Leo." I went on shoveling it into my mouth and shrugged.

"Father Dunstan might call round this evening," said Grandmother after a moment. "He has been very supportive." I went on eating. "He would like to speak to you. He is worried about you." The words dropped into silence again. I took another piece of bread, wiped it round my empty bowl, and pushed it into my mouth. "He has been very helpful to me," she said. "I hope you will talk to him. Would you like some more of that?" I nodded. Eating was something to do, and I set myself about it with a ferocity.

"I spoke to Maria yesterday," Grandmother said, setting down another piece of bread and another bowl of soup in front of me. I began eating again. "She asked after you. She's a very nice girl. Apparently that baby of hers has been ill." I didn't look up. "Nothing serious," Grandmother said anyway. "Only a cold or something like that. She seemed quite tired out; apparently he has been crying without pause."

The silence came down again. "So, did you get to the border?" she asked. "How is the war going?" I shook my head. "You did not reach the border?" I shook my head again. "Why did you come back?" I shrugged. I could not explain that without words. "You did not do something bad, that they sent you back?" I shook my head. They did not send me back; that at least was true. "Ah, well . . ." She drifted into silence again.

A couple of minutes later there was a knock at the door. Grandmother got up to answer it, evidently relieved, and the tight atmosphere broke. It was Father Dunstan. "Hello, Margaret," he said. And then, catching sight of me, "Leo. You are back from the border? I did not expect to see you so soon." I gave him a curt nod. There was deep sorrow in his voice. I wished he wouldn't pretend to be sad when he wasn't the one who should be sad. He wasn't the one whose brother had died. He barely even knew Stirling.

"It's kind of you to visit, Father," said Grandmother.

"It is no trouble."

She shut the door behind him and motioned to the sofa. I noticed then that there was still a green fist-shaped bruise on his face where I had hit him. The window that I had broken was boarded. He had probably fixed that, and the table too. "How are you coping, Margaret?" he asked her as she sat down in the chair opposite him.

"Oh . . . ," she said lightly. "Well . . . quite well . . . thank you, Father."

"Good," he said. "I am glad to hear that."

"It will be better now that Leo has returned," she said, smiling at me. I turned away from them.

Father Dunstan began talking about arrangements for the

memorial service, and I started toward the bedroom door, but Grandmother said, "Leo, I want you to be part of this too." I turned to them. "We chose the words for Stirling's cross without you, and I felt guilty for that."

"Come, Leo," said Father Dunstan. "Come and sit over here." Reluctantly, I drew a chair over to them and sat down.

"Now," said Father Dunstan. "I have made all arrangements for the service to be on Friday at twelve o'clock, as is usual." I thought about that and tried to work out what day this was. It might be Sunday, or more likely Monday. I gave up. When I listened again, Father Dunstan was talking about hymns and Bible readings. "Do you want to choose them?" he asked.

"I don't know." Grandmother looked worried, close to tears.

"Perhaps I could suggest some," said Father Dunstan.

"Yes. That would be best. Thank you."

They did not need me here. I got up, and they did not try to stop me.

It was growing dark outside. I sat on my bed and watched it. I felt strange and distant, removed from everything. If it had been an ordinary week, we would have been at school all day; we would have been laying out our uniforms now as darkness came down, while Grandmother built up the fire and lit the lamps. Instead, all that life was gone completely. I watched the sky darkening, and realized that I had no assurance that the sun would rise. Nothing was certain anymore if Stirling could be gone and I could do nothing about it. I closed my eyes. I could not see my life before me anymore. I prayed for something—a sign or a voice to tell me I was dreaming. No sign came. I could not even conjure those stories about England that had carried me through the hills. My mind was empty.

It was dark in England also, and the first stars were emerging, and Anna and Ryan were standing on the shore of the lake. The fences of the big house ran down to the water, so Anna could not cross into the grounds. "We will have to speak low or my uncle will hear," Ryan was saying across the fence. "I'm supposed to be studying astronomy."

"Your education is strange," she said, glancing toward Lakebank, where a single window was lit. "These things your uncle makes you learn."

"I know it. When he first came to England, he read about the noble gentlemen who lived a long time ago and what their sons used to learn. And it seemed to him a good kind of education to give me."

"So it's because you're landed gentry that you learn these things?"

He looked up. His eyes were blacker than the darkness. "Who told you we were landed gentry?"

She shook her head. "No one did."

"We're not," he said then. "We came into some money—my uncle did—ten years ago. It is almost gone now."

"So you just live here running down your money?" she said. "What will happen when it runs out? You will get a job?"

"Not me. My uncle might, because he is trained as a butler and he has the false—well—" He stopped then and looked away.

"False what? False papers?" He shook his head. "You were going to say false papers." The darkness made her bolder. "I will never understand you, Ryan," she said.

"Probably you won't."

She glanced at the book in his hands. "What's that?" she said. "What is the other book, inside the astronomy one?"

"Oh, that one is Shakespeare."

"Is that part of your education too?"

"No. My uncle would be angry if he thought I had been reading this instead of studying the stars. He thinks Shakespeare is a waste of my time."

"Why is that?"

"It is not my culture. And my uncle does not have much time for half the things Shakespeare writes about. He thinks grand plans are more important. I used to agree with him, but now—".

She met his eyes in the darkness. "Now what?" she said. He did not reply. The silence drew on and neither of them broke it. Then a door slammed in the house, and they both started.

"Now nothing," he said. "I should get back. My uncle will be watching to see that I complete the work." He turned. "Here he comes now."

"Shall I leave?" she said.

"Wait for me. I will speak to him and come back as soon as I can. Please stay."

Anna walked a short way off into the shadow of the trees and then turned back. She could still hear their voices.

"What is this?"

"What, Uncle?"

"This book." There was a silence, then an impatient cough. "Reading this English poet again. What will that teach you? Nothing. He writes about love."

She could not hear Ryan's reply. Then they were closer to the fence, and his uncle was talking again. She stood still. "Ryan, you must not forget your duty," the man was saying. "You have done no archery for near a week. You have done no history, no geography, no fencing. Nothing. At least, you have done none of it properly. You have been halfhearted about everything."

"Why can I not have a holiday?"

"You know why. A thousand times I've told you, damn it. Listen to me." Their voices were rising.

"I am listening. Uncle, you have been strict these past weeks and I'm tired."

"You have a limited time to learn these things, and you have to learn them. You have a duty to others. You are not allowed to think of yourself. You cannot go running off to see this girl."

"It is barely two days since I met her, Uncle. Do you really think—"

"I do not know what to think. It has been two days without useful work. You have been there four or five times. You were looking for something to distract you from your work even before she appeared—"

"That is not true." There was a pause, then he spoke more earnestly. "She has my heart and soul."

"Ryan, with your games of romance, you are risking a deal more than your own heart."

"You make it sound like a mortal sin to do what I want. All I ask for is one friend. Do you want me to be lonely?"

"Listen to me, Ryan."

"I said I'm listening."

"There is only one girl you should be involved with. That is the one who has the silver eagle, and—"

"It's been ten years, and you act as if it will be tomorrow. Your grand plans, Uncle—you even order who I must love. Or what if she is the one? You did not think of that." There was a silence. "Or what if she really is a relative of your brother, as you say?"

"It makes no difference if she is. That is in the past now. You do not need to spend all your time with her. What you need to do is fence, study the stars, and practice archery. And you need to know everything about your country that you can possibly know, or else—"

"Or else what? What Malonian gives a damn if I'm not the world archery champion or I don't know who won the Battle of the Eastern Fields, or—"

"Cassius Ryan Angel Donahue." There was a pause, and then the man laughed, but half exasperatedly. "I am serious, though. Do you have any idea what it is like in Malonia under Lucien's rule? Do you? Because I have been trying to tell you but you do not listen."

"But, Uncle—"

"But what? The people want a king who can dance, make patriotic speeches, ride a horse, fence. They don't want someone new or different or unique. They want someone safe. Do you understand? Until you are certain you can meet your responsibilities, no more going to see this girl."

"I never asked for—"

"It makes no difference. You cannot choose your duty, and you would do well to accept it."

"But listen—"

"Enough." His footsteps were fading across the gravel of the beach. "The discussion is finished. Map the positions of the major constellations, and think about the significance of these patterns for those who are expecting revolution. I will be in the library, working."

There was a silence. Then the door of the house, far away across the lawn, banged shut. In the darkness, Ryan said, "Anna?"

She came out from the trees and walked back to him. "I thought you might have gone," he said.

"You told me to wait."

"Did you hear—"

"Yes." He did not reply. "Ryan, what were you saying about me? That I am a relative of your uncle's?"

"You should not have overheard that," he said. "But I will explain. It is only fair to explain."

She twisted her fingers through the chain of her necklace. He watched the moonlight glinting on it and frowned slightly, as though he was thinking of something else. And then his eyes changed. "What is it?" she said.

"I never much looked at it before, your necklace. Is it a bird? Let me see." He caught hold of it. "And that jewel has always been missing?"

"Yes. But, Ryan—"

"Tell me where you got this," he said.

"My Nan gave it to me when I was a baby."

She turned away. He caught her arm. "She is the lady in the photograph, isn't she? The one who looks like you? And she gave you this necklace?"

She did not answer. "Please, Anna," he said. "Tell me about her."

She hesitated, then turned back to him. "There isn't much to tell. She was the one who brought me up when I was little. And then—she passed away. It was a car crash, near here. I was in it as well, and—"

"But tell me where she got the necklace from," he interrupted.

For a few seconds neither of them spoke. Then she said, "I should go. . . ." She raised her hands to her face.

"I'm sorry, Anna. I see I have upset you; I did not mean—"

"I hardly know you, Ryan. I don't want to tell you about my Nan any more than you wanted to tell me this afternoon about your parents."

"I am sorry. I did not realize this was something that mattered so much to you, or I never would have—"

"Of course it's something that matters to me!" she said. The moonlight showed up the tears on her face. "Ryan, you don't understand anything! You were angry for half an hour this morning when I just mentioned your parents."

"I told you, I wasn't angry with you."

"Then who were you angry with?"

"No one. I wasn't. I don't want to discuss this, please." And then she saw the tears in his eyes, threatening to fall. "I don't want to discuss it," he repeated. He looked away and raised his hands to his head as though in exasperation. "Anna, why do you have to bring all this back to me?" he said. "I'm not going to explain the history of my life to you. And if I was, I would have to know where your grandmother got that necklace from first."

"Why?" she said, more quietly. The moon disappeared behind a cloud, and in the darkness they were separated.

"I can't explain," said Ryan's voice. "I wish I could, because—" He paused. "I want to tell you. Honestly, I do."

In the darkness, his hand found hers. "Then tell me," she said.

And then someone was calling from the lighted window. "Ryan, come in! Now. Straightaway."

They looked at each other for a minute. Then Ryan turned. "I have to go."

He glanced back once as he walked away from her; then his uncle called again and he broke into a run toward the house.

Anna turned and walked away down the beach, without looking back. But she could still feel exactly how his hand had caught hers, like a lasting imprint on her palm.

❧

I was lying on my bed, staring at the ceiling, when Father Dunstan came in, so at first I did not see him. I was thinking that the last time I had lain here, which seemed to me so recent, was back in the days when I used to be the Leo that I was—the ordinary boy who had a brother called Stirling. And now, so soon—three days later—I was an only child who had lost a brother. That wasn't really me. It was so sudden. It was not just Stirling who was gone. I was not myself anymore. I had lost a part of my identity—a large part. I was forgetting who I was. I had only ever been Leo in relation to Stirling. I had a strange feeling that I was a lost soul, in the wrong situation, in the wrong body. I did not recognize myself in the mirror. Everything was different.

Father Dunstan shut the door, and I heard him and sat up. "Sorry, Leo," he said. "I wanted to talk to you." I swung my legs over the side of my bed, rested my elbows on my knees, and stared at him. He drew the chair round so that he could sit in front of me. "I wanted to ask you about the service," he said. "Your grandmother and I both thought it would be nice if you said something." I gave him a questioning look. "Perhaps you could take one of the readings from the Bible, or you could talk before the service starts. I know that it would be difficult, but you were the one closest to Stirling in the world, and those who loved him would like to hear what you have to say about him. I know that it is difficult at the time, when something like this happens, but people often regret not taking their chance to do this." He looked uneasy when he saw my face. "Could you do one of the readings, perhaps?" I just went on looking at him. "Of course, you do not have to. Think about it, that's all." I nodded reluctantly.

"Leo, there was something else," he said. "You are not talking." I shook my head. "Remember, the longer you go on with something like this, the harder it is to stop it." I stared at him and said nothing. "And it can lead to misunderstandings. Sometimes it is better to talk about things rather than contain them." When still I did not reply, he spoke again. "How about if you agreed to speak now, and we talked about this, and then after that, if you still think it is the right thing to do, you can remain silent again?" He did not understand. "Will you write, then? I want to speak with you." I nodded eventually, though I did not want to write. That was not the point. The point was that I did not communicate at all.

"Here," he said, handing me a pencil from his pocket and a crumpled piece of paper. "Why are you not talking?" he asked me.

"Why the hell is it your business?" said the voice in my head.

A lot of reasons, I wrote, my hand trembling from the pressure I exerted on the pencil. The lead broke.

He took a penknife out of his pocket, sharpened the pencil silently, knocked the shreds of wood onto the floor with the back of his hand, and then, handing it back to me, said, "What kind of reasons?"

So I don't have to answer stupid questions, I wrote.

"Any others?"

I am tired with words, I wrote. *There are not enough.*

"Not enough for what?" he asked.

To say what I want to say.

He sat silent for a moment. Then he said, "You know, Stirling would not necessarily wish you to do this. Perhaps he would have preferred you to speak, if only for the sake of supporting your grandmother and reading at his memorial service. He would want you to do what is right."

"How dare you say that?" said the voice in my head. "When you just said, the moment before, that I was the closest to Stirling in the world. How can you know what Stirling would have wanted?"

Anyway he is dead so he will not know, I wrote.

"Do you think that?" he asked quietly. "Do you not think that he can see you, or know what you are doing?" I didn't answer.

"Often it seems the right thing to do, to become absorbed by a vow like not speaking," he continued. "But it might actually be a trap, preventing you from getting back to normality."

How can I get back to normality? I wrote.

"Normality may have to be redefined," he said. "But eventually, though it does not seem like it now, you will get back to some degree of ordinary life."

So I should talk?

"That is up to you," he said. "Only, I think that Stirling would be glad that you spoke for the sake of others, rather than angry that you broke the promise."

We sat in silence. I traced a line on the paper from one

corner toward the other, but it never got there and I gave up and dropped the pencil. "Are there any other reasons that you decided not to talk?" he said. "As a sort of punishment, perhaps?"

He waited, but I did not pick up the pencil again and answer him. "It's important to remember that there is no reason for you to be punished, Leo," he said eventually. "You were not to blame for Stirling's death, and punishing yourself for it will do no good." He looked at me.

I picked up the pencil again and wrote, *You can't make me talk.*

He sighed. "I know it, Leo. But I think that it would be the best for you. How about if you talked only when it was necessary? Only when you need to communicate. You don't have to talk about your feelings. You could just answer questions people ask you, for example."

Sometimes I don't want to answer. Then what?

"You could just say so."

I will think about it, I wrote.

"Thank you, Leo," he said. "Thank you. Good lad."

"Don't patronize me," said the voice in my head.

"Sorry," he said, seeing me frown. "But thank you. And about reading at the service . . . I would like you to do it. I really would. Stirling would have too, I think."

I said I'll think about it, I wrote, and then I shoved the paper and pencil back at him and lay down on my bed and turned to the window. He bent down to pick up the pencil from where it had fallen. "Thank you, Leo," he said. I bit my lip to keep back a loud sob until he had left.

✳   ✳   ✳

I did think about speaking at the service. I went to Stirling's grave the next day. I sat at the end of it and looked at the wooden cross with Stirling's name and wondered what I should do. Suddenly he was cut out of my life, where once he had been so important, and I could no longer do anything for him except the dull, dead things—taking a bunch of flowers, clipping the grass on his grave, or perhaps speaking at his memorial service. I wanted so badly to talk to him, like I used to. He was the only one I ever really talked to. I wanted to ask him if I should read at the service, like I would have done before.

"What should I do, Stirling?" I asked, in my head. There was no answer. "What do you think I should do?" I imagined him as he was when we laughed about something, or when he asked me a question, or when he talked about the Bible. What would he have said? "Should I speak at your memorial service, Stirling?" There was a silence that was not just the lack of response; it seemed the opposite of a response. "This is stupid," said the voice in my head, and I went home.

Grandmother was not there. I assumed that she was downstairs in the bathroom or out at the market, perhaps. But there was nothing to do at home, and when a couple of hours had passed, and I had checked that she was not in the building or the yard or the bathroom, and a storm was rising outside, I decided to go out to look for her. I wrote a note—*Grandmother, Gone to look for you. I will be back*—and left it on the table.

It was beginning to rain. It had been raining on and off since I had got back from the barracks at Ositha. Clouds had been gathering all day, and suddenly they burst. Thunder and lightning cracked against the buildings, as if they were an enemy force attacking the vulnerable island city. I did not know where I was going, but I concentrated hard on thinking about where Grandmother would have gone, and I thought, strangely, of school. There was no reason for her to have gone there, but I went west anyway.

$$\sim\!\!\sim\!\!\sim$$

I cannot remember walking through the city, but I remember running up the street toward school. The rain was falling hard, and the lightning flared against the buildings. I could hear shouting and laughter and someone chanting a song. It must be afternoon break, I realized. That school was still going on seemed to me stupid. But they were all there in the yard, those boys I used to know.

I suddenly saw Grandmother silhouetted against the fence. She was staring into the yard. A couple of the younger boys were glancing at her uneasily. I ran up and touched her arm. "Harold?" she asked. I shook my head and tried to pull her away. She was talking to me urgently, but I could not understand.

"North!" said someone then, and I realized it was Seth Blackwood crossing the yard at a jog. I went on trying to pull Grandmother away. "Why haven't you been in school?" he called. "We were all wondering. It isn't your brother, is it?"

I did not answer. Seth reached the fence and looked through it at me. "You should take this lady home," he said, lowering his voice. "The teachers are edgy these days, because of the assassination attempt and the situation with the war, you know." I must have looked blank, because he started telling me about it—about how a madman had tried to assassinate Lucien, and after that my platoon had been sent back to school with all the other cadets. I didn't listen to much of it. But I remembered suddenly what had happened at Ositha and what the sergeant had said about prison. I did not want to meet any of the teachers.

I prized Grandmother's fingers from the fence and steered her away. She began to sing as we walked. I motioned to her to be quiet. She was not watching me. She started muttering something to herself, and her eyes darted as she talked, as if there were demons in her. I almost spoke, but I bit back the words and pulled her by the hand, and she followed me.

"You should talk," said the Voice. "You should talk to her." I ignored it. I heard someone shouting behind us, maybe Seth Blackwood, or else one of the teachers. I pulled Grandmother into a run, though she could hardly manage it.

Somewhere on the way home, she came back and began asking me what was happening. But I could not speak. I went on dragging her along behind me.

When we got home, I bolted the door. Then I fetched a piece of paper and explained. I told her everything, even that she had been calling me Harold.

"Is this true?" she said when she had read it. She put her hand to her head, looking frightened. "I have no recollection . . . I cannot remember what I did. . . . I went out to go to the grave-yard after you had left . . . but beyond that, there is just dark-ness." She sat down heavily opposite me at the table. "I think I had an idea that Stirling had been kept in late. I wanted to go and fetch him." She began to cry then. "Leo, I fear that I am losing my mind."

Perhaps it is only because of Stirling, I wrote. *You are not old.*

"I am sixty-five, Leo. That's old. And then where will you be?"

Where will I be when?

"When I am dead."

You are not going to die, I wrote. *You are just upset.*

"You're probably right," she said, but she still looked frightened. "At least I have never done this before." I didn't tell her about the time at the graveyard, when I was back from Ositha. I didn't see any benefit in it. "I'll ask Father Dunstan when he comes tomorrow," she said, and pretended to put it out of her mind.

Father Dunstan told Grandmother not to worry. I don't think that he could have told her anything else. I said it wasn't madness, but I think now that it was. Why not madness? I was losing my own mind in those days. It's easy to do. Easier than going on living, pretending everything is still as it used to be.

Father Dunstan asked me again about speaking at the service. I agreed, reluctantly, to take one of the readings. "Thank you, Leo," he said. "It would mean a lot to Stirling." I didn't know how I was going to speak, but I knew that I was going to manage it somehow. I had to do it.

The next day was worse. I woke early, before the sun had risen, and the very darkness of the room and Stirling's empty bed and the shadows in the corners made me suddenly wish that I could die rather than count the seconds until sunrise. I lay there and wished again and again that I had run faster, until I almost thought that I had, and then I remembered that I hadn't and that was the reason for Stirling's death. I cried for hours. I got up pale and sick, with swollen eyes and a heavy heart. I looked in the mirror and wondered dismally how I had ever thought myself handsome.

Grandmother asked me to go to the market. We were

almost out of food. "How are you, Leo?" asked Mr. Pearson at the fruit and vegetable stall. "And how is your brother, little Stirling?" I couldn't speak. "What is it?" he asked, seeing me struggling with the tears. "Are you unwell?" I waved my hand to dismiss the question, and hurried away before anyone saw the tears fall.

There was nothing to do in the house. In Stirling's Bible, I found the passage that I was supposed to read for the service, thinking to practice it. But I began to cry again, because in the front of the Bible was written, in my father's own hand, *To Stirling on your christening. May you grow up safe in the light of God's law. With all our love, Mother and Father.* I remembered him writing it, for one thing, when Stirling was still a baby; and for another thing, all of them—Mother and Father and little Stirling—were so far away. And it hurt to see his stupid wish, that his son could be kept safe, because no one could be kept safe by God's law alone. Because God was in heaven, and we were on earth, and he could not reach out to us even if he wanted to. And God liked to test people, to see what it took to break them. And God's law is not a light, I thought. It's a burden that none of us can lift. If people try, it only crushes them.

The worst thing was thinking of Father and Mother, in Alcyria or further away, who thought Stirling was still safe. They had left him when he was two years old. Father was a wanted man and they had to escape quickly; they were going to send word in a month or two, to tell us to follow. If they did, it never reached us. Grandmother thought they must have been caught crossing the border, and she would not let us set out after them. She was convinced that they were dead.

I hadn't looked after Stirling for them as I should have

done. Mother wouldn't have let him catch silent fever. Father would have run all the way from the eastern hills, no matter how tired he was.

I read through the passage that I was supposed to speak, and tried to imagine how I would read it. But I worried now that I would break down and cry, break down at the front of the church, and everyone would see me. So I shut the Bible and sat and stared out the window at the unchanging view, until Grandmother cooked dinner. I hardly ate anything. I felt guilty that I was nervous about reading at the service. But it was not just reading; it was the whole thing. Everyone would be staring at me, watching how I reacted, and it was our last chance to say goodbye to Stirling forever.

"Help me, Stirling," I said in my head that night, unable to get to sleep for worrying. "Help me. I can't read. I just can't. I won't be able to speak." I tried to imagine Stirling's answer, but it was no good. Stirling thought of kind things to say, and wise things, and I couldn't think of those things myself. "I wish you were with me, Stirling," I said in my head. "I never realized how much I need you." I knew he couldn't hear. I cried myself to sleep.

I dreamed that I was standing at the front of the church, but I was dumb. As if I had silent fever. No words came from my mouth, no matter how much I tried to talk. And then I dreamed that I was falling into Nothing, and woke up shivering and sweating.

But when I eventually drifted back into sleep, I had a completely different dream. I was sitting opposite Stirling at the table, and it was snowing outside, like it had in December, when the fire drove out the early shadows and I began to teach him to read. He handed me the Bible and pointed to a passage, and I read it. " 'And I saw a new heaven, and a new earth . . .' "

"How did you learn to read so good, Leo?" he said when I finished, and I heard his voice so clearly that I thought he must really be speaking to me and woke with a start. I was smiling when I woke. And then I remembered. Perhaps it was stupid, but for a moment, although I knew he was dead, I didn't feel as if he was gone.

*A*t the front of the church, standing at the lectern in the colored light from the window, I spoke the last words: " 'And there shall be no more death, neither sorrow, nor crying, neither shall there be any more pain: for the former things are passed away.' " There was a silence, and my footsteps echoed as I walked back to sit down. Maria, at the back of the church, began to cry. I sat down again in the front pew, beside Grandmother, and she took my hand. "You make me proud, Leo," she whispered.

When I read, I didn't read as myself. I didn't think of Stirling being dead or of what the words meant. I just read them. I thought of Nothing. And I managed to get through the reading that way. I managed to get through the whole thing that way. Which is why I barely remember anything about it now. I was so wrapped up in not crying that I hardly thought about anything else. Maybe it was the wrong thing to do, but at the time I could see no other way to endure that service.

When Father Dunstan began his sermon, I tried to concentrate, but I kept being distracted. I wondered if I had remembered to shut the door of the apartment. It was crazy, because I had gone back twice to check it, and I didn't care if anyone broke in anyway, not anymore.

"When something like this happens," Father Dunstan was saying, "our life is irreversibly altered. We cannot explain something as terrible as Stirling's death. We begin to question everything. Nothing makes sense to us anymore. In the words of the writer of the book of Ecclesiastes, 'Everything is meaningless.' In the face of such a tragedy, everything can become meaningless.

"The Teacher, the writer of Ecclesiastes, is weary of life. He has seen the unfairness and the inexplicability of it. He has searched for wisdom, but found only that everything is meaningless. At the beginning of the book, there seems little hope. But as it progresses, we see a new meaning in life. The meaning is God. The Teacher argues that everything is meaningless without God.

"So what is his conclusion? What does he come to, after his examination of life? At the end of the book, the conclusion is quite simple: 'Fear God and keep his commandments, for this is the whole duty of man.' And that, I think, is what we must do. Fear God and keep his commandments.

"It would be difficult for any one of us to try to explain why Stirling died—what purpose his death served. But I feel sure that, when we reach heaven, it will become clear to us. God adds a new meaning to our earthly life, one which is beyond us now. But what we do know now is what we have to do.

"God wants us to continue with our life, even if we are not sure where we are going at times. He wants us to obey the words of the Teacher. Although we cannot explain why we carry it out sometimes, we know what our task is. 'Fear God and keep his commandments.' There is nothing in the scripture about understanding God, for that is beyond any of us. There is nothing that tells us that we must know exactly why we carry on, all the time. Only that we must do this: continue to live, in the way that God wishes us to, until the end of our days.

"Truly, everything has a meaning, and though we may not see it now, in time it will make sense to us. Although we are struck with the incomprehensibility of Stirling's death, we can carry on as God, and Stirling, would want us to. We can carry on with our lives, by striving our utmost to fear God and keep his commandments."

Then I stopped listening. He talked for more than twenty minutes, and that is all I can remember.

"What did you think about Father Dunstan's sermon?" Grandmother asked me after the service. I did not know what I thought. My mind was empty.

But I remembered his words. And now I think that maybe what he was trying to say was right.

On the way back from the service, someone came stumbling up behind us. We had been moving slowly, as if we were walking against a current, but we stopped now and turned. It was Maria, clutching the baby to her chest. She stopped in front of me and looked as if she was about to speak and then shook her head and stared at me in silence.

She was different somehow. Baby Anselm clenched his fist and stretched it again. I watched him and thought that even he had changed. I remembered that barely a week had passed since we had fought over something inconsequential, me and this girl I used to know. I tried to remember what it was, but I couldn't. She went on looking at me. "Leo, I don't know what to say," she began eventually. "I wanted to talk to you, and then you left for the border. Leo, that this should have happened . . ." She shook her head and fell silent. I watched her tears and my own landing in the dust of the road, like when the first rain begins. I watched them as you watch a stranger's tears. Whenever I remember that day, I remember it as something that happened to a stranger. Not because of the years that have passed; it was like that at the time.

Grandmother took Maria's hand briefly, and then Maria took mine. I think I let her, but I can't remember now.

And then I was thinking of that day when the truancy officer had called, when Maria and I had sat together in the apartment and later Grandmother had stood and rocked the baby. And now we four were standing in the road in mourning dress—tears lying in the creases in Grandmother's face, Maria sobbing openly, the baby silent and expressionless as if he knew. Maria's hair was covered and she had taken the jewels out of her ears. I started to remember then what I had said to her. Something about righteousness, or the baby. Could I have said that? I didn't know anymore. The old Leo was still stranded somewhere beyond the shock and silence of the last few days, wondering faintly if he should apologize. "What I said to you . . . ," I began, tears running down my face. I coughed and started again. "Before, what I said to you . . ."

Maria shook her head, almost angrily, and gripped my hand. "Leo, don't," she said. "How could that matter now?"

*T*he next day was strange and empty. I got up and dressed, but that took all my strength, so I lay back down on my bed and stared at the ceiling while the minutes passed. Grandmother came in several times, but I did not move. "Get up, Leo," she said eventually. "Don't lie there. Come with me to the market."

I sat up and looked at her. "We are going out," she said, more briskly. "Put your overcoat on."

I did not want to. She picked up the coat and tried to put it over my shoulders, roughly. I shook my head and covered my face with my hands. She gave up, looking as exhausted as I felt, and knelt on the floor and cried.

Something had fallen out of the pocket of the overcoat. It was that black book, the old book that I had read to Stirling. She picked it up, sniffling like a child. "Leo, what is this?" She leafed through the pages, then closed it and sobbed louder. "I will never understand you, Leo," she said. "You will not speak one word to me, and yet you have been writing all these stories."

I shook my head. I had not. But after she had gone trailing back to the living room, still crying, I picked it up and turned over the pages. And even just glancing at the words, I could see what the story was. It was the same as the dreams that had been haunting me these past days—Aldebaran, the prince, and Anna. And more, pages more, as though the writer thought I still cared about that.

I ripped the book in half, down the spine, so that the pages scattered on the dusty floorboards. It made me sick to see those words there as though things were normal. What did this fairy tale mean to me now, after all that had happened? I did not want stories anymore. I wanted to be left in peace.

But later, when it was growing dark, I gathered the pages again. I put them together between the two covers in the pocket of my overcoat, as I would have done before. That was the story I had read to Stirling. Whether or not I cared about it, he would have. He would have wanted to find out what happened next. He cared about them like real people, these three we read about in the desperate days when he was ill. And I could not throw away that book.

And I could not stop myself from dreaming. Perhaps I did not exactly want to. Because while I was lost in these strange dreams, my heart did not know that Stirling was gone.

～～～

It was growing dark in England, and the wind had risen, but Anna was out in the yard, dancing under the security light. And suddenly Ryan was there, at the edge of the darkness. She stopped. "What are you doing?" he said.

"Practicing. Monica thinks I am in bed. I have no time in the day, and in the evenings she doesn't let me use the dining room in case I disturb the guests."

They looked at each other in silence. "I have not seen you for days," said Ryan then. "I am sorry. I promised to explain, and then my uncle—" He shrugged and sat down on the low wall. "I will tell you now what I was going to. Will you listen?"

"Yes."

A group of guests, dropping the last ends of their cigarettes, passed them and went in at the hotel entrance. Ryan followed them with his eyes, then turned back to her. "Firstly, about

Aldebaran . . . ," he said. "Arthur Field, as you know him. He is not in truth my great-uncle." He paused. "I am going against him to tell you this. I think maybe he is yours." Anna opened her mouth to speak, but he raised his hand and continued. "His brother, Harold Field, was here in England a long time ago. Do you know of that man?"

"Harold Field? He was my grandfather. I never met him, but I know that was his name."

"Are you sure?"

"Yes, I'm sure."

"Aldebaran thought so too."

She turned suddenly. "Where are you going?" said Ryan.

"Let me get Monica's photograph of their father," she said.

She ran to the deserted kitchen and took the picture from the windowsill. Ryan was waiting at the door when she got back. "Here," she said, handing it to him. She stood in silence while he examined it. It was a faded photograph, taken by a passerby on Graysands Beach. Her Nan, in her late twenties, was standing beside Anna's unknown grandfather, her hand on his arm. The man was looking straight into the camera with a charming grin. One hand held baby Monica casually on his shoulders; the other was in four-year-old Michelle's hand.

"I see," said Ryan quietly. "Do you see it? They are so alike. This could be a younger version of Aldebaran himself."

There was something about this man, her grandfather—that was what Anna had always thought—something about his easy, self-assured expression and the way he looked so directly at the camera, as if he was challenging it, that was different from other people. And that was the same, she realized now, as Arthur Field.

"He knew," she said. "That was why he hit his head on the car hood when I told him that Monica's name was Devere."

Ryan nodded. "He knew that was the lady's name. But he did not want to tell you about this."

"Why not?"

"He doesn't want to be connected with anyone in this country. He wants to disappear without complications. But he does not understand that you may be involved whether or not he wishes you to be. Not just because you are related to him, but because of my history."

"What is your history?"

"It is difficult." He handed the picture back to her and turned to look out over the dark water of the lake. "It is difficult to tell you about these things, Anna. I will try to be honest. Can we walk along the road for a while? It will be easier to explain."

They started out toward Lakebank. "I told you that my parents are dead," said Ryan. "They were shot, ten years ago. My uncle was the one who arranged it. My real uncle, back in Malonia, where I come from. My mother's elder brother."

Anna turned to him, but he went on walking steadily and kept his eyes lowered. "He had them murdered?" she said eventually. "Is he in prison now?"

Ryan shook his head. "It was political. My father was a very important man. My uncle wanted his place." He stopped in the dark road and looked at her. "Things are serious, Anna, if I go on. Do you understand me?"

"Yes, I understand you."

"My father was the king, and his father before him. I am the last son in the line of Donahue. I am the heir to the throne. In

Malonia I was a prince. Now I am an exile." He met her eyes again. "You may not believe me. But will you listen?"

She did not reply, but she went on watching him as they walked on into the dark. "My father came to the throne very young," said Ryan. "He had already ruled the country for five years when he was my age. About a year later he met my mother. She came from a noble family; they govern a state off the west coast of Malonia." He glanced at Anna as if to check that she was listening, then went on. "The noble family of Kalitz has always disputed with the family of Donahue. At the time when I was born, this enmity was very bad. My mother and father were young and they loved each other. They were married when they were fifteen and seventeen. They thought that they could overcome the hostility between their families. But my mother's family used her marriage to get closer to the royal family and further their plot to overthrow the government and seize power."

Ryan fell silent. "So how does Arthur Field come into it?" said Anna eventually. "Who is he in this story?"

"He was a great man in my country. Second but one in the secret service, and he had great powers. His taken name is Aldebaran; that is how everyone knows him. He was exiled before me, and he took me in when I was sent here to England. So you could say that I owe him my life."

"What do you mean by powers?" said Anna.

Ryan tried to explain.

"You can't really believe that!" she said. "That he can read minds, and prophesy. Ryan, seriously—" And then she remembered something. When they had met on the road that day, Arthur Field had known when the fog would lift before it started lifting. And that her real name was Ariana.

"Aldebaran wrote a prophecy concerning me," said Ryan. "That is part of it too. He wrote that I would not be killed but exiled, and that anyone who harmed me would be punished for it, blow for blow. So no one dared. My uncle had my parents killed; he took over the country; but he did not dare to harm me. He exiled me too. He sent me to England."

Ryan turned to her then. "But you come into the story, Anna. You are part of this. Because in the prophecy, Aldebaran connected me with the silver eagle, a valuable charm that is very famous in my country. Aldebaran got hold of this silver eagle, and brought it with him to England. It looks like an ordinary necklace, set with silver and blue jewels, the kind of talisman every noble family owns. But it has power locked in it—magic power."

"Magic power?" said Anna. "Ryan—"

"You have these things here in England," Ryan said. "Don't try to tell me you do not. You understand these things as we do."

When Anna did not reply, he continued. "The silver eagle is part of the prophecy concerning me. Aldebaran took one jewel out of the necklace and kept it, and threw the rest into the sea."

"The sea?" said Anna. "Where? Near here?"

"Very near." Ryan watched her steadily.

"Why did he throw it away," said Anna, "if it was such a valuable necklace?"

"It would have been too dangerous to keep it with him. He believed that the jewel and the necklace would find their way back together. He foresaw that this silver eagle would be restored to us by someone dear to me—someone I loved, even. That was what he prophesied; he thought it would be a sign. But it has been ten years, and nothing. He was beginning to think that he had made a costly mistake and lost the necklace forever. And then—" Ryan

313

stopped and turned to her. "And then you walked up to us in the fog, and I could tell there was something about you; straightaway I knew. And here you are, with a silver necklace, a charm in the shape of an eagle, with a missing stone. And I can't help wondering, Anna."

She took her necklace out from her collar and examined it in the fading light. "What did he say when you told him all this?"

"I didn't," said Ryan. "I told him nothing about your necklace. I wanted to speak to you first."

"That was why you wanted to know where I got it from?" He nodded. She hesitated for a moment, then spoke: "My Nan found this necklace on the beach." He did not answer, so she went on. "She used to walk there with Harold Field, my grandfather—on Graysands Beach. She kept going back there after he disappeared. There was one time she was certain she saw him, but it was so far away that she decided it was a mistake. And then she found the necklace, and she thought it was a sign; she thought so too. She took it to the police but no one claimed it, so they gave it back to her."

"It was Graysands Beach where Aldebaran threw the silver eagle into the sea," said Ryan. "I know it was. But how did the necklace come to you?"

"She gave it to me when I was born." She turned to him. "What happened to Mr. Field's brother? What happened to my grandfather?"

"He passed away," said Ryan. "I am sorry. In Malonia he was a soldier. He rejoined the army after he came back. He was killed in action a year later. He never returned to England."

"But what about the man my Nan saw on the beach?" said Anna. "That was years after my grandfather left."

"Perhaps he did come back," said Ryan. "When people die, they don't just disappear; I'm sure of it. Perhaps they can move in time and space, between the worlds. Like those with powers, the great ones, can."

"Between the worlds?" said Anna.

They were at the gates of the big house. The building was dark, except for one second-floor window. They did not go in but stood in the deserted road, the darkness almost complete now. "Have you ever heard of Malonia?" said Ryan. "Is the name familiar? Some people here in England think they have heard it somewhere."

She shook her head. "I thought my grandfather was Australian. I have never heard of that place."

"It is strange to hear you say that," said Ryan. "Sometimes when I wake up in this foreign country, I find it hard to believe that I have lived here ten years. Where I come from, there are rumors of England. Explorers claim to have been there. When people are reported missing and believed dead, legends spread that they may not have died at all—that they have passed through into England by chance or accident. And the great ones, those with powers—they can move into other places. Stories like that are well-known. It is a fairy-tale land, and most of us pass our lives without thinking much about it. It is not part of the real world. When I was a little boy, I did not believe that it existed."

"How far away can your country be?" said Anna.

He opened the gate and she followed him. "I will try to explain."

But by the time they reached the house, she was not certain that she understood.

They went in at the side door. Ryan did not turn on the light until they were in the old library with the door closed. "My uncle will hear unless we speak quietly," he whispered.

Anna laid the picture of her grandfather on the table, and her necklace beside it. "Here," she said. "Look at it. Does this look like a valuable necklace to you? They are just glass, these jewels."

Ryan took a chain from around his own neck and laid it next to hers. His own had a single jewel on it—a blue jewel. And it was identical to the largest stone that was set in her necklace. It was the missing jewel, the bird's right eye.

Anna turned to him but could not speak. Ryan raised his hand to his forehead, startled too. "They are the same," he said. "They might look like glass to you, but in my country these are valuable jewels."

"Ryan, stop it now," she said suddenly. The necklaces were drifting together on the table.

He raised his hands. "I am not touching them. I told you, Anna. There has been a link between them since before we were born. They have great power in them."

"They must be magnetic," she said, her heart beating faster.

"The chains are gold."

At that moment they heard footsteps in the corridor. "Ryan, are you there?" called Arthur Field. They both turned.

Aldebaran opened his mouth, then could not speak. The silver eagle was lying on the table. His dead brother's photograph was beside it. "This picture is Anna's grandfather," said Ryan, standing up. "And this is the necklace that her grandmother found on Graysands Beach."

There was a silence. Then Aldebaran approached the table. "Of course the necklace would go to a relative of Harold's," he muttered, shaking his head. "Of course. There tends to be an order to these things."

He picked up the necklace and turned it over in his hand, then looked up at Anna. And then suddenly his face darkened. "Ryan, you should have told me," he said. "You should not have brought it here."

"Uncle, I thought—"

Aldebaran looked about, then spoke low, as though people were listening. "In the name of heaven, Ryan! You know that this house is watched."

✎∽◦∾✎

At the far edge of the grounds of Lakebank was a ruined chapel. They sat there now, around an old army storm lantern—Anna, the prince, and the great Aldebaran. The necklace was in Anna's hand, but Aldebaran kept his eyes on it. "Let me try to explain," he was saying. "You are my great-niece, and you are implicated, and I ought to explain about this prophecy I wrote. And about the worlds that exist, the way I see them."

"I tried to tell Anna," said Ryan. "The exile on me is not just distance; it keeps me locked in England. And it would take great power to get someone back home who was exiled the way I am."

"When you are growing up, you hear stories," said Aldebaran. "In our country, there are many stories about England—about this world that surrounds you. The carriages that drive by themselves, the lamps that do not waver, a place where the people no longer fear that magic is real. As you grow up, you learn to believe that England is a fairy tale. Those who have disappeared have died, not vanished; those who claim to have been here are liars. But the great ones—those who are trained as what you call magicians— have to learn to take up again those things that you set aside in childhood, because we work in this field. In the realm of myth and

317

legend, trying to make possible what others believe impossible, or at least highly doubtful."

"Uncle, you are not making this clearer," Ryan began, but Aldebaran raised his hand. The lamp flickered and sent shadows leaping across his face as he went on.

"These great ones, these men and women who study magic, find that England is not a legend. Far from a legend, it is there, in some dimension apart from us. There are many places that only the great ones can see, and that most people are unaware of. And yet to believe that we can do without these places is absurd. The worlds drive each other forward. They depend completely on each other. Look at that star there." He pointed. She followed his gaze. "Leo, we call it—or part of your English constellation Leo. If someone was in Malonia, at a point that is somehow close to this place, that person might begin to think about the star Leo. For no other reason than the fact that I just mentioned it here. Your world and our world, even Malonia and England themselves, are linked very strongly. You speak Malonian here and call it English. You give the same names to your children, close enough. These things pass through."

Anna and Ryan listened in silence. Aldebaran went on: "The stars in your country, and the constellations, they all have names that make sense. Not so in Malonia. We named them later, and every time an astronomer tried to think of a name, something suggested itself. We absorbed your English star names, imperfectly but clearly. We have a strange assortment of names now, not knowing the reasons. Jupiter and Venus are nothing in our country."

Aldebaran frowned into the darkness. "Or my nephew. He was a very famous writer. I do not have printed copies of any of his books. But they all came to me, in visions and dreams. The books drifted straight from his head into mine, and I wrote them down. If you have powers, you have a stronger connection with your relatives, because a part of you is the same. That is why it was foolish of me to throw away the silver eagle when I had relatives here who could easily be the ones to find it—" He broke off. "But even across that distance, I could see what Harold was thinking, what he was writing. Thoughts are passing between people—and between places—all the time. Everything is. Spirit and thought, all these invisible things. And sometimes people also can pass through."

Anna turned the necklace around in her hand as Aldebaran talked. The light jumped over the skeletal chapel—over red stone arches and carved walls and, above them, the remains of a high vaulted ceiling with the stars shining through. The stone was twined with flowering creepers, and the white blossoms swung in the breeze, reflecting the light. Beyond the ruined window, Anna could see another light shining. It was growing brighter all the time. "Do you know what this place is?" Aldebaran said.

"This chapel?" said Anna. "Monica said it was a tourist site years ago, until the owner of Lakebank bought the land."

"He bought the land because I told him to," said Aldebaran. "I was that man's butler. And I told him to buy it because this is one of your unexplained places, and I wanted to investigate it. There are strange ruins everywhere in England; it is remarkable. Some of them are just that—ruins. Some of them, like this chapel, are places that are closer to my homeland, to Malonia. Places where the barrier between the worlds wears thin."

"The barrier between the worlds?" said Anna.

Aldebaran shrugged quickly. "It is a way of speaking. People say that there is a network of doorways into England from our country, but in reality it is less simple. The great ones—those trained in magic—have always been fascinated by the idea of England, and many of them have passed into this country. I have found, living here for so long, that there are places where I can see more clearly back into Malonia. One is the stone circle up on the hill. One is this chapel. I cannot go back but I can see, faintly."

"What about Ryan?" said Anna, watching the light grow still brighter. "He doesn't have powers; how can he move between places like you said?"

"Ryan is exiled by one who has powers," said Aldebaran. "My idea—and it may be wrong—is that this necklace of yours, which has the power of great men and women in it, would be enough to carry him back."

"He has good reason to think it," said Ryan, turning to Anna. "When you hold this jewel of mine, the one that comes from your necklace, you can almost see Malonia. I know you can."

Aldebaran shook his head. "I do not think it will be as simple as that, Ryan."

Ryan took off his own necklace and handed it to her. "Try," he said. "Doesn't the air change, and the darkness? If you watch carefully. Can't you hear faint sounds?"

Anna took the necklace and they sat in silence. Her own was still in her other hand. She was watching the light beyond the window again. And then a shadow crossed it. She stood up. "What is it?" said Aldebaran, his voice suddenly faint. Anna went to the door of the chapel. She could see what the light was now. It was a gas lamp. And others were emerging, in the darkness of the forest. "What are those lights?" she said, and turned.

Ryan and Aldebaran were gone. The lantern was gone. She was in a stone church. And the flickering light that had been the lantern now came from a rack of candles standing where

Aldebaran had been. She dropped Ryan's jewel and caught hold of the wall to steady herself. And it was a solid wall; it did not vanish.

She could hear voices close by, and she stumbled toward the door of the church, thinking they were Ryan and Aldebaran. But there was no one there. Beyond was a square, empty in the moonlight. In the darkness of the center was a fountain—a statue of a horse in a large round pool. But the pool was empty and crusted with green algae, and the horse's mouth was choked up with algae so that no water sprayed from it.

Then she saw where the voices came from. Two men were standing in the shadow beside the church—strangers in blue uniform. One was a young man with a chubby, boyish look about him. The other had his back to Anna. "We will close half the city," he was saying, and his voice sounded older. "It is safer in the current climate. Are you with us in this? Will you come with us?"

The young man shook his head. "I am undecided. It is a great thing to ask of me, and—"

The older man raised his hand suddenly and the other stopped. Anna could see the side of his face now. He was a handsome man, with defined features. Then he turned, and she saw the other side. A scar ran from his forehead to the bottom of his cheek, and where there should have been an eye, there was only a ragged socket. The scar had healed so crookedly, and must have been so deep, that the two sides of his eyebrow were far out of line. And he was looking at her. "Do you see what I see?" muttered Ahira. He took a step toward Anna and reached out his hand. "Faintly, do you see it?"

The young man turned and frowned. Anna backed away, toward the church door. Behind her, someone put a hand on her shoulder. She stumbled and dropped the necklace. "Anna!" said Ryan.

She was in the ruined chapel. The gas lamps around the square had vanished; the two men were gone. "What happened?" she said, reaching for her necklace. It was lying in the dust, and she did not know why.

"Do not touch that!" said Aldebaran suddenly.

"I could see two men," she said. "I don't know—was I dreaming?"

"You had that necklace in your hand, and suddenly you were drifting away from here." Aldebaran picked the necklace up as if it burned him, and took the lamp with his other hand. "Come on."

"It was strange," Ryan muttered to Anna. "It frightened me; I can't explain, but you were growing faint. You did not hear when I spoke to you. Where were you, Anna?"

"It was an old church, and there were lamps shining outside. And there were two soldiers—a young man and a man with a scar across his face and a missing eye."

"Ahira," Ryan said. "You saw Ahira."

"Who is he?"

Ryan spoke without looking up. "He is the one who shot my mother and father. I gave him that scar and took out his eye. I threw a knife at him."

"Hurry," said Aldebaran before Anna could reply, and they went up to the door of the house. He closed it behind them and bolted it four times. Then, still holding Anna's necklace, he disappeared upstairs. In the silence, they listened to his footsteps—up one flight, then the next, then—faintly—another.

"Is he taking it?" said Anna.

"That is what he prophesied," said Ryan. "That it would come back to him."

Anna started to say that she would miss the necklace, then stopped. She had a strange feeling that nothing was real anymore, and the lightness about her neck seemed just a part of that—no more. "He doesn't really understand these things," said Ryan. "Not even he understands them. No one does. He thought that he would study the necklace and find out what the great ones who made it had in their minds. But you cannot predict what these magic objects will do once those who made them are dead. They gain their own power."

"My necklace?" said Anna. "I never thought . . ." And again they fell silent.

Aldebaran crossed the attics of Lakebank, stirring up dust that no one had crossed for ten years or more. He went to the farthest corner, where an old box lay under the shadow of a beam, and opened the lid. Inside were several British army medals from a war whose name Aldebaran had forgotten, and beneath them were letters—letters from Raymond's greatest friend, who had died in action. Aldebaran had always regretted reading them. He put that out of his mind now. He laid the silver eagle among the medals and frowned at them for a moment, then closed the lid. Then he crossed the attics again and went slowly back down.

Ryan and Anna looked up when he appeared on the stairs. "It is late," he told Anna. "You should return home. I will walk with you."

"Then I'll come too," said Ryan.

"No," said Aldebaran. "You will stay here in the house. The

situation is growing dangerous. I cannot believe that Talitha will not act, if we really are being watched here."

"Uncle—" said Ryan as though he was afraid.

"I promise you, this will not be like last time," said Aldebaran, putting a hand on his shoulder. "We are prepared. There is no question of torture or soldiers ransacking the house. But we must be careful."

Aldebaran and Anna walked in silence into the dark. Ryan ran to the library window, and she turned back and saw him standing there, his eyes on her. He opened the window and called to her then: "Anna, come back."

She went to him. He leaned on the windowsill, looking down at her, the light behind him so that she could hardly make out his face. "What is it?" she said. He shook his head.

She reached out and put her hand on his, and he took hold of it and kissed it, then leaned out the window and kissed her. "You are caught up in dangerous times," said Ryan. "I wanted to tell you, Anna: be careful."

She nodded and gripped his hand for a moment. Then Aldebaran called, "Ryan, be sure to lock that window fast." Anna turned and followed him. Ryan closed the window and locked it, but he watched them until they were out of sight.

"I am sorry for what my brother did," said Aldebaran abruptly as he shut the gate behind them. "I have been thinking about it all evening. I am sorry for all of this. I wanted to find Harold's family and make things right with them. I had no intention of implicating you in these concerns of my country. I wrote the prophecy, and I threw away the necklace, and I failed to see . . ." Then he turned and looked at her, as though he was seeing her differently. "Although it is your country too. You are partly Malonian." He frowned at the road and spoke again, to himself rather than her. "I pray that all will turn out well."

They walked the rest of the way in silence. "Ryan told me you wish to be a dancer," said Aldebaran as they approached the hotel.

"Yes. I want to go to dance school. This year, if I get in."

Aldebaran nodded. "There was a girl I taught once who could have been a musician, but she married young and put her love before those things. That girl was Ryan's mother, and you know that she died."

"Yes, Ryan told me."

Aldebaran turned to Anna. "She was almost a daughter to me. I have no children, and I am separated from all my family here. But I am proud to have a niece like you." He studied her face. "This may be dangerous," he said. "I will not pretend. But I promise to take care of you."

Monica had locked the doors of the hotel. Anna climbed up the tree and through her bedroom window instead. Aldebaran waited until she switched on her light; then he turned and walked back to Lakebank. She stood at the window and watched him disappear along the road.

Ryan was at the library table, drawing on a scrap of paper, when Aldebaran walked in. Aldebaran picked it up and examined it in silence. It was a careful sketch of Anna's face. "Love brings down many captives," said Aldebaran.

"'And lifts up many princes also,'" said Ryan, snatching back the paper.

Aldebaran laughed, then stopped. "That is not Shakespeare," he said. "That is one of our poets."

"Diamonn," said Ryan. He set aside the picture. "Uncle, what does this mean? All of this."

Aldebaran sat down opposite him. "I will communicate with the leaders of the resistance. I will suggest that the plans for revolution should be brought forward. We have the silver eagle; I think that the power in it could carry an exile like you home; Lucien's government is in crisis. There is no better time than now to think about going back."

"Going back?" said Ryan. "Is this your grand plan? That just when I become attached to this country, we leave it forever?"

Aldebaran handed him a book. "Read this," he said. "These are the latest reports from the city. Things are growing serious. Perhaps we should set aside astronomy and archery and concentrate on the current situation."

Ryan took the book in silence. Aldebaran went to his desk but remained standing, looking into the empty glass case in front of him. "What can I do?" he said eventually. "You have to return, Ryan. We cannot stay here forever. And yet—"

"Uncle, I know," said Ryan, opening the book.

Anna did not sleep easily that night, without the necklace in her hand. She tried to imagine her old life at home: waking at five, hearing the traffic already whining, and practicing before school out on the playing fields, because more than anything she wanted to be a dancer. That old life seemed distant now. But when she slept eventually, she dreamed of the same things, as though nothing was different: her family gazing up at her while she danced across a stage edged with white lights. She could see them all, the relatives she knew and the shadowy man and child who were always there. Only this time those two faces were clear. The husband's face was Ryan's, and the child had his eyes.

That Sunday morning I woke early. I could not sleep for the weight on my heart. It was still pitch-dark. I was sure that I had dreamed something, but I didn't know what it was, and it was gone as I tried to catch it. It was quiet as the grave that night, silent as the cool, lifeless earth deep down where no sound of the living can reach. It was so silent that I could not think. Then, slowly, the noise rising like the footfalls of a stealthy army in the dark, it began to rain.

That afternoon it was still raining hard. The streets were streaming with mud and almost deserted. No one would go out in such weather. Except soldiers. They were the only ones who passed. I sat at my bedroom window, watching the rain and thinking of nothing. There was nothing to do, and I couldn't concentrate anyway. I would read the same sentence of the newspaper ten times, without understanding it. I could hear Maria and Grandmother talking in the living room, the low rise and fall of their voices, but I did not want to be with them either.

I thought I might visit Stirling's grave. I put on my overcoat and went into the living room. "You are not going out in this weather?" said Grandmother, following me with her eyes as I searched for the keys. I nodded. "Where are you going?"

Maria was beside her at the table, her hand resting on

Grandmother's arm. "Here," she said, and handed me a piece of paper.

The graveyard, I wrote.

"You will get ill, going out in the rain," said Grandmother. "You will get very ill. And there are soldiers about even though it is Sunday; there must be something wrong. Leo, stay in the house." Her voice was quavery and tearful. She caught hold of my arm. "Please, stay here."

I shook my head and went to the door. "I think he will be all right, Mrs. North," said Maria. "It is not cold outside, and it looks as though the rain will be stopping. Would you like me to build up a fire anyway, for when Leo gets back?"

Grandmother nodded and grasped Maria's hand. While they were laying out the coal in the grate, I left. I hurried down the stairs and out into the street. It was something to do, walking, and it made the pain in my heart duller and easier to bear. And I would rather be standing in the rain beside Stirling's grave than trying to read the newspaper again and again while the silence made my head ache.

As I started along the side of the square, two soldiers stepped out of a doorway. "Where are you going?" said one. I did not reply. "This area is closed for an important military operation," he said. "Did you not hear the announcements? Did you not read the newspapers?" I made to carry on walking. They did this sometimes, but I was not going back home because they told me to.

They glanced at each other uncertainly; then one of them caught my arm. "Unless you are going directly back to your house, you should not be out here," he said, struggling to keep hold of me. "If we see you again, you will be escorted back with an official warning." He pushed my arm roughly and let me go. I could feel their eyes on me as I went on.

In the next street I met two others, and three more in the next. These three would not let me carry on toward the graveyard. They stood in front of me until I turned back the way I had come.

I was suddenly tired, and I did not have the strength to go on. I sat down in the doorway of a house and rested my head on my arms. A moment later someone was tapping on the window—a wealthy-looking woman, glaring at me for sitting on her doorstep. I got to my feet again.

I walked a couple of streets farther, then sat down under the high wall of the locked Royal Gardens. The rain was running down my face but I did not care. I sat and closed my eyes and wished for the hundredth time that Stirling was with me. Stirling would not stand for this desperation. He would have said something to bring me back. I could not tell myself those things.

Sitting there with my eyes closed, I began to see a hill where the sun was shining, and the girl Anna and the prince. I had been a hundred miles from thinking of these things, and they were suddenly in my mind, as though someone else had put them there. I stood up and looked around, then thought of the book and took it out of my pocket. It was in two halves now— two shabby leather covers with loose pages between them.

What was the use of fairy tales and dreams now that Stirling was gone? This book could not bring him back. I was suddenly angry with it, this book that had told us all kinds of meaningless lies about a country that did not exist. Aldebaran was dead; we had no English relatives; the prince had been shot ten years ago. And yet this strange story was still haunting me and I could not shake it off.

I drew back my arm and hesitated for a moment. And then I threw the book with the last strength I had, over the fence into the Royal Gardens. I heard the pages scatter among branches, with a sound like a bird's wings, and then silence.

That was it; the story was gone. I turned and walked home.

❧

Aldebaran was gazing out the window without seeing the English sunlight. His mind was on his homeland, and the rain falling there, and his English family, who he could barely see. And a black book. He did not notice that Ryan was gone.

Anna was cleaning one of the guest rooms when through the window she saw Ryan approaching. She left the bed half made and ran down to the yard. "You should not have come here," she said, stopping in front of him.

"I had to see you."

"Aldebaran made you promise to stay in the house. Ryan—"

He caught hold of her hands. "It will be all right."

Monica was calling to Anna from somewhere in the building. Anna glanced at him, and they started across the lawn, away from the hotel, toward the waterfalls. "Even so," said Anna. "What happened before to make you so frightened? Did you say they sent soldiers here?"

He hesitated, then spoke. "They came to the house; I don't know how. Talitha must have arranged it. I was only a little boy. Aldebaran hid me out in the ruined chapel and told me to wait for

him there. A day I waited, and half the night, before I went back.
He was lying on the floor, very sick. I thought that he was dead. I
thought that I had lost him as well. . . ." He stopped. "I almost did.
But the next day he was sitting up in bed, telling me that Talitha
could never really harm him, and I chose to believe that. They
worked together for thirty years in the secret service, years ago,
before I was born. Perhaps it was true what he said. Perhaps he
knew her too well to be defeated by the things she thought of."

They started up the shaded path beside the waterfalls. "Why
didn't they look for you?" said Anna.

"It was a clever prophecy that Aldebaran wrote. Those who
believe it will not risk harming me because Aldebaran said that the
same harm would fall on them. And besides, the revolution is
Aldebaran's plan; he is the powerful man and the leader of the
resistance. He is the one they want. I am just there to fulfill
the prophecies he has written. Do you see what I mean?"

Anna was glancing back through the trees. "What is it?"
Ryan said.

"I don't know. I thought I saw something." She shook her head
and they turned and walked on. "But what did you want to talk to
me about?"

He folded his arms and unfolded them, then ran his hand
through his hair. "I wanted to speak to you without Aldebaran
there," he said, half smiling. "I hardly seem to have the chance now.
Listen, Anna—"

She glanced back down the hill again. "Did you hear that?"

There was a silence. They could hear nothing. "Anna, are you listening to me?" said Ryan. "Here, this is what I came to give you. Take
it." He put something into her hand. It was a folded sheet of paper.

Anna turned back to him and opened it. On the page was a

drawing. A portrait of her. She stared at it in silence, tracing the pencil lines. He was watching her carefully. "What do you think?"

"How do you know my face so well?" she said, looking up at him.

He laughed quietly, as though that was obvious. "Anna, I came here to tell you—" And then he stopped. There was someone standing on the path behind her, in the shadow of the rocks.

Anna turned. In the silence of the English wood, Ahira and Ryan stared at each other. Another man stepped out of the shadows— the younger soldier from the square. The third was a stranger with bristly blond hair, also in blue uniform. All of them were armed.

"Ahira," said Ryan, reaching for Anna's hand but missing it. His eyes were on the soldiers. In another second, the man with the scar across his face had a pistol out.

"Don't move," he said.

Ryan moved anyway, suddenly, toward Ahira. The blond man shouted something. There was a thud. Then Ryan was on the floor, blood running from his forehead. Ahira stood still, the pistol still raised from bringing it down on Ryan's head.

Anna dropped the picture and stumbled toward Ryan, but the blond man caught hold of her and bent her arm back so that she could not move. The youngest man fell to his knees. "What the hell did you do that for? Do you know who the boy is? If you've killed him—"

"Shut your mouth," said Ahira. "Get up. Stop wailing and get up."

"He's just unconscious!" said the man who was holding Anna. He was tying her hands, and every time she struggled, he smacked her hard across the head. "If you make a sound, I will shoot you," he said.

"What are you doing?" said Ahira. "Why are you tying her up? Darius, what—"

"This is the girl. She has the silver eagle."

"Let go of her!" Ahira raised his voice. "Of course Aldebaran would not be so stupid—"

"We will have to take her," said the young man. "She will go to Aldebaran if we leave her. Sir, we should go now, while Talitha can let us back through. I do not like this place, and you should not have harmed the boy—"

"Go, then," said Ahira, turning away from him. "Darius, take the girl with you."

The man still had hold of Anna's wrists. He adjusted something on his pistol and put it to the side of Anna's head. "Do not speak, please," he said. "Walk quickly. Do not look back."

Aldebaran came back from his thoughts "Ryan?" he said. There was no answer. He got up from his desk and went to the door of the library. "Ryan, come here!" he called more loudly.

He was troubled suddenly. He went through the house calling Ryan's name, then took his keys and started out along the road. He climbed over the wall and ran up through the wood, toward the waterfalls. By the time Aldebaran reached where Ryan lay, Ahira had gone. And the others were in the ruined chapel, quickly leaving England behind.

❧

*W*hen I came back to Citadel Street, a carriage was passing, flanked by soldiers. The horses struggled and labored in the streaming mud. I stopped in full view of the soldiers and folded my arms and watched it pass. I did not care anymore.

Someone was struggling in the carriage. I stepped closer to

it and saw who was inside it—Ahira himself, and two other military men. One of them, I thought I recognized—a man high up in the government who they called Darius. And a prisoner. A girl, bound and gagged. She struggled closer to the window and met my eyes for a second. And in that second, I recognized her.

I had thrown away the book; I had tried to drive the dreams out of my mind. And no sooner had I given up on the story than I had come back home to find Anna in the real world, a living girl—a prisoner of Lucien on her way to the castle. I stepped toward the carriage as it stopped at the point in Citadel Street where carriages could go no further. Then soldiers were in front of me, pushing me back so that I could no longer see. "What are you doing?" one was saying. "You should be in your home." I struggled, but it was no good. Ahira and the other two were mounting horses—the girl too, still tied hand and foot, was bundled onto Ahira's horse—and in another moment they had vanished.

"Where do you live?" the soldier was demanding, pushing me roughly. I pointed to our building and he let me go. "We will keep an eye on you," he said. "And make sure you get there safely."

Grandmother was alone in the apartment, but the fire was lit. "Come in and take off that wet coat," she told me cheerily, though there were new tears still lying on her face. I moved as if I was dreaming. I went to the window and leaned far out. I could see the horses moving slowly up the castle rock. Was it because Stirling was gone that I had lost hold of my mind? I had not seen that girl; it was impossible.

But in another few minutes, I had stopped caring about it. I was thinking of Stirling again, and Grandmother was crying with her face in her hands, and someone needed to get the dinner but neither of us had the strength. And whether she was real or not, that girl was a hundred miles away from anything that mattered to me now.

⤜⤛⤚⤙

"If you ask me, we should have shot Aldebaran," said Darius as they marched Anna through the castle. "The boy is nothing without him."

"No one asked you," said Ahira shortly.

"You cannot shoot a great one," said the young man.

"Why not?" said Darius.

"You just can't. It's like shooting a priest."

"I'd kill a priest if he stood in my way," said Darius with a laugh.

"And account for it in hell," said Ahira darkly. "Now shut your mouth."

They walked on in silence, along the torch-lit corridors underneath the castle. The youngest man lit his cigarette from one of the torches as they passed, and Ahira frowned at him but did not say anything. He marched ahead, and the younger soldiers glanced at each other. "Over there are the dungeons," said Darius to Anna, tightening his grip on her arm. The shadows leapt and wavered. There was a sudden wailing noise, and Anna started. "See?" said Darius. "That is a traitor to the king. He is a dangerous maniac, of the Unacceptable Class. He is to be executed as a public example tomorrow." He pushed her up to the door. Inside the cell was an old man, crying.

"Do you want to know how they execute them?" said Darius, pulling her on along the corridor.

"No," said Anna.

"I'm going to tell you. Ten bullets—just like that—and not one of

335

them misses. They stand you out in the yard, and they count down to when they shoot. From thirty—very slow. You should see them. They go whiter with every count. Piss themselves, some of them. Some of them throw up. It's strange, what it does to the mind." His hushed laugh echoed around the corridor. "Some of the women pass out. We shoot them anyway. I have executed countless traitors."

"Stop telling her," said the young man. "She is not your girl, that you have to boast to her. And she does not want to hear."

"It may interest her," said Darius. "It may yet be what happens to her."

The young man laughed uneasily. "Darius—"

"I'm serious. She is part of the prophecy. If Ahira believes in it, then it makes as much sense to shoot her as to bring back the silver eagle. Sir?" He raised his voice and Ahira turned.

"What is it?"

"I was just remarking that perhaps it would be wise to kill the girl."

"I think that the king and Talitha know better what is wise and what is not," said Ahira. "Stop trailing behind. I'm not a bloody schoolteacher. Darius, come here and tell me what Talitha told you in the square."

"Aye, where were you?" said Darius, leaving Anna with the younger man and jogging to catch Ahira up. "Ten minutes we were waiting in the carriage before you appeared back in the real world."

"It is nothing to concern you," said Ahira, raising his hand to his head. "Tell me what Talitha said."

"Aldebaran has been stirring up trouble. Revolution is imminent." Then he lowered his voice so that Anna and the young man could not hear.

"We have cleared half the city and taken Talitha away from

the battlefields for a day or more," said the young man, as if to himself. "We should have been certain that we were bringing the silver eagle back at least." Ahira glanced at him and he fell silent.

They started up a dark staircase, in the heart of the castle now. After another few minutes the young man spoke again. "Sir, you should not have hurt the boy."

Ahira did not ignore him this time. "Will you shut your mouth?" he shouted, making Anna start.

"I'm sorry," the young man said. "I'm sorry." His hand on Anna's arm was shaking.

"The boy will be all right," said Ahira very quietly. As she struggled up the stairs, her hands tied behind her, Anna began to pray that it was true.

They came up in a wide hall lined with carved panels. Guards opened a door for them, and Ahira pushed the younger soldiers through, then hesitated for a moment. "Listen," he told Anna, lowering his voice. "Do not be afraid." He was looking at her so strangely that she stopped still. "Go on," he said then, in a different tone. "Hurry. The king cannot wait forever."

Unsteady light was jumping over the walls of the low room. The firelight and the candles dazzled Anna's eyes, and she looked up and saw that they were reflecting off a golden throne. A tall man sat there, leaning back casually with his arms behind his head. He was wearing a crown. But he had two guns in his belt. He sat up and looked at Anna in silence, and she stared back at him.

She was staring because this man looked like Ryan. His features were almost the same, except for his eyes; even from here, she could see that they were a clear blue. But he had a kingly air about him that Ryan did not have at all. He stood up now, and the three soldiers bowed. "Curtsy to the king," whispered Darius. Anna hesitated, and he hit her across the head. She bent into an automatic curtsy.

Lucien now walked toward them, his eyes fixed on Anna. "This is the one Aldebaran wrote about," he muttered, then raised his eyebrows in the same way Ryan did, but with none of the humor. "Where is the silver eagle?" Lucien asked, turning to Ahira.

"She does not have it," said Ahira. "We have already—"

"She does," interrupted Darius.

"Quiet!" said Lucien, and he turned again to Ahira. "You are certain?"

"Yes." Anna wondered why he was saying this. He was not certain. He had barely spoken to her.

"We should search her," said Darius. "We cannot be certain else." Lucien nodded. Darius smirked and proceeded to search her, putting his hands into the back pockets of her trousers and running them down her legs. She stepped away from him.

"She does not have it," said the youngest soldier. "Get away from her. She's only young and she's scared of you." He was only a couple of years older than her himself.

"He's right," said Lucien. "Darius, I sometimes wonder about you. Have you no sense of pride?"

"Calm yourselves," said Darius, laughing and raising his hands.

"Are you talking to me?" demanded Lucien. "That is no way to talk to me."

"Forgive me, Your Majesty . . . I did not . . ."

"You are forgiven."

"I thought, Sire," ventured Darius, "that it might be wise to kill the girl. She is a part of the prophecy too, is she not?"

"I don't think that killing the girl would give any clear message to the people," said Ahira.

"He is right," said Lucien. "The silver eagle is real and solid. If we had it, Aldebaran's prophecy would mean nothing."

"Sire . . . ," murmured Darius. "Under torture, the girl might tell us where it is."

"We have no time for that," Lucien said, his voice rising. "Have you failed to understand the situation? The president of Titanica has sent half his army to the Alcyrian border. The common people are growing rebellious. We must fight two enemies, and Talitha has not the time to hunt for the silver eagle because of a prophecy that may or may not be valid."

"But, Sire . . . ," said Darius. "If you try to do too many things, you may end up doing nothing at all. That is something Ahira often tells you."

"Don't tell me what to do. If we suppress the people, the Alcyrians will break through the lines. If we beat back the Alcyrians, the people will rise up against us."

"Then perhaps killing the girl is the only choice left to us," Darius persisted.

"No!" Lucien said. "What will that solve? Nothing! We don't want the girl; we want the silver eagle."

"But has she given it to him yet?"

There was a pause. Then Lucien spoke again. "I will not take any action until I have spoken with Talitha." He seemed to be thinking for a moment. "Lock the girl in a cell; use an empty room if the dungeons are full. Do not give her food or water; we will need all the stores if we are besieged. I will ask Talitha what she sees fit to do next."

Ahira stepped forward. "Shall I take her?"

"I will," said Darius.

Lucien shook his head. "Ahira will do it. But go quickly; I need you back here." Ahira nodded, took hold of Anna's arm, and steered her out the door.

Thunder had begun outside, and lightning flashed, illuminating Ahira's face as they passed a window. The scar and his empty eye socket stood out starkly in the colorless light. Ahira led her through the castle, then into a dim room. He bolted the door, lit an oil lamp on the table, and said abruptly, "Sit down."

Anna went to the corner of the room. Ahira watched her in silence and the lightning flashed again. "Listen," she said suddenly, hearing her voice shaking. "Tell me, was Ryan all right? You didn't kill him after we went down through the trees? Please tell me . . ."

He stared at her as though he was surprised. "He is not harmed. He was waking when I left; I made sure of that."

Anna sat down and could not get up again. Ahira looked at her for a moment, then sat down himself, opposite her at the table. They stared at each other. "Your name is Anna," said Ahira then. "Am I right?" He laughed shortly at her expression, then stopped and frowned. "And shall I tell you how I know? Because the prince opened his eyes and said your name."

"Ryan did?" she said. "Ryan said my name?"

"Is that what you call him?" said Ahira.

There was a silence. "Why are you here?" said Anna. "I thought you were going back to them straightaway."

"I need to speak to you first." He got up heavily and untied her hands. Then he went to the window. Outside, somewhere beyond their sight, horses were moving through mud and men were shouting to each other. "I had never been to England before," said Ahira. "Seeing the prince there—it was strange. I had not seen him for ten years. Since the day I shot his parents. Listen to me."

"I'm listening," said Anna quickly.

She did not dare to look away. "You know that there is a prophecy concerning that boy?" he said. "Aldebaran wrote that whoever harmed the prince would receive the same harm. Do you know it?"

"Ryan has told me about it."

Ahira nodded. "I used to believe in that prophecy. The day we took the castle, I was the one who stopped the others from harming the prince. And then I began to forget it. In any case, I thought only of physical harm. But what harm more could I have done to that boy than shoot his family in front of his face? I realize it now. And they are talking of shooting you as well."

He turned to stare out at the storm. "After I hit that boy, I suddenly had—I don't know—a vision. That was why I remained on the hill. I could not move. I thought I was dying. This scar on my face—it is all the retribution that has fallen on me. I shot his mother and father. And the prince cares about you—I know he does—probably more than anyone else. I have one relative. The rest of my family disowned me when I joined Lucien's government. You probably do not blame them for it. You probably think I am an evil man. But I too have cared about people. I too have loved."

Anna did not reply. He turned back to her. "It may just be superstition, but I am afraid. There is something strange in the air. Riding here through the city, I heard the wind and the rain calling my name. It was not just my imagination; I really heard it." He sat down again opposite her and leaned forward, breathing fast. "You know Aldebaran; you have met him. Is he capable of doing that? Tell me what he can do."

"He can see what you're thinking," Anna answered carefully. "And the future."

Ahira leaned back and covered his face with one hand. "He is a very powerful man. My mind has been in torment since I hit that boy. I know that the prophecy will soon take effect; I am sure of it. These ten years have been borrowed time for me—escaping a punishment that will surely come, while all the time I thought that I was safe. Will I lose the only family I have? Would that be justice? I don't know how these great ones think when they write their prophecies, and I have no power to change destiny." He stood up again. "I will not let them kill you," he said. "That is why I cannot let them kill you. I can't have your blood on my hands as well as his mother's and father's. Do you understand what I am saying?"

"I don't know."

"I care about my family just as much as the prince cared about his," Ahira went on. "Perhaps I should write to my one relative. Perhaps I should let him know . . ." He turned to her. "Should I? Tell me."

He was leaning forward on the table in front of her, waiting for an answer. "Yes," she said eventually. "You should write to him."

He nodded. "Because if I do this—if I protect you from harm or even help you to escape—it will become dangerous. And I may not come out alive, and then it will be too late to set anything right. Our country is in a bad situation—you must see it. If the rebels bring the boy back and overthrow the government, I will be one of the first to be executed. But if I do not try to set right what I have done wrong, a worse punishment may fall on me whether we keep hold of the country or not."

There were footsteps outside suddenly. Someone was in the corridor. They both fell silent, listening.

There was a hammering on the door. Ahira crossed the room and opened it. Darius was there. He looked at them both and smirked faintly. "And you say that I have no pride," he muttered, catching Ahira's glance.

"What do you mean by that?" said Ahira.

"Nothing, sir. Nothing. The king needs you. At once."

Ahira stood in the doorway, still watching Anna, while Darius tied her to the chair and blew out the lamp. He watched her until the door closed between them and the younger man bolted it. And then she heard them both march away.

❧

*T*hat night I woke up about eleven. I had gone to sleep early, for the rain had brought a cheerless dark over the city, and I slept without dreaming. I was wide-awake now, and everything was suddenly peaceful. I could not explain it. I felt as though everything was going to be all right. There was no reason for the change, but I was calmer than I had been since Stirling had died, as though if I had picked up the newspaper, I would have been able to read it straight through.

Then, suddenly, I knew that Grandmother was gone. She was not in the house. I tried to hear her breathe, but I couldn't from this distance, so I got up and went into her room. I was right. Her bed was empty, the covers cast aside. She was nowhere in the apartment. I ran back to my room and pulled on some clothes. I picked up my keys, checked one last time—she was gone for sure—and went out.

The apartment door was ajar, and so was the front door downstairs. I shut them behind me as I went. Perhaps she had gone to the graveyard. I turned into the street, blinking against the light of the streetlamp. There was no sign of her. I turned left and broke into a run.

I found her in a narrow, dark street nearby. She was wearing only her nightgown, which clung to her thinly in the night breeze. I was so frightened I didn't even think about not talking. "Grandmother?" I called. "What are you doing?" She didn't hear. She was muttering furiously to herself. I reached her and took off my jacket and put it about her shoulders to cover her. She did not seem to see me. "Grandmother, come home."

She allowed me to lead her away, but suddenly she began shouting. The words she yelled weren't recognizable as real ones. They were harsh in the silence, and I tried to quiet her, but she shouted all the louder. A man came to the window of one of the houses and frowned sleepily out at us. "Shh, Grandmother," I told her.

Then two soldiers rounded the corner. Our eyes met. I tried to pull Grandmother away, but she stood still in the middle of the street. Casting a hasty glance behind me, I saw the soldiers turn from their route and begin to approach us.

"Grandmother," I muttered. "Shh. Be quiet. Quickly, let's go home."

"Hey!" shouted one of the men.

"Keep walking," I muttered to Grandmother.

"Hey—lad! Where are you going this time of the night?"

"Home," I called.

"Wait here," one muttered to the other, and he strode down the street toward us.

"Stop where you are!" the soldier told me. I stopped. "Where are you going with this madwoman?"

"She is not mad," I said.

"She is an Unacceptable. She ought to have proper care taken of her."

"She is not mad," I told him again.

"She is disturbing the peace," he said.

"That's why I'm taking her home," I said wearily.

He was beside us now, and he pushed at my shoulder aggressively. "Do not dare to take that tone, arrogant young bastard."

I stumbled and swore at him.

"What did you say?"

"Nothing." We began to walk away, Grandmother hurrying ahead of my guiding hand and glancing back fearfully at the soldiers.

"What did you say?" he demanded.

"Nothing."

"Hey! Stay where you are, I told you. Do you want to be arrested also?"

"You are not arresting either of us," I said. "We are leaving now."

"Stay where you are." He caught hold of Grandmother and stopped her. Immediately her screams shattered into the wet quiet. "Shut your mouth," he told her. She went on screaming.

"Stop!" I cried. "Let her go!" I grabbed at him.

"Get off me!" he shouted. Grandmother went on screaming. The jacket fell from her shoulders, and her gray hair slid from its tight knot, wild about her frightened face. I grabbed the soldier's rifle across his back, the closest thing I could catch hold of, and pulled at it hard. "Get off!" he yelled again.

"Let go of her!" I shouted. The rifle strap was choking his neck; he coughed, and his hands loosened their grip. I went on tugging at it. Grandmother's screams grew wilder.

Suddenly the strap broke. I fell down in the mud and so did Grandmother, from the sudden force. Her screaming stopped abruptly. I got up, dripping mud and still holding the soldier's rifle, wiped the water and earth from my eyes, and ran to her. She did not move. "Grandmother?" I said. I fell down on my knees beside her. She had fainted and was still unconscious. I turned her over, wiped the mud from her face, and shook her by the shoulders. The soldiers had disappeared into the night. "Grandmother!" I went on urgently. "Wake up!"

While I knelt there, I heard a sound, louder than the hushed drips from the sleepy houses, and getting louder still. It was footsteps. Steady footsteps, coming closer. I looked up and saw that a dark figure was approaching steadily. The figure glided up the street, with long strides, and all the while its face was in shadow. But by the inclination of its head, I could tell that it was looking straight at me. The whites of its eyes glinted in the light of the streetlamp as it approached. I stayed still, crouched on the ground like an animal, shivering in the mud.

Then, "Leo?" said the figure. "Leo! I did not recognize you. What are you doing here?" It took down its hood, and I saw that it was Father Dunstan. "Leo! What is going on?"

"Father!" I exclaimed. "It's Grandmother. She collapsed, and I cannot wake her. The soldiers came and—" He dropped down beside me.

"Margaret?" he said, taking hold of her shoulders. "Margaret, can you hear me?"

"Father, Father," I was saying suddenly, as though I was a child and he was my own father. I clutched his arm.

"All right. Calm down, Leo. Go on trying to wake her."

I tried to talk to her, but my voice sounded so feeble that I barely heard it myself. Father Dunstan took Grandmother's wrist, sat motionless for a moment, then nodded quickly. "I can feel a pulse."

"Then why won't she wake?"

"It must have been the shock," said Father Dunstan. "It can bring on attacks like this."

"Attacks like what? Father—"

And then, suddenly, she coughed and blinked. I let go of the priest's arm and caught hold of her hand. She did not grip it back. Her face was colorless, flecked with a few dark spots of mud. Eventually she looked up at me and mumbled, "Harold?"

"It's me, Leo," I told her. She began to cry.

"All right," said Father Dunstan. "Let's get her back home."

We managed to support her between us, though she was hardly able to walk. She was covered in mud and her face stood out pale, trembling and glistening with tears in the lamplight. She muttered, "Harold, Harold," over and over as we walked, like a prayer. "All right," I said, and gripped her arm more tightly. "We are almost home."

I heard myself say that from a long way off. My ears were ringing suddenly with a strange silence.

✳ ✳ ✳

Back in the apartment Grandmother went on shaking and crying. She collapsed on the sofa, staring into the cold fireplace with tears running down her muddy face. I fetched blankets and cushions and propped them around her, but that didn't stop her shivering.

Father Dunstan lit a lamp. Something in my left hand glinted, and I realized I was still holding that soldier's rifle. I dropped it by the door. The sound made Grandmother start and cry out. She went on asking for Harold and then mumbled something about Arthur. It occured to me distantly that she must mean Aldebaran. Father Dunstan boiled water for tea, and Grandmother drank some, still crying. "You have some tea too, Leo," he said, pushing a cup into my hand. "You have both had a shock." I drank some automatically and noticed that my hands were shaking. I stood up to ask him what to do, but I could not speak.

"How old is your grandmother, Leo?" Father Dunstan said then, drawing me aside.

It was stupid, but I couldn't remember. I had known once, before all this. "Sixty?" prompted Father Dunstan. "Or older?"

I started counting on the fingers of my right hand. "Sixty-one?" said Father Dunstan. "Sixty-two? You do not have to speak." He went on guessing. At sixty-five I nodded.

He stood silent for a long time. In that silence I heard Grandmother begin to tell me some story about her childhood, in a high, weak voice that did not sound like her own. "She is old, Leo," Father Dunstan said then. "And shock is not good for someone so old."

I just looked at him in silence. And then Grandmother came

back. She stared at us, felt the mud in her untidy hair, and started up from the sofa. "Leo!" she said. "What happened? Father?"

Father Dunstan knelt beside her and took her hands. "Rest there for a moment, Margaret," he said. "You have had a shock; that is all." He began to tell her, and she listened, tears rising in her eyes again.

"I was never like this before," she said, crying again, when he had finished. "What are we going to do without Stirling? I never had these strange turns, or felt so tired, when he was here."

"It is understandable that you are not quite yourself," Father Dunstan said. "These past days have been very difficult for you, Margaret. You need to rest, and you will begin to feel more normal." He went on talking to her, and she listened anxiously.

Moving slowly, I fetched a shawl for her and helped her wash the mud from her face. Father Dunstan made more tea and he and Grandmother talked quietly. I sat in silence and watched my own hands shaking. "I have to go," said Father Dunstan eventually, taking out his watch. "I was on my way to see a very sick child. I don't want to leave you like this, but I have no choice." In the half darkness of the room, he caught my eyes briefly, as if to tell me something. "You will be all right?" he said, turning to Grandmother.

"Aye, of course," she said. "I feel fine now, Father. I don't know what happened, but I'm sure it is nothing to be anxious about." But I could hear her voice quavering.

"Take care of your grandmother," he said, putting his hand on my shoulder for a moment. And then he left.

We sat in silence, without looking at each other. My hands

were shaking worse than ever. "Leo, Leo," said Grandmother then, trying to take them in hers. "Don't be afraid. It's all right now. I am myself again. It was just those soldiers."

It was not fear that was making my hands tremble and my heart beat fast. I thought I could see the room growing darker in front of my eyes. I could tell suddenly that I was going to do something like I had before—throw a chair through the window or hit my head against the wall. But Grandmother was so weak and frightened; I was terrified of shocking her again. I thought that if I sat still and kept my eyes closed, I would be safe. I willed myself not to move.

The lamp went out. I didn't dare to get up, so we sat in darkness. I could hear Grandmother's breathing—deliberate and irregular, as though she had to think about it—but nothing else. And then there was a sudden bang at the door.

Grandmother tried to get up. I raised my hand to stop her from moving. "Go and answer the door, Leo," she said weakly. "Please go. It must be Father Dunstan back again."

I forced myself to go to the door. "Hurry," said someone outside. It was not Father Dunstan's voice. Light showed under the door, flickering strangely. I struggled with the catch, then got it open.

Outside was a soldier with a burning torch in his hand. He stood close enough that I could feel the heat on my face. "Good evening," he said. "Are you the main occupant of these premises?" I didn't answer. He smirked faintly and went on. "An Unacceptable has been traced to this address. I am here to bring you the warrant for her arrest and detainment under the Unacceptable Classes Act Clause 24."

He handed me a folded sheet of paper. It fell through my

fingers. He shrugged and went on with his recitation. "Soldiers will arrive in the next few days to collect her and take her to an appropriate center. You are advised that—"

Behind me, Grandmother started to cry. She was sobbing loudly, rocking back and forth, her face in her hands. The soldier raised his torch and took in the mud in her hair, her filthy nightdress, and the dark, shabby room. Then he laughed and shook his head. "Poor old bitch. This is life, eh?"

"I'll kill you," I said out loud.

He raised his eyebrows and gave me a jovial punch on the shoulder. "Just try it."

There was a silence while we stared at each other. I clenched my fists until my knuckles burned with pain. "Leo, come away from the door . . . ," Grandmother was murmuring.

"Thank you for your cooperation," said the soldier, turning to leave.

I swayed in the doorway and tried to remain still. Then I could not. I pushed him against the wall, then snatched the torch from his hand and threw it hard down the stairs. Next thing, I had hold of his shirt as if to strangle him. I stumbled on that rifle in the doorway, and I suddenly had it in my hand, trying to bring it down on his head, but he caught my arm. My heartbeat was thumping in my forehead; he was swearing; Grandmother behind us was crying out, her voice high and frightened. "Leo, stop!" someone else was shouting then, trying to separate us. And then louder, "Don't hurt Anselm! Don't hurt Anselm!"

I collapsed onto my knees. There was blood on my forehead; he must have hit me. Maria had separated us. She was kneeling in front of me now, in her nightdress, the baby screaming in her arms. The soldier was hurrying away down the stairs.

"I heard noises, and I came to see," Maria was gasping. "Leo, I didn't want you to get into bad trouble; you looked like you were going to kill him. Who was that man? What did he want?"

She reached for my hand. I did not want her to touch me. I staggered away from her, still shaking. I was frightening myself now but I could not help it. I got up and ran down the stairs, struggling with the safety catch on that rifle. I could still hear Grandmother sobbing, and Maria was calling after me to come back. At the bottom I tripped and crashed down hard on the floor. I staggered to my feet again. I pulled open the front door and ran out into the alley.

The street was empty. The soldier had gone.

I fired a shot anyway, into the silence. Then I fell down in the alley and rested my head in my hands.

❧

"What was that?" said Lucien, on the balcony. The distant gunshot had sent a bird snapping through the treetops of the roof garden below.

"A troublemaker in the city," said Talitha. "The law enforcement will be there, no doubt."

Lucien nodded, but his eyes had darkened. The others stood in silence and watched him. Ahira was a short way off, frowning into the night. Darius and Anna had just come out onto the battlements, unnoticed. Cannons pointed into the starlit sky from this highest balcony, and Anna glanced at them now. Darius stepped forward. "The girl, Your Majesty. You sent for her."

Lucien turned. Talitha remained where she stood, her back to the others so that Anna could not see her face.

Lucien took a couple of steps toward Anna. "You do not have the silver eagle?" he said. "Not on your person, here in Malonia."

"No," Anna said. Lucien stared at her for a moment. Then he muttered something to Talitha, and she turned to look at Anna.

Anna was startled. Ryan had said that Talitha had been in the secret service for thirty years with Aldebaran, but that was not possible. This woman was young—perhaps only thirty—a beautiful woman with very red lips and dark eyelashes. She did not look like someone trained in magic. She did not stand resigned and wise either; she put her arm about Lucien's shoulder and ran her mouth idly over the side of his face, and he pressed his face into her neck as he talked.

Talitha replied, in a low voice. Anna started suddenly. She had thought that something was inside her head. A spider was crawling inside her skull, over everything that she had ever thought or felt. Talitha was staring at her strangely. Anna tried to look away and think of nothing, but she could not do it; she could not look away.

"She does not have the necklace . . . ," whispered Talitha to Lucien. Then she lowered her voice still further so that no one else could hear. The others waited. Ahira glanced at Anna briefly, then turned and looked out over the silent city.

"What if the girl has not actually given the jewel to Cassius?" said Lucien.

"What if?" said Talitha. "It will make no difference. The necklace is what is important. The gift means nothing. This is science." She paused. "One interesting thing though, Sire. This girl is not irrelevant. She is an English relative of Aldebaran's."

"What does this mean?" said Lucien. "That we can hold her as a hostage? To make Aldebaran give up the silver eagle? You mean to say torture . . ."

Talitha went on muttering, and Lucien nodded at everything she said. Then he turned to Anna and considered her for a moment. "It is regrettable, but there is no other course that we can take. We cannot kill Cassius; the silver eagle is hidden and we do not have time to retrieve it by any other means."

"I will communicate with Aldebaran," said Talitha. "I will give him half an hour. Long enough to panic; not long enough to think. After that, we can kill the girl anyway and nothing will be lost." She turned to the two soldiers. "Tie that girl up."

Darius hurried away down the stairs to fetch ropes, then appeared again and tied Anna's hands and feet, smirking. "Do that carefully!" Talitha said suddenly. Darius stopped where he was, still winding the rope around Anna's ankles. "This girl is a close relative of a very powerful man," said Talitha.

Lucien turned to her. "Does she have powers? This English girl?"

Talitha glanced at Anna again. "Yes," she said. "Yes, she does." Then she looked away. "One of you, keep your rifle trained on her."

Darius swung his rifle off his shoulder and raised it, then pretended to fire a shot with a quick laugh.

"I will do it," said Ahira, putting his hand on the gun. "You are supposed to be at the border, and it will take you the night to get there."

Darius stared at Ahira for a moment, then shoved him hard with his shoulder. Ahira grabbed the rifle, and at the same moment there was a gunshot. The bullet ricocheted off the castle wall. Ahira wrested the gun from Darius's grip. "Go to the border," he said firmly. He put the gun back into the soldier's hands, flat, but stood between him and Anna. Darius looked to Lucien.

"Go," said Lucien. "Ahira will come later with me. You are needed there."

"But surely, it will only take—"

"Go! Stop arguing and go!"

Darius disappeared through the doorway, muttering, and clattered away down the stone staircase. Silence fell. "Aldebaran," said Talitha into the silence.

"Can he hear you?" whispered Lucien.

In England, in the dark library beside the lake, the great Aldebaran started and looked up. The rising wind and the waves of the lake had called his name.

Lucien paced up and down the balcony. "What is Aldebaran doing?" he said after a while.

"I cannot tell," said Talitha. "I will send troops to the ruined chapel at midnight. If Aldebaran is there, they will take the silver eagle from him."

There was silence again on the balcony. Anna's eyes were fixed on Ahira. He glanced at Talitha, then turned to Anna and mouthed something about ropes. She tried to pull her hands free, and he gave a quick nod.

The ropes had been tight enough to cut her wrists, but they were loosening now. She concentrated her mind on them and the knots slid outward. Then Talitha turned. "I will tighten those," she said.

Anna started to gasp but could not breathe in. The ropes were tightening about her wrists and ankles, but not just the ropes: the air was suddenly tightening around her as well. Her heart was thudding strangely, first in her head, then in her chest, then in her stomach. She could not breathe, and she felt the air crushing her bones. Her chest was stabbing with pain. She fell sideways onto the floor, the air pressing down on her as heavy as steel.

Then Talitha turned away, and Anna was lying in the dust, gasping in air again and shivering. "Aldebaran cares about his family," Talitha said. "Fifteen minutes he has now. I think this will work."

"Is it really necessary to torture a young girl, Talitha?" began Lucien. "I mean to say—" Talitha raised her hand, and he fell silent.

"Where are you going?" demanded Ryan as Aldebaran ran down the stairs.

"The chapel. Stay in the house."

Ryan rubbed his bandaged head and got up, though the room swayed in front of him when he did it. "Uncle, you will not tell me what is happening. Tell me about Anna; is she safe? Please—"

"I have no time. I have to go. Stay here."

Ryan grabbed Aldebaran's arm, running after him into the dark. He swayed then, and Aldebaran caught hold of him to stop him from falling. "Go back to the house. Now, Ryan!"

"Tell me why you are going to the chapel."

"I can't tell you. Ryan, if you don't let me go—" Something fell from Aldebaran's hand and landed, glittering, on the grass. There was a silence.

"That is the silver eagle," said Ryan. "Uncle, I don't understand what you are doing."

Across the lake, the church clock chimed twelve.

Talitha, on the balcony, shook her head. "Aldebaran has not come?" said Lucien.

"I was not sure," said Talitha. "Aldebaran does not care enough about his family, perhaps." She turned to survey Anna. "We have lost nothing. But we will have to kill this girl anyway. He will have his resistance people here storming the castle if he thinks there is a chance that she can be rescued. We cannot give him time to think. I will go down and tell them to call the troops back from the church. I will be back here in a few minutes."

Lucien turned to Ahira. "Untie her and stand her against that wall."

"I will take her down to the yard," said Ahira, untying Anna's ankles and wrists. "I will do it there. Or perhaps we should not be so hasty. Perhaps we should hold her in a cell for another night."

"No! We have no time; you heard what Talitha said. Aldebaran could use this to provoke the people to revolution—a noble cause, rescuing the prince's true love. We must finish this and assemble the army at once. Do you not understand?" There was more than a trace of panic in Lucien's voice. "The enemies among us have been in contact with him for months. The army uncovered one of their bases today, with stacks of communications, detailed plans. We are on the brink of revolution. The boy must not return. We have to stop Aldebaran's words from being fulfilled. It's not enough to go into hiding and kill him when he gets here. We will never get power back once we have lost it. We have to show them that there is no future except for King Lucien. Shoot the girl quickly. Let us do what we can about this problem, and then turn to the Alcyrians."

Ahira took a pistol from his belt and aimed it at Anna's head.

Lucien turned to look out over the balcony again. She opened her mouth to speak but she could not. Ahira looked straight into her eyes for a moment. Then she shut them.

Stumbling through the dark forest, Aldebaran heard the gunshot and fell to his knees. Ryan ran up to him, catching hold of his arm again. "What is it? Uncle, what is it?" And Aldebaran turned to say that he had told Ryan to go back to the house, but he could no longer speak.

Anna opened her eyes. Lucien, silhouetted on the balcony, fell to the floor.

His blood was running over the stones, toward her feet; she clasped her hand to her mouth and could not move. Ahira lowered the gun and turned back to her. "Don't speak." His voice was shaking. He grabbed Anna and pushed her through the door.

They stumbled out of control down the staircase. "Talitha will know," Ahira said. "Soon, she will know. Run fast and stay with me."

They raced through the dark corridors and stairways of the castle, whipping up the flames of sleeping torches as they passed. Ahira kept one hand on her shoulder, the pistol still raised in his other. At the side door, he paused and surveyed the empty yard.

Somewhere high above them, someone cried out suddenly—at first a shout, then a wail that did not fade in the night air. "Run," said Ahira. "Stay with me. That is her; that is Talitha."

He pushed her toward the stables. "Smith!" he called out to the nearest soldier. "Get me a horse, quickly."

The man was barely older than Anna, with sunburn peeling on his nose. He fetched a horse and put the reins into Ahira's hand, bowing slightly. Ahira swung Anna up onto the horse and climbed on behind her. He bent to speak to the man. "The king is dead," he said. "Alert your people. Alert your revolutionaries." The man stared at him, raising his hands as though he was afraid. Then Ahira kicked the horse into a gallop and they were at the gates. "That boy is with the resistance," said Ahira. "I have been watching him for a long time. He will tell the right people."

There were shouts as they turned from the gate onto the road, and gunshots from the windows above. The ground burst with bullets around them. The horse skittered sideways as it turned the corner, and Anna was looking suddenly over the edge of the rock face. But it scrambled back into a gallop and went on. Then there was shouting, closer, and hooves were rapidly leaving the yard above them. Anna was slipping on the horse's back. "All right," said Ahira, throwing one arm around her waist. "Listen, believe that the bullets will miss. You have powers; you can protect us. Please." He shouted at the horse and it galloped faster. Then they were in the town and sheltered for a moment from the falling bullets. A crowd of people leapt out of their way as they passed.

Ahira directed the horse into a narrow street, without letting go of Anna's waist. It stumbled and lurched forward, and her heart jumped, but Ahira did not let her fall. The noise behind was suddenly growing fainter. "When we get to the church," Ahira muttered, "don't look back at me; just go. Leave me to whatever comes. All right?"

❧

After I stumbled down the stairs, I remained in the alleyway and could not get up. Maria came down, and Grandmother, but I did not move. "Leo, you are shaking," said Grandmother. "You are not well. Tell me what it is." The baby screamed. I sat there with my eyes closed and would not answer them, though they came down several times.

"We will be upstairs," said Maria eventually. "I understand if you want to stay by yourself, Leo." And they left me there in the silence.

I was trying to force myself to stay still until I was calm. I managed it for a long time; it felt like hours had passed while I sat motionless. But then I had to do something. I had to, otherwise I would go insane. Hot tears were burning in my eyes. I wanted to find that soldier. Or anyone. I did not care anymore. I could feel my hands shaking as though they were someone else's, and hear my heart beating like a stranger's heart. It made me frightened, but I went on. I stumbled out into the street.

People began surging past me. They were as far away as ghosts. "Revolution! Revolution!" they were chanting. One of them tried to pull me along with them, but I pushed him away. Then they were gone, and again the street was silent.

My heart had turned cold. I hated everything suddenly—the dark street around me and those people who had passed, the castle on the rock above, the blue flags flying, and every one of the soldiers. The soldiers most of all. I fell down in the mud of the alley again and pressed my face to the ground. I tried to drown myself. I really did. I was so angry that I could not go on living without doing something terrible. But I thought that if I lay there long enough, it might still be all right.

Lying there, drowning in the wet earth, I realized that I could hear shouts. Not only shouts, but horses' hooves also, and gunshots. I rolled over, still lying in the mud, and stared down the street. In that moment—that last moment of stillness—I saw everything as if it was caught in glass. A horse, going at a gallop. On the horse were two people. One was that girl, Anna, their captive. Behind her was the soldier. Lucien's man, Ahira. Not just a soldier, but the worst of them all. I hated him above all others. I was so angry that the stars shivered, and I saw lightning though there were no clouds. That was why I did it. That was when I decided. And even in that moment, I was praying silently, Don't let me do this.

I put the rifle to my shoulder. I aimed it at the man's head. He could not see me, because he had no eye on the right-hand side of his face, and that was the side that was toward me. Still, everything seemed frozen. I couldn't think. But I didn't need to. I closed my eyes and pulled the trigger.

Time stopped with that gunshot. "Get to the church!" Ahira gasped in that moment. Then he landed hard in the road. In the darkness of an alleyway, someone moved.

The horse pounded off again. Anna was slipping now, without Ahira to hold her. She lost her grip on the horse's mane. She tried to turn back to see what had happened, but the horse was galloping faster now. As it turned a corner, she jolted into the air and fell.

She was suddenly on her back in the mud, staring up at the stars. For a moment she made out the English constellations, startled to see them here. Her heart was beating so fast it hurt her, but she was not injured. She lay there, gasping not enough air into her lungs. Then she sat up. The horse had disappeared.

She could see the domed roof of the church below, only a few streets away. She got up and began running, but her legs were weak now. The torture Talitha had inflicted had left her muscles shaking, and as fast as she ran, she could hear the hoofbeats coming closer above her. And gunshots. Anna came out onto the edge of the square, fell to her knees, and crawled into the doorway of a house. After that she did not dare to move. They were closing in, down the alleyway above her. Ahira was shot, and they could shoot her too. There could be snipers on the roofs and machinegun posts in these dark houses. She could not tell. She glanced around the square, suddenly dizzy, and the stars tracked across the sky as though they were falling.

In that moment, lying there in the doorway, Anna did not think about whether she would die. She was suddenly thinking about powers. About what Talitha had said, and what Ahira had said. Believe that the bullets will miss. It was only forty steps to the door of the church, and she could run that far. She stood up and closed her eyes, still in the shadow of the doorway. And then she ran out into the square.

Someone shouted, but Anna did not turn. She could hear gunshots now, and a strange whistling in her ears, and dull thuds ahead in the wall of the church. She ran faster. One of the horse statue's ears shattered ahead of her. A gas lamp exploded behind. In a house close by, a child screamed. Then something caught the side of her head and she stumbled. But she was inside the church. Anna fell down and crawled between two pews. And suddenly silence and darkness surrounded her.

⁓⁓

I came back suddenly. The anger left me. I was flat in the mud of the street, dazed and shivering, with a rifle against my shoulder. Ahira lay motionless in the road.

In the silence he moved feebly and lay still. Then I realized it: I had shot him. I stopped breathing.

And after that, I don't remember so well what happened.

I had the stupid thought that perhaps he was not dead. I stumbled over to where the body lay. No. He was dead all right. I was shivering uncontrollably now. I wondered if I was possessed. If someone else had taken me over and ordered me to fire that shot. Nothing seemed real. I sat down beside him in the road and told myself it was only a dream.

There was a gold ring on his finger, glinting in the light of the streetlamps the way my own christening bracelet was. This close, I could even see the lines on that famous man's hands, and the fine streaks of gray in his hair. I had not shot this man, I kept telling myself. It was impossible.

Then I could hear horses approaching behind, and shouts. Soldiers. I crawled into the darkness of the alley and watched them. They reined in their horses and leapt from them, talking urgently. I got to my feet without knowing what I was doing and staggered back up the stairs.

I collided with someone at the apartment door. It was Maria, asking what was going on. I was shaking and I could not stop. The darkness outside the window was thick with gunshots. Grandmother got to her feet and came toward me. "I can hear the soldiers talking out there," she told us urgently. "They will come to take me away. I am not mad! Maria, they want to take me away, after all that has happened already." And she began to cry again. Maria put her arms around Grandmother, her eyes on me as I moved about the apartment with that rifle in my hand.

"Leo, you are covered in mud," Maria said. "What is it?

What did that soldier want, the one who was here earlier? Your grandmother did not say."

Grandmother was explaining, her voice choked and quavering. "Come up to my apartment," said Maria. "They will not find you there, Mrs. North. My father is back and he won't let them in."

Grandmother nodded slowly, blinking the tears out of her eyes. "Thank you, Maria." She turned to me. "Leo, will you fetch me some clothes?"

I was dreaming again, worse than ever. Nothing was real and I did not care. I fetched clothes for her, and a thick shawl. The night was warm, but my own skin felt as cold as steel and she was shivering too. In my head, seconds were counting down relentlessly all the time. I thought of soldiers battering down the door, to take her to a center for Unacceptables, or to take me to prison. Because I was a criminal now, a murderer. I had killed that man.

I shook my head, pressed my fingers into my eyes until I saw white lights in my forehead, and forced my hand to release the gun. The clattering on the floor made Grandmother start. And me, even though I was the one who had dropped it. Maria was staring at me anxiously. I picked up the water jar from the table, trying to behave as though there was nothing wrong. But on the way back to the kitchen, a fit of shaking came over me, and I dropped it. It shattered on the floor.

"Oh, Leo!" Grandmother exclaimed. "That will be expensive to replace!" She sounded almost like her usual self, and it was the more ridiculous after what had just happened. "Why can you not be more careful like . . . ?" She trailed off. She had been going to say "like Stirling."

"Leo," said Maria quietly. "You are not yourself. Come upstairs and sit down for a while. Or tell me what is wrong." She went on watching me. "Do you just need to sit by yourself?" she said. "Is that it?" I nodded, trying to reassure her. I could feel my teeth rattling against each other. "I will be back in a minute," she said. "I will just help your grandmother upstairs."

When she had gone, I picked up the rifle again. I pulled back the bolt to reload it, then realized that there were no more bullets. That had been the last. I almost laughed at that, though it was not funny. Then I thought of something. I went to the bedroom and opened the window seat chest. Underneath that private's uniform was the pistol, still loaded. I took it out, checked the safety catch, and put it into my pocket.

I went out and down the stairs, keeping tight hold of the handrail to stop myself from falling. I tried to force myself not to look at the place where Ahira had landed, but my eyes moved to it by themselves. The body was gone. There was a dark patch where the blood refused to combine with the mud and disappear. I think I would be able to walk to that place even now and find to the nearest inch where he landed. It was burned on my mind already and I could not erase it.

I heard gunshots in the city. They were becoming a familiar sound, as though they were part of the weather. Smoke was rising from somewhere. The stars overhead were very clear, drifting over the sky as I walked; the buildings looked more solid in the moonlight than anything real, like an empty stage set. Everything looked like that. As I walked, I began counting the steps I took. Then the Voice spoke to me. "Go back," it said. "Go back to Maria and wait until you are calm. Don't go on walking." I ignored it.

The gunshots in the city had subsided when I reached the graveyard gate. As I stood there, the deserted graveyard seemed endless, the city back across the bridge more than infinity. Stirling's grave was the only safe place. I found it and knelt beside the wooden cross. The moonlight was falling across the grass and shadowing the letters of the inscription. It was only then that I really thought of Stirling. Before that I had hardly been thinking at all. And I began to realize what I had done.

I could not stay there; I had to go on walking. I decided suddenly to go to the hills. No one would find me there. I walked, without thinking, away from the city.

❧

*I*t must have been nearly dawn when I stopped, though it was still as dark as ever. I was out of hearing of the church clocks in the city now. The last time I had heard them, they had chimed three. I was too tired to go on. I collapsed on the grass and stared at the stars.

I felt nothing—but I would, soon enough, and I knew it. All the way from the city, I had been trying to tell myself that. I had shot Ahira—really shot him; it was not just a dream. I could do nothing to change it. My life was ruined and there was no way to repair the damage that was done. And if I went back now and tried to carry on as if things were normal, I would have to know every day that I had shot him. The same way I knew every day now that Stirling was gone. I could not go back. It was too much; I did not have the strength.

I sat up and took the pistol out of my pocket. I emptied out the bullets and counted them, then put them back in and took off the safety catch. It would be an easy thing to do. You can pull the trigger of a Delmar .45 with your little finger. It would be easy even to pull it by accident. Perhaps that would be the best way, I decided. Continue thinking, and then pull the trigger while I was not concentrating on doing it, so I would not think of the pain. I was always frightened of pain. I'd never have made a soldier.

I put the gun against my head. I tried to summon the strength to do it. Just enough strength to pull the trigger, and that would be the end of it. The real end this time. I closed my eyes.

~~~~~

In the forest, Aldebaran and Ryan were kneeling motionless. Ryan started up then. "Did you hear that?"

"What?" said Aldebaran, making no attempt to hide the tears running down his face.

"There was a sound, Uncle. Up by the old chapel."

Ryan ran ahead. Aldebaran followed him. They reached the door of the chapel and stood in silence. There was someone lying inside. "Anna," said Ryan then. "Anna, Anna." He ran to her and took her head onto his knee. He put his hand against her face and it came away dark with blood. He was crying now himself. "Help me, Uncle!" he shouted.

Aldebaran fell to his knees beside Anna. "She is breathing," he said. "These are only surface wounds."

Aldebaran picked Anna up and they started down through the

forest. She woke and saw his face and tried to tell him something, then closed her eyes again. Ryan was praying. "Run ahead and call an ambulance," Aldebaran told him.

Anna opened her eyes when they reached the shore of the lake. The stars were beating in time with her heart. And then they went dark.

In that strange country, the moon rose from behind a cloud as though it was gliding. It illuminated every tree and every ripple of the lake and shone down on the ambulance that was moving along the road beside the waters. And over the Malonian eastern hills—over another, smaller valley—the moonlight grew brighter and sharpened to the same color, as if there was no division between the worlds anymore.

～⁓⁓

In the days after Ahira was assassinated, a hundred people would claim that act for themselves. Perhaps they were right. It was not really mine. It was as though someone else took control of my arm and my mind. I must have spent half a second aiming the rifle, but the bullet struck true. And Ahira fell, a long way away. I could almost have believed that it was someone else who shot him.

But I must be honest: in that half second when I aimed the rifle, I knew what I was doing. I felt as though things had become clear to me. It was not Ahira who I shot at, not only him. It was Sergeant Markey, for what he said about our mother, and the truancy officer who drove me back to school with threats, the sergeant in Ositha binding my hands tight enough to cut them, the men who closed the city and would not let me go to my brother's grave, the two who

368

knocked Grandmother down in the mud, the private who brought that warrant to the door and looked at us as though we disgusted him. And I fired the shot because they drove me to it. They brought it on themselves. That was how I felt in that half second of stillness. As though it was not me but him who was responsible.

The dawn will be rising soon, and still I sit here reading. You must be asleep by now, thinking that I have gone home. Or perhaps you are watching at a window. It is the darkest point before the sun rises, and I am the only one left now. The balcony is silent.

I remember how the city looked that night when I ran to the hills, strange and distant and too solid. I did not realize what I had done, not then. I have had enough time to realize it since. I wrote this because you asked me why I did it. You asked me to explain.

I would not have shot Ahira if Grandmother had not wandered out that night. If those soldiers had not come at that exact minute, when I was already desperate. If I had kept my mouth shut and not sworn at them. Even after everything, after Stirling was gone, I might not have done it. Was it just chance, then? I don't know. In that moment, when everything stood still, I hated Ahira. Maria told me I would never get to hate him as much as she did. She was wrong. I did. I don't know why.

I don't have the heart to read on, but if I don't, I'll have to let you read this. And I can't do that yet. Not after so long. I will read to the end, now that I have started. I cannot think what else to do anymore.

*O*ut in the hills I sat up suddenly, without knowing why I did it. There was someone close by.

I let my finger fall from the trigger of the pistol, but left it resting against my head. A girl was moving along the other side of the valley. The moonlight turned her eyes to silver and carved deep shadows in her hair. Everything had brightened suddenly. The stars above made the whole sky clear blue; the stream shone like liquid silver. The moonlight was streaming through that small valley, flowing over the girl on that side and me on this side and every blade of grass between us. Even my own hand on the gun was shining. It made me dizzy. I sat motionless, watching her. Then she turned and saw me.

"What are you doing?" she said. In the silence her voice carried clearly.

I realized suddenly that she was the girl I had seen with Ahira, the girl who had been haunting my dreams for weeks. "Anna," I said, standing up. I watched her in silence, and she gazed back at me across the valley, a ghostly figure shining in the dark. "Are you an angel?" I said then. She didn't answer. "Who are you, then? The Voice?"

"What voice?"

"Are you a spirit? Are you dead?"

"I don't know anymore," she said.

"How can you not know?"

And then I realized that I didn't know anymore if I was dead either. Perhaps I had actually pulled the trigger. It's easy to shoot even when you don't completely mean to do it. Just a trigger you can pull with your little finger.

And when I thought of that, the hills vanished and Ahira was falling to the ground again. It was not just a vision—it was really in front of my eyes, and closer than before. I shook my head. It wasn't me who fired that shot, I thought then. It was someone beyond the control of my mind. I didn't order my hand to shoot, or will the bullet to fly straight. Perhaps a real soldier had been hiding close by in the dark and had fired at the same time I had, someone who could shoot faultlessly and was used to killing.

"What are you doing?" Anna said again, away on the other side of that small valley. I blinked and remembered where I was: out in the eastern hills in that strange bright moonlight, not lying in the mud watching Ahira fall. I didn't answer.

"Don't shoot yourself," she said.

I tightened my grip on the gun. "You can't stop me," I told her.

"Take that gun away from your head."

"Why? No one would care if I did this."

"How do you know?"

I shrugged. "There are some things you just know."

"Take the gun off your head. Please."

I did it, but partly because my arm was aching. She was walking down the hillside toward me now. I hesitated, then began to walk down to meet her. "Why were you doing that?" she said. "Please tell me."

All the time we were walking toward each other, she did not take her eyes off mine. I told her everything that had happened in the days since Stirling had been gone. And then we were facing each other across the stream. I stopped still. The moonlight was caught inside the water; the stream was carrying it along in a bright channel. I switched the pistol from my right hand to my left and then back again. "Are you going to try to stop me?" I said.

She shook her head. "I can't stop you."

"What are you doing out here in the hills?" I asked her.

"I don't know. Maybe I'm dying. Everything went dark and now I'm here."

I ran my fingers over the cold barrel of the gun without really noticing it. "This isn't heaven," I told her.

"No."

Time passed. The water went on flowing between us. After a while I sat down on the bank, and she knelt opposite me. I stared up at the stars. They seemed to be sliding on their courses, as if they were not anchored anymore. "Do you even believe in heaven?" I asked her.

"What else is there to believe in if you don't believe in that?"

"But that doesn't mean it's true. You are saying you believe in it because you want it to be true?"

"No—because when people die, they don't just disappear."

"What does that mean?" I demanded.

"That there is somewhere else. It's one of those things you were talking about, the things you just know."

I sat up straight and looked at her. "That's where I want to be—somewhere else. Maybe heaven, probably hell. I've had enough of this. I want to be somewhere else." I wanted to be somewhere my heart didn't hurt like this, like it did now—pain too much to bear, that made the days seem months and the weeks seem years and turned everything bitter. "That's what I want," I told her.

She shook her head. "What I want is more time."

"More time?"

"Yes. If I'm dying now, there's nothing I can do to change it. I don't know if I am. But I want to go on for a while at least."

"Why?"

She started telling me about her future, about how she wanted to dance. I told her that my mother used to be a singer and a dancer a long time ago. She started telling me about how fast things change and how fast time passes, as if that would convince me to throw away the gun and go home. But thinking about the future made me the more convinced never to go back. The future to me was nothing anymore. Fifty or sixty more years without Stirling, and then without Grandmother either. And the guilt of what I had done would catch up with me when this strange tiredness lifted from my mind—and then what?

"There's too much future," I told her. "I'm too tired. I can't live for that many days; I'll go mad. If I'm not condemned to death or put in prison . . ."

"You don't know what's going to happen in the future," she said.

"I know roughly what's going to happen in the future. And there's no possibility that it can be good. I want to start again."

"But dying isn't a new start with this same life; it's something else."

"How do you know what it is?" I was suddenly angry. "And you can't tell me what to do when you don't know a damn thing about me."

"I'm not telling you what to do. Listen—don't people need you back at home?"

I shook my head. No one needed me; I had failed them all. I hadn't run fast enough from the hills, and I couldn't bring Stirling back. Grandmother had needed me with her, but I had turned my back and marched to Ositha and left her alone to grow frail and helpless. And I wouldn't be able to stop the soldiers taking her away.

"Won't someone need you in the future?" she said. I didn't understand what she meant. She must have seen it in my face, because she went on: "There might be someone you're going to help, or someone who will need you one day years from now, and if you were dead, you wouldn't be there to do it."

"Did you ever wish you were dead like this?" I demanded. "No, I don't think you did."

She didn't answer. Then she said, "It was a long time ago, and I was only small."

"What did you do about it?"

"I started counting the days to make the time pass."

"Right," I said, without much interest. "And then what?"

"I don't remember, but one day I must have stopped counting."

"Why did you count the days?"

"To teach myself how to survive in normal life, I suppose, when everything was different."

"How old were you then?"

"Five years old."

"Five years old and counting the days passing?"

"It's not a big tragedy. It's just my life. Maybe there are reasons why you want to die and you don't. Maybe there aren't. I don't know either way. But I lived ten years more after that and now I'm here talking to you."

She still seemed silver and distant in the rising dawn, as if she was not really there at all. I put out my hand to touch her, but I could not reach across the stream. And I didn't dare to do it anyway. I thought that it might make her vanish. "You are some kind of angel," I said then. "So please, just tell me what to do."

"I'm not an angel. But I'll tell you what to do."

"What?"

"Put down the gun and go home." And then she began to fade. "Listen," she said. "I don't know if I'm dying or coming back. I don't have any choice. Maybe I'll regret all the things I didn't do, but there's no way I can change it. Everyone dies in the end. Everyone ends up in the same place, and usually they don't have a choice about it. Killing yourself is not the same." She was speaking fast, as though she wanted to tell me these things before she left me forever.

She went on. "My father was twenty; he was a good man

and he's gone. My Nan was fifty and we all needed her, and we still need her, and there's nothing we can do about it now. It doesn't make sense. People die when they could have done so much if they had stayed alive. And for some reason I got more time and they didn't. Maybe it's just chance that I was left and they went, or maybe there's a reason, but you can't change it either way if you're the one left to carry on."

"You haven't done what I've done," I told her. "I'm fifteen years old and I shot a man. Now tell me how to carry on."

I didn't say it bitterly. I wanted her to tell me. "Please," I said. "Tell me how to carry on."

And then she was fading. I reached out. "Take hold of my hand," I told her. "If you take hold of my hand and prove to me that you're real, then I'll put down the gun and go home."

She was too far away. I got up suddenly. "Don't leave me yet," I said desperately. I stepped toward her, into the stream, and for a second I didn't even feel the water around me.

And then I was alone in the eastern hills, up to my waist in a cold stream in the dark, with a gun in my hand. The moonlight was gone.

I began to lift the pistol again. And then I thought about Stirling, eight years old and gone, and all the things he would have done—and all the things he had done already, all the things that made me miss him like this now, like it was too much to bear. And then I thought about Ahira, and the moment when I realized he was dead and it was my fault—and no matter what evil he did, no matter how little his future might have been worth to the world, I had taken it from him and he could never do anything else again. And my heart hurt too badly for me to go on living, and the weight of what I had done was already too much to stand, but suddenly I couldn't do this either.

Because some acts were easy to commit and yet could be regretted forever—that was what I realized then. I had shot Ahira and I would pay for it. And killing myself was too great a thing to do. It was the same thing.

I let go of the gun. The water carried it away, dashed it against a rock, and then pulled it beneath the surface. I felt more despairing than I had in all these past days since Stirling had died. It's strange how easy it was to pull the trigger of the rifle and shoot Ahira. And how hard it was to get up, turn around, and walk back home.

Aldebaran brushed the tears from his face as he jogged down the steps of the English hospital. And Anna stirred and looked up into the light. She had been dreaming.

Ryan ran to her. She saw him drifting in her vision, his head still bandaged, and tried to sit up, then collapsed back down again, out of breath. There were tears on his face. "Why are you crying?" she murmured.

"I was worried. They said that you were all right, but I was not certain." He knelt beside the bed and watched her face. "Anna."

The surroundings were sharpening in front of her eyes. A bleak white room, with a large window. "Where are we?" she said.

"In hospital. Do you not remember?"

Her head was aching and the room still shifted in her vision. The early sunlight through the blind was lying in stripes across the floor. She put her hand to her face, then started when she felt the stitches in her cheek. "Ryan, what—"

"They are just scratches, really," he said. "Gunshot wounds. One in your shoulder, one in your arm, one in your cheek, one in your side. None of those bullets hit you, Anna. They only grazed the surface. How is that possible?"

"I don't know. Am I really back here? Ryan, I thought I was gone."

She reached for his hand. There was a drip attached to her own, and he took it carefully. "You were unconscious," he said. "Aldebaran thought it was shock; you passed into Malonia and back again, and it might be too much to do that. And the things that happened—Anna, I am sorry. I should have done something. I did not think they would take you."

"It was not your fault. You couldn't have done anything."

He looked as if he was about to speak, then stopped and shook his head.

Anna put her hand to her neck, out of habit, and found the necklace there. "Aldebaran put it round your neck before the ambulance came," said Ryan. "He thought you might need it." He brushed the last tears off his face, but more fell.

"Don't cry," said Anna. "Ryan, I am all right."

She tried to sit up again. He propped up the pillows behind her. "What did you tell Monica?" she said. "How did you explain these?" She touched the stitches on her cheek.

"I said that we got lost out on the hills and fell in the dark. To explain the bruise on my head and your injuries. I don't think the doctor believes it, but . . ." He blinked the tears out of his eyes. "What could I have said? How can you tell the truth when no one would believe it?"

"I didn't know if I would see you again," Anna said. "I didn't think I would wake up. The last thing I remember, I was in the church and I thought I was shot. But I had the strangest dream. . . ." She shook her head. "I can't remember it now."

Then she thought of something. "But Aldebaran was here; I know he was."

"Yes, until a few minutes ago. When he knew you were going to be all right, he had to go home." Ryan glanced toward the window, but Aldebaran had already passed out of sight. "He is going back to my country. Things changed, Anna, last night. They say it is a revolution. Lucien is dead, and the others—Ahira and Darius Southey and half the military leaders. Not Talitha. No one dares to kill a great one. But she is captured, and Aldebaran is no longer an exile."

A doctor appeared suddenly at the door, and Monica behind her. Monica stood for a moment and stared at Anna. Then she was running across the room, her heels clattering on the floor. "Thank God, thank God," she was saying, her own tears falling on Anna's face. "What the hell were you thinking? You wandered off into the hills without even telling me! Anna, I didn't dare to phone Michelle! You are all she has; what would I have said? And—"

The doctor put a hand on Monica's shoulder to quiet her, then leaned over to speak to Anna. "Do you remember what happened?"

Anna glanced at Ryan, and he repeated his story. "Is that right?" said the doctor. Anna nodded. The doctor frowned but she did not argue. She examined Anna's cheek for a moment in silence. Ryan caught Anna's eyes, then glanced away.

"Strange," the doctor said then. "These grazes are all the same. They look almost like—I don't know. I would have said gunshot wounds."

The great Aldebaran, walking over the hills in the early sunlight, looked back for a moment toward the town where the hospital stood. And then he started up through the trees, toward the old stone circle, where once he had opened his eyes to a strange country. As he walked, he stopped hearing the birds singing and the wind that ran through the trees. Ahead he thought he could hear other faint sounds—voices in the air, speaking in an accent that he recognized. And England, like a dream or a nightmare, began to fade around him.

I sat down on the step outside the door of Maria's apartment. It was very early in the morning the day after I shot Ahira. The sunlight was slanting through the high window of the stairwell, and I sat and watched it. After a while, the door opened. "Leo!" It was Maria's voice. I turned slowly. Grandmother was beside her.

"We were so worried," Grandmother began, taking my hand. "Were you out in the city, Leo? Did you hear the gunshots?" She hugged me to her briefly; then Maria helped me to my feet. "Things will be better," said Grandmother. "I will bake a loaf of bread, and you can go down and fetch the water for tea. Things will be better from now on."

I knew they would not. But just knowing that left me with a strange kind of calm. It seemed a stupid lie to meekly help her home after what I had done, but I took her arm anyway and we started down the stairs.

I watch the last lights burning in the city. It is almost dawn now, but the daylight holds off awhile longer. I go to the parapet and stare at the lights, imagining the people in those houses—all the thousands of people—sleeping now, or calling good night to their families, or pouring a last drink and sitting down to talk. Are any of them awake now because their hearts are troubled? Perhaps. I cannot tell. I turn the last pages of the book, but for a moment I cannot read on.

After I had got that far with the story, I decided not to tell you much more. I was exhausted with telling you this history and remembering these things. What happened in the days after I came back? I cannot remember exactly. Some of it is still clear; other parts I have lost entirely. I know that I tried to act as if things were normal. Real life pulled me back in, and I didn't know what else to do. I told no one and went back to Grandmother and Maria.

If I had carried on despairing every minute of each day, it would have been easier to stand than that normality. I was ashamed to live, the same way I would feel ashamed to be one of the people sleeping guiltlessly in those houses, or to have gone down and danced in the bright rooms below. I have no right. It is hard to justify my crime to you. All I can say is that I am paying for it.

My story goes on—but not yet. I will read about the others first.

Anna woke suddenly. She was shivering as she had on that dark balcony above the city. The clock on the other side of the lake was chiming two. A breeze caught the curtains and made them rise and fall. She picked up her necklace from the table. She had slept all that day and most of the night, but now she was awake and breathing fast.

"Anna?" said a voice outside her door then. It was Ryan. "I heard you call out. Are you all right?" She turned on the lamp and got up to unlock the door. Ryan was there in the dark corridor, dressed and with a book in his hand. "My room is across from yours," he said. "Listen, Monica will be angry if she hears us talking at this time of night. I just wanted to check nothing was wrong."

"Come in for a minute."

She shut the door behind him. "Thanks," he said. "She does not even like me staying here; I don't know what she would say if she thought I was disturbing the paying guests."

"You are a paying guest yourself," said Anna. Aldebaran had insisted that Ryan leave the house while he was gone, in case it was still watched, so he had come to Hillview.

He sat on the chair beside the bed. Still blinking in the lamp-light, she wrapped the blanket around her shoulders and went to shut the window. "A storm is getting up out there," said Ryan. "Was that what woke you?"

She shook her head. "It was just a nightmare. I didn't like being in that hospital. It reminded me of . . ." She shrugged. "Other times. Sorry if I woke you."

"I was not asleep. My uncle has left me with enough work for a year. Politics and laws, and I have to know them. He is not too far away to check up on me."

She sat back down on the bed. He reached out briefly and took her hand, then let it go again. "Things will be different from now on," said Anna. "I will practice dancing harder than ever. I could have died, and I didn't. Do you know what I mean?"

"I know." He closed the book in his hands and set it down on the floor, then leaned forward in his chair and watched her.

"What is it?" she said.

"Anna, are you all right now? When you were in Malonia—I don't know—it must have been frightening. Is that what you dream about? Is that what gives you nightmares?"

She pulled the blanket tighter around her. "Maybe it is that, partly. In the daylight I had almost forgotten. But when I fell to sleep, I could see it again. I could see all their faces as if I was really there. It was more real than a dream."

Ryan nodded. "After I was exiled, I used to dream that I was back there. I used to see my mother and father again and think, Just give me five more minutes and it will be real—I will get back home somehow, back to how things used to be. But I never had five minutes more; I always woke."

There was a silence. Ryan looked away then. "I was thinking about Talitha today," he said, in a different tone. "The revolutionaries have captured her and she will be imprisoned for life. One of my duties will be to publicly sentence her, as one of the first criminals convicted during my reign. An old tradition."

"You will be responsible for that?" said Anna.

"I will be responsible for many things. I am scared to think too much about it. I cannot speak judgment on one of the great ones, even her. She is a very famous woman, and she frightens me, in spite of her beautiful face."

"She is young," said Anna. "I thought you said she worked with Aldebaran in the secret service."

"No, she is his same age, or a year older. Talitha is very powerful, and the signs of age are easy to prevent if you choose to do it. Even Aldebaran does, I think—not much, but you would not say that he was seventy."

Ryan folded his arms and looked out at the moon lying silent over the hills. "Aldebaran thinks that the mistakes of the old government are what we must learn from now. Talitha was not wise enough. Lucien was not admired. And they were too personally involved." He shook his head. "He has surrounded me with prophecies and myth and set me up as a lonely figure. The opposite of what Lucien was. I hope it will work, but—" He turned to her. "Sometimes I wish I was an English boy. I have been separated from everyone, even here in England. And now I have you, and everything has changed. I don't want to be a leader. Sometimes I don't even think I believe in those things. But all I am doing is stepping into a place set up for me. Do you see what I mean?"

"Yes, I see. Have you talked to Aldebaran?"

"I cannot change anything now. But even so, I am more glad than I can say to be able to talk to you like this." He got up then and went to the window. "Anna, shall I stay here until you fall asleep? Let me do that; I don't mind."

"All right. Thank you."

After a while had passed, she said, "Lucien looked like you. I never told you."

Ryan smiled sadly at that. "Aldebaran says he looked more like me than my father did. That is how life goes." He shook his head. "The whole thing is strange. If I had lived here in England a few more years, I would really have begun to think that the rest was just a dream."

<hr />

"Leo, what are you doing?" said Grandmother. It was afternoon, I could tell from the light, and I was sitting on the windowsill as I used to do often. And I was writing. "I thought you were asleep," she said. "What are you writing about?"

I did not know. I had been asleep, but now I was writing in the margin of the newspaper, as though I had something urgent to set down. And the handwriting did not look like my own. It looked like the mysterious writer's—the great one who Stirling and I had spent so long talking about, the one who had written in that book that I'd thrown away. I turned the pages, startled. I had written all kinds of things. The names stood out from the rest—Aldebaran, Ryan, Anna.

I folded the pages and put them in the windowsill chest without reading them. All that time I had been frightened that someone was trying to communicate with us—a powerful great one, even Aldebaran himself. I did not know what to think now. Was that all the great mystery was, the mystery that had sustained us through Stirling's illness and carried me home from Ositha? Just a story I had written because I was desperate and haunted by strange dreams? I realized that the last of the magic had drifted away. I found I didn't care.

"The gunshots have stopped, thank heavens," said Grandmother. She was sitting in her old chair, as she used to. She had drawn back the curtains, and the room was so bright and strange that my eyes began watering. We had kept them shut these past days. I stepped into the shadow of the boarded window. "Did you notice it, Leo?" she said. "Did you notice the silence?"

I nodded and sat down at the table. "Maria came past while you were sleeping," said Grandmother. "She says she thinks it is safe to go out now, and the newspapers may have started up again. She went to find out what has been happening."

None of us had known, these past days. We had stayed in the building and sat up at nights while bursts of gunfire shattered the darkness and glass exploded far away. Every night it was like that. Some people said it was the Alcyrians, or rebels, but those were just rumors. Father Dunstan came once or twice.

If he knew what was happening out in the city, I could not remember him telling us. The streets were deserted. Not even the soldiers were moving about.

"They never did come back," said Grandmother, as though she could tell my thoughts. "Those soldiers never did come to take me away. Their threats are greater than their actions, these young men." She smiled, but shakily. I nodded. Even so, I checked for the hundredth time that the door was bolted.

"Things are changing," said Grandmother. "I'm sure they are. I am too old for this, I must confess. I am glad that it is quiet at last today. You cannot even hear the gunshots from the northeast border." She crossed the room slowly and sat opposite me. "They say they have closed the schools," she said. "You would not have gone back anyway, would you?"

I shook my head.

We sat in silence for a long time. Then she got up and forced her mouth into a smile. "I know I had one of those strange turns earlier, but I am better now," she said. "I made some dinner." She hurried to the kitchen, brought back two bowls, and set them down on the table. Then she said, "How long was it this morning before I was myself again? Tell me the truth, Leo."

She passed me a three-week-old newspaper, now covered in my own scrawling handwriting. They were ordinary messages: *Later; ask Father Dunstan about it; half an hour; I will make the dinner.* All the words I could no longer say. I examined them, turning the newspaper around to read all four margins. "Leo," said Grandmother. "How long?"

I picked up the pencil and wrote, *Two hours.*

"Two hours?" She smiled too cheerily. "Less than yesterday, then. That is good news."

It was not exactly the truth. I reduced the figure every day. "I remember some of it," she said. "I was not so far gone as I sometimes am. You were holding the baby, weren't you? Maria was talking to me, and you were holding the baby."

I nodded. That was true. *Maria can bring you back better than me sometimes,* I wrote.

"Yes." She stirred the soup in her bowl. "She is one of the kindest people I have known. I don't know what we would do without her, especially now." Her voice quavered, and she bent her head over the bowl. It was still less than a month since Stirling had died. I felt as though in these past four weeks I had lived a hundred years. And yet I could not get used to it either.

"Will Father Dunstan visit later on?" said Grandmother. I shook my head. He had been there in the morning, while she had told me she didn't recognize me and asked us again and again to fetch Harold. *Tomorrow,* I wrote. *He said that he would come tomorrow, if the city is still quiet.*

She nodded, then sighed. "I am so tired suddenly. I'll go to bed after dinner, I think. You won't mind, Leo?" I shook my head and took a spoonful of my soup, the usual vegetable stew. When I tasted it, I almost spat it out again. She had made it with cold water.

After Grandmother had gone to bed, the wind rose outside. I lit the lamp, put it on the table, and sat and thought of nothing. I could hear the neighbors passing on the stairs outside the apartment, and then silence and darkness fell. About nine o'clock Maria came to the door to check if we were all right, then went on upstairs with the baby.

I don't know why, but I sat down at the table and started writing all over the remaining margins of the newspapers. I

388

wrote letters to everyone I could think of—to my father, about how he should never have left us; to Ahira, about why I had fired that shot; and then to Stirling. To Stirling I wrote all kinds of things—how the wind sounded outside and what the boarded window looked like and how the grass was growing on his grave, and little flowers too, small white flowers that Grandmother said were beautiful and should stay there even though they were weeds. Then I held the letters to the oil lamp and burned them one by one. The varnish of the table sent up a hot, acid smell. I had to leave the apartment.

I put on my overcoat and set off for the graveyard. I didn't look to the left or to the right. It wasn't until I was almost upon the Victoire Bridge that I realized that the bridge was no longer there. Two crossed planks of wood had been nailed across the gap between the houses, and the same across the graveyard gate, and in between was nothing but the drop to the river below. The Victoire Bridge had been smashed away.

I went round by the North Bridge. I sat beside Stirling's grave and looked at the letters engraved on the cross. The grass on the grave was growing taller. The wood was softened with the first traces of lichen and mildew. I sat and thought about Stirling. I hadn't heard his voice or seen his face for three weeks or more. It was longer than I ever remembered being away from him. When he was a baby, my mother took him south to visit her relatives for a week; another time, when I was in the sixth year of school, my platoon went on a three-day march in the west country. Apart from that, we had been together every day since he was born.

The day after Stirling had died, and the next day, and the

next day, I had thought I was in a dream. As if I might wake up—as if Stirling might walk in through the door—and it would turn out to be a mistake. But the dream went on and I didn't wake. I wanted to stop time, to somehow drag it back to the point when things made sense. The world moved on too quickly, and every passing day forced my hope that Stirling might come back further and further away. The grass was growing; the words on the stone were fading; days had passed already and would become months and years. And this tiredness had come over me—this dreamlike, sick tiredness—and I just let it.

So in the end all I could do was sit on Stirling's grave while the darkness grew darker. Then I turned around and walked home.

I would be lying if I said I noticed the strange flags on the castle. I didn't. And I didn't notice the slogans on the walls. I noticed the soldiers, though. They had gone. There were no soldiers in the city. I looked about for them, around every corner, but they were not there. The streets were deserted.

❧

*W*hen you are dreaming, you never know when you will wake. Sometimes it startles you. That was how it was with the strange tiredness that had surrounded me since that night when Ahira fell. I was back in the apartment, and I knew I would not sleep, so I piled up the plates from dinner and took them down to the yard to wash them. I could have brought the water up in the jar, but I did not have the strength.

It was silent out in the yard. The shadow of the water

pump fell long across the ground. I washed the plates in the moonlight, then stacked them and went quietly back up the stairs. I could tell from the silence that everyone else in the building was sleeping. Even Grandmother was; she had been asleep when I had got back from the graveyard.

I reached the apartment and put the pile of plates on the table, then turned to shut the door. And then suddenly I was no longer dreaming, and I realized what I had done. Less than a week ago, I had shot Ahira and watched him die by my feet in the mud of the road—and here I was washing up plates as though everything was normal. I had not thought much about it while the gunshots and the explosions had kept us awake and frightened. Now it seemed suddenly as though I was falling back into normal life. But how could I? How could I ever believe that things would be normal again?

I wished with all my heart that I could leave this apartment and never come back. Everything was gathering dust. Grandmother's sleeping face, in the half-light, was strangely faded and old. I had no assurance that my family was protected anymore. Grandmother was losing her mind. Stirling was gone. I had shot that man. My life was destroyed, and I was acting out normality as though I could ever put it back together again.

I paced through the empty apartment. Stirling's boots, with their carefully arranged laces, and Grandmother's old chair, standing still and empty, as though she was already gone, made me sick with fear. I felt suddenly that I could not go on here. I wanted to get up and walk away. I wanted to be exiled from all this. I had come home because I was afraid of what would happen to Grandmother if I left her alone, and because I could not shoot myself; I could not do it. But now I was slipping back into the normal things, as though I had already forgotten Stirling and Ahira's blood was on someone else's hands. It made me sick to think of it—that I had dressed this morning and gone down to fetch the water, and I was a murderer. And no one knew.

"Leo?" said a voice behind me, and I turned. I suppose I must have left the door open, because Maria was beside me, with Anselm in her arms. She laid a newspaper down on the table. "I wanted to show this to you," she said. "I could not sleep."

It was our old newspaper, with a different title. I looked at it without seeing it. "Here," she said. "They are all of them dead." She pointed to a list. They were Lucien's famous men—military commanders. "It makes me sad to think of it," she said. "I don't know why."

Ahira's name was there. It stood out from the list as though I'd known him. There it was in printed letters. I had done that. I had put his name there in the list of the dead when I had pulled the trigger of that rifle.

I grew sick and began to shiver. I pushed the newspaper away, catching hold of the table to steady myself. And then I thought that there was nothing to stand on anymore, that I would just fall through the world and disappear. I knelt on the floor and cried and cried with fear.

"Leo," Maria said. "Oh, Leo. It's not fair. That this should have happened to you. All you wanted was to look after Stirling and now . . ." She trailed off, reached for my hand, and took hold of it tightly.

But maybe I deserved it. Maybe I deserved everything that happened to me. That was what I felt like then. I deserved anything, for being a murderer. I wished desperately that someone would punish me. I wished that someone would take their revenge. I wanted to turn myself in to the soldiers and be sentenced to death.

I was the one who had taken revenge to begin with, but I had been too angry and I had gone too far. I would have given anything I had not to have done it—to be back there in the mud of the street, paralyzed with hatred for every soldier in this country, and to be given the choice again. I shut my eyes and prayed to go back, but I knew it was hopeless.

"Don't stay here on the floor, Leo," Maria said. "Let me help you." And she put the baby down on the sofa, though his crying rose. I managed to get up and collapse again in Grandmother's chair. I had stopped crying, but I was shaking violently. I pressed my face to my knees. She put her arm about me until I stopped trembling.

Anselm carried on crying. She went and got a chair, and pulled it up beside me. It reminded me of the day when she had come to Sunday dinner and Stirling had thought of going on a picnic. Everything was so terrible and so hopeless now. "Anselm needs feeding," Maria said over the noise. "Sorry, Leo—do you mind?" I shook my head. Watching her feed the baby, I wondered how I had thought I loved her. Love didn't mean anything to me anymore. Just meaningless words—all magic had left everything forever.

Anselm began to fall asleep, and she laid him down on the sofa. "Sorry, Leo," she whispered. "Now we can talk." But I couldn't. She got me a piece of paper, but my hands shook too badly to write.

"I'll just talk about ordinary things," she said. I nodded. I didn't want to hear about ordinary things, but I did not want her to leave me here alone either.

But she didn't talk about ordinary things. She said suddenly, "Everything's so confused, Leo," and she started crying as if her heart would break. I thought she meant my life, but she sobbed, "Sometimes I feel so lost." She clutched my hand. "I just wish . . . I just wish I'd never done half the things I've done, but it's too late. I used to have such a beautiful life, and I ruined it all."

I picked up the paper and wrote, *Tell me*. My writing looked like a kid's, it was so shaky. We're both lost, I thought. We were trying to guide each other but neither of us knew the way out.

"I can't tell you," she said. "I'm sorry—you don't want to hear this." It made me think of when we had talked in the yard that time, when she had been here only a short while. I wished now that I had spent that time with my family, Grandmother and Stirling, the way things were before. "You don't want to hear this," she sobbed again.

With a great effort, I wrote, *I do*.

"Can I tell you everything? You won't mind? Only I feel as if I'll go mad sometimes, not telling anyone." I nodded, to tell her to go on. I wished she would talk about herself, not me. I think she realized it.

"It's just . . ." She took a gulp of air. "I'll try to explain. I feel so ashamed, Leo." She took another gasping breath. "I used to have such a beautiful life. I didn't have to worry about anything, and I had a pony, and a lovely house, and my mother and father were always happy. I was a completely different person. I used to look at places like this and think the people who lived in them just weren't real. I told you already about how I was rich, before." I nodded. "But I think when I told you, Leo, I gave the impression it was a long time ago."

She shook her head. "You know, when you have a beautiful life, you think it will last forever. And I wasn't just rich, I was happy. But I can see now that no one's happy for very long. Something spoils it." She wiped the tears from her face with her palms, but they went on falling. "I'm all right; things aren't so bad now. I know there are other things besides being happy. Other things to live for. There have to be, otherwise how can you bear it?" Then I realized she wasn't only talking about herself.

"I know that, but sometimes I just wish everything was simple like it used to be. I used to go to balls and parties with all sorts of rich and famous people. And I'd meet young men, and flirt with them, and see my father looking sort of embarrassed and pleased at the same time, you know, and I used to dream about marrying a rich man. All I worried about was what I would wear or whether I would remember to curtsy. I worry so much these days. And I know it's my own fault, but . . . Can I tell you about Anselm's father?" I nodded.

"I met him at a ball, at his house. We danced together. That was when I was fourteen. I was such a silly, frivolous girl; I didn't really think about anything, and I didn't consider who he was or whether I liked him. I just liked dancing. And he led me out of the ballroom, and I just thought we were going out to the balcony. And I went along with it, because I liked the way he looked at me, like he really loved me, and I liked the way everyone else talked about it behind their hands.

"And he led me farther, away from all the guests, and I

knew why—of course I did. I must have done." She stared intently at her hand clasped in mine. They were both shaking, and I could not tell whose had started it. "I was pretending to myself that I didn't realize what he was thinking. I don't know. And he took me to his bedroom. I should have just run away, but I was afraid because he was so important. An important man in government, and my father always said that you should be careful of those. And anyway, I thought maybe I loved him. I was quite wild. Several boys had asked me to marry them, and I'd come close to it with some of them. But it's different with boys your own age."

She was shaking as badly as I was. "Oh, Leo, it was such a terrible mistake. Sometimes I just go over it in my head and I think I'm falling, and I imagine that I ran away, but I didn't. As soon as he locked the door, I realized it was a terrible mistake. I was too scared to say anything, and then it was too late and he wouldn't listen even when I did. And now I've ended up here.

"I used to worry that my father would die out at the border and it would all be my fault. When Anselm's father found out I was pregnant, he asked me to marry him, but I couldn't. I hated him. I hated him as soon as he locked that door. And I was frightened of him. I said I'd marry him, but I got so ill with worry that my father just wouldn't let me. My mother said I should, but my father swore he'd die before I married that man. And so Anselm's father got angry, and he told Lucien, and Lucien made my father lose his job at the bank and have to become a soldier. And I was terrified to tell anyone, in case he might have my father killed. So no one knows who Anselm's father is except my mother and father and me. And I just can't bear my own baby being half a man I hate."

She was still sobbing. "I thought I'd got over all this, but then my father came back from the border and I heard that Anselm's father was dead, and now I'm so confused I don't know what to think. It's just brought everything up again. And I've been going almost mad, unable to talk to anyone about it. I feel almost as if I loved him, and I feel guilty for not marrying him, but I don't know why. I hated him."

Then I remembered something. I started shaking harder than ever. I picked up the paper and scrawled desperately, *Who was Anselm's father?*

"Oh, Leo, I can't tell you. I can't tell anyone. I just can't." She looked at me with pleading eyes, and I knew then that she was going to. And I wrote suddenly, *Don't.*

I was shaking badly, and she was shaking too, and she put her arms around me, and we both cried. Like two lost children, and no one to comfort us. "I know you must despise me, Leo," she sobbed. "I can't bear Anselm being that man's son. I thought I'd be glad to see him dead, but I just feel so guilty. He was killed . . ." She pressed her face to my shoulder. "He was killed early on, the first night when the rebels were fighting the soldiers in the streets. A lot of government men were killed that first night."

I tightened my grip on her arm. She pulled away from me, tears still falling down her cheeks, and picked up Anselm. The tears fell like jewels onto the baby's face. "Leo, listen," she said. "I have just read that newspaper. Everything is changing again." She was still sobbing while she spoke. "I don't know what I think anymore. But it's true—the king is coming back. Lucien is dead. They are calling it a revolution."

*M*uch later, when she had stopped crying enough to speak properly and my fit of shaking had subsided, she told me everything that was in that newspaper, as well as she could. I would not believe it. Then she led me to the window and opened it wide and pointed up to the castle. "Didn't you recognize the flags?" she said. "Orange, like they always used to be, until we were five years old. Don't you remember?"

I had blotted out most of my childhood after my mother and father had gone away. But standing there by the window—leaning out to glimpse a sliver of a distant tower with a flag flying from it in the moonlight—standing there and looking up, I remembered.

I thought I was going to tell her then. I thought I would tell her about Ahira. But I could not. I picked up the paper she had handed me, and hesitated. And then I wrote instead, *Let me tell you something. A story, about something that happened before Stirling was gone.*

It was strange how the words I wrote could sound so measured and sane while the tears were running down my cheeks and my heart felt as though it was broken. I was trying to take us both away from that dismal room, to another place. I prayed that it would work and started telling her, in writing that shook as badly as Grandmother's, about the book that I had found. About how the story had appeared, and the words that Stirling and I had read. And all of it—even that I had torn the book in half and thrown it away. And that it was me who had written those words all the time.

"You have powers?" said Maria, the tears still breaking up

her voice. "I knew. I think I always knew." She cried harder. "If I was like you, I would stay there all the time. I would dream I was in England for the rest of my life, rather than have to live here." She gripped my hands. "Can you see England now?" she said. "Tell me about it—please, Leo."

But I could not. So I put my arms around her instead, and she hugged the baby to her, and we waited for it to get light.

The moonlight glinted in the tears on Ryan's face. Anna sat up and looked at him. The light was what had woken her, running out across the lake, over the lawn, and in at the window, so that the room grew pale as ice. She could not tell how many hours had passed. He had been watching the stars from her window as she had fallen to sleep that night, and now here he was crying. "What is it?" she said.

He started and turned. "I thought you were asleep." He brushed the tears off his face hastily. "I don't know, Anna. I seem always to be reduced to tears these days. My uncle would never stand for this behavior." He tried to laugh but could not quite bring himself to do it.

She sat on the edge of the bed and watched him. "What was it that made you cry?"

"It was what Aldebaran wrote about being back at home." He had a book in his hands, but he closed it now. "It made me want to go back to my country. It made me remember. I have been here so long, I started to think this was my place."

He put down the book and blinked the tears out of his eyes. "And you dancing this evening. Perhaps I drank too much at dinner.

Maybe that was it. Does Monica always celebrate expensive book-ings like that?"

"She does now. Things have been bad here for a while, and then a group booking for September—it might be what carries us through."

He nodded, still brushing the tears from his face. "I'm sorry," he said. "I don't know why I was crying."

"I understand," she said. "You don't have to tell me. I know that you must miss your home."

He caught hold of her hand. They sat in silence. "I suppose you have finished making up that dance," he said then.

"Yes. Tonight I finished it."

He wound his fingers through hers, frowning as though he was concentrating only on that. Then he let go of her hand and closed his eyes and said, "Anna."

Out across the lake the clock chimed two. The stars had grown brighter and closer outside the window, but neither of them noticed. "Ryan, listen," she said, and touched his shoulder lightly. But she did not go on.

He put his hand to the side of her face and looked at her for a moment. Then he drew back again and shut his eyes. "You know how I feel," he said. "Maybe I should go. It is late."

"Don't go."

He turned his back to her and sat on the edge of the bed. She put her arms around his shoulders suddenly. Her cheek was against his, and she could feel his jaw move as he swallowed. She thought about stepping away from him. Instead, she kissed the side of his face.

And then he turned and he was kissing her, saying, "Anna. Anna."

The moonlight caught them in its beam. "Tell me to leave," he said. "Just tell me and I will." She shook her head.

The light was as solid as water, turning his face to silver, and her own arms around his neck looked like someone else's in that light. Then she was lying beside him, and he watched her face for a moment without moving. "Anna, do you love me?" he said.

"Why are you asking me?"

"Because I have to know, otherwise—"

"Yes," she said. "Of course I do."

He laughed quietly, as though he could not believe her, and then looked up and met her eyes. "I am going home," he said. "Tomorrow maybe, or the next day. I didn't know how I could tell you—Anna, I love you. I honestly do, and I would far rather stay, I swear—" He stopped and shut his eyes. "I don't know if I should be here. Should I leave?"

"Stay here," she said. "Don't say anything else, just stay."

In the silence of the early morning, when the hotel lay dark and still for a few hours, Ryan said, "If I go back home . . ."

"Yes," she said, her head against his chest, listening to his heart beating. He ran his hand along her shoulder thoughtfully.

"If I go back, what about you? I will stop believing in this place. I will think England was just a fairy tale. And how can I, when you are here? You will probably be a famous dancer, and I will never see it."

"I don't know about dancing anymore," she said. "It's you now, all the time."

They lay in silence. She began to drift into sleep. "I wish we were married," said Ryan suddenly.

"What?" she said. "Are you still awake, Ryan?"

"Yes." He turned to look at her. "I wish we were married. I seriously do. Then nothing would separate us. I'm asking you now, Anna—"

"What are you asking?"

"If you will marry me."

She reached up and ran her hand through his hair, then let it fall again and closed her eyes. "Yes," she said. "Yes, I will."

"Anna, are you serious?" he said. She did not answer. He nudged her, then laughed quietly and stopped. Anna was already asleep, but Ryan lay still, wide awake, his arms about her, and watched the dawn rise over the lake.

◦◦◦

Anna woke early and suddenly. Ryan's face was resting against hers. His left arm was under her head, and his right arm was about her. She moved it carefully. She picked up her clothes and went to the window. In the darkness, everything had been enchanted. Now, in the morning light, it seemed faintly stupid. Birds were darting through the trees beyond the window, their singing sharp as ice in the still air. Anna leaned her head on the window frame and looked out.

Ryan stirred and opened his eyes. He raised his head and looked at her, then fell down again onto the pillow and covered his face with his hands. "I'm sorry," he said then. "I honestly am. I don't know—I should have left when I said."

"You shouldn't have left," she said.

"Come here," said Ryan, sitting up and looking at her. She crossed the room and sat beside him. He regarded her cautiously. "Are things still same between us?" he said.

"Of course they are."

And then she caught sight of the photographs on the table behind him, her own copies of the pictures Monica had downstairs. Her father's open smile seemed suddenly the highest judgment on her. She didn't look at her Nan. She caught hold of her necklace and went back to the window. "What?" said Ryan.

"Things get out of control," she said. "You don't mean to do anything wrong, but they go too far. . . ."

"Who are you apologizing to?"

"I don't know. Ryan, I don't think we should have—"

"All right," he said. "So we both drank a bit, and you were tired from finishing your dance and working all day, and I was homesick. If that was how this happened, all right. But it does not alter how I feel. What about you, Anna? Does it change anything?"

She watched the sunlight on the floorboards. "I have to talk to you," he said quietly.

They dressed in silence. It was just past five o'clock, and the building was still. Anna stood at the window and watched the mist drifting across the lake. "Anna, listen," Ryan said. "You know what you said last night?"

"What did I say last night? I said a lot of things."

"When we were talking, just a couple of hours ago. When I asked if you would marry me."

She turned to him, but she could not read his expression. "You never asked me that."

He turned away from her and began making the bed. "Ryan, are you joking?" she demanded.

"Don't say that!"

"Ryan—" She snatched the sheet from him so that he had to look at her. "We're fifteen years old."

"The law is different in my country. Fifteen, you can get married."

"Did you really mean to ask me that, Ryan? Or were you half asleep and talking about nothing?"

"Of course I meant to ask you."

"I thought you said that you were going back home. How can you do that if you marry me?" She stopped then. "You mean come with you."

"Yes, that's what I mean."

She sat down on the bed and looked at him. "I tried not to sleep last night," he said, walking to the window. "I was lying there wishing that the sun would never rise because suddenly I didn't want to be anywhere else except there with you. And then I thought, why not? Why not go together? You have seen the city. You are partly Malonian. Why not?"

"The city," she said. It only made her think of Talitha's strange young face, and the soldier called Darius, and the blood running over the stone of the castle. They were like pictures from a dream. "What would I do there?" she said.

"We would be together. Anna, I have been wishing I was back there my whole life, but it means nothing now if I won't see you again."

"It's easy for you to think about going back, Ryan," she said. "You are just taking up a place that is already there for you."

"What—because I am the prince—the king? Because it is supposed to be my destiny?" He shook his head. "It is nothing like that. Someone made that phrase up—'the eyes of a king'—and everyone hung on to it, and it just stuck. Maybe it was Harold North who first wrote it—I don't know—one of those influential writers. And next thing, the nation was trying to fit me into Aldebaran's prophecy, and he was here in England working out his grand plans for my life. Everyone wanted it to be my destiny—that's all. It has become my duty to go back, certain. But that is not the same thing. It is something I have to do out of responsibility, not because I am anyone great."

"Only the other day you were telling me I had to be a dancer. Did you mean that?"

"You can dance anywhere, Anna."

"That's not true. And everything I have ever had is here. How could I leave to go to a place that I don't even think of as real? I don't know if I could even stay there. I think I would wake up back in England."

"But I can't stay here with you," he said. "Come with me. My heart will break."

"Will you please talk seriously?" she said. "Sit down and talk seriously to me."

There was a silence. "Maybe you said you loved me and never meant it," he said then. "But where I come from, if you love someone and tell her so, she doesn't become just some girl you left behind. If what happened last night happens between you, you are going to marry her. You stay together and are never parted, not for anything. But maybe you never meant what you said."

"I never said anything I didn't mean," she told him, raising her voice.

"And what, then? Tell me what to do."

"Ryan, if you were an English boy, I would wait three or four years and then marry you. But this is not simple."

He opened his mouth to tell her that love was simple. And then he changed his mind. "We have not known each other long," said Anna. "You have to leave; I have to stay. I don't see how we can change it."

They watched the sun rising higher. He ran his fingers down the cut in her cheek, which was already healing. "Anna?" he said. "Tell me how your life will be after I leave. I want to know that."

So they stood by the window and she told him. In the years afterward, he would try to imagine those things: the flat she lived in on the edge of the city; the playing fields below, where she practiced dancing in the early mornings; her oldest friends and where their own flats were—next door, or a floor above, or in the building opposite. "Keep telling me," he said. "I am trying to remember everything you say."

But she stopped then. Someone was approaching on the road. Ryan turned to look. A tall figure, striding toward them at a steady pace. Across the lawn, Aldebaran stopped and looked up at the window.

Then someone was knocking on the bedroom door. "Anna, are you awake?" Monica said. "Come and help me start the breakfast."

Ryan glanced at Anna. "I will get my things and leave," he whispered. "You go down and help Monica. We will wait for you at Lakebank."

～c～c～

The house was locked and silent when Anna crossed the grounds. Then someone called her name, and she turned. Ryan was coming down through the trees toward her. She stopped in front of him. He studied her face. "Are you leaving?" she said eventually.

"I cannot go anywhere without that necklace of yours."

She put her hand up to it and almost laughed; then her face grew serious again. "I forgot about that. With everything else."

"Everything else," he said. "Yes. Last night—"

She shook her head. "But why are you wearing these clothes? Are these Malonian?"

He nodded. "They are almost like my English ones. I will get used to them."

Then Aldebaran was beside them. "We will leave in a few moments," he said, turning to Ryan. "I have made strict arrangements to avoid trouble. The army is not yet so experienced as I might wish."

Ryan's eyes were still on Anna's. Aldebaran turned to her. "Our people have been here already and taken everything we need. Since I will not see you again—"

"Won't you?" she said.

"I will not come back. There is nothing for me here. For either of us. Ryan will have to put England out of his mind now." He glanced at her. "Not entirely out of his mind. But we will not return."

Ryan caught her eyes and started to say something, then stopped. Aldebaran put his hand on her shoulder. "I will remember you, Anna," he said. "You have been caught up in strange times these past days. We all have. But I am proud to have a niece like you. One day you will be a great dancer."

"How do you know?" said Anna.

"I know," said Aldebaran. "I can always tell."

Anna was staring at him, but he turned briskly to Ryan. "I will be waiting for you. Come quickly." He took his hand from her shoulder. "Goodbye, Anna."

Aldebaran turned and marched up through the trees. They watched him pass from shade to sunlight and back again, between the dense branches. Up by the chapel, against the sun, he turned and looked out over the valley. A moment later he was hidden from view. She thought she could see him again, briefly, at a window, but they watched for a long time and he did not appear again.

Ryan turned back to her. "Here," she said, taking off her necklace. She forced her hands to clasp it around Ryan's neck, but for a moment they would not let it go.

"Perhaps one day we will be married," Ryan said. "We should be together."

"Maybe we should." She could not even take his hand, her heart was aching so badly. She folded her arms and watched the ground under her feet.

"Anna, last night," he said. "I was not thinking. I should have—" He stopped and began again. "What if you—"

"It's all right," she said.

He looked as though he wanted to continue, then gave up and shook his head. He took something out of his pocket. It was his own necklace, with the jewel that was missing from Anna's. "Keep this one," he said. "It will make no difference if I give it to you. Anna, I would promise to be faithful and come and find you years from now, but I don't know what things will be like after I go back. I don't know anymore."

She took it from him in silence. "Anna, listen—" he began, but she put a hand on his shoulder and he did not continue.

Then she started and looked up at him. "Do you have a bullet-proof vest on under that shirt?" she demanded. He took hold of her hand and wound his fingers through hers, but she kept her eyes on him. "Ryan, do you?"

"I will not need it," he said eventually. "It is just a safety measure. Aldebaran insists, that is all."

"But will you be all right?"

He gave her his nearly arrogant smile. "I live a charmed life. I'll always be all right." And he laughed, but shakily. "Come," he said. "We should start up toward the chapel."

Her hand was still on his shoulder. They started up through the trees. Then he was walking faster, and Anna tried to keep pace with him, taking hold of his wrist. "Ryan, wait," she said. They were struggling through dense branches and thorns, and she lost hold of his arm.

The clouds raced over the sun and a few raindrops fell. Anna struggled up toward the chapel. Ryan vanished between the trees and then appeared again farther up. The rain was falling quickly now. She ran toward the edge of the clearing and the chapel door. But when she reached it, he had walked farther on. And then she could not see him anymore.

Aldebaran was kneeling at the altar. Ryan walked up behind him silently, hearing the rise and fall of the thousands of voices outside. "Uncle?" he said, and put his hand on Aldebaran's shoulder.

Aldebaran turned. "We are home," he said. "And England already looks like just a dream." He stood up and ruffled Ryan's hair, as though he was his own son. "Shall we go out?" he said.

They walked side by side. There were flowers over the church doorway, and leaves were laid on the ground—a pathway from the door out across the square. Orange flags were flying on the castle towers. The square was packed with people; the crowds stretched halfway up Citadel Street. The girl closest to the door—a pretty brown-haired girl with a baby—was crying. A few others had seen Ryan approach the door, and a tentative cheer rose.

Ryan tried to turn, but Aldebaran caught his arm and led him onward. Then they stepped out into the sunlight, into the cheering that burst like painful screams from the crowd, into the falling flowers and the triumphant music. Ryan had wanted to turn back because he had thought that he heard Anna calling after him to wait. But a moment later he had stopped thinking about that.

In the English wood, Anna could almost reach them. She heard faint voices in the air and started toward them, but they vanished. She thought she could see Ryan again for a second, a long way off now and about to turn. And then there were crowds moving like spirits around her—thousands of people there, though she could not quite see them. She took hold of the jewel around her neck, as Ryan had done when he had said that he could almost see Malonia. But it came no closer. Even the traces she had seen drifted away from her. The wood was silent.

As Anna crossed the lawn past the deserted house, someone was running to meet her: Monica, waving a few sheets of paper and shouting something. "What is it?" said Anna.

"Did you know Ryan and Mr. Field were leaving for good?" shouted Monica. "You never said! Anna! He left me this letter! He left me this! I only found it when I went back to the kitchen just now. Anna, did you know?"

"What?" said Anna again. Monica stopped in front of her, breathless, and laughed, then held out the papers, but her hands were shaking too much for Anna to read them.

"They have all the right signatures," said Monica. "I've just checked with the lawyers. These are valid documents." Monica glanced up at the house. "Where is Mr. Field? I have not missed him?"

Anna nodded. "They have left."

"Did they leave in a taxi? I passed one on the road, but I would have thought they would take the car. Then it's too late to speak to him?" Anna nodded. "What are you doing here?" said Monica. "I thought you came to say goodbye."

"I was just walking. Tell me what that paper is, anyway."

Monica laughed out loud again and put the pages into Anna's hands. "Look, I don't know what the hell he did it for. I told you he was eccentric. Anna, Mr. Field has given me his house." She spun around, taking in the acres of forest and the wide lawns. "All this."

"He gave it to you?" said Anna.

"If this is valid, which the lawyers say it is," said Monica, "it means that you can go home and practice all you want for your audition. I'm going to Lowcastle now to talk to the lawyers about it."

They walked back together. After Monica had left, Anna began sweeping the floor of the dining room. The guests were passing the door, dragging suitcases and shouting to their children as if it was an ordinary day. After a long time, Monica returned and danced around the room, without caring anymore about damaging the floor. She was telling Anna about the new hotel she would open at Lakebank, the biggest hotel in the valley. Anna listened. Then she put down the broom. "I think I should practice for the audition," she said. "I want to go home."

Monica stopped dancing. "You're a good girl, Anna," she said. "I'm lucky to have a niece like you. Mam was always so proud of you. Go home and practice; I can get a temporary worker. And if you don't get this scholarship, I will sell some land and pay for you to go to dance school."

Darkness had fallen completely when the bus slowed at the edge of the playing fields. Thunderclouds were thickening over the towers of the city. Raindrops began to fall. The bus driver hummed along to the radio, tapping his fingers on the steering wheel. Anna picked up her suitcase and stepped out in silence.

The lights of the tower blocks were brightening. After the bus had vanished, Anna stood on the corner of those old familiar streets and looked up. The window of her flat was lighted, and she could see her mother crossing the room. She started across the playing fields, under the light of the streetlamps, then up the stairs and along the walkway to her door. After it closed, England was silent, except for the heavy raindrops that were falling like beads of glass, and cars gaining speed around some corner far away. That was all.

❧

"*D*o you think it was real?" Maria asked me once. "What you dreamed about England—do you think it was real?"

I did not know. I had wondered about it once, I remembered. Stirling and I, walking home from school, had talked for a long time about whether England was real. And when I had read that book to him, when he had been so ill and frightened, he had believed in it. I suppose it passed the time. It was a story. And now the book was gone, anyway.

Maria wiped the tears from her face then, and got up and boiled water for tea. She was talking about the prince's return, about how the newspaper called people to come to the square that morning and see it. I did not hear all of what she said. I was wondering how she could do this—cry so desperately that night and, when the morning came, force herself to get up and make tea. She moved across the lighted kitchen like Grandmother did, like someone many years older than she was.

The baby murmured, and she called quietly, "Leo, will you hold him?"

I picked the baby up. He blinked at me and stretched out a hand. I felt stunned and tired, like someone who has been too long in a battle and wants to lie down and rest. But I picked the baby up because she told me to.

I have no right to hold this baby, I was thinking all that time. I could hardly stand it. But she was busy in the kitchen and I could not call to her, and there was no one else to take him. So I did not let him fall. Is that how you put your life back together? Because you have no choice about it, in the end.

⌑

When I look up, I can see the gray light beginning along the eastern hills. It is an unforgiving light; it draws everything slowly out of the darkness—the city, still sleeping; every stone of the castle; and my own hands on the book. My story is almost finished. There was hardly anything left to tell after that point.

Maria saved me in those first desperate weeks. Grandmother was growing frailer, and sometimes her mind drifted for two days at a time. Maria was the only one who could help her. Often I sat with the baby sleeping in my arms while she talked Grandmother back into the real world. And she stood by my side when I thought I was going to fall and disappear into Nothing. I was so frightened in those days. Fits of shaking came over me when I thought about Ahira.

Stirling and I used to talk about Anna, our English relative whose story came to me. I don't know if I really spoke to her in the hills, or if it was just another dream. But I would have gone through with it otherwise and pulled the trigger if she had not been there. I think it was right to go back. I've done so many things wrong, but I think now that killing myself would have been only another mistake. It would not have canceled out the others. I don't think it would even have taken away the pain.

Once, a long time after, I dreamed of Anna again. I could see her in the English city, traveling somewhere, light crossing her face and then darkness. That was the last time I thought about England. I wrote them here, the last things I saw.

Anna was turning the jewel around on her necklace as the bus edged through the streets. From the window she could see the evening star, and she wondered if Ryan could see it too. Then she stopped thinking about that and closed her eyes.

The bus stopped not long after, at the edge of the playing fields. She got down slowly. "Anna!" said someone from the shadows. A boy's voice. She turned.

"Bradley," she said. "You made me jump."

He grinned and came to meet her. He was one of the friends whose names Ryan, far away, was already struggling to remember. "I saw the bus and came down," he said. "I wanted to talk to you. I have hardly seen you in the last couple of weeks."

"It's this new school," said Anna. "I get home late."

"I am only one floor up from you. And I have been missing you—we all have."

She linked her arm with his. Bradley lit a cigarette and they started back toward the building. "Look at your uniform!" he said. "It is a change, this school. What do you think about it?"

"I can hardly believe I am there sometimes," said Anna. "We dance four hours every day, and you should see the studios. And there are nine dance teachers. But—"

"But what?" Bradley was watching her closely. Anna shrugged and sighed. "This is what I wanted to talk to you about," he said. "You seem distracted, Anna. You seem different. You have been talking about going to dance school since we were five years old. And now—I don't know—you are acting strange."

"I'm not acting strange . . . ," began Anna, without conviction.

"Is it this boy, your Ryan that you told me about? Are you missing him?"

They walked in silence up the stairs and along the walkway to Anna's door. "I haven't been feeling well, that's all."

"You've been ill?"

"I don't know what it is," Anna said. "I just feel sick and strange these days. This morning, I was sitting there putting on my shoes and I had to be at the barre for the register. I knew I had to be there, but I felt too sick and I couldn't get up."

He turned to her, about to speak. And then he stopped. Anna looked at him.

"I should go in," she said then. She unlocked the door and hurried inside, without meeting his eyes. Bradley was still standing there as she crossed the hall to her bedroom and closed the door behind her. "Ryan," she said quietly. The silence did not change.

A long way away, Ryan looked up from his desk. He stared out into the dark, his hand on the silver eagle at his neck. Then he let it go again. He bent his head over the page and signed his name, Cassius Donahue, above the capitals HIS MAJESTY KING CASSIUS OF MALONIA. The ink glittered. He pushed the pile of letters away and again stared out over the city.

Aldebaran had said he would forget England soon enough; everyone did, once they left it. And England had blurred to him already, like a memory from his childhood or a familiar dream. But that was not the same as forgetting. He could not forget.

I was trying to strangle someone. I could not see his face; he was just a soldier. We were struggling on the ground, and in a circle around me were faces I knew—Grandmother and Stirling, Maria, Father Dunstan, even Aldebaran—all of them shouting at me to stop. And I wanted to stop—I was trying to—but my hands would not release him. I could not force them to let him go. Then I was trying desperately to wake up. I knew that if I could wake myself in time, I would be able to stop myself from killing him. But my eyes would not open either. Ahira's face was close to mine, bleeding white and staring at me lifeless.

I woke suddenly and almost threw up with fear. I would not sleep again after that dream. I got up and stood in front of the window. There were still stars in the lightening sky, and the moon was weak and pale. Everything was silver outside. The first frost of autumn had come that night, creeping onto the roofs of the city and into the shadows of the houses. I stood at the window until the sun rose.

I had dreamed of the same thing many times and would dream about it many times again. But I remember how I woke that morning, because that was the day you came back.

There was a knock on the door soon after the building began to stir. I had not heard anyone come up from downstairs; I had been thinking and had forgotten that I was here at all. Grandmother was sleeping, so I went to open it. Standing on the step was a gray man. He smiled, and when he did, he looked like a skull. "Leonard? You must be Leonard." I didn't answer. "The last time I saw you, you were hardly more than a baby."

I just looked at you. Then you took a book from your pocket and said, "Is this yours?"

The smile and the formal greeting were just a pretense. You knew about us. I stared at the book in silence. A black leather book, shabby and scratched now, and fastened together roughly down the spine with glue and steel staples. "I tried to put it back as it was," you said. "But even the great ones cannot mend what is broken."

I took it from you and turned over the pages. They were all there, some of them faded now and others muddy and torn. "Do you want this back?" you said. "Should I have brought it?"

I did not answer, but I let you in. In the next room I heard Grandmother stir. A moment later she was hurrying through the door, still in her nightdress, saying something about Harold and Arthur in the same distant way she always did. Only this time it was not madness, because you were really there. "Margaret," you said, and then she was crying and throwing her arms around you, and you were saying, "It's all right. It's all right." But she would not let you go. You said, "Margaret, it's all right. I'm back to stay now." And I think you were crying too, but I am not certain. I understand why you were crying, Aldebaran, if you were. Grandmother is the same to you as Stirling was to me.

When Grandmother had gone to lie down, much later, you turned back to me. I was still clutching that book in my hand; I had not put it down since you had given it back. You sat down at the table and called me over. I put the book down and sat awkwardly opposite you. "I have missed too much," you said. "I have missed your whole life. Leo, tell me what has happened here since I have been gone."

The voice in my head was shouting. But I didn't really answer. I just stared at you. Then I realized you could hear that voice.

"What is it?" you said. I shook my head. "If you will not speak, write. I want to know."

You got me to write. Maybe it was because I was scared of you—I don't know. Maybe you used your powers. I hated you for it then. Everyone was trying to save me: Anna, who had sent me back home from the hills; Maria, picking me up from the floor when I cried; even Grandmother, as much as she could. And you. Were you the Voice that spoke to me across the worlds, that brought me back from Ositha and told me stories of another place? Aldebaran, you never confirmed it, but I am almost certain that you were. And now you had searched the Royal Gardens for every page of that story and gathered them and put it back together. You knew about me, even if only faintly. You always had.

"What has happened, Leo?" you said. "I have been away a

long time. I should have been here; I did nothing to help you. And Stirling—"

You ran your hand over your face and kept it there. And then I wrote, *I have done a very bad thing. Please let me tell you. I can speak to no one.*

You looked at me in silence. I was startled at what I had written. I did not want to tell you this; I closed my eyes and prayed that I would not. I had swallowed this secret, and it had become unreal, because the days had passed and I had not told it. I was afraid of what would happen if I told a single person what I had done. But I had to, suddenly. I picked up the pencil again and wrote.

You sat looking at my words for a long time without speaking. And then you glanced up at me, and I thought I saw the same fear in your eyes that must have been in mine. You shook your head. "Leo, I—" And then you handed the paper back to me. "Tell me everything from the beginning. I cannot understand; Leo, explain to me why you did it."

I did not take the paper from you. I opened the book instead. There were gaps in the writing—there had always been—enough pages to begin to explain. Without knowing what I was doing, I started to write on the first page. I began when I thought all this began: with the snow. Four months back—that was all it was. You watched me write. Then, after a while, when I could not see how to go on, I put the book aside.

"I had no idea how you were suffering," you said. "I was so far away from the real world that I could hardly see. Leo, the struggles you must have had, both of you, since Stirling—"

It is not your fault, I wrote in the margin of the newspaper. *We cannot blame you for being exiled.*

"I blame myself," you said. "I was always in a dangerous situation; I got what had been coming to me for a long time. I never thought Margaret would be left alone, or that you would . . ." You looked at me as though I was your own son. "If only I had been here. If only—"

Then I did not want to talk about that anymore. *Tell me about the book,* I wrote instead.

You went to the window and spoke to me from there, without turning. "Those stories," you said, "the stories you wrote in the book—they were the things I tried to show you. I was far away, but I thought you and Stirling would like to see into another place. An English fairy tale, if you like. I wanted to speak to you." You shook your head then, sadly. "Perhaps it was useless. I have failed you all; I should have been here. All I could do was try to show you what my own life was like. And I did not give you the words. The words are your own."

I opened the book and looked at the handwriting properly then. It was half mine and half someone else's. It cut deep into the paper like my own had, long before, when I used to go to school, but it sloped forward also. "Here," you said, and wrote a few words yourself on the margin of the newspaper. The slope of the letters was yours.

Why did you throw it away, Leo? you had written.

I thought about that. *What did an English fairy tale mean to me anymore?* I wrote eventually.

And then I thought of what Maria had asked me. *Was it real?* I wrote. *Did these things really happen in England?*

You shook your head. "I don't know. It is hard to explain. Doesn't anything begin to look like a dream after it is past?"

I shook my head at that. Not to me. To me what was past

was still here. It was not dead and gone. The night when I shot Ahira, the moment when I came back and Stirling was lying there so still, Grandmother crying and crying with mud on her face. All those things were real. And the days before that, the days when things were still all right. When we walked to your false gravestone and the sun shone on the east of the city, or that day with Maria and Stirling and the baby when they thought we would go on a picnic. These things were still real.

After you had left, when darkness fell, I picked up the book again and went on writing. You had asked me to explain, and I had started something now that I could not set aside.

Maria goes to confession every week. She told me once that I should go. She did not know what I had done, but she knew there was something. She could always tell. Anyway, I never went there, to kneel in the darkness of the church and repent of my sins. But I wrote in the book; I went on until it was quite dark, and rose again the next morning and went on writing. I went on even after the winter set in, and through the spring, and into the next summer. Every time I ran out of space, I would skip forward to the next blank page. I didn't read what I had written. I just went on. I counted the days by the words I wrote, and learned to survive.

I went on writing even after you had lost all hope of an explanation and stopped asking me, even after everyone had accepted that I did not speak. Everything found its way into the book—the old words that I had read to Stirling, the recent dreams that I had to write again from memory, my own life. Aldebaran's story, Anna's, the prince's, and mine.

I stopped thinking about England after that day you came back, Aldebaran. In the end, it did not matter to me anymore. I could no longer find the magic that had once surrounded that place. The prince's return passed me by. Whoever ruled the country, Stirling was still gone—Ahira too. But I did not say that to you.

Because I knew it like a theory: things had changed. Even if the revolution came too late for me, it altered things. Maria's father returned from the border. His leg was damaged forever and he was no longer smiling, but he is alive now, not buried out there in that graveyard at Ositha. Anselm goes to Sacred Heart Infant School rather than the West Kalitzstad Military Academy—and even if they have bullet marks in the outside walls and too few books, he will learn to read and write, not fire a gun. They closed down the high-security schools and sent the children with powers home. If I had wanted to, I could have trained in magic. Grandmother grew frailer, but no one came to take her away. She cannot walk far now, so sometimes we carry her old chair down to the yard. It is still a dark place. The yard has not changed; nothing about this building has. They say when the king returned, he planned to put running water in all the houses. He has not done that yet.

And they opened the Royal Gardens. People who are better at living than me, better at forgetting, go there for picnics.

*R*eading this now, I see that I did not explain why I did it. I did not explain it at all. The more I tried, the less I understood. For a second I wanted Ahira dead, but I willed the bullet to miss. How can I explain why I did something evil? Why I did something that would ruin the rest of my life with guilt? There are many reasons, and there are none. I don't want to make excuses, Aldebaran. I made a mistake. I'll pay for it the rest of my life. It will never go away. If only someone had taken the rifle from me; if only Ahira had followed a different route that passed Citadel Street by . . .

But what else can I say? There is nothing.

I finished the story today. It has taken me five years. I am twenty now. Today I spoke again, for the first time. And I planned to show you the book, but I didn't. I couldn't when it came to it. You didn't ask me to. Instead, you asked me to go with you to the castle. A ball for the king's guests, you said it was.

I thought I would refuse. But I suddenly said, "I will go with you." My voice surprised me. It was not how I remembered it sounding when I was fifteen.

That's where I am now. At the castle. As soon as I arrived, I wished I hadn't come. I never much cared about parties and dancing, even when I knew how to smile, and laugh, and talk. But I came to please you, Aldebaran, because there are other things besides being happy. Other things to live for.

So I tried to stand in the room and speak to those strangers. But I suddenly thought I was falling. I really tried, Aldebaran, but I couldn't. I thought I was going to burst out crying. I went and stood in the roof garden, where it was quiet. The music and the light were still spilling out the open door. I stepped away, into the shadow, and looked up at the stars.

They name the great ones after the stars, don't they? Those trained in magic, who take a new name, take it from the stars. But I was already named after a star. Leo is a star; in England it is a whole constellation. When I looked at them from that roof garden, I didn't know which one.

I remembered then that I used to want to see the view from the top of the castle. It seemed to me stupid to remember it, that I would care about seeing a view. How often I used to think about it. But I could see the highest balcony from where I was, and I could see the steps that led to it. I crossed to them and began to climb.

As I came through the door, I almost collided with a man with a *dagger drawn in his hand. The king. "Forgive me," he said, with something like fear in his eyes. "Those stairs . . ."*

"I came to look at the view," I said. It concerned me nothing that he was royalty. He could see it.

"Leonard North?" he said. "Aldebaran's great-nephew?" I nodded. He held out his hand. "Cassius. I have been wishing to meet you."

I took it. "King Cassius," I said. He laughed at that.

The final chords drifted up, resolute, on the violin, and then scattered clapping. "You are not dancing?" he asked me. I shook my head. "I am not either," he said. "I would rather stand up here and watch the stars."

I nodded and looked out over the parapet again. You can see everything from there—every place I've ever been in my whole life. Below are the treetops of a walled roof garden; below that the towers drop to the yard, and the rock, down into the city. The city, farther on, drops to the river. "This is the highest point for miles," said Cassius. "The stars are closer here."

"They say the stars are the same in England."

I don't know why I said it; perhaps I was thinking about his story in that old book. He turned to me then but did not speak. "Yes," he said eventually. "Yes, they are exactly the same." He looked out over the city. "I always saw it as a kind of sign. Perhaps I am foolishly romantic."

I just shrugged at that. Then I said, "People expect that of you. You know what this country was like under Lucien."

"I don't know. I never did." He smiled, though he looked tired. "It is a disadvantage, and I don't mind telling you."

We stood there for a while in silence. Then he turned to leave. "Do you think that they will miss me? I will be back by one."

I shook my head, though I did not mean anything by it. Then he turned again, and was gone. I heard his footsteps fading down the stairs, and then silence.

A while later you came and spoke to me. I thought about giving you the book then. But after you had gone, I decided that I would read it again, from start to finish, one last time. So I sat down there beside the lamp and began.

Standing here, on the highest tower, I realize that a lot of the things I have said or thought have been wrong. I shut the book. I'm not going to show it to you now—not yet. It's too difficult. And there are some things that don't need to be explained. I wrote this book for you, Aldebaran, but I wrote it as if it was for a stranger. When I thought of you reading it, I couldn't write at all. And I'm frightened to show it to you, because you're the only relative we have left, and I don't want you to think ill of me. I hope if you read it someday, you'll understand.

I said that Stirling's life was like a book—a book cut off in the middle. But maybe it's not cut off. Maybe he's only skipped ahead to the next chapter. That's what I think now. Because how could that be the end of it? Even in this world, he is not entirely gone.

I want to make this an ending, Aldebaran. I'll write all of this into the book—all that I've thought now when I read it—and I'll show it to you one day. So what is it in the end, my story? Shall I call it a happy ending or a tragedy? The sad endings are the real endings, where everything finishes and Nothing rises up like mold into what was once beautiful. The happy endings are not endings at all but beginnings—beginnings of something better than what came before. And this is both, because this isn't a book, it's my life. I can't say my life's not sad. I'll still cry. I'll still wish I was somewhere else. I'll still count the days sometimes. Only I want to go on. I want Stirling to look down on me as the brother he knew. To be the same Leo, for better or worse, that he left behind.

And I look up into the sky, the wide sky and the high, silver stars. And I can see the star called Leo now—I can see it clearly. It is the one that is shining the brightest of them all. That is what I think, just for a second.

The sun is rising in the east and all the guests have gone home. A maid is collecting empty glasses from the roof garden, and their quiet clinking is the only sound. Clouds are rolling over the sunrise, so that the balcony is troubled by their shadows. I can hardly expect them not to pass over me. But perhaps it is something to accept that they always will.

I said that the clinking of glasses was the only sound, but there is a small bird too. On the parapet, close by, this bird is singing. It's been singing for some time, but I didn't notice. I think that I'd notice only if it stopped. I reach out my hand to touch it, but it flies away just before I can. But only a second before, and it doesn't fly far.

There are a lot of things in my head, and some of them don't make sense, but it doesn't mean I'm losing my mind. I'm not happy like I was before. But happiness isn't everything. The stars are fading. I know which one is Leo. I thought, only a couple of hours ago, that there are some things that you just know. You can never prove them. Perhaps uncertainty makes you all the more certain. And proof was something created by humans, but it's easy and natural to know things in your heart.

I also thought that there was no magic in the world. And I think that now, perhaps, the magic is harder to find than it was when Stirling was here and Ahira was just a face on the newspaper. But sometimes I glimpse it. Times like now I glimpse it. Just for a second.

I wonder if the magic is beauty, or truth. Or the little bird's song.

Or happiness. Or maybe it's love. One of those distant things. I wonder as I go down the stairs. I wonder as I walk through the deserted streets. I wonder as I go into the church. I kneel down and pray. "Forgive me, Ahira," I whisper. Perhaps it's stupid, but I imagine that he does.

When I get back to the dismal apartment, I can feel the magic slipping away again. I brush some of the dust off Stirling's overcoat. It's funny, because that coat is the size of an eight-year-old, but he'd be thirteen now. But really, he's beyond thirteen. He's beyond an overcoat. He's not in this dimension anymore. He's beyond these calculations we place on things to keep ourselves sane.

The rain is falling like steel. I open the window and watch it. Then I think that the magic is all those things that I thought of, and more than that. The magic is heaven. It's beyond my explaining. I used to think that beyond meant far away. Unreachable. But it's not. It's over a stream that can be jumped, or through a doorway into the next room. That's all beyond is. Beyond is a line—like magic, like madness. That's all.

Because heaven's not high above us, beyond the stars. It's everywhere; it's close; it's all around us. All around us, in another dimension. And in some places the barrier wears thin.

A woman sits at her dressing table, leaning her head on her hand. She stares in the mirror at her own blue eyes, at the tired bulges under them, and at her forehead, which is creasing already. Then she winds her fingers through the chain of her necklace and watches the light glitter on the single jewel.

A boy runs into the room, holding out his arms. Anna lifts him onto her knee. "Your dancing was lovely tonight," he says, looking up at her.

"Did you think so, Ashley angel?"

"Yes." His face is serious. "You're the best dancer in the world." She laughs at that. He holds out a newspaper to her. "Grandma read it to me. She said to show you. You're in the newspaper, Mam!"

It's only the village newsletter, but he wouldn't know. Anna takes it from him and reads the headline. "'Local Hero'?"

"That's you," Ashley says, grinning up at her.

She runs her finger along the lines as she reads. " 'After the repeat performance on Saturday, Miss Ariana Devere is planning a tour with the Royal Ballet.' " Before the laugh has escaped her lips, she sighs instead.

Ashley looks up at her. He has his father's eyes, she thinks. It has become a habit, thinking that, and she hardly notices it. "Mam, can we go for a walk?" says Ashley.

"It's late! You should be in bed, Ash."

"I'm not tired."

"You won't be able to get up early tomorrow if you stay up late tonight."

"I don't want to get up early tomorrow. I want to go for a walk."

"No. It's too late."

"Please."

She shuts her eyes. "A short walk, then. Where do you want to go?"

"Up to the stones on the hill."

"All right. It won't take long."

"I used to want to be a dancer once, you know," she says as they walk.

"You are a dancer," says Ashley.

"No, only for fun. But I used to think I would be a famous dancer. I even started at dance school, for a few weeks."

"You could be famous, like the newspaper said."

"It's a joke," she tells him. "It's because people wouldn't expect

432

me to be good at ballet—because I work in a hotel, you know. And because of how seriously everyone takes the village talent show."

"I don't understand. You are good at dancing. You won it. You could be a famous dancer. You are good."

"Not good enough," she says.

"Why don't you practice, and get good enough, and then be a famous dancer?"

"I don't have time."

"Uncle Bradley said you should. He said so yesterday, on the phone. He said you can always find time."

"Uncle Bradley says a lot of things that he really shouldn't."

"How can you find time? How can you lose it? It doesn't make sense."

"You know Uncle Bradley talks a lot of rubbish sometimes. It's best not to listen to him."

After that he is silent, jogging beside her, every so often looking up to see if the frown has left her face.

Dusk is falling when they reach the top of the hill, hand in hand. Anna turns and looks down at the lights of the houses. There is a stillness resting over the valley like mist, but they are above it on the hill, and there are restless sounds all around as the night creeps in. She stands still, with Ashley beside her. The farthest lights are the windows of the Lakebank Hotel, Monica's place, and the dark hill above them is where the old chapel is. And the sliver that reflects the moonlight is all that can be seen of the lake from here.

When they turn to the stone circle, they both see the difference in the stones. There is an extra one where there used to be a space. And then it moves, and they see that it is actually a man standing a little way off with his back to them.

A tall man, with black hair already fading, standing in the shadow between two stones so that the moonlight does not reach him. Ashley grips Anna's hand and presses closer to her. They are both frightened to step into the circle, as if it is enchanted.

At some small noise, the man turns. She just stands and looks at him, and he looks at her.

When Anna has thought about this, what would happen if they met again, she has imagined telling him. About the years she has struggled: the shame, the pain, the disappointment. Trying to get through her first term at dance school, getting sicker and sicker— or when she had to leave; maybe that was the worst. All the people she had to tell, and the things they said, which made her stay at home rather than face any more remarks and glances. Going to hospital checkups alone and giving birth alone while he was somewhere else and didn't know. All the friends who went away and came back breezily, talking about their weddings and their new houses while she jiggled the baby on her knee. And most of all, dancing: the girls she had met in that first term at dance school and what they were doing now—the shows they starred in, the schools where they taught. And the dreams she still had, as though she wasn't shut out of that world forever.

It was only luck. She could have done those things. Or if she could not have done them, she never had the chance to try. She had the potential, and the determination, and the right beginning. Everything but the luck. And what she can bear least of all is that he never knew. She has imagined it many times, standing there and telling him and forcing him to listen.

He looks as if he wants to speak too. But in the end, they don't say anything.

Ryan steps forward and holds out his hand. She reaches out and takes it silently. "I never came back here," he says. "I meant to come back but I started to forget this place. Anna, we should not have parted the way we did."

"We should have been together," she says, and grips his hand more tightly. "Are you really here? Is this real, or is it just a dream?"

There are tears in Ryan's eyes, and he looks away from her before they fall. Then he sees Ashley standing at the edge of the circle watching them, almost crying himself because he does not understand. Ryan crosses the empty grass and kneels and looks into his face. Anna puts a hand on Ashley's shoulder. "Ryan, this is—"

He raises his hand to quiet her. Suddenly he can tell by the boy's eyes. Dark eyes, and proud, in spite of his frightened tears; strong eyes, like his own. The eyes of a king.

It's hard to shut the book, but I'm going to do it. And it will be hard to let you read it, but I'm going to do it. And maybe, Aldebaran, you'll think it's a sad story. But it's not—it's really not. It's my life. Everyone's life is sad. Everyone cries. Everyone thinks they're falling sometimes. But in the end, we learn to survive.

THE LAST DESCENDANTS TRILOGY

CONTINUES IN

VOICES IN THE DARK

READ ON FOR A SNEAK PREVIEW OF BOOK II IN

THE LAST DESCENDANTS TRILOGY

NIGHTFALL,
THE TWENTY-NINTH OF
DECEMBER

❧

I want more than anything to tell you the truth about my life. I am a criminal and a liar. But I swear to you that this will be a true account.

That was how I began as the coach drew away from the city, south and west into the darkness of the moors. The woman opposite me was pretending to sleep, one arm around the shoulders of her little boy. The old man next to me kept sighing and shaking his head. He was saying the rosary; the quiet clicking of the beads was the only sound. We were all avoiding each other's glances. The snow and fire behind us made wild patterns on the glass. Every few seconds, the old man glanced back and sighed again, as though he had left a good life behind him. Fires were blazing on the walls of the castle, throwing black smoke over the stars. I imagined that he had some ordered existence in the city, and this ritual was all that he could carry of it with him into the unknown.

I owned nothing but the clothes I wore and the contents of the pockets. I kept checking them to see that everything was still there. I had given the driver fifty crowns and my christening bracelet as payment; by the time we set off, it was nearly midnight, and the queues at the harbor stretched a mile. But I still had a pencil and a stack of papers and a box of matches and a candle and the medallion Aldebaran had given me.

We did not speak to each other. This would be a long journey, long and cold, but we were still strangers and had nothing to say. The old man beside me had his rosary beads, but ever since I was a young boy, I had put my faith in stories; they came more easily to me than prayers. When we set out on this journey, I had thought that perhaps I could write everything down and explain it. And yet the words did not come easily this time. It was nearly impossible to write with the lurching of the coach, and my heart was heavy. I put the paper back into my pocket and tried to sleep.

"Get down from the coach!" someone shouted when we had traveled a few miles. It was only the driver, cursing at a broken wheel and glancing about him with his rifle raised. Ahead were the lights of a village. We would have to stop for the night here, the driver told us. If he fixed the wheel now, the horses would be too cold to continue, and besides, this road was dangerous. We would go on to the next inn and stop there. The woman made some protest about this. A cold wind was sweeping over the snow, driving it in gusts against the windows of the carriage. We stepped down, shivering. The little boy clung to his mother's overcoat. I offered to take one of her cases, but she shook her head. The driver unhitched the horses and led them beside him, and we walked in silence toward the lights.

None of us had money for a bed, so we all ended up in the front room of the inn. This was just a windswept village in the middle of nowhere. The little boy and his mother slept in a corner with their heads on the table. The old man got out his rosary again, then put it away and ordered a bottle of spirits and sat there drinking it and watching the snow fall. I listened to the wind growling and thought about what I would write. Then I got out the paper and pencil and began again. But it was no good. I sighed and crossed out the start of it.

The inn sign creaked and rattled in the wind outside. I could not write; every time I tried, it was wrong. When this had gone on for some time, the old man got up and came toward my table, holding out the bottle of spirits. "Here," he said. "Maybe it will cure your writer's depression."

"It's kind of you."

He poured me a glass, then waited to see if I would let him sit down at the table. I drew out a chair. He settled slowly, flexing each finger so that the joints cracked. I could tell from his face that he had once been handsome, and his eyes were quick and kind. I sipped the spirits and waited for him to say something else.

"Where are you going?" he asked eventually.

I shrugged. "I don't really know."

"Neither do I. I am trying to find my family. Maybe they have gone to Holy Island; that's what I am thinking. But there again, they could be somewhere else."

"I'm supposed to be going to Holy Island too," I said. "But . . ."

"But you don't think you will," he said. "Now that you have set out."

"How did you know?"

"Ah," he said. "A lifetime of studying human nature. Now, tell me what you are trying to write."

I thought about this for a long time. "A letter to my brother," I said eventually. "I've done a very bad thing. I don't know if he'll forgive me, but I want to explain. And I want to tell him . . ." I hesitated.

"Go on," said the old man kindly.

"I want to tell him the truth. He's only a baby now, but I want to record it, for when he grows up. I was never told the truth, you know? And I think if he knows it, he will stand a chance."

He nodded for me to continue.

"And I want to tell him about our life in the city," I said. "Because that's all gone now. He'll never know it."

"Admirable," said the old man.

"Not really," I said. "Not if you knew."

"So tell me," he said. "Maybe it will make it easier to write if you tell me first."

"Do you think so?" I said.

He shook his head. "I can't tell. It depends."

"It is a long story," I said. "It would take a while to explain."

"This will be a long journey," said the old man.

I folded the paper and drank the rest of the glass of spirits. It burned in my chest like fire and gave me courage and made me melancholy at the same time. He introduced himself at last as Mr. Hardy. I told him my name was Anselm. We sat there talking about nothing at all for a long while, and the wind cried like voices in the dark outside. Then, as the darkness drew on, I started to tell him the story. There was nothing else to do on this bleak night. I told him how it started with our shop and with the graveyard and with the old days on Citadel Street, and there I got confused and fell silent, trying to think where it began. "With Aldebaran's funeral," I said eventually.

"Aldebaran is dead?" he said, and started as though he had been struck in the chest.

"Yes," I said. "He died in July. Did you not know?"

He shook his head. Everyone in the country knew it, but this man had somehow missed the fact. He went on shaking his head and said, "Aldebaran is dead" again, but this time it was not a question. "Tell me this story," he said. "I want to hear."

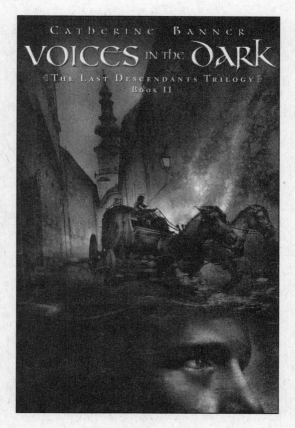

Available now!